"Because of his experiences, Walborn is able to provide the reader with a unique perspective in his story telling that includes vivid portrayals of taboo subject matter related to the mental health field and critical commentary on psychiatric care across the United States. His familiarity with the large asylums of the past, the severely mentally ill, and psychology creates a work of fiction that seems utterly too real. "

—Jason Gum, M. I., author of *Preserving and Responding: Glenville State College*
Glenville State College Archivist
and Reference Librarian

"Walborn does not fear writing about the politics of mental health care. Within his iconic style of writing he demands action from the reader to foster research and appropriate training in mental health care of the mental health practitioners. This is a must read for anyone who has sought or practices mental health care."

—Kandas A. Queen, Assistant Professor of Business

D1167263

Two Days at the Asylum

Inspired by True Events

Frederick S. Walborn, PhD

Clinical Psychologist

Publisher Page
an imprint of Headline Books, Inc.
Terra Alta, WV

Two Days at the Asylum

by Frederick S. Walborn, PhD

To order additional copies of this book or for book publishing information, or to contact the author:

Headline Books, Inc.
P.O. Box 52
Terra Alta, WV 26764
www.HeadlineBooks.com

Tel: 304-789-3001
Email: mybook@headlinebooks.com

Publisher Page is an imprint of Headline Books

ISBN 13: 9781946664235

Library of Congress Control Number: 2018936452

PRINTED IN THE UNITED STATES OF AMERICA

This novel is dedicated to the seriously and chronically mentally ill who need our help.

Foreword

I hope *Two Days at the Asylum* will be an entertaining read; more importantly, I hope the reader will become enlightened and take some action to help the severely and chronically mentally ill who are homeless due to the closing of the munificent asylums.

One-third of the homeless population is suffering from schizophrenia. One in five of prisoners in our expensive prisons are seriously mentally ill.

At the close of the novel is a site where the reader may make a ten dollar or more charitable contribution to foster research, education, and intervention programs. The focus of the APF (American Psychological Foundation) Visionary Grant has historically been working with serious mental illness, imprisoned, homeless, and understanding and eliminating stigma and prejudice of mental illness.

DAY ONE:
(Thursday, July 17th, 1969)

1

The wounded mosquito flew in a haphazard pattern outside a screened window. It was the third day of its life. The mosquito will be dead in exactly 36 hours.

A large rip in the rusted window screen guaranteed an easy entrance for the insect.

A genetic tear in the mosquito's left wing interfered with its flight pattern. Missing its first attempt to fly through the opening, it hit the screen and bounced off the screen. On the second attempt, the mosquito flew into the darkness of the room.

A woman and man sat inside the gloomy room. One bulb in the three ceiling lights of the room functioned. Untouched beads of sweat rolled down the faces of the two people. Neither person spoke.

The mosquito attempted to make a direct flight to the sweating man. Its wounded left wing resulted in a flight resembling an aerial dog fight with itself. Eventually, the mosquito made it to the head of the long-haired, bearded man. The insect buzzed around the right ear of the man.

The man did not move or speak.

The jaw of the woman dropped. Her eyes tightened as she watched the bizarre display of barrel rolls, vertical climbs, and quarter loops of the insect flying around the man's ear.

The high pitched buzz of the mosquito ceased when it landed on the man's beard. The six-legged insect made a precarious journey toward the man's mouth.

The gnat's thin legs marched on the man's exposed chin.

The woman's eyes fixated on the hiking mosquito.

The psychologist broke the silence. "Jesus! Will you kill the damn thing?"

"I think I know why we are here," replied Jesus in a monotonic voice.

The mosquito rode Jesus' moving chin.

The sweaty, long-haired, bearded man looked like many of the hippies of the day. There was a childlike quality to the man. His boyish blue-and-white striped shirt and his blue jean pants rolled up around the ankles, accentuated the effect of him being naive. He cheated a glance at the chiseled calves of his psychologist.

The psychologist crossed her athletic legs. "If you don't kill the thing I will slap it off your face."

On cue, the mosquito did a barrel roll off Jesus' chin.

"Are you listening to me?" asked Jesus. "I think I know why we are here."

"Here, as on Earth?"

"Did I say Earth?"

"No, you did not say Earth."

"I mean there could be other intelligent beings." Jesus turned and gazed in the direction of the barred window with a tear in the screen. "Well, there probably are other intelligent beings in the universe. The Air Force has their Blue Book program."

Jesus sat more erect.

The psychologist watched the left-wing-wounded mosquito fly into a wall. She sighed and shifted in her wooden chair. "What Blue Book program?"

Speaking at a faster rate, the bearded man said, "The government conspiracy program where the Air Force is trying to determine whether all of the UFO sightings are a threat to national security. You know, all that stuff about Martians' sticking probes up peoples' asses."

Pulling a swath of her dampened black hair around an ear and not wanting to pursue the issue of why a higher species of life would travel light years to a planet with the ultimate goal of sticking something in someone's ass, the psychologist turned away from the antics of the mosquito and faced the man.

She asked, "Okay, what is the purpose of intelligent beings?"

In a hurried manner, "Well, I don't know. I mean I don't know if it is limited to intelligent beings." Turning his head toward his psychologist, "What do you think?"

The psychologist chuckled. "What do you mean? I'm getting confused. You say you have discovered something or understood something. You made it sound as if you found the essence of life."

Jesus grinned. "I just don't think you will be able to grasp the essence of it."

"Well, I do have a Ph.D."

In a chipper voice, "Yeah, but books can get in the way of knowledge."

In a patronizing voice, "Are you going to tell me what the purpose of life is?"

Jesus leaned toward his psychologist. In a deeper pious tone, "I use to think it was change; now, I think it's giving."

"So the essence of life is giving?"

Jesus looked toward the floor and did not speak.

A few seconds passed.

He raised his head and with one hand pulled back his dampened hair over the top of his head. He looked back in the direction of the barred window.

The mosquito was at the window attempting to leave the room. Mesmerized by the sharply angled light rays coming in the dusky room, Jesus stared at the reflected light.

The psychologist turned and watched the mosquito bouncing off the screen of the window.

Jesus stared at the light rays.

The psychologist watched the mosquito land on the screen and walk toward the opening of the screen.

Jesus stared at the light rays.

The psychologist turned her head toward her patient and emphatically stated, "Jesus."

Her voice softened, "The essence of life is giving?"

The bearded man looked at the psychologist and exposed his light blue eyes. He interlocked his calloused fingers in his lap. "We are here to find our individual strength; and then, to give to our fellow human beings, creatures, and trees. We are all interconnected. I could not strike the mosquito because it is as integral to the growth of the universe, just as you and I. Rarely do people actually listen to the silent voices of the universe."

"Do you believe I do not listen to you?"

"Sure. I mean you can only do so much. Sometimes you miss me by a mile. You have missed me right now by a thousand light years. It's time for a cigarette break. I'm going to go."

"Okay, Jesus."

"Peace is with you."

When Jesus said goodbye, he waved a hand salutation in a Jewish priestly blessing of a raised hand in the air with his palm exposed, and he separated his two sets of fingers into a 'V' shape. His gesture was similar to the Vulcan sign of Mr. Spock in the recently discontinued Star Trek television series.

Jesus methodically walked out the room.

The patient's name, the name on his Admission papers was Noah Holiday. His diagnosis was manic-depressive disorder. When Noah became manic, he became delusional and believed he was Jesus. Noah was a frequent flyer of the Weston Asylum. He returned to the hospital about every three months.

Dr. Katie Carmel was a clinical psychologist. Her planned two-month stay at the asylum had grown into two years. She was trying to help Noah Holiday to break free of his delusion of being Jesus. Instead of questioning and fighting his delusion, she endorsed his delusion. She assumed he was Jesus. By being empathic with his false beliefs of being Jesus, she hoped his delusions would melt away.

Sitting alone in the make-shift psychotherapy office of two wooden tables, wooden chairs, and a crazy mosquito; Carmel grabbed the sides of her head. She attempted to mentally gain a focus. *It seems the more attention I give him, the more he acts like a pubescent boy, or a Wall Street trader. He only cares about hitting on me. I don't know if this empathy thing is going to work.*

She grasped the side of the table with both her hands.

The bold mosquito landed on her left forearm.

"Son-of-a-bitch." Carmel raised her right hand and struck down with the speed and force of a lightning bolt. The mosquito escaped and buzzed above the head of the psychologist.

Carmel was different from the other professionals of the Weston Asylum—as evident by her clothing and demeanor. The nurses and physician assistants wore the classic white shirt, white pants or dresses, and white shoes. The professional staff could wear street clothes. The typical clothes of the professional women at the asylum were the long moo-moo dresses, bright mod clothes, tight mini-skirts, or blue-jeans. The men usually wore T-shirts and bell-bottom blue jean pants. Based on their clothing, it was sometimes difficult for a newcomer to determine who was a professional and who was a patient.

It was obvious, Carmel was not a patient.

She wore a tight yellow dress with small white polka dots. She had purchased the dress from Montgomery Wards. The dress was designed to be sexy, but not too sexy. She had decided to make this mixed-message classic dress into an open sexual statement that declared she was comfortable with her sexuality.

Having been raised by parents who had lived through the Great Depression, she had learned the value of a dollar. A Singer sewing machine provided Carmel the opportunity to do sewing alterations to help the dress match her body. The sleeves had been cut a little shorter to accentuate her thin; yet, powerful arms. The top part of the dress was so tight she didn't need a bra. The original hemline came down to her knees; she shortened it a couple of inches. The hemline of the dress belled four inches away from her thighs. To an asexual observer, she looked like a gong in a bell. To sexually active people, she looked like a gong in a bell—only sexual.

Once composed, Carmel bolted from the wooden chair and her dress swung as she strutted out of the doorway of the room. The vein of her upper left arm was pronounced as she slammed the steel door shut. Without looking at her keychain that hung from her thin waist belt, she selected the correct key and locked the door.

Carmel turned away from the door and saw what every hallway in the asylum looked like: dirty, yellow, buttery colored walls with gray patient doors equally spaced apart. In the middle of the distance of the hallway was a wooden desk. A nurse wearing all white sat behind the desk.

The psychologist, in her fitted yellow polka dot dress, sashayed down the expansive hallway of the Acute Unit. Her knees rose to hip level; a foot struck the concrete floor directly in front of the other foot making a distinctive "click…click…click."

All of the heads of the hallway turned in the direction of the pronounced sound, except for the nurse behind the desk.

The nurse did not turn to acknowledge Dr. Katie Carmel.

The mosquito made an indirect flight into the tear in the screen. She flew to her eggs in the rain gutter of the stone building.

In 36 hours, the mosquito will return to the same room, with the same two people.

Due to unforeseen events, the mosquito will be killed by the psychologist—or Noah Holiday (AKA, Jesus).

2

July 17th, 1969 was a special day at Weston, West Virginia. It was Community Day at the Weston Asylum. This was a unique one-day event of the year at the hospital. The president of the hospital, for a token fee of fifty cents, opened the door so the locals could come inside to view the workings of the magnificent building.

The president's goal was for the visitors to leave with the idea that the Weston Asylum was a good home for the patients. And more importantly, the townsfolk would vote to pass a bond to increase funding for the asylum. *The locals would not want these crazies to be wandering around their streets.*

Standing outside the asylum that day, two men talked on-and-on about the quarter-mile-long insane asylum. A man wearing a tailored brown suit said to a man wearing a wrinkled blue suit, "I went to the library before coming today and did some research on the place. Did you know this is the second largest, hand-cut, stone masonry building in the world?"

Blue Suit gawked. In a voice similar to Gomer Pyle on the television series *Andy Griffith Show,* he said, "I did not know that. What is the largest building?"

"The Kremlin."

The man wearing the brown suit reached out a sweaty hand in a gesture of welcome. "My name's Milo." Blue Suit grasped Milo's hand with both of his hands and vigorously shook it. Blue Suit's eyes twinkled with life; he grinned ear to ear and exposed his yellowed teeth and a front silver crown.

Following an uncomfortable moment of staring at each other, waiting to hear the other man give his name, Milo finally turned back toward the massive building.

Due to the heat and humidity, the distant ends of the building were a softer tone of grey. Milo fixed his hands on his backside, his elbows bent back, as he perused the grand building. "Look at that. Those blocks of limestone must weigh over 400 pounds. Can you imagine cutting each one of those stones? The stones fit so tightly you can't even see any mortar. They don't build things like they used to."

Blue Suit shook his head. "Nope. We can send a man to the moon, but we can't build a house worth shit. Did you hear Bill ordered one of those Sears houses?"

"Fuck no."

"Fuck yes."

Milo smiled at his new friend in the auspicious setting of the insane asylum. Blue Suit asked, "What's the world coming to?"

"Who's Bill?" Milo asked his new buddy.

There was a pause in their conversation.

Milo's face dropped. "You mentioned Bill buying a Sears house. I thought you knew Bill—Bill Reed—we must be talking about different Bills."

"I just made up Bill and his Sears house for the sake of conversation," said his new friend. Blue Suit looked around. "Well, I have to go. Group therapy starts in a few minutes." Blue Suit turned away from Milo. He walked away, his arms flailing.

The dropped jaw Milo watched as his newly found companion, now a patient, gleefully walked to the stone structure. Before he could fully grasp what happened, the massive two wooden doors of the main doorway of the insane asylum opened.

The townspeople gathered outside the covered entryway, awaiting their turn to go into the hospital. Some were wide-eyed and silent. Some were wide-eyed and over-talkative. Milo walked to the group.

A young woman with scarecrow-thin arms and legs gingerly walked out onto the front portico. In the future, she would be diagnosed as suffering from anorexia nervosa. The diagnosis did not exist in 1969. A mod shift hung on her. Bright orange and yellow colors splattered the otherwise unflattering dress. Groovy orange stockings covered her ostrich-thin legs. Her skin had a white pearl appearance.

Dr. Dewey Nash, the president of the hospital, selected Ashley to be one of the tour guides. Ashley was a social worker who worked in the Admissions Unit.

Meandering down the worn stone steps, she spoke to her anxious audience in a West Virginia sing-song twang. "My name is Ashley and I welcome you to the Weston Asylum. I am so happy you came to visit us today. Each guide can take only twelve people at a time. I will take the first twelve who line up in front of me."

A male visitor who came out of his hollow only to get flour and other necessities pushed his way to the front of the group. Standing in front of the Twiggy-look-alike he asked, "Are you married?"

She glared into the man's pupils and affirmed in a stern voice, "Sir, this is a mental hospital where we respect people. If you do not think that you will be able to control your rude comments— I suggest you leave—now."

Ashley fixed her gaze on the man for a few seconds to give him a chance to respond. Never losing eye contact, the man responded by increasing the rate of chomping his chew of Red Man. She subtly rolled her eyes to the heavens. *This is a battle to lose. If there's a future concern with this character—I'll take him down—and win the war.*

The man stared downward toward the buckled sidewalk.

Ashley's sweet, peppy voice returned. "Oh, you are a good group. Thank you for not pushing one another and don't worry, you will all get inside today to see the great work that is done at the asylum."

The president of the hospital, Dr. Nash, had thought of everything. To obtain an intimate feeling between the visitors, the tour group's size was held to a maximum of twelve people. All of the 666 doors of the hospital were oiled in an attempt to stop any creepy haunting sound of metal against metal.

Ashley stood to the side counting heads as the townsfolk walked up the worn stone steps. She was astonished there was so much diversity in her first group of the day. The first to enter was the Red Man chewing fellow. The next two were a middle-aged couple. Milo wearing his brown suit was the next to enter followed by his wife. His wife wore a dress with sunflower prints arching over her pronounced stomach. The fourth and fifth visitors were a couple of long-haired hippies. Six and seven were a couple of Mennonite faith, as evident by their clothing. The woman wore a plain long black dress and sported a hand-sewn head cap. The Mennonite man dressed in all black wore a black Billy Jack hat.

Ashley took a mental break in her counting. *This is going to be a fun interesting group.*

Eight and nine she knew. The man was president of the Bank of Weston, Richard the III. The dark-skinned bank president sported a small green alligator sewn on his white casual shirt. His wife, Jez, had burnt red skin. Her skin was prematurely thin and was burnt a darkened red. The exposure of the cavernous wrinkles in her upper too-tanned breasts testified to too many fun-filled ventures at Myrtle Beach.

Ashley leaned over and reached down to help the tenth visitor up the steps. The elderly man smiled and shook Ashley's hand, "I'm Dan." He firmly shook her hand and let go. "Honey I swim one mile three days a week, and on my days off I hit the weights. I think I can manage a step; but, I do thank you." Not to be outdone, the elderly lady behind him said, "Hi sweetie. I teach dance in Buckhannon three days a week. You can always remember my name. I'm Debbie, the dancer." The elderly dancer hacked some phlegm and flicked away her finished cigarette into the yard.

The twelfth, and final, visitor was a middle-aged demonstrative woman wearing pink overalls and sporting pig-tails. Ashley turned to follow the large woman into the main entrance of the asylum.

The round-faced, obese, pink-overall woman abruptly turned and glared at Ashley. She demanded, "Missy. That is my daughter

Juli Jo. She comes too." Ashley turned her head downward in the direction of a pubescent girl dressed in pink with pig-tails.

Ashley's brain filled with conflicting thoughts. *Dr. Nash said to limit the groups to twelve. What if he found out I allowed thirteen? Thirteen is an unlucky number. The pig-tailed dressed in pink kid has to be the pig-tailed dressed in pink woman's offspring.*

Ashley stood more erect and fixed her dress. "Of course child, please join us."

Ashley's innocent addition of the thirteenth visitor, the pig-tailed girl; will result in acts of mischievousness, chaos, compassion, and ultimately in the summons of numerous emergency vehicles to the asylum.

3

The thin Ashley followed the shuffling group into the double-door entry. Her orange shoes deftly touched the concrete floor. The walls of the wide hallway were painted robin-egg blue. Their tour guide commanded, "Folks!" All the heads turned in unison to look back at Ashley and she calmly said, "Were going to start in this room." One of her delicate arms pointed to a room on the left.

The thirteen bodies, not twelve, entered a room that looked like a large living room from one of the past lumber baron mansions in West Virginia. Red velvet couches and chairs lined the walls. A green velvet couch, two green chairs, and a fainting couch circumscribed the green marble fireplace. Framed black and white pictures adorned the walls. A mosaic carpet partially covered the wide-planked hardwood floor. In the five floor-to-ceiling windows perched square fans set on full speed blowing out the hot air. Numerous electrical extension cords, filled to capacity, snaked along the juxtaposition of the floor and walls.

The sweaty visitors wandered around the ostentatious room. The woman wearing a dress adorned with designs of four-foot long sunflower plants, yellow high heels, and red lipstick said to her husband Milo, "There's no dust anywhere. This place is like a museum or a hotel." Milo turned to his wife and said, "The fireplace chute has to go up at least four stories. Why isn't there a bunch of soot on the walls? Look at that fireplace; there are no stains anywhere. I bet it doesn't even work."

Ashley watched as the hippie guy's dilated eyes attempted to take in the energy forces of the asylum. He reached out a hand toward the tank-top hippie gal. "I need another brownie." She reached into her hand-stitched purse and she said to her partner of life, "Let's pace this." He took the brownie and broke it in half and reached out with half a brownie to his partner. "We're good?"

Twelve of the thirteen heads of the visitors turned as two workers from the cafeteria wearing the compulsory white uniforms entered the room. The young thirteenth head was trying to open a locked door. The white-clad workers carried silver trays. On top of the trays were silver pitchers containing cold lemonade and silver bowls filled with lemon-lime mints and peanuts. The cafeteria workers were instructed by the president of the asylum to liberally serve the refreshing lemonade; the purpose was to cool off the visitors and to lessen their anxiety.

Ashley reclined in a chair. She crossed her orange stocking legs as she watched the townsfolk gather around the two white "servants." President Nash wanted his people, the people of Weston, to feel special. Part of the president's instructions to all of the tour guides was to make sure they learn the visitor's names.

Ashley pulled a small notepad and a pen out of a large pocket of her orange and yellow dress. "Folks, since we are going to be spending the day together I would like to learn all of your names. Again, my name is Ashley. I am terrible with names, so I am going to have to write them down and use some heuristics to remember your names."

"You're gonna use her sticks to remember our names?" questioned the squat Red Man chewing fellow. His eyes squinted. "You gonna beat our names out of us?"

Ashley dropped the notepad and pen to the floor. For the second time, she locked eyes with the disruptive man. "Sir, a heuristic is a clue to solving a problem. In this case, my problem is trying to remember everyone's names. I know you want to have fun and be noticed during this tour, but I must ask you to contain yourself."

"Well, why didn't you say 'clue' instead of 'her sticks.' That's just confusing."

"Okay, I need a clue to remember people's names. So, what is your name?"

The guy's jaw dropped as if she'd asked about his history of receiving or giving abuse.

The room was silent waiting for his response.

"Call me Red Man. That's what all my girlfriends call me."

Ashley let it go and picked up her pad and pen. She scribbled 'Red Man' with some questions marks following. She turned toward the elderly lady. "You have already helped me; you are Debbie, the dancer. And, I have already figured out a 'clue' to remember the man's name who is with you, Dan the Man."

Happy that she was singled out of the group, Debbie perked up and said, "Dan and I have been married for 52 years."

Polite applause emanated from the group.

Looking toward the man in the brown suit Ashley said, "I remember you because you manage to wear a suit in this unbearable hot day. I commend you."

"My name is Milo. You can remember my name because I sell Combine Accident Insurance to farmers in Ohio. Where there is a large silo, I know there is money. I'm Milo the silo."

In a fun-filled voice, "Oh you are a dear. Yes, I can remember Milo the silo. And, who is the woman with you?"

The obese woman wearing four-foot sunflower plants on her dress and sporting red lipstick spoke up before her husband could speak. "I'm Maddy." Not wanting to be outdone by her husband, "You can remember Maddy because I am mad about life. I love life. I am thankful every day I live."

Not wanting the attention the histrionic woman craved, Ashley looked in the direction of the sixth visitor, the pig-tailed little girl dressed in pink. "And, you are Juli Jo."

"I'm Juli."

The overweight twelfth visitor to enter the hospital said, "Now honey, when you are a woman you can change your name. It is still Juli Jo."

Not wanting the tour to turn into a group therapy session, Ashley changed the subject. "And, who are you?"

"I'm her single-parent mother," said the likewise pig-tailed pink-clothed mother. "My name is Jana."

Ashley crossed her thin legs. "Oh, I can do this--Juli Jo and Jana. You're a team in this venture of life."

Not wanting a further response from Jana, Ashley turned toward the hippie couple. "And you guys are? The hippie gal with the brownies in her purse spoke up for the two of them. "He's Hagar and I'm Harmony. Well, my name at the suffocating freedom courthouse is Helga Rose Riperdolvin. I prefer Harmony."

"Of course you do. That is a beautiful name," said the trying to remain composed Ashley. Wanting to get on with the tour, as she wrote down the names on her notepad, she said, "Those names I think I can remember—Hagar and Harmony." Trying to diffuse any further tension in the room Ashley concluded, "Those are beautiful names."

Ashley looked in the direction of the two black-clothed Mennonites. The man wearing a black Billy Jack hat spoke first. "We are here from Pennsylvania visiting relatives." Pointing in the direction of the black dressed and head cap woman he said, "She's my wife, Sarah. I'm Seth."

Writing down the names of the Mennonites, Sarah and Seth, Ashley silently questioned the diversity of the room. *These people have a lot of unresolved shit.* "I think I can remember you are Seth and Sarah." She made a point to mention the husband's name first.

Looking down at her notepad Ashley smiled and said, "Except for the sole visitor, Red Man, all of the couples' names begin with the same letter. What's the odds of that? This must be a positive sign that this will be a good tour based on Carl Jung's ideas on synchronicity.

On her notepad she had written:
Red Man ???

Debbie the dancer
Dan the Man

Milo sales rich silos (brown suit)

Maddy the mad about life (sunflower dressed)

Juli Jo (Juli)
Jana (pig-tailed and pink like daughter)

Hagar (high)
Harmony

Sarah
Seth (Mennonite)

The easily excited Ashley withdrew her notepad back to her lap and wrote—Richard the III and Jez. "I know, as many of you local folks might know, Richard the third and his wife, Jez. They are the benefactors of many programs in town, including this hospital.

The rich couple stood more erect waiting for polite applause that never materialized. Following the uncomfortable silence, Richard the third said, "Please, it's just Richard."

"What kind of name is Jez?" asked the Billy Jack hat Seth. Not waiting for a response, "Is that short for Jezebel? Are you a whore?"

His counterpart, Sarah, backhanded Seth in the chest. "We are no longer in Pennsylvania. Keep your words to yourself and pray for her."

The too-tanned spirited Jez would not be humiliated in the gathering of hicks. "You backward idiots have no right to judge. How long did it take you to get here in your horse and buggy— three days? If you ever decided to join the rest of us in civilized culture and read the scriptures, you would know that Jezebel was the beginning of the women's movement."

Ashley stood up.

The visitor group turned in her direction seeking guidance. Ashley straightened the lines of her dress with her arms. In an evangelistic voice she commanded, "These I will bring and make them joyful in my house of prayer; for my house shall be called a house of prayer for all peoples. Isaiah 56:7. If any of you listen to your weekly sermons, if you listen to people, you know we are all in the same boat. In this house, this hospital, if you can do nothing else, I hope you may appreciate the gifts of life you have been provided."

The visitor group did not expect a sermon from the anorexic social worker. A dumbfounded silence filled the room.

Ashley resumed to her seat looking down at her list of names. Her mind easily wandered, *"This once fun group of diversity is going to turn out to be a fucking mess."*

4

A scream broke the stillness in the room. "It's the devil!" Every head in the room turned to the direction of the scream.

The source of the scream was the eleven-year-old pig-tailed Juli Jo. Attired in pink stirrup pants and a pink top she pointed at a framed print of *The Nightmare* by Henry Fuseli. The painting was of a green creature squatted on the chest of a sleeping woman's body.

The seated Ashley giggled. "That is a painting about our dreams. Have any of you had a night terror? It is different from your usual nightmare because it happens in the early morning hours and the dream seems so real. The colors are especially vivid and some people feel like there is a weight on their chest like the green creature in the painting. You have these dreams because you are having a dream during non-REM sleep."

The visitors whispered to each other. Ashley clarified, "You have a night terror because you are dreaming when you are not supposed to be dreaming."

The townsfolk felt more comfortable in the strange surroundings due to their knowledgeable tour guide, the relative coolness of the room, and the rare opportunity to be catered. A lighthearted conversation began amongst the folks.

Ashley had been forewarned by Dr. Nash that a pattern of uplifted conversation might develop and she must allow the visitors to continue for a few minutes praising the facility. Then she could begin her memorized tour.

"I thought it was going to be like a prison," said Jana. Her pink cladded child, Juli Jo, countered, "Aren't the people supposed to be in cages? Do we get to see them?"

Richard, the bank president with a motto of an alligator on his shirt, said to his wife, "My sister in El Paso thinks we're a bunch of hicks in West Virginia. She needs to come out and see my bank and this building. The Southwest just has some mud dabbed structures that are painted pretty colors."

Jez, his overly tanned wife, had heard numerous times her husband's petty comments about his sister living in Texas. Jez changed the subject. "If they know how to treat us then they must know how to treat these crazies with some respect."

Richard could not let it go. "I told my sister in El Paso we don't have a bunch of peace signs and gang graffiti on our bridges in West Virginia. I finally had enough of my sister's shit and told her the last two times I saw any graffiti painted on the bridges in West Virginia was the one that said, "Jessy loves Jake," and the other said, "Jesus loves you."

The Mennonite Seth said to his wife, "Do you think we have sinned by being here?" His wife, Sarah, replied, "You're being stupid again."

"Get out of there," screamed Maddy to her husband. Milo pulled away from being inside the fireplace.

The elderly couple held hands and looked out one of the large windows. Ashley overheard Debbie say to her partner, "I know I had earlier reservations, but perhaps some mentally ill people need this type of setting."

Hearing the thoughtful comment by Debbie, the petite Ashley rose from her chair. She sauntered to the tall wooden doorway of the room. Tapping her empty glass with a spoon three times she gained the needed attention of the visitors.

The return of the sweet voice of Ashley gained the visitors' attention. "I want to thank all of you for taking time out of your busy schedules to come and visit us. We are proud of the work that we do to help these tormented people. They come to us suffering from psychosis, manic-depression, severe depression, and dementia. We have come a long way in developing new scientifically improved methods of helping these folks to lead a better life and for many to be cured."

The Red Man chewing fellow, sitting alone on a couch laughed. "This is all a joke. You people don't do shit. You just lock them up and hope you don't get hurt and keep them confined, so we don't get killed. You just want us to pass a bond to fund this stupid place. You've got a damn cemetery out back. I guess those folks are cured on their way to heaven."

Ashley's eyes narrowed. She decided it was a time of war instead of just being a battle with this man. In a too calm of a voice, she said, "Sir, what is your degree in psychology?"

The messed-up-hair man rubbed his hair into a further mess. "I don't have a degree."

Social worker Ashley briskly walked to the couch where the man was sitting. She glared down at the man, "Sir, sometimes it is better to listen than to talk. This is the third time I have attempted to help you to listen. The fourth time you will be escorted out."

The yellowed toothed man smiled. "Can I be escorted out with you?"

Ashley turned away from the man and walked with a forced determination out of the room. The visitors were left without their tour guide.

The room was silent.

The visitors looked at the other faces in an attempt of gaining recognition of what had just transpired. None of the visitors chanced a look at the man on the couch.

"Code Blue visiting room, Code Blooo visiting room," broadcasted a reassuring woman's voice over the intercom system of the hospital.

The histrionic Maddy screamed.

Wearing all white clothing a white man and a black man appeared in the doorway of the room.

The skinny white man sported a Beetles hairstyle and round sunglasses.

The black man walked past the Beetle-look-alike and up to Maddy. She screamed again.

Ashley rushed back into the room and stood beside the black man. She placed a hand on the cannon-ball shoulder of the black man. "Mack, would you please help the man sitting on the couch realize that he does not need to be a part of the tour?"

Without requesting details of the need for the man's departure, the black man in a deep hollow voice said, "Of course Ashley."

The white cladded charcoal-black man walked to the couch. The visitors parted a path reminiscent of Moses parting the Red Sea. The John Lennon sunglasses white man remained by the doorway and watched.

The black man towered over the man on the couch. In a cavernous voice, the black man said, "You need to leave."

The white man swallowed the last of his chew. His face lost all color. He vomited on the carpet.

Maddy screamed again. Milo frowned at his wife. The other visitors remained motionless in silence.

The black man seized an upper arm of the once Red Man chewing white man and pulled the man up. The black man in control of the situation looked at Ashley. "I will make sure this mess is cleaned up." He scanned the faces of the visitors and said in his deep voice, "Folks don't worry any. As you can see by this man's mess, he did not need to be here. This was not wanted nor expected. I, we (he did not bother to look at his impotent partner standing at the doorway), are used to taking care of the unexpected. We are here to protect our professionals and to protect you. I promise you will have a safe and enlightening day."

Ashley moved out of the doorway so the physician assistant could escort the man out of the room. As the men were leaving, she said to the black man, "Mack, you have no idea how much you being here means to me."

The social worker drastically created a new persona. She turned to the visitors and acted as if nothing had transpired. Calling a code to take a US citizen down and vomit stinking on the floor appeared to be of no significance to Ashley.

The thin figure straightened her mod shift and walked to a framed print of a man being dunked in a river by a large wooden contraption. "If our disobedient visitor would have been patient enough he would hear that before the Civil War most people suffering from severe and chronic mental illnesses were misconceived as being sinners who God needed to punish. Their symptoms were believed to be the work of the devil. Some of the treatments consisted of torturing the patient so the devil would no longer desire to live in the patient's body. As a result, many of the treatments were, shall we say…insane?"

Most of the twelve returned a reassuring chuckle. The all black attired Mennonite couple's faces were blank stares. The Billy Jack hatted Seth silently questioned. *Is that girl making fun of our religion?*

Ashley nimbly walked to an early picture of the Weston Asylum. "As you have probably already noticed there are many pictures of the facility as it was being built in the middle of the 1800s. During and after the Civil War large mental hospitals were built in almost every state east of the Mississippi River. They discovered that if patients were treated in a compassionate and respectful manner, then most of the people could be cured."

Eleven of the remaining twelve visitors stopped eating their mints and nuts. Hagar, the hippie, stood beside a table where the silver plate had been placed and was munching down the remaining mints and nuts.

Jana walked away from her daughter who was trying to look up the chute of the chimney. The middle-aged pig-tailed woman took a step in the direction of Ashley. "I have only an eighth – grade education, but I think everyone in this room is thinking what I am thinking. I've heard many horror stories of what happens within these walls."

Dr. Nash had forewarned Ashley this question might arise and she had been prepped by the president of the Asylum to answer, "Some of the horrendous frightening stories I have heard. Most are simply not true. You must remember that the people living here are not themselves. Some even come to us believing they are Martians or even Jesus Christ."

She gained the needed nervous laughter she hoped for.

The social worker pointed to a framed profile of a woman. "The original intent of the building of these facilities was compassionate. The sole driving force of this movement was Dorothy Dix, **a woman**. During the early 1800s, she had witnessed the cruel imprisonment of the chronically mentally insane with criminals in prisons. Her righteous idea was to build a facility where people suffering from severe and chronic psychological disorders could do something productive in a structured and safe environment. By the end of their day, they could feel good about themselves. During their stay at asylums, the patients were turned into productive workers. Many of the patients were farmers growing corn, beans, and tending the cattle, chicken and hog farms. Other patients worked at various supportive jobs. Some of the asylums were completely self-sufficient except for the slaughtering of the beef cattle." Ashley spoke in a stronger voice, "Instead of kicking these troubled souls out to the woods or imprisoning them we gave them a purpose, a meaning to their lives, all of this happened due to the workings of a woman, Dorothy Dix."

The elderly Dan drawled, "The farms have been closed for years."

Ashley lightly touched the upper arm of Dan as she walked to a picture that looked like a surgical room. The social worker returned to the president's scripted reply. "New methods of treatment were discovered. One was frontal lobotomies. The psychiatrist who created this horrific form of treatment did win a Nobel Prize only to be later killed by one his patients. Lobotomies were one of the reasons the farms closed. The people whose brains were cut were of no longer of use because they could never remember anything—they had no short-term memory—but they were more docile."

Standing in the corner of the room Ashley did a dramatic 330-degree turn. Her dress could only bell outwards an inch because it hung on her like a gunny sack. She pointed at a picture of President John F. Kennedy and returned to her rehearsed speech. "In the 50s there was a new breakthrough form of treatment, psychotropics. Many of our patients just need medication. If they just take their pills, then life will be good. Therefore, it seemed there was no need to keep the expensive farms; and, it became cheaper to buy the food in bulk."

The petite social worker went rogue from the all-powerful Nash's prepared speech. "These new medications are going to be the demise of the Weston Asylum. Kennedy signed the Community and Mental Health Act of 1962 that provided for the building of pill dispensaries in almost every county east of the Mississippi. Because of that bill, we are going to see a return to the days of what Dorothy Dix witnessed before she insisted on the appropriate care of these people. Someday this hospital will close and instead of the patients being sent to the woods as they were in the early 1800s, they will be sent to the streets. We will also once again see these suffering souls needlessly being sent to prisons instead of getting the care and purpose of life that our hospital once provided."

"That's sad," moaned Jana, the pig-tailed pink-dressed woman.

"It is saa…," Ashley briefly stopped talking in an ill-attempt to regroup. "Please forgive me. I cannot see into the future." The once composed Ashley was out of sorts and even begged of the group, "Please do not tell Dr. Nash what I said." She straightened the sides of her dress.

The pig-tailed girl of the group, Juli Jo, looked up from the fireplace and asked, "Said what?"

"Nothing." Regaining her composure, the porcelain-skinned tour guide resumed her high-pitched sweet voice. "I guess we should begin the tour. I can walk and talk at the same time. Let's head out for a tour you will never forget."

5

Ashley led the group of twelve townsfolk out of the visiting room and back into the wide entry hallway of the Weston Asylum. In preparation for Community Day, the color of the main hallway had been repainted two months ago to a cheerful robin-egg blue.

The majority of the walls in the grand building were bare. The entry hallway was one of the exceptions. Framed prints of paintings adorned the walls of the main hallway. The themes of the prints were of sunlight breaking through clouds striking hay fields, farmhouses, and country churches. There was no glass protecting the prints from the elements and the framed prints were screwed into the walls.

In her orange and yellow dress, Ashley led her group to the center of the hallway. The group stood at a major crossroad of the building. All of the four floors of the Weston Asylum met under the tower clock.

When Ashley reached her destination, she turned and faced her group with both of her thin arms highlighting the two staircases to her sides. She saw something she did not like. Her audience was looking at something or someone behind her.

The common folks of central West Virginia saw a fast-paced dark figure advancing toward them. The group froze. Cigarettes ceased to rise to mouths. Visitors forgot to breathe. Their pupils widened. Untouched sweat poured down their faces.

An outline of a figure came sashaying down the hall. The figure had a distinctive walk. The cavernous monstrosity of the hospital was silent except for the distinctive resonant sound of the heels of the walking figure. The high heels of her white patent heel shoes were driven to the floor with force, "click...click... click."

The dark figure was silhouetted against the white glass panes of two doors at the far end of the hallway. All faces locked in a desire to see who was going to emerge from the shadows. Carmel's knees rose slightly higher as she walked at a faster clip and her hips had an added twist.

The mesmerizing figure abruptly emerged from the shadows into the light.

Katie Carmel in her tailored, yellow polka-dot dress, was used to the attention that she created.

Ashley was accustomed to Carmel's ostentatious entrances. She did not bother to turn toward the approaching figure of the psychologist.

Carmel walked to the side of Ashley. The psychologist's yellow polka dot dress and attitude dwarfed the social worker in her orange and yellow mod colors.

Refusing to turn to face Carmel, Ashley spoke to the twelve visitors, "This is Dr. Carmel. She is one of our newer and younger psychologists on staff." Ashley's head partially turned without making eye contact and continued, "Dr. Carmel, would you have a moment to speak to our visitors?"

"Of course, I would love to," said Carmel in a quick and sarcastic reply.

Dr. Carmel had just left a meeting with president Nash. During the meeting, Carmel had insisted the opening of the hospital for townsfolk to gawk at the patients was an inhumane gesture and president Nash was treating the patients as if it was a human zoo. When leaving the meeting, she screamed, "I cannot believe this is the 60s."

Carmel's pearl white eyes skimmed to meet the eyes of the people who would come to a human zoo. She wanted to scream at the people and tell them they were sicker than her patients.

The psychologist took in a full breath and slowly exhaled. Her eyes looked past the group and focused on one of the religious-themed prints on a wall of a god-sent sunray protecting his flock.

Dr. Carmel spoke. "I am a clinical psychologist and I work on our Admissions Unit and I also do psychotherapy with our patients on the Acute Unit. I take it that is where you will next be herded." Carmel looked down toward Ashley. Ashley raised her head up and down.

The new person in power over the group continued, "When people first come to the hospital they go to the Admissions Unit. Typically, we have them for three days and then our team of professionals will decide where they need to go. Some will go home or back to jail. Many will stay here at the hospital and we have different units dependent upon the patient's particular needs."

Carmel stopped talking and stared at the pink stirrup pants and sleeveless girl.

Juli Jo stared at something or someone by the staircase to the left. The girl's wide opened mouth and rounded eyes suggested something not good.

A figure from the staircase moved with the stealth and ease of a spirit from the staircase to within centimeters of Carmel.

Without turning her torso, the composed psychologist leaned her head to the left. Standing next to her with his head tilted slightly upward was Noah Holiday (AKA, Jesus).

She gave him a slight grin conveying, "*You got me.*" He smiled back with a full goofy grin.

Noah Holiday (AKA, Jesus) said, "Kate, I needed to find you because we need to do some last minute details before the people go on their tour."

Carmel knew this was not going to be good. When Noah was in a manic mood, he would refer to her as 'Kate' because he had previously found out she did not appreciate being called that name.

Noah Holiday's referring to Carmel as Kate is the classic reaction formation defense mechanism that Anna Freud, not Sigmund Freud, introduced to society. People in love adopt an opposite attitude of severe teasing for the ones they love. It's similar to the teasing of lovers on a sixth-grade playground or on match.com.

The smirk left Noah's face. He took in a deep breath and said in his best professional voice, "This will only take a second. We just need to tune these babes up for the company."

Noah Holiday does the thinkable but unthinkable.

His wide-opened hands grabbed the full breasts of Dr. Katie Carmel. He affirmatively squeezed twice and then lowered his hands to his sides.

Carmel and Noah Holiday stared at one another. One had a look of a guilty boy who was waiting for his punishment. The other had the stoic blank stare that nobody could interpret.

Cigarette ashes of the visitors fell to the concrete floor. Pouches of underarm sweat-stained their clothes.

What followed might be due to the psychologist's embarrassment. Or, it could be because she was still upset at president Nash opening the hospital for these visitors to come to a human zoo.

Dr. Carmel blinked and surveyed the group of astonished faces. In a professional yet apologetic voice, "Please forgive him. He is just hungry and I didn't breastfeed him today."

She took a decisive step back from Noah and commanded as if she was talking to a dog, "Come Jesus."

Carmel turned away from the astonished crowd and in her hardened pace descended back down the hallway from where she had come, "click…click…click."

Noah Holiday dutifully followed a step behind her.

He was the first to speak.

"That was cool."

"Shut up."

6

When the burnt skinned Jez heard Dr. Carmel tell Jesus to "shut up" she screamed.

Not to be outdone, Maddy fainted. Fortunately, Milo caught her shoulders before her head struck the concrete floor.

Ashley took immediate command of the situation and walked to the side of the woman and man. "Please step back and give the woman some space and cool air."

Ashley stood over the couple with her hands on her hips.

Milo was on his knees and cradled his wife's head against his chest. With care, he shifted her head to his thighs and removed his brown jacket. He bundled the pressed brown jacket and laid it on the concrete floor and rested his wife's head on his jacket.

Ashley's lower thin lip slightly dropped. Between the woman's false eyelashes Ashley thought she caught a glimmer of the woman's eyeballs similar to the game children do when they pretend to be asleep. Ashley took a step next to the lying woman's shoulder and stared directly down into her eyes. The woman's eyes shut.

Milo removed a white handkerchief from his pants pocket and lightly tapped the perspiration on his wife's forehead and lips (even though there was no sweat on her red lips).

When he tapped his wife's lips, Ashley thought she saw the man pucker his lips in the act of kissing.

Ashley looked up and scanned the other visitors' heads to get verification that this was all a scam on the woman's part to get attention. The other visitors did not look at Ashley. They were all staring at the pathetic woman. Three of the people quietly prayed. The black dressed Sarah handed Milo a Weston Asylum booklet she had taken from the waiting room. "Here, use this as a fan to give her some air." As the man fanned his incapacitated wife he looked up in the direction of Ashley. "She'll be fine. She does this at gatherings especially when she gets hot." In a futile attempt to display his psychological knowledge and that he had the situation under control he said to Ashley, "Her mother's touched."

Milo unbuttoned the top four buttons of her dress. The Mennonite Seth solemnly requested, "Let us pray." He lowered his head without seeking recognition of whether the other visitors wanted to pray. "Oh, Father in heaven—." Ashley interrupted his prayer. "Sir." The man looked up to Ashley. With the grace of a ballerina, Ashley floated her head up and down and crooned, "I am sure she will be fine." The man unknowingly mimicked her vertical head gesture and raised his head up and down in agreement.

Another visitor group shuffled in through the main doorway of the asylum to begin their tour.

The young but mature Ashley thought this charade had been going on for too long. She looked down at Milo with his suit jacket used as a pillow for his histrionic wife. "Perhaps in her delicate condition Maddy is going to need some longer type of care. I will get one of our doctors to see if we can provide her some care and maybe let her stay a couple of days."

On cue, Maddy's eyes fluttered and opened. "You okay baby?" asked her husband. In a drowsy voice, Maddy said, "I think so." The Mennonite Seth laid his hand on her forehead. "God was always with you." When the man laid his hand on the top of the lady's head, Ashley thought she caught the black-hatted man peer down the woman's unbuttoned top.

Knowing president Nash would be waiting for them, Ashley waved her pencil-thin arms to the two wooden staircases. "Okay, we need to go folks. The other group is catching up with us. We are going to go up one of these staircases where you will then be allowed entrance to one of our functioning units."

The group of twelve splintered off and waddled up their way up the two hand-carved staircases. The ornate staircases that were lumbered from trees of the extensive Asylum property were obviously of a different era. The handrails were so low that many of the townsfolk had to bend their backs to reach the overly wide and dysfunctional wide handrails.

Last year, during Community Day, one histrionic patient had managed to get on the roof of the four-story facility. When there was a large enough crowd she screamed at the top of her lungs, "President Nash is the devil. You must rise up against him and destroy him before he destroys us." She removed her robe and stood naked in a crucifix stance for a few seconds. A swan dive turned to flailing arms and legs in a futile attempt to stop her fall to the sidewalk. Similar to so many suicide attempts, right after the decision to jump, cut the wrist, swallow the pills; there is the thought to not die. Her death was on the front page of the *Charleston Gazette* newspaper.

To prevent another happening like last year Dr. Nash had the more agitated patients moved and locked up out of view. And, for a little more reassurance, he had a discussion with one of his psychiatrists, Dr. Blowfish. They agreed that the hospital should not take any risks this year, so they upped the Thorazine on all of the patients suffering from psychosis and added Thorazine to the treatment regime of some patients who were not suffering from psychotic symptoms. Thorazine was effective for reducing a person's hallucinations and delusions. And in the case of Community Day, it was a sedative drug. The docile patients remained in one of the Acute Units, 246, for the tour.

The paranoid Nash had investigated **every** assurance that nothing as terrible as last year would occur during this Community Day.

Ashley gracefully walked up the flight of wooden stairs. The walk up one flight of stairs left many of the visitors huffing and puffing. Five of the townsfolk were extremely overweight.

Once the visitor group had managed the climb up a flight of stairs, the lithe social worker pointed her thin index finger in the direction of a steel door with a small window. Checker board patterned wire was encased in the middle of the glass pane. "This is one of our Acute Units, 246. If you smoke, you may have one last cigarette before we enter the unit. We do not allow smoking on the units. The patients go outside to a screened-in area to smoke, but we will not be going to those porches. And, we will be on the unit for about an hour."

With Ashley's comment that the visitors' would have to go without a cigarette for one hour, six visitors lit cigarettes: Milo, Maddy, Hagar, Richard, Jez, and Debbie. The smoker group splintered away from the nonsmoker group and huddled around a floor ashtray on the balcony.

The smokers heaved in long puffs as if it were going to be the last of their brief lives. Ashley walked over to the now twelfth instead of the thirteenth visitor. The tour guide/social worker leaned down to the pig-tailed girl. "That is such a cute pink outfit."

Out of the corner of her eyes, Ashley saw the girl's mother in pink overalls walk to her. With a calloused hand, Jana grabbed a shoulder of Ashley and the woman slightly tugged, "Can we talk for a second?"

Ashley did not like to be touched by men or women. Thinking the larger woman had an issue with a friend or relative that she needed a professional opinion about Ashley responded to her in a professional chirpy voice. "Of course."

The two walked to the opposite side of the balcony of the smokers. The pink bibbed-overall coal miner lightly grabbed both shoulders of Ashley. "Honey, I'm concerned."

And here it comes; she's going to ask me about some advice for some strange relative.

"You're just too thin."

Ashley's jaw dropped. *What the fuck?*

"Child, even though you're cute as a button you look like one of those Holocaust victims. We got plenty of food from our garden and a few cattle. I just don't want you to go without food no matter how hard your financial situation might be. We live in the yellow house just across the bridge outside the entrance of the hospital. You are always welcomed."

Only one other person in Ashley's life questioned Ashley's anorexic symptoms. Her best girlfriend she had known since grade school pestered Ashley about her recent alarming weight loss. For Ashley, her best friend's concerns were relatively easy to dismiss.

Ashley did not know how to respond to this invasive yet supposed compassionate holier-than-thou woman. *Who the hell is this fat cow telling me about my weight, especially during a tour?* The pencil-thin arm-and-leg social worker looked in the direction of the visitors huddled around their beloved floor ashtray. *Those are the sick ones with their cancer sticks. Why is she picking on me?* Her thoughts turned tangential. *She's so damn fat she's going to die of a heart attack probably during the next flight of stairs. She has no idea that life is about making a decision and sticking to it. It's that simple. She couldn't even get past the eighth grade. She looks like a sick version of her stupid spoiled kid.*

The chunky woman leaned closer to the stick figure and hushed so the others would not hear, "Do you still have the—monthly cycles?"

Ashley's sweet voice returned. "I bleed like a cut stag pig."

1

A distinctive clicking sound of a key turned inside the heavy locking mechanism on the other side of the steel door.

The visitors' faces turned to the small window in the doorway. Most of the smokers extinguished their cigarettes in the floor ashtray. Hagar the hippie and Debbie the dancer drawled another puff of their cigarettes.

The steel door swung open and slammed against the wall.

A figure stood in the doorway and in a thick Bella Lugosi voice said, "We've been waiting for you."

The visitors had already seen this man in his Beetle haircut and John Lennon sunglasses in the visiting room of the asylum. Some of the visitors' faces turned to Ashley for guidance and reassurance. Ashley's eyes penetrated the man's sunglasses with a stare of disgust and contempt.

The pearl-white-skinned social worker glided to the side of the man dressed in white. The visitor group did not move closer to the doorway. Ashley straightened her dress to verify there were no bulges in the lines of her asexual dress. She said to her group, "You already met Mr. Trick Greene downstairs. He is a physician assistant here at the asylum. The staff and nurses wear all white. The professionals may wear street clothes. We could not function without our physician assistants. They do a little bit of everything to help out on the units."

Ashley left out a major detail of a physician assistant's job description. The title 'physician's assistant' was a glorified name for men who enjoyed settling down the patients who became physically agitated. They were glorified bouncers in a mental hospital setting. When a patient threatened or hit someone, there were physician assistants on most of the units to help calm down the situation. The accustomed job for a physician assistant was to take the patient down onto the floor and place them in a hold until one of the nurses could administer a hypodermic needle with a powerful dose of Thorazine that would snow the patient.

Ashley's two arms pushed Trick Greene back into the unit he had arrived from. His arms and legs flapped in the air similar to the scarecrow in the *Wizard of Oz*. The social worker walked into the unit and with her back still turned to her group said, "We are supposed to have two physician assistants join us while we walk through one of the most productive units in the Asylum." She walked and stood by Trick Greene. "Is Mack on this unit today?" she pleaded.

"Hell, I don't know."

The social worker turned and waved for the group to enter the unit. "Come on in. We'll wait here a few moments to see if another physician assistant joins us."

The visitor group did not move. Finally, Jana pushed her way between the visitors and lumbered through the doorway. She turned back to her pink-clad pig-tailed girl, but the girl was not standing outside the doorway. Juli Jo was a full ten feet inside the unit. Her mother screamed, "Juli Jo." The girl dutifully ran to her mother's side.

The visitors waddled their way through the doorway being only too polite to allow the person standing next to them to enter the unit before them.

The visitors saw what every one of the units of the Weston Asylum looked like, a long and wide hallway with a nurse sitting behind a desk midway down the hall. The visitors' heads scanned the people on the unit. Deadened eyed patients stared into space and zombie figures shuffled around the long wide hallway. A few of the patients sat at round tables.

In preparation for the visitors, the staff had liberally sprayed lemon-scented aerosol cans throughout the unit. The scent was so overpowering elderly Dan the Man sneezed.

The walls were a buttery yellow color. The label on the paint can, when an extensive repainting had been done in the 1950s was 'Navajo Yellow' suggesting a bright yellow. Over the years the color of all the units had deadened to buttery yellow; or as the nurses referred to the drab color, piss yellow needing water. Rows of navy gray doorways lined the two long walls.

The splashing of the bright orange and yellow colors on Ashley's dress contrasted with the drab surroundings. Ashley walked five steps further into the unit. "You are now on Acute Unit 246. This is the unit where many of the voluntary patients and patients on a 60-day hold are placed. Dr. Carmel also does psychotherapy with some of the patients on this unit. You met her earlier downstairs when the patient—when she had to leave."

Trick Greene in his John Lennon glasses and Beetles haircut stepped to the side of Ashley. "I am usually on this unit, Ashley is not."

"Trick is correct," Ashley agreed, "I do not usually work on this unit. I am on the Admissions Unit. That is the first unit that all of the patients usually go for a stay of three days."

Ashley took a step sideways from Trick. "Mr. Greene. You apparently need some recognition. Go ahead; if you can control yourself tell our gracious visitors what good things happen here on the Acute Unit."

The round sunglasses man grinned. "First of all, I want to thank you for coming to our humble home. Here, at the lunatic asylum happy home, our goal is to make everyone happy." Ashley sighed in disbelief.

"Here, here—." Trick pointed and ran to a patient who sat in a chair. The patient did not move and he stared at the Navajo, buttery, piss-yellow walls. "This is Demetri or something like that. He just got sent to our unit from Admissions. But, the important thing is that this guy is from Russia and we will provide him the same top quality of care we do Americans. None of us can speak Russian. Even though the doctors are not sure why he is here, we still provide him the highest quality of care. Now some of you might be asking, 'Why are we paying the bill for a Ruskie?'"

Trick abruptly stopped speaking and squeaked. An incomprehensible force clamped onto Trick's right upper arm. Involuntarily Trick's shoulder reached to the height of his ear. Trick had felt this force before. Trick knew the other physician assistant, Mack Johnson, had arrived.

Mack Johnson was a 5 foot 10-inch black male. He was the physician assistant who earlier in the morning had removed the inappropriate man in the visitors' room. White shirt, white pants, and white shoes accentuated his coal-black skin. The forty-something-year-old man's body could easily be that of a middle linebacker in his 20s. Johnson sported 18-inch guns in his upper arms. The most distinguishing feature about Mack Johnson, when he was wearing clothes, was his deep, cavernous, reverberating voice. When he spoke, people tended to listen, even the agitated patients.

Mack affirmed his hold differentiating Trick's bicep from his triceps. The powerful black man grinned at the visitors and casually commented, "It is good to see all of you again. I hope your day is going well. Please forgive my colleague. He has a tendency sometimes to let his mouth engage before his brain."

A few chuckles, some silence, and some outright laughter vented from the thankful visitors.

"Please Miss Ashley continue with your tour and Trick and I will be of any assistance that we can possibly be." Mack let go of Trick's arm. Trick Greene's shoulder dropped.

The married Ashley walked to the side of the Mack and laid a hand on his bicep. The size of his arm dwarfed the thin fingers of her hand. "This is Mr. Mack Johnson. He will also be escorting us through the unit." Ashley unconsciously and blatantly blinked her eyes. "You will be going with us Mack, won't you?"

"Missy, I am here for you and our visitors."

Midway down the long hallway of Unit 246, from behind the nurse's desk, a dapper fiftyish looking man wearing a bold-striped, three-piece suit with a 2-inch wide red tie stiffly walked toward the visitors. Striking veins of white hair marked the temporal sides of his richly waxed black hair. An ultra-thin mustache lined his thin, caustic, upper lip. He smiled as he paraded down the hallway, but his smile was crooked. And, one of his eyes was fully open looking like a glass eye and the other eye looked normal. President Nash's imbalanced face was due to partial paralysis of his face resulting from having polio as a child.

All of the visitors had heard stories of President Nash. Only a few had ever seen him around town.

When the president reached within five feet of the visitor group he ran a hand through his waxed hair. In a high-pitched finely enunciated voice he took control. "I am Dr. Nash. I am the president of this fine institution." His one good eye scanned his audience. "Ashley, I am glad you were able to keep the group to twelve."

She slightly nodded her head, "Thank you, sir."

The president's presumptuous clothing in the drab surroundings and his nasal voice captured the attendance of his visitors. "We use to do lobotomies at this hospital. At that time we had no other means to help these poor people who had sinned beyond remorse and we were acting in the faith of our God that we could make what time they had on this planet to be at least somewhat tolerable before they succumbed to the fires of hell."

Nash's voice grew to that of a tent evangelist and his arms reached to the heavens. "Yes, these people are mentally ill. Yes, many of these people are also physically ill." His arms fell to his sides and his voice slowed and deepened. "But, at the core, these people are spiritually ill. We provide a Bible free of charge to each of our patients."

"Amen," solemnly validated over half the visitors.

The crooked-faced Nash took a dramatic pause in his allocution to look into the eyes and souls of his audience.

He thought he was well on his way to getting the desired effect. More importantly, he had his gut instinct that the people heard him. They had that numbed, country-church, beaten-down look in their eyes. They knew they had sinned because their preacher had told them so. Because the country folk were told weekly they had sinned it was without question that the patients in this fine institution must have sinned more than them. And—a doctor told them the patients had sinned.

Nash saw a pig-tailed girl in his audience who did not hear his words. The president of the asylum intuitively knew the young child's vision would come during her adolescence as did his.

Nash returned his gaze to his adult audience and shrieked, "But we don't do lobotomies anymore."

A tiny squelch burped from Maddy. President Nash, Milo, and the other visitors paid no heed to the false scream.

Nash walked to a younger patient sitting in the hallway. The sleepy looking man looked like the typical college student from a few years back. His hair was finely parted on the side and he wore a short-sleeve blue plaid shirt. Nash asked, "Sir, may I use you as an example?"

"Are you going to hurt me?" The half-closed eyed man looked at the president, then looked at the visitor group, and returned his apprehensive gaze toward the president.

"My son, nobody is going to hurt you here. Why are you here?"

"I hear words."

The president of the asylum was glad he selected this patient. Before Nash had left the nurses' desk, he had asked the nurse who was a good candidate to use as an example. She told him the patient in the blue plaid shirt had just arrived from Admissions, but his speech was logical and coherent. More importantly, the nurse said, "He's been the most cooperative nice man I have seen here in weeks." President Nash had been concerned the patient was snowed. The nurse clarified he was somewhat drowsy but just a good guy.

President Nash pointed at the casually dressed good looking man. "This man hears words." The president said the pronunciation as if the man was not there. Without knowing anything more about the man's history or even his name, President Nash shrilled out the following sermon in his high-pitched bird-like voice, "Ten years ago we would cut on his brain in the basement of this facility. That was before my time. Now, here at the Weston Asylum, we provide psychopharmacology. We give our patients medications so they may return home and live a productive life. A decade ago they discovered Thorazine and Imipramine. These are wonder drugs if there ever was. Thorazine helps these poor tormented souls to stop thinking evil thoughts and the Imipramine lifts them from their melancholia. In a matter of days, mankind will reach the moon. In a matter of years, we will discover drugs that will completely cure schizophrenia and depression."

The pink dressed girl pulled up on her stirrup strap pants. Juli Jo said, "That lady said," pointing toward Ashley, "Drugs are going to close this place."

The one full-eyed president looked at Juli Jo. "My child, if we were to close these places where would they go? They would end up in the streets and prisons." President's Nash's voice regained its strength. "We are all citizens of the greatest country in the world, the United States of America."

The intensity of Nash's voice once again reached a crescendo. "Of course we cannot keep helping these sinful people and eventually to find a cure without you passing the upcoming bond. I hope that you will also tell your friends, family, and church members the great things you are going to discover that we are doing here."

The lop-sided faced, boldly-striped suit man took a dramatic step backward and slightly bowed his head. "Thank-you for letting me talk with you today."

He received a loud applause from seven of his visitors. Screams of "Amen!" echoed off the Navaho yellow, buttery, piss-yellow walls.

He abruptly turned and walked out the door the visitors had entered.

In her bright orange and yellow mod shift, Ashley walked to the front of the visitor group. She guided the visitor group down the hallway of the drug-induced zombie patients sitting and standing along the walls. A nurse walked in their direction to tell them more about how the Acute Unit functioned.

Before the group had taken a couple of steps Mack boldly brushed a cheek of Ashley. She turned her head in his direction and then turned her head in the direction Mack was looking.

Ashley's face turned to that of terror. The skinny eleven-year-old Juli Jo was talking to the patient that president Nash had earlier used as an example.

The pig-tailed, pink stirrup pants girl had slowed her walk to gain distance from her mother. Once she knew she was not detected the girl had walked back to the nice young man president Nash had used as an example.

Within a couple of feet of the seated man, Juli Jo said, "You don't look crazy."

"Thank you."

"I'm Juli Jo."

"I'm Bob Burns."

"If you aren't crazy then why are you here?"

"I didn't say I was not crazy. But, I didn't say I was crazy. I hear voices."

"I do too. I hear my Mom when she calls me. Well, I hear you too."

"I hear voices when someone doesn't talk."

Juli paused to comprehend what she heard.

The girl broke the silence, "You do not."

"Yes, I do."

"Can I hear them?"

"No."

"Is it God?"

"I doubt it."

This was a lot for an eleven-year-old to try to understand. It just didn't make sense.

Juli Jo looked into Bob Burns' eyes. "What do the voices say?"

"Bang and escape."

"That's it, bang and…"

"Juli Jo, get back over here," came a scream from Jana.

Juli Jo hurried back to the group. As the visitor group herded its way down the large hallway, Juli Jo turned back toward Bob Burns. She waved and the sleepy-looking young man smiled and waved back.

Bob Burns moved an index finger vertically in front of his mouth suggesting, *shush, it's a secret.* He silently mouthed the words; *it's okay.*

One floor above the visitor's tour of the Acute Unit, an important daily meeting was late to begin. One of the participants was not present for the meeting.

The sharp "click...click...click" of the white patent high heel shoes announced Katie Carmel was on the Admissions Unit. Her fast-paced knees drove high into the air, and her shoes forcefully struck the stained concrete floor. She paraded with the narcissism of a woman modeling new clothing on a catwalk. The brazen strut on the Admissions Unit pounded a little faster than usual.

The visitors were not allowed access to the Admissions Unit. A free lunch in Cafeteria A was going to be provided for the visitors. Dr. Nash did not want the visitors to see patients when they were fresh off the street; and, he did not want the visitors to meet the professionals who worked the Admissions Unit. He had a free catered lunch on the Admissions Unit so visitors would not witness the bizarre and bold antics of the patients, staff, and professionals on the Admissions Unit.

Only a unique type of person would work in a mental hospital. It took a different type of person to work on the Admissions Unit at the Weston Asylum. The professionals on the Admissions Unit were tough-skinned souls who didn't take crap from the patients, and they didn't take crap from the other members of their beloved Treatment Team.

Dr. Carmel's strut moved to a gallop, "click..click..click." Due to the earlier episode with Noah Holiday (AKA, Jesus) tuning up her breasts, she was pushing the clock. An elderly blue-haired patient reached out to the psychologist. Carmel in a hurried voice said, "I'm late, I'm late for a very important date." The patient yelled, "Fuck you!"

The intensity of the Admissions Unit was equivalent to that of an Emergency Room. Unlike having to do a quick stitching for a wound, the professionals of the Admissions Team had three days to be mind readers and determine whether the patients would harm themselves or someone else. Two months ago the Admissions Unit released a patient that suffered from manic depression and would sometimes be psychotic during his spells of mania. The afternoon of his release from the Admissions Unit he killed his mother because he thought she was the devil. Some psychotic people can hide their delusions (*Kill your mother. Free the world of the devil.*) just as well as neurotics can hide their irrational thoughts (*Have another piece of cake. You deserve it*).

The front of the yellow polka dot dress hung tight to her thighs and the back of the dress flagged behind as she passed the nursing desk midway down the corridor. The nurse behind the desk yelled, "Psycho called and asked if you were on the unit. I told him I thought I saw your Buick was in the parking lot."

"Thanks."

The scheduled 0900-1100 Admissions Treatment Team meetings were always lively. Professionals from seven different areas of expertise (psychiatry, psychology, nursing, social work, physical therapy, occupational therapy, and nutrition) shared the information they had obtained about the patients. The goal of the team was to determine what to do with the patients before the patients' 72-hour court-order ran out.

One of the professionals on the team may adamantly believe a patient should be released and yet a different professional obstinately believe the patient should remain in the asylum. The power structure of the Admissions Unit, the credibility of the professional, was not based on the type of college degree a person had achieved. Instead, a professional gained power within this exclusive club based on the number of battles they had won during the Treatment Team meetings. Social workers could easily trump a psychiatrist if they had information the psychiatrist had not obtained.

Psycho's going to be pissed. Carmel's trot turned to a full run, "click.click.click." The athletic figure threw her body against the last Navy-grey door on the right. In one quick move, she lifted the keychain hanging from her thin belt and unlocked the door.

The psychologist arrived at the Admissions Treatment Team room. The time was 0902.

The Admissions Treatment Team room stood in contrast to the rest of the asylum. The room was filled with sunlight. Six-foot tall windows lined the two walls of the expansive corner room. Unlike so many areas in this massive building, there was lots of light and space. Two 12-foot long hickory tables constructed from trees on the property were arranged in a 'T' pattern. At the top of the 'T' sat the major players of the treatment team. The almighty psychiatrists and psychologists sat at their informally assigned seats at the table, similar to parishioners sitting in their regularly assigned pews at church.

Circumscribing the walls of the room were numerous overstuffed chairs and two couches for members who came late and for some of the minor players of the team. The seats around the room and at the end of the T-table were affectionately called 'the peanut gallery.'

In this light-drenched room were two plastic rubber plants. A half empty box of maple-square donuts was at the top of the 'T' and at the lower end was an empty box of Twinkies.

Carmel hurried into the room. Most of the faces watched in disgust because the psychologist had gained enough power to delay the beginning of their sacred meeting. Some of the faces purposefully did not turn in her direction to acknowledge her presence.

The yellow-with-white- polka-dots dressed Carmel sashayed to her chair to the right of 'Psycho' where her empty chair was waiting for her. She managed to catch a glimpse of a man in his 30s posed on a couch. His relaxed demeanor in this highly charged room was suggestive of someone with power—or stupidity. Actually, …nobody sat next to him on the couch because the scent of his Hai Karate cologne was so strong. His greased red hair complimented his light baby-blue polyester suit.

His reaction was that of seeing a long lost friend and he openly exposed a wide goofy grin in the direction of Carmel.

When the goofy man turned to Carmel, he exposed one of his physical weaknesses, when he had on clothes. His two large ears protruded out the sides of his head like a caricature of a monkey. And fate could not be any crueler; his name was Dr. Heering. Carmel and Heering had a one night stand one year, nine months, 11 days ago. Heering would like it to be a two-night stand.

Dr. Heering was the chief psychologist of the hospital. The people of the treatment team believed there were more important things for him to do than to sit during their daily treatment team meetings. His input was minuscule and the acceptance of his input was even less. He never individually met with the patients. Once every two months, the Team may have needed to consult him regarding an administrative issue, but these questions could easily have transpired over a quick telephone call to his office. It was not clear to anyone of the Treatment Team why Dr. Heering attended the meetings.

A squat woman sitting at the lower end of the 'T' sighed for all in the room to hear.

Carmel pulled her dress under her thighs as she sat to the right of Psycho at the head of the hickory table. Looking to Psycho, "I apologize for being late. There is no excuse." The man dressed in all black did not look up from a patient's chart he was reading.

Psycho was in charge of the Admissions Unit and he sat in the middle of the head of the 'T' so he could clearly see everyone in his room, and so everyone in the room knew he held the power in the room. Psycho had been a psychologist in the Navy. Aboard Navy ships, the officers who held key positions went by their work stations or duties. The person who oversaw all the supplies was always called 'Supp.' The person who oversaw the operations of the weapons was always called 'Weps.' A psychologist aboard one of the larger ships was called, 'Psycho.' The name stuck for the leader of the Admissions Team.

Historically, psychiatrists assumed the administrative power in the hospitals. During the early 1960s psychologists had gained power within the hospital hierarchy and they were not going to let go of their power. Psycho, a psychologist, held the key position of the hospital.

Psycho's clothes for the day were all black: black shirt, black tie, black pants, and black shoes. His clothes had been dry cleaned and severely starched with creases. Black shoes shined like black mirrors. Two pronounced veins promulgated from his forehead. The forty-something man could easily pass for a thirty-year old fit man, except for his prematurely balding head.

Even though the time was two minutes past 0900 hours, the extreme heat and humidity already was working on the people in the room. Most of the players in the room had beads of sweat on their foreheads. The number of intakes had been unusually high the last few days.

A drop of perspiration fell from Psycho's veined head to the paper lying on the table. He slowly lifted his head and turned toward Carmel. "I don't care why you are late," said the man dressed in black. "You've delayed my meeting and you have wasted tax-payers money because of your behavior." He barked, "Give me ten!"

Silence in the room.

Carmel raised both of her opened hands in a gesture for Psycho to slap her hands.

"No! Give me ten push-ups!"

She did one of those knee-jerk quick-witted reactions and said, "As soon as I get a break I will go to the grocery store and get you ten Push-Ups." One of her dark eyebrows rose.

A slight smirked appeared on Psycho's face.

The room filled with laughter. An older man at the 'T' looked dumbfounded.

The red-headed Dr. Heering wiped the sweat from his forehead and believed it was now okay to be sarcastic. "I will miss this place so much when I retire."

"Don't worry, you won't be missed when you do retire," said one of the bold peanut gallery professionals.

Psycho was a die-hard behaviorist. The behavioral, psychological movement came to its zenith during the 1960s. The major belief of the behaviorists was that people were no different than just a bunch of trained monkeys and that thoughts, emotions, and free will were not relevant to the therapeutic arena. Whereas, Carmel was a devout psychodynamic therapist and believed that life was mainly about relationships, particularly early relationships; people's past and especially traumas can set a weak foundation for future human development.

The two professionals, Psycho and Carmel, frequently exhibited a love/hate relationship during the Admissions meeting.

Two drops of sweat landed on the paper in front of Psycho. He removed a white handkerchief from his pants pocket and smudged the drops. To prove he was in power and not a hurried man, Psycho turned his head to look at Heering, the Chief Psychologist, who sat on the couch. "If I may conclude our conversation before we were interrupted by Dr. Carmel's late entrance, they will just be reinforcing drugs and violence. Untold lovesick numbers will succumb to the supposed bliss their songs tout. I am going to use my vacation time for something much more rewarding than going to a pig farm in upstate New York to listen to some music."

A raised peace sign and a "groovy," defiantly slurred from the Chief Psychologist's mouth.

Psycho sneered at Heering. Psycho was about running a smooth operation and he allowed Heering's hippie gesture slide. "Now that Dr. Carmel has arrived perhaps we can begin our meeting."

A variety of power gestures evolved in the hospital and Carmel was not going to let this little stab slide. "Psycho, it is what it is. I suggest we simply get started unless you wish to discuss with Dr. Heering some more of your unconscious desire to be able to grow long hair and attend Woodstock."

The professionals representing the seven specialties howled.

9

The time was 0912 hours and the Admissions Team leader wanted to get his delayed meeting started. Without moving his shoulders, Psycho turned his head to his left. In a clear stern voice, the balding Psycho said to the psychiatrist, "Let's get it going. Dr. Blowfish, what is the status of our Russian friend Demetre'?"

Blowfish in his tan Sears-and-Roebuck three-piece suit spoke in a sheepish voice. "I moved Demetre' to Acute Unit 246."

"You can't do that." Psycho's shoulders turned and squarely faced off Blowfish.

"I know."

"What the fuck do you mean you know?"

"I know I can't move him to an Acute Unit without everyone's signature."

"But you already said you moved him to 246."

"I did, yesterday."

Psycho looked in the direction of the couch toward the Chief Psychologist with the protruding ears, Dr. Heering. The useless Chief Psychologist leaned on the arm of the couch, and he gazed at a crow on the windowsill. Psycho did not want to waste his time with the impotent Heering. He turned his head and shoulders back to Blowfish.

"How can you move a patient off this unit without the Team's signatures?"

Blowfish's voice gained some strength. "I signed it yesterday because the unit is getting filled up and we are coming up on a weekend. I didn't want to open another unit if we didn't need to. The social worker, Ashley, has been trying to contact the family but the brother who speaks English will not be able to come until Monday. Ashley is so busy today with the visitors I had another social worker move him."

A squat no-neck figure at the lower end of the table looked down at her charts.

Psycho's mouth pulled to a side. *The fucker's going against my rules. He's challenging me.*

All eyes in the room were on Blowfish.

The Sears-and-Roebuck psychiatrist grabbed the lapels of his jacket. His shoulders and eyes squared off against Psycho. Not seeing a crack in the persona of Psycho, Blowfish looked at the other faces in the room. "Now I need everyone's signatures for his transfer to the Acute Unit." Dr. Blowfish handed the patient's chart to the professional to his left in a gesture to gain the signatures of the treatment team.

The act of Blowfish transferring a patient without the members having an opportunity to provide input on the move was a direct blow questioning Psycho's power and the importance of the team members. Besides, Blowfish's move was unethical.

Psycho glared and sternly stated, "Besides raping the rest of this team of their evaluations do you recall that a Russian interpreter is coming from Morgantown this afternoon?"

"I forgot."

An infrequent ring of the telephone in the Admissions Treatment Team room interrupted the conversation.

A social worker answered the phone, "Yeah, let me see." The social worker turned toward Psycho with a leer on her round face. "The Russian interpreter from West Virginia University is at the front lobby and they want to know where to send him."

Exacerbated by one of his psychiatrists getting out of control, Psycho said in a too soft of a voice, "Tell them we were expecting him this afternoon. I will be down to meet with him at 1103 hours."

Paying no heed to Blowfish, Psycho looked around his room of pupils and authoritatively stated, "I will have Demetre sent back to admissions from the Acute Unit. The interpreter will be on the floor at 1130 hours. We will proceed as we usually do when we use an interpreter, psychiatry and psychology has first dibs and after that, it is first-come-first-serve. So, make sure you utilize him while he is here. Once all of us are done with our evaluations, we will meet tomorrow to determine where this man will go."

The authoritarian voice continued when Psycho looked back at Blowfish. "Dr. Blowfish, may I meet with you in my office at 1300 to get a full disclosure on this incident?"

The red-faced Blowfish figured he had enough of this nonmedical psychologist telling him what to do. Blowfish, more importantly, believed he had the administrative support from President Nash to stamp out any ruling by the psychologist.

The psychiatrist goes for it against the psychologist. "Listen, you little behavioral prick. Don't you know when someone does you a favor? I was making your life easier."

The wrinkles of the crow feet of Psycho's eyes disappeared and in a too-calm-of-a-military-voice. "Let's go ahead and meet right now." As he stood up from his chair, he asked the impotent-bird-watching Chief Psychologist, "Would you please join us?" Dr. Heering looked in a stupefied manner toward Psycho.

Blowfish shuffled some papers in an agitated manner. He was not overly concerned because he knew that the president of the hospital, his golfing buddy and co-Deacon at the 1st Baptist Church, would take care of this matter. Blowfish knew, as did Nash, money governs our values, thoughts, emotions, and behaviors. Blowfish was only trying to save the institution some unnecessary expense of opening another Admissions Unit.

Psycho stood beside Blowfish as the psychiatrist slowly stood. Psycho gently touched the back of Blowfish and pushed him to walk to the door.

Psycho was the last to reach the door. He turned and in a confident voice of endorsement asked, "Dr. Carmel, will you please take over for me and get Demetres' ass back here?"

"An absolute pleasure sir." As the three men were leaving the room she requested, "Psycho, would you please leave the door open so we might get a breeze?"

The two veins in the forehead of man in black were pronounced. He hesitated.

"A nutritionist said, "It's hot as hell in here and we need a breeze." Carmel promptly read Psycho's mind, "We will close the door if any patients meander down this way of the unit."

Psycho walked out the doorway and left the door open.

Carmel shifted the patient list to her side of the table. She deputized a social worker to call the Acute Unit and get Demetre' back to Admissions.

Carmel easily became all business. "Let's review Dr. Pedro's cases."

The aged psychiatrist slowly turned his head to the side and he blinked his tissue-thin eyelids as he looked in the direction of Dr. Carmel.

Dr. Pedro was a thin, gaunt-looking figure. He worked for a psychiatrist-for-hire company. When a psychiatric facility could not fill a psychiatrist position, they utilized the services of a psychiatrist-for-hire company for a quick fix. Usually, the psychiatrists of these firms had a questionable history. Their tour at the different facilities was usually a few weeks to a few months.

There was a permanent red rouge pattern on his bony cheeks. His droopy eyelids didn't conceal his dull sunken eyeballs.

The interim Admissions Team leader questioned the aging psychiatrist, "Dr. Pedro, have you seen Clark Mark?"

"Unfortunately Dr. Carmel, I did not have the opportunity to meet this man."

A social worker chimed in from the peanut gallery, "Mark is one of Ashley's patients and she is out doing Community Day. I met with Ashley before work and she said last night Mark had poured super glue in both of his ears to make the voices stop. He's over at infirmary."

The social worker, nick-named 'Toad' by the Team was a squat-looking no-neck woman who was despised by many of the Admissions Team members because she was an obvious wanna-be; that is, she believed she was clearly more knowledgeable about mental disorders because she had smoked some marijuana when younger; and, she clearly made it known to all of the Admission's Team members that she excelled at interviewing patients and gaining much-needed information. Toad rarely interviewed patients and she got most of her information when she called family members or pumped other people on the Admissions Team for information.

Carmel wanted to keep the meeting moving and questioned, "Has anyone else seen Mr. Mark?" No response from any of the professionals.

"Well, I guess he's a keeper," declared Dr. Carmel. "Please get over to the infirmary and do the best that you can to complete his assessment. He is a 72 hour. Do we know where he got the Super Glue?"

Toad quickly responded in an authoritarian weighty voice, "The patient advocate has been notified and we are looking into it."

Carmel moved to the second case of the aging psychiatrist, "Dr. Pedro, have you seen Bob Burns?"

Before Dr. Pedro could answer; Toad, the stumpy social worker again spoke, "He's not on the unit."

Carmel's eyebrows rose. She looked quizzically toward Toad. "Where is he?"

"He was also transferred to Acute by Blowfish," said the grinning social worker.

The psychologist looked at Dr. Pedro, the stumpy social worker, back to Pedro, and then back to the social worker. "But, I thought Bob Burns was Dr. Pedro's patient?"

Simultaneously Toad and the elderly Dr. Pedro shrieked, "He is!"

Carmel pulled the two sides of her dampened hair behind her ears. "Blowfish moved Bob Burns who is Dr. Pedro's patient?"

Carmel shifted her body in her chair. She was unhappy how this meeting was going. The psychologist did not want to be dependent upon the aging psychiatrist-for-hire for a determination of the patient's future. Carmel's snow white eyes looked into the yellowed eyes of Dr. Pedro. "Did you see Bob Burns before he was transferred?"

The for-hire psychiatrist initially nodded his head in a negative fashion and then he nodded his head in an affirmative manner. Carmel glowered at Pedro and he quickly clarified, "I forgot, I did see him yesterday before he was transferred. I have not had a chance to do my notes on him yet. You know, I see so many patients it is easy to get them confused."

Aggravated at the psychiatrist's feebleness Carmel requested of the team, "Did anyone else see Bob Burns while on the unit?" Blank faces stared back at Carmel.

Dr. Carmel's chest rose. Instead of requesting a social worker to call, Carmel asked a member of the team to pass the phone up to her. *This is already a fucking mess. I need to personally take care of it because Shivangi is going to be bitching.* Carmel pushed the speakerphone function.

The interim psychologist looked in the direction of Toad. "What's the number of Acute?"

"0712"

Carmel punched in '0712' on the phone.

"Acute Unit." A heavy masculine voice answered the phone.

"Mack, this is Dr. Carmel, why are you at the nurses' desk?"

"It's a long story."

Since Mack forewarned her Carmel simply asked, "Is Dr. Shivangi around?"

"Yeah. She's in the chart room bitching about you guys in Admissions."

In a calm voice, "Would you please transfer me to the chart room?"

All of the faces of Admissions stared in the direction of the interim director to see how she was going to handle two inappropriate referrals to Acute.

The head of the Acute Unit answered the phone, "Shivangi."

In the best sweet voice she could muster, "Dr. Shivangi, this is Dr. Carmel on Admissions. We had a patient, a Bob Burns, mistakenly referred to your unit before the Team could evaluate him. Would you please send him back to Admissions?"

Shivangi questioned in a heavy Indian accent, "I thought it was the Russian, Demetre'?"

"Yes, Demetre' needs to be returned. We also need Bob Burns returned so everyone can complete their evaluations."

Dr. Shivangi completely lost her Indian accent, "What the hell are you people doing up there?" Shivangi hung up the phone.

Carmel redialed '0712'. "Mack, will you get me the chart room again?"

Before Carmel could speak, "Did you people decide to go crazy during this heat when we have Community Day on my Unit? All my beds are full and we are going to open another floor because of the stupid judgments of your glorified Admissions Team. What is it? Do you need to piss or not?"

Carmel leans closer to the phone in the center of the 'T' shaped tables. In a composed voice, "I do not need to piss. But, Dr. Blowfish decided on his own, without any of our Team's signatures to move Demetre' and Burns to your unit." Carmel then used the first name of the Dr. overseeing the Acute Unit, "Sarah, I hope you understand the Admissions Team was not any part of this. We are just trying to correct a mess."

Carmel waited for a response. The sweating Director of the Acute Unit realized if she sent two patients back then she would not be forced to open another floor.

"I'll send them back. You people do better in future." Not waiting for a response Shivangi hung up the phone.

Carmel needed to find a pace for the meeting. "Toad, would you please read the Admissions Note from downstairs of the man we will hopefully get back from Acute, Bob Burns."

Toad in her newfound importance shuffled through the pages of the chart and read, "Patient is a 23-year-old Caucasian male. Patient is active for auditory hallucinations hearing the words 'bang' and 'escape.' Otherwise, this physically healthy man exhibits no other signs of positive or negative symptoms of schizophrenia. Speech is fluent, logical, and coherent. This man has a BA in history from..."

The psychiatrist-for-hire Dr. Pedro interrupted Toad's reading of the Admission note and screamed, "Yes, yes I remember this nice young man. He's a polite boy who even seemed to care how my work was going. He asked about my work as a rotating psychiatrist. I told him I liked rotating to various hospitals because it gave me an opportunity to visit different states. It also..."

Dr. Carmel interrupted Dr. Pedro, "Do you have any pertinent psychiatric information on the patient?"

Someone snorted in the peanut gallery.

The incompetent traveling psychiatrist unflappably continued, "Right. Bob Burns is between jobs and it seems that he is just out trying to find himself. He reminds me of one of those boys on *My Three Sons*. Jobs in history are pretty much nonexistent. Unless you go on for your doctorate and teach at some college or university the jobs are fairly limited. I guess you could be a curator or maybe work for some dig in Egypt, but they probably finished digging up everything there is to dig up. I mean how much can you dig before you run out of pyramids and statues?"

Dr. Carmel leaned over the patient list on the table with her elbows on both sides of the list. Her downtrodden head was held by her hands.

The psychiatrist of Bob Burns rambled, "I mean there are other findings in Egypt, but there is just so much mankind can do."

Carmel raised her head and in a clear demonstrative voice interrupted, "Dr. Pedro, why is Mr. Burns here? Is he trying to find himself?"

"I think so."

Still trying to find a much-needed pace to the meeting Carmel firmly grasped the edge of the table. She looked out one of the numerous windows, "Wouldn't a career counselor be a little better for him than an insane asylum?"

Pedro raised a yellowed fingernail in the direction of Carmel. "Usually, yes. But, there is something going on with this young fella. He hears voices."

"Well, now we're getting somewhere." Carmel's face relaxed.

Dr. Pedro rubbed his white whiskers of a day growth. "Bob, Mr. Burns, hears 'bang' and 'escape.'"

The interim director demanded, "Does he hear a loud bang like a cannon?"

"No, no, no. He hears the words 'bang' and 'escape.'"

"That's it?"

"Yes. I believe it will be a great opportunity for this man to stay awhile and to do some psychoanalysis with him. It is obvious that it is an oedipal issue and that 'bang' is a thinly veiled unconscious desire to bang his mother. You know, to have sex and to simultaneously shoot her, to violently kill her. He wants to escape from these horrendous conflictual impulses of having sex and killing her; he wants to escape. I think I might be able to help Bob and I would like to transfer him to the Acute Unit. He said he is willing to stay if it would help."

"You're an idiot," declared an exacerbated voice from the interim Admissions Unit Director.

"What?"

Carmel flatly places two of her hands on the table and looks intently in the direction of Pedro. "You want to keep a man in the hospital solely because he hears two words? And even though you just met this man for a few minutes, you somehow know it has to do with childhood conflictual issues with his Mommie? Please, tell me you are joking."

The elderly psychoanalyst giggled. "Of course I am not joking. You should well know by now that psychosis is only an escape from conflicts that cannot be resolved due to the non-caring schizophrenic-creating Mom. Current research supports common sense. This man, Bob Burns, is a classic example and I hope to write an article on it."

All eyes of the treatment team were on this-this most recent dog fight. Even though they knew Carmel was going to take the old guy out, they just wanted to see how.

Carmel barked, "You've only met this man for a few fucking minutes and you already cured him and you are going to write an article about the cure?"

Pedro's eyes soured into a pout and he begged, "Let's keep him on the unit for a few days and see how he does."

Katie Carmel looked at the social worker and questioned, "Is he voluntary?"

"Yes."

All of the Admissions Treatment Team knew a rare voluntary admission was easier to handle than an involuntary.

"We'll see how he does. Please, once he gets back to our unit, everyone interview this man. We've lost a day."

Carmel needed to find her pace to the meeting. "Next is Ms. Jenkins. I believe she is Dr. Blowfish's patient and her 72 hours runs out today. What do we know about her?"

Toad read the Admission Note, "Patient attempted suicide by rolling her wheelchair into traffic." Toad, who had worked on the unit for over six years, was familiar with this patient. After reading the brief Admission Note, Toad looked up from the chart and added her personal information about the patient, "She's a frequent flyer. Ms. Jenkins is constantly doing histrionic gestures to get admitted to the hospital. The last time she was here we rolled her over to the 'bad boy bad girl' unit to remind her how she did not want to stay here. She voluntarily left after a day on the unit. It worked for a couple of months and then she was back. We tried for as long as I know to keep her out of the hospital."

"So, how's she doing on the unit?" Before anyone could respond, Carmel asked a second question. "Can we discharge her today?"

A blood-curdling scream came from the Admissions Unit hallway. All of the members of the team looked to the door leading to the hallway. The members of the Admissions Unit were similar to a mother who knows the various screams of their infant; they all knew this was not a good scream.

In a single move, Carmel rose from her chair, threw her chair backward to the wall, and raced to the opened doorway.

10

Carmel sprinted into the Admissions Unit hallway.

The treatment team members remained seated, stared at one another, and chattered about the scream. A social worker stood up and walked to the hallway. The remainder of the team followed.

When Carmel jettisoned out the opened doorway, she saw a common situation. A couple of doorways down from the Admissions Treatment Team meeting room, a physician assistant lied on his back. On top of him, belly-up, was a frequent flyer psychotic patient. The physician assistant had contained one of the patient's arms. Katie Carmel immediately knew what to do because she had worked with this physician assistant numerous times taking down patients.

She threw her body on top of the flailing patient. The sandwiched patient swung punches, kneed whatever he could strike, and head-butted Carmel. Blood immediately flowed from a gash in her thick left eyebrow. The physician assistant underneath the patient continuously screamed in pain.

Carmel's eyes fixed on the patient's eyes. The patient kicked the air searching for an object to strike. His one free left fist searched for a solid object. He tried a roundhouse to her head. She blocked the blow. The patient followed with a roundhouse to the side of her abdomen. It struck home. Carmel's body slightly moved to the side. Carmel's eyes remained fixed on his eyes. The patient followed with three more stabs to her side. On the third stab, she grabbed the patient's left wrist and pressed his arm against the body of the physician assistant. The man kept violently kicking. The physician assistant wailed in pain.

Over the intercom system of the hospital, the calm voice of a woman, announced, "Code Blue 382, Code Blooo, 382."

The Admissions Treatment Team circled the three, similar to the common high school fights of the 60s. But, none of the physically capable people helped secure the situation. The no-neck social worker screamed, "Knee him in the nuts!"

All of the patients in the hallway sat or stood motionless. Due to the abuses they had experienced and witnessed in their past, they had learned how to melt into the surroundings.

The patient looked like a man possessed. His eyes were tense and his voice graveled in groans. The two had secured his arms but the patient kept kicking his legs and thrusting his knees searching for a way free.

Carmel managed to get her legs between the man's legs and she spread her legs in a futile attempt to contain his kicking. One of the patient's legs broke free and then the other.

In the process of trying to control the patient's kicking, Carmel exposed how she was apparently in too much of a hurry in the morning to include all of her clothing.

Two nurses ran from the rooms behind the nurses' desk in the middle of the hallway. The nurses attempted to contain the violent patient. Each nurse attempted to contain one of the patient's kicking legs. The nurse on the left screamed and buckled in a fetal position. Seconds later the other nurse fell on her back pulling her lower leg to her chest.

A third nurse came running from behind the nurses' desk with a hypodermic needle of Thorazine. She did not bother pulling down the patient's pants and quickly administered the shot into the side of his buttocks.

The patient was subdued in seconds.

Within three minutes of the Code, twelve other people were on the Admissions Unit to help contain the crisis. The professionals of the Admissions Treatment Team stood at a safe distance from the recent melee.

Standing up from the physical altercation, Dr. Carmel received enthusiastic applause from the Admissions Treatment

Team. She gained the all-important faith of the team. As everyone knew throughout the hospital, Carmel was the only professional, except for the majority of nurses and the hired physician assistants, who would assist with agitated patients.

Upon hearing a Code Blue, three of the standing physician assistants who had run to the unit lifted up the patient and carried him to the solitary room on the unit.

Dr. Carmel straightened her polka-dot dress and reached down to help the physician assistant still lying on the floor. He screamed, "No!"

"You're hurt?" A look of surprise was on Carmel's face because she assisted this physician assistant during numerous other take-downs.

The prone physician assistant said in a remarkably calm voice, "The guy grabbed and tore my bicep; I can't move my arm." He attempted to move his lower right arm. He screamed similar to the original shriek the Admissions Team had heard. With his good arm, he pressed against the cool concrete floor and stood in the motions of a rickety old man. "This guy was a rough one."

When the two faces met, "You're bleeding."

Carmel raised a hand to the sting above her eye and wiped away a wash of blood. "I'm good. A couple of stitches if that."

The two nurses who attempted to be first responders rolled around on the floor and remained screaming in pain.

As will become apparent later, the original frightening scream heard by the Admissions Treatment Team came from the injured physician assistant. Before the arrival of Carmel, the patient had managed to rip off a major tendon of the physician assistant's bicep muscle. The physician assistant will go on Workman's Comp for six months. Both of the nurses who tried to contain his kicking will go to the medical hospital for their knee injuries due to the patient kicking them in the knees. Miraculously, Carmel remained injury-free except for the cut above her eye and a couple of bruises on her side.

White-clad nurses swarmed to the bodies of the physician assistant and the two nurses.

Carmel stepped backward as the nurses went to work. She had believed the physician assistant, with over twenty years at the Asylum, was invincible. A tear rolled down a cheek.

Some of the zombie patients risked moving closer to the most recent malady; but, not too close.

Carmel believed she could do nothing else about the situation. Walking back toward the Admissions Treatment Team room she said in a composed voice to the people behind her, "We have too many patients to review to be standing here in the hallway. Let's get back to work."

Carmel sat at the head of the 'T.' *They are reminded I'll take risks when they don't. I am different. This is good.*

The Admissions Team members were quick to find their seats.

Carmel looked down at the list of patients to review. Carmel's bright white eyes faced the group, "Ms. Jenkins is back, this time in a suicidal wheelchair. What are we going to do with this frequent flyer?"

Carmel, as were many of the professionals of the Admissions room, was familiar with patients who malinger a suicide attempt so they might return to the structured confines of the hospital setting.

Cutting through the usual protocol of reading the intake, Carmel asked the team, "Is Jenkins making another gesture to get back into the hospital."

Toad, the social worker who thrived on gossip, had some information none of the other members were aware. "According to one of the nurses last night she threw a chair at another patient. She claims to be suicidal."

"Does anyone have more information on this patient?" requested the now beloved leader of the Admissions Treatment Team.

Nobody spoke.

"We don't have time to babysit. If she's threatening, then send her to where she wants and she probably needs to go to Acute. Meet with her then sign the chart if you agree."

An affirmative nod rose in unison from the Admissions Unit Team members.

None of the Admissions Treatment Team members recognized the most recent decision by Carmel was very little different from Blowfish's earlier decision. Because Carmel had obtained the power seat at the head of the 'T', most of the professionals were going to follow her decision even though they might believe differently after interviewing the frequent flyer.

The contradictions of the asylum, of life, never fail to exist. It's about power plays.

Similar to the cognitive processes of someone jumping off the Golden Gate Bridge, a fleeting thought intruded Carmel's synapses. *It was probably a bad decision.*

ll

The visitors' group had just completed a tour of the Acute Unit. The visitors were not impressed with their visit to an active psychiatric unit. They saw a lot of sleepy looking patients who didn't say anything. President Nash had instructed the psychiatrists on the unit to give all of the patients, including the non-psychotic, a hefty dose of Thorazine.

The visitors' group bundled at the end of the Acute Unit. Because of the extreme heat and humidity, they stood a distance from each other. During their tour of the Acute Unit, the visitors heard from experts that the reason people were different, or insane, was due to a chemical imbalance. One of the nurses on the Acute Unit had told them, "The fortuitous but scientifically advent of psychotropics during the 1950s stopped the horrendous screams from the asylum."

None of the professionals or visitors connected how frontal lobotomies, or killing crazy people, also stopped the screams.

The orange-and-yellow dressed tour guide stood by the last grey door on the right of the Acute Unit. Ashley removed a set of keys from a large pocket in her dress. As she unlocked the door, she said, "We are now going to take a break in the shade and hopefully there will be a breeze on the front lawn." Ashley pulled the heavy door open and she looked at Hagar wearing a tied-died T-shirt standing next to her. "Go down two flights of stairs and there will be a bar in the middle of the doorway. Push hard and you will be back on the front lawn."

It was late morning and the red-eyed Hagar did not move. Ashley had seen such nonresponsive movement of friends at parties. "It's okay," she said as she touched his shoulder. "The worst thing that can happen is you get lost in the basement. Just go down some stairs and when you see a door with a horizontal bar then push on the bar and you will be outside." Harmony, wearing a tank top, grabbed the tied-died T-shirt man's hand and smiled at Ashley. "Got it."

Upon entering the entrance to the exit, the hippie couple's eyes fixed in awe of the geometrical winding staircase. The walls and the stairs were painted the same color as all the doors in the hospital, a Navy grey. The staircase dropped eight steps, turned, and then dropped another eight steps and turned. Inside of the handrails was a caged wall that went the distance from the fourth floor to the basement.

Because his lover held his hand, Hagar risked a step down the staircase. Without looking at the woman who held his hand he slurred, "Man, this is like the Penrose picture in our bedroom."

The long-haired woman looked at him and asked, "You okay?"

"Yeah, this place is just so groovy."

The two young people in their twenties managed to find a rhythm so they could safely walk and lead the visitors down two flights of stairs.

Not wanting to rush the two troubled leaders of the group down two flights of stairs Ashley said to the next man in line, "Take your time. We are in no hurry."

As he walked past Ashley, the elderly Dan asked, "Why the caged walls?"

"It's a long story," she said. Ashley did not want to go into any unnecessary details.

The staircases were used to transport patients from one unit to another. Previous to the expensive caging of the numerous staircases, a number of patients, when being moved to another unit, jumped off a staircase to their deaths. The Weston Asylum had too high of a number of effective suicides compared to other single-story asylums. The federal government threatened to cut back some of the recent legislated Medicare funding of the facility unless the number of effective suicides were reduced.

The cages were added and the number of effective suicides of the institution dropped by over one-half.

The slow descent of the leading couple created a bottle-neck by the gray door. Ashley overheard some of the visitors' comments as they strolled past her into the caged staircase.

Debbie reminisced to Dan about growing up with an asylum in town. "I remember as a child when we drove by this place. The screams that came from the windows scared me as a child. I had nightmares."

"I did too," replied her husband. "You don't hear the screams like you use to. Those medications are wonderful."

Sarah, the woman of the Mennonite faith wearing a head cap hushed to her husband, "They actually seemed like nice people." Her husband dressed in all black and a broad-brimmed hat frowned. "You know the friends we are visiting said the best thing that ever happened to this community was the closing of the farms of this bedeviled place. The day they announced the closing of their farm's local corn prices went up four cents."

"Yes, I know my husband," returned his faithful wife.

The next person to wait her turn to what had developed into a precarious walk down two flights of stairs was Juli Jo, the pig-tailed girl dressed in pink. She looked up at her mother. "How do they know if someone is crazy?" Before Ashley could hear the answer of the child's mother the two began their descent down the staircase.

The next visitor stood next to Ashley. He was a little too close even though he was accompanied by his wife. Richard, the president of the Weston Bank, wanted to be sure he was recognized. He hesitated and said to Ashley, "You excelled making all of us feel comfortable. What you did in the visitor's room by calling two thugs to control the situation was an act of feminine grace of the old South. You, my lady, are a lady."

His wife, Jez, took a definitive step into the staircase. Richard took a step, hesitated, and turned back to look into Ashley's eyes, "President Nash has talked about the great things you do here. I hope you realize you are an exceptional person."

Only one couple was left to what had become a long and precarious descent down two flights of stairs.

Milo, the Combine Accident Insurance salesman, signaled with an extended arm for his wife to go ahead of him as he said, "This one patient made so much sense. I asked him…" Maddy elbowed Milo in his ribs.

In an attempt to complete what he was saying, "Honey, I know I was not supposed to talk to them, but I asked this one guy what it was like in the asylum. You know what he said?"

"You were not supposed to talk to the crazies," scolded Maddy.

"The patient looked sane as hell and he said it was less bad than the asylum I live." Milo laughed at his own joke. Maddy did not laugh. They did not further speak as they walked through the doorway.

Ashley kept a distance and followed the group down the staircase.

One of Maddy's yellow high heels caught the edge of a step and she tripped head-first. Milo froze and watched. Richard caught her before her head struck a metal step.

The sunken eyes of Ashley rounded. *These people can't even walk down a flight of stairs.*

12

It took more than the expected time, but the bungling visitors did safely walk down the two flights of stairs. When Ashley arrived outside, she witnessed utter chaos. Maddy dashed in the direction of the multi-colored parked cars and screamed, "This place is crazy! Everyone is crazy! My husband does not care! Nobody cares about me." Her husband Milo did not move. He crossed his arms with his jacket between his forearms. He looked in the direction of Ashley and said, "It is what it is."

Pink-cladded pig-tailed Juli Jo screamed at her pink-cladded pig-tailed mother, "I hate you! I look like a prissy. I am going home to change clothes. The preadolescent darted toward the front gate.

The hippies pulled back and forth on a purse. Ashley could not hear what their quarrel was about.

The skin burnt Jez yelled at Richard, "And so you think I am too fat?"

The petite social worker lost it. She screamed, "People—people you're acting like a bunch of children. You must think of others. This day is not about you. It's about our people here at the asylum. Our people, your people, need you. You're acting crazy! Stop what you are doing—now."

Ashley's eyes teared.

Maddy dutifully walked back toward the group. She turned and Juli Jo ran to the open arms of her mother. The hippies quit yelling but each hung onto the purse. Jez was not done and her eyes squinted in the direction of the eyes of Richard. She still sought verification from her husband that she was *not* fat.

As the visitors coalesced into a group, Ashley calmly said, "People—it's hot—we're tired. Let's take a break over at the gazebo or under some trees."

The two affluent couples, Milo with Maddy and Jez with Richard, walked and marked their territory on the gazebo. The remaining visitors stood under the trees.

Two cafeteria workers walked toward the group. They brought two silver trays with silver pitchers of sweet-tea and glasses. Behind them was Trick Greene carrying two silver buckets of cashew nuts.

Three dressed-in-white workers walked up the step of the gazebo and placed their silver on the boarded seating that circumscribed the gazebo.

The visitors standing under the trees considered the invitation of a cool drink as verification that it was okay to be in the gazebo.

Jana, the pink dressed demonstrative pig-tailed mother, said to the group, "Look at that. They brought us cashew nuts. I love cashews. The only time we get cashews is at Christmas. They sure know how to treat people right."

Ashley took some delight in the woman's statement. She thought she was doing a good job. Ashley hoped that Dr. Nash would be proud of her.

The social worker resumed her duty as tour guide, "We don't want you to eat too much because in a little bit we will be providing a ride around the main building to the cafeteria for lunch."

A blue half-bed pickup truck crept across the lawn. A huge object lumbered in the back of the truck. When the object swayed, two maintenance workers bodies wavered in an attempt to keep the object erect. A third maintenance worker walked beside the pickup. The truck drove closer to the visitors and it was difficult for the visitors to see the object because the cab of the pickup obstructed their view. Within 10 feet of the gazebo, the truck stopped.

A man wearing a black tuxedo with long tails stepped out of the passenger side of the truck.

Ashley's voice was full of enthusiasm, "Everyone, this is Dr. Averto. He is from the music department at Glenville State

College. Their music program is becoming one of the most significant in the country. He wrote a grant on a new type of therapy, music therapy. He agreed to come today to play some music for us.

The maintenance worker on the ground lowered the tailgate of the truck. Flattop, affectionately known by his workers, was the Head of Maintenance. The two maintenance workers in the back of the truck scooted the object to the tailgate.

The man in the tuxedo yelled, "Be careful you buffoons! There is only one other harp in all of West Virginia."

Flattop was not accustomed to people yelling at him nor his workers. He yelled back in the direction of Dr. Averto, "I **swear, on a stack of bibles**, nothing is going to happen to your harp."

Flattop commanded to his two subordinates in the back of the truck, "Okay, when we get it sticking out over the edge of the tailgate I will stabilizing the harp and then one of you will jump down. The three of us will pick this mother up and lower her." One of the two maintenance men in the back of the pickup said, "Got it."

Flattop forcefully tugged the heavy object in his direction. The expensive harp leaned to a side. One of the men in the truck grabbed the strings of the harp in an attempt to keep the harp upright. The strings bowed in the direction of his body.

Dr. Averto screamed, "Let go of the strings, you buffoon!"

The maintenance worker let go of the strings.

All of the weight of the heavy harp was on the other maintenance worker in the truck. Flattop ran to the side to assist the other maintenance worker to balance the incredibly heavy music instrument. Due to Flattop's quick response, he and his worker managed to get the harp vertical in the back of the pickup truck.

The frustrated Flattop yelled, "When I count to three, **together** we push the harp to the edge of the tailgate.

"One, two, three!" The two in the truck worked in unison and scooted the heavy harp past the end of the tailgate. One-half the harp hung in air.

"Do you idiots know what you are doing?" screamed Dr. Averto.

Flattop calmly said, "We've moved bigger and heavier objects than this. Don't get your panties in wad."

Flattop said to the slightly deaf worker on the back of the truck, "Jake you stabilize it while Zeke jumps down."

The partially deaf Jake heard his name, so he pushed on the harp. Zeke was in the process of jumping down from the truck. Flattop was not prepared for Jake pushing the harp.

The harp tilted downward toward Flattop. He was alone in his attempt to balance and hold the heavy object. It was too heavy for him. Flattop jumped out of the way.

The weaker top of the harp struck the hardened drought-ridden ground and bounced.

Flattop rolled.

The harp fell to the side where Flattop had laid.

The expensive harp banged into the yard and bounced a couple of times. A chorus erupted from the strings.

Hagar said to his partner, "It's all about strings, harmony, and change."

His not-as-stoned partner rolled her eyes into her head and held the purse close to her side.

Dr. Averto ran and fell on his beloved harp.

The three maintenance workers stood the harp erect.

Averto plucked a number of chords. "She seems to be fine." His hands delicately massaged the wood of the harp to verify there were no cracks.

"It might not have been pretty, but we got it here for you," said Flattop.

Following Dr. Averto running, lying on his harp, and scolding the maintenance workers; the musician regained his presence knowing his baby was not injured.

The visitors had never seen a harp. They had seen pictures of angels holding small lyres in the Sunday School lesson books but never something as majestic as a full sized harp.

Once Averto had his harp and three-legged stool in place, all of the visitors except for one couple, sat on the grass similar to kindergarten children waiting to be enthralled. The couple who refused to sit on the grass was Jez and Richard.

To further enhance the experience cigarettes were lit by the smokers.

The thin Ashley in her bright orange and yellow gunny sack dress walked up to the side of Dr. Averto who squatted on his small stool. "Before our accident," Ashley moved her eyes away from Flattop, "I mentioned how Dr. Averto is a music therapist and volunteers his time for us at the Weston Asylum." A thin arm of Ashley lightly flew in the direction of the seated man, "Dr. Averto."

The visitors after having survived being within the confines of one of the actual units of the asylum, being served cool, sweet tea and cashews, and being outside under a shade tree with a slight breeze; were feeling good. They expressed their good mood by a resounding applause for the musician.

Dr. Averto sheepishly smiled and in a thick Italian accent said, "Thank you for having me come. I was more than happy to welcome. I come here to teach patients music. They get their own Flutophone that is provided by a research grant. The principle is simple. Many times words cannot express how we experience, how we feel. The problem is we feel alone with our misfortunes and pains. Music can make that expression so others might hear their inner voice. Some of the patients make monstrous music and some make so sweet. But, enough of that, I now play for you."

Once comfortable with the fitting of the massive harp against his upper left shoulder Averto said, "We make many sounds."

Averto plucked a few chords and he delightfully questioned, "Can hear the water running over the rocks?"

Averto played the strings again and he achieved the approving nods and smiles. They could hear the water cascading over the rocks. The West Virginia mountain folks were familiar with the playful running of water down a mountainside. He continued plucking the cords in variations of the running water theme, "Ahh, so cool and calm; it is so peaceful. Listen and let it come to you, let it cool you."

The Mennonite couple and the hippie couple closed their eyes.

From the balcony of his second-floor apartment, Dr. Nash watched the events that unfolded by the gazebo. He was happy because a deacon from his church was in the visitor group, Richard, the banker. The president of the Weston Asylum was hopeful his investment would eventually pay off with the raising of new bonds.

After a few minutes of the running water theme, Dr. Averto stopped playing the harp, and pushed the weighty harp off his shoulder, turned it slightly to the side so he might gain a full view of everyone.

Averto asked his audience, "Does anyone here fish?"

Almost everyone, including eleven-year-old Juli Jo, raised their hands like a bunch of school children. The standing bank president and co-deacon with Nash did not raise his hand. His severely-tanned and wrinkled wife had walked away from the group. In a histrionic gesture, she alone watched the traffic on Highway 33.

Dr. Averto was a professor of the mountains and he knew some people could hear and some could not. He wanted to reach the interested few in the limited time he had.

Averto's fat calloused fingers plucked the strings. He asked of the interested, "What does this remind you of?"

Hagar slurred, "It's my leaky faucet."

The professor did a decisive pluck of two strings with two of his fingers.

Hagar laughed, "That is definitely my bathtub."

Dr. Averto looked at the hippie and raised a forefinger to his mouth signifying 'hush'. Harmony grabbed her partner's upper arm.

Averto plucked another string; a few seconds later, another; then another, another; until, he was a maniac violently plucking strings.

"I know, I know what that is!" yelled the elderly Dan. The physically fit man proudly screamed, "It is the rain as it is coming across a lake. You first hear a few drops hit the water, then more, and more, and then…you're soaked." Everyone laughed in full agreement.

The round-faced Averto pushed the massive weight to his side. "We all experienced, yes?" Most of the heads of his audience moved in an up-and-down motion. "And now I play you welcome music. Welcome to Weston Asylum music."

The professor easily transitioned to Handel's *Water Music*. The visitors were all smiles. This once crazy house was turning out to be a nice sane place. Life was good at the Weston Asylum.

Ashley happened to look in the direction of the clock tower on the main building. Seeing the president on his balcony, she did a full-arm big wave. He returned a 'great-to-see-ya' wave with a smile; the smile was a half-smile due to his polio as a child.

13

President Nash's half-smile in the direction of the social worker at the gazebo was short lived. He ambled into his plush apartment on the second floor of the asylum. His half-smile turned into a half-frown. Dr. Blowfish (the psychiatrist who moved patients to other units without the Admissions Treatment Team's authorization) reclined in a Queen Ann chair in the president's apartment.

Earlier in the apartment, there was a meeting of Blowfish, President Nash, Psycho (Navy psychologist in charge of the Admissions Unit), and Heering (chief psychologist with the big ears).

Psycho and Heering had left the impromptu meeting.

Obvious to everyone at their meeting, except for Blowfish, was the necessity of retaining the treatment teams' signatures before a discharge off the Admissions Unit. Following their meeting, Nash had gone outside to his balcony to gain time to think how he was going to further clarify with Blowfish that he overstepped his authority.

Following his gaining some composure from the balcony venture, Nash towered over the seated Blowfish. He screamed, "Dammit man. You can't go moving people off the Admissions Unit without everyone signatures." Veins stuck out in Nash's neck. "I do not want to be called into another one of your fucking petty meetings with Psycho and Heering. They're not players. They don't understand like you do. They don't get it that we need to keep these beds full if we are going to stay open. I don't like having unplanned meetings. You screwed this one up Blowfish.

Follow the written and unwritten rules of that rogue Admissions Unit."

Blowfish looked up from the floor. With sad puppy eyes and a boyish tone, Blowfish pleaded, "Sir, be careful, your high blood pressure."

"Shit!"

"Sir, I was just trying to clean out the Admissions Unit before the weekend…"

"Can't you hear me?" Nash's voice softened. "You know you can't do anything with those people on Admissions. It's like corralling a bunch of cats."

The president took a seat in a chair next to Blowfish. Their heads turned down and slightly cocked to the side toward the other. It was unclear how this conversation was going to end.

Blowfish rubbed his jawline with his left hand.

It took everything Blowfish managed to muster not to scream, *you don't play by the fucking rules!*

Dutifully Blowfish agreed, "Yes Sir."

Nash, in the best of a smoosch job that he could muster, "Are we still teeing off at 1:00?"

"Yeah."

"Then we're done."

Blowfish walked out of the president's apartment.

Nash returned to the balcony of his second-floor apartment. He saw Ashley and the townsfolk laughing and having a good time with Dr. Averto. *Community Day is off to a fantastic start. What can go wrong?* Just as soon as he allowed the optimistic thought that nothing could go wrong, a nagging feeling, or an intuition, supervened. *There is something or someone in the hospital who is going to destroy me.*

Retaining her sweet sing-song voice, the porcelain doll-faced Ashley recited the rehearsed speech to her audience. "Let me tell you more about the facilities here at the Weston Asylum. As some of you may know the city of Weston was offered to build an insane asylum or to build a college. We choose to build the hospital. What is now Glenville State College could have been in Weston. Out back are several ancillary buildings including a medical building, forensic building, a building for mentally retarded patients, a building for the chronically mentally ill, and the cafeteria where we will soon be leaving to lunch." Inside the main building, there is a barbershop, hairdresser, dental facility, and library. In a one day tour, there is not enough time to see all of the facilities."

Her dark eyebrows rose, "But we will return to tour the library that is a smaller scale of the library at the Biltmore mansion in North Carolina." Dan and Maddy unwittingly mimicked Ashley's raising of her eyebrows.

Toad, the squat social worker who had been at the Admissions Treatment Team meeting, walked toward the visitor group gathered at the gazebo. When she was within 30 feet of the group, the needing-attention social worker yelled, "Ashley!"

Ashley in her bright orange and yellow dress turned around and smiled.

Toad waddled to the side of the thin Ashley and in a dramatic manner, her two stubby arms grabbed the thin arms of her best girlfriend. Knowing she had commanded the full attention of Ashley, and more importantly, the visitors, Toad in a harsh voice said, "You need to move the Russian Demetre' back to Admissions."

One of Ashley's orange stocking legs stomped on the ground. "Did that asshole move him to Acute?"

Hearing the girl-next-door tour guide cuss, the mouths of Maddy, Jez, Seth, and Sarah jaws dropped. Juli Jo laughed from hearing the word *asshole.*

The Hippie couple stood in a daze with each once again holding the purse.

"Excuse me for a minute," said Ashley to the group. "Please, keep playing, Dr. Averto." The professor began playing the light but soothing *Night of the Lilies.*

The two social workers stepped a few feet from the visitor group and the compliant Ashley did not want the townsfolk to think she was abandoning them. She looked back toward her group and said, "There is still some more green tea and cashews in the gazebo. But, don't eat too much because we will soon be getting on a hay wagon that will take us to the cafeteria for lunch."

Debbie, the elderly dancer, lit another cigarette. The too-tanned couple lit their cigarettes. Milo and Maddy lit their cigarettes. The hippie couple walked back to the gazebo for more cashews.

The two social workers walked to one of the large oak trees so they could talk confidentially.

Toad was the first to speak, "Yep, he moved him last night."

In a pissed-off voice, "I told Blowfish yesterday afternoon that Psycho would not go for it."

Toad was excited by her best friend being upset and by this most recent scandal at the asylum. In an excited voice Toad recalled the morning Treatment Team escapade and said to her one true confident of the hospital, "Blowfish decided to grow some balls and he cussed out Psycho during Treatment Team. He called Psycho a 'little behavioral prick."

"No!"

"Yes!"

Toad liked being the first conveyer of gossip.

The two social worker chums shared delighted giggles under the oak trees.

Toad in her excited laughing voice further added, "And then Psycho calls a meeting with Blowfish, Heering, and the president."

The two social workers howled.

Toad was on a roll with the most recent hot gossip. "Psycho didn't take Blowfish's shit and called the meeting right **then**. The three; Psycho, Blowfish, and Heering left the Team meeting. Carmel was left in charge and she sucked."

"Why do you hate Carmel so much?" asked Ashley.

"I don't hate her any more than any of the other narcissistic asshole psychologists."

Having completed her mission of serving as the main source for spreading gossip within the asylum, and unconsciously splitting various departments into conflict, Toad recalled the main reason she was supposed to talk with Ashley. "They want you to go up and take care of the paperwork to move the Russian Demetre' back to Admissions so the interpreter and everyone can meet with Demetre" at eleven-thirty."

"Shit. That's right now."

Toad lied, "I know, I tried to find you as quick as I could."

Ashley asked, "Can you cover for me here?"

"Sorry, I got to work through lunch. I got two people being kicked back to jail by three and I need to make sure the sheriff's department picks them up."

"What am I supposed to do with the visitors?"

"Let Trick take them to the cafeteria."

Ashley pulled down on the sides of her already straightened dress. "Sounds good, what could Trick screw up in the short amount of time to get to the cafeteria?"

14

President Nash had been planning for this Community Day after the conclusion of the previous year's Community Day. Trick Greene being a tour guide was not a part of Nash's strategic plan for Community Day.

Toad walked confidently back to the building with her shoulders pulled back and her stubby arms swinging in the air. Ashley returned to the visitor group and announced the reason for her brief departure. "I have to take care of some minor business, but I am the only person available to take care of it. Mr. Greene will take you to the cafeteria. I will meet you there in 45 minutes to an hour."

The man behind the John Lennon sunglasses slurred, "Groovy. I can tell them more about the place."

Ashley straightened the sides of her dress. Maddy, rubbed her round tummy and pleaded, "You're not leaving us?"

"I said I will meet the group in the cafeteria as soon as I can." Ashley frowned at the woman who had become too attached to her.

Trick did not have a scripted tour. Not missing a beat, he pointed to something across the street. The new tour guide said, "I was raised just over there in that house."

Similar to the social worker Toad, Trick Greene had always thought that he was under appreciated at the asylum. Finally, he was given a hint of authority.

In a deeper tone of voice, Trick Greene walked toward the gazebo and stepped up onto the first step. Overlooking his audience, he said, "Yes, I was raised in that house right over there." He pointed to a quaint greenhouse across the street from the front lawn. "I am the third generation to work here. I could tell you some stories. Matter of fact," he leaned toward eleven-year-old Juli Jo and whispered, "I saw my first naked woman when I was about your age. She was running across the yard just right over there. She was having a good ole time."

Jana took a step in the direction of Trick. She stopped any further advancement because Jez and Debbie giggled. Richard roared with laughter. He asked, "Did you catch her?"

"Hell, I was just a kid. I wouldn't have known what to do with her."

Trick Greene's broad grin exposed his white teeth. He liked the attention. He wanted more.

Trick strode into the interior of the gazebo and pointed in the direction of the northern end of the main building. The townsfolk walked around the gazebo to see what he was pointing at.

In an excited voice, Trick declared, "There's the time with the John Deere. Did any of you hear about it? It was years ago?"

Some of the heads dared a negative nod. The Mennonite couple looked at one another wondering where this Beetle look-alike with dark-round sunglasses was going.

The man dressed in white leaned over the railing of the gazebo and said in a soft voice, "They tried to keep it hush. Apparently, there was this one guy, when the farms were still active a few years ago; he finished plowing the soil with a Type A John Deere. You know the one with two cylinders that sounds like a Harley Davidson? It sounds nothing like a Triumph. You know the difference. The Triumph is British. The Harley is all-American."

Trick was not a story-teller. He got a bunch of blank stares because of his unnecessary details.

The limber physician assistant leaped over the gazebo railing and leaned on the railing. "Back in the day, as was customary, whoever finished the farm work for the day had to get the tool or machinery ready for the next day. So this patient unhooked the plow, filled the tractor up with gasoline, and then he decided to go for a ride. As most of you know, the farm was up there on that flat spot on the hill."

Trick pointed to a bulldozed hill behind the huge limestone structure. The top of the hill had been bulldozed flat and the soil was pushed to the hollows creating one open field that provided plenty of sunlight.

All of the visitors' faces were locked onto Trick Greene. Believing he had gained some impetus to his story Trick continued, "There's some other fields in the hollers but that's the main field up there. There's a gate in the back of the main building that goes toward Glenville." He again pointed in the direction of the end of the main building. "When the patient drove the tractor to the back gate he told the security guard he was supposed to go and get the oil changed. The security guard should have known better because we have our own maintenance department. The security guard allowed the patient to leave on the huge tractor. The patient drove the tractor through the roads of Weston and a number of folks after the fact said they saw him driving. They said he was real courteous and he stopped to let people cross the road. They didn't find him until six o'clock the next morning in Roane County, 60 some miles away. Somebody called and said he was just sitting there on the tractor alongside the road. He'd run out of gas."

Trick's story brought a roll of laughter from most of the visitor group. The Mennonite couple frowned.

Trick was on his needed roll.

Feeling more comfortable with the visitors, Trick settled into a pronounced Southern accent and concluded his story. "When our folks finally caught up with the patient they asked him, "Why did you leave?" The crazy patient said he just felt like going for a drive. When they asked him where he was going he said it really didn't matter; he just wanted to go for a drive. Now that's not crazy or is it?"

"What is crazy about wanting to go for a drive?" demanded Sarah in her Mennonite head cap.

"Exactly," agreed Trick. "Who hasn't wanted to just say, "to heck with it,"" and go for a drive?"

With that seemingly empathic question, he got a lot of appreciative smiles and affirmative nods. He felt connected with the visitors. Trick had gained the much-needed attention he so desperately desired. He was in his groove.

Feeling good, Trick looked toward Dr. Averto and decided to enliven the group up a little more and he requested from the professor, "Do you know any Beetle songs?"

"I know them all."

"Please, play one of your favorites," as if the now all-powerful Trick was willing to share his power.

The professor played *Here Comes the Sun* on his harp.

By the conclusion of the song, Trick had gained some time to recall other interesting stories about the Weston Asylum. He walked to the side of professor Averto and said, "Ashley is one of our better social workers, but she left out some of the better stories. Several years ago some odd things began happening around the old place. There was the incident where some patients got access to the warehouse where we store the food products. They confiscated the forklift, drove it to the building with the indoor swimming pool, drove through one of the large French-door windows and they dumped sixty of the eighty-pound bags of flour into the pool. Sixty bags of flour weighing eighty pounds each. In the following morning, the pool was like a huge bowl of cookie dough."

The visitor group howled. Even the Mennonite couple laughed.

The insurance salesman, Milo, blurted out, "These crazy people do crazy things."

Thriving on the attention, Trick leaned low and said to his attentive audience, "Remember a few years ago when the farms were still active?"

Since he already told a story about the farm he only got a couple of affirmative nods.

In his over-zealous voice Trick continued with a third story. "You know how I told you it was the responsibility of the person who finished using the farm equipment to get it ready for the next day?

Eight of the twelve visitors raised and lowered their heads.

Trick walked back to the steps of the gazebo and stood on

the first step. The group of visitors had to turn and walk a few steps in his direction. Looking down at his visitor group he said, "Well, this one patient got done planting corn for the day and he filled the four planter bins up with seed corn for the person the next day. Each bin holds about two bushels of seed. Well, some patients that night took out half the corn seed with a bucket and tossed the seed into the nearby woods. Then they filled the half full bin with sunflower seeds. They mixed the corn and sunflower seeds up real good. It wasn't until a month later the sprouts were coming up that anyone noticed. It was a glorious site to see these sunflower plants in the middle of a corn field."

All of the visitors howled.

The Mennonite couple knew they liked their rows to be straight and the weeds to be few. To mix a seed with a different variety of seed was…an unheard sin.

"How'd you know he used a bucket?" questioned eleven-year-old Juli Jo.

"What?"

"How did you know he took the seed corn out with a bucket. Couldn't he'd used a bag?"

"What?"

The pink stirrup pants and sleeveless top girl demanded, "Can't you hear? How did you know he used a bucket?"

"I don't know. He could have used anything. I just put that in the story so it would make some sense. He had to put it somewhere. Anyway, one final story and then we need to go." Looking in the direction of Averto, Trick asked, "Would you please play another Beetle's song while I tell these fine people one more story?"

Averto smiled and played *Let It Be*.

From his perch on the first step of the gazebo, Trick pointed to the groups' right. "See that bush over there? The same year as the mixed seed incident, a patient trimmed that bush into the resemblance of a man's anatomy, if you know what I mean?"

The group wailed once again. Because the elderly fitness fanatic man was caught off guard, he burst into a laugh and choked on his own spit. Black Hat chuckled so hard that snot shot out of the Mennonite man's nose.

Trick Greene left out some important details about the four events.

The first event, with the patient taking the tractor for a ride—did happen.

The other three events: flour dumped into the swimming pool, sunflower seeds mixed with corn seeds, and the trimmed phallic bush; also happened. However, the way Trick presented the later three stories was as if the patients did the events. The last three acts of vandalism were not due to the conniving workings of the patients. Trick and some of his high school prankster buddies had committed the last three acts of defacement.

15

"Now we must enter our coach to go feast," said Trick Greene. He waved in the direction of an approaching John Deere tractor pulling a hay wagon. The old tractor stopped and the wagon tongue jerked into the tractor. "Hop on the wagon and we will take a ride out back to the new cafeteria."

Juli Jo jumped on the tongue of the wagon and leaped onto the wagon. She sat on one of the hay bales waiting for the others to arrive. Her Cheshire cat grin acknowledged her being first on the wagon. Two men assisted Maddy onto the wagon. Her husband on one side steadied her arm; Seth placed a veined hand on her spacious rump and pushed. Once standing on the bed of the wagon, Maddy looked down at the Mennonite man, and in a coy voice said, "Thank you, kind sir." The histrionic woman narrowed her false eyelashes. Milo glared at Seth.

The limber elderly dance lady, Debbie, moved with the grace of a deer. She stepped on the hitch, easily stretched a leg to the wagon, and catapulted her body to the wagon. She took a draw from her half-finished Old Gold cigarette, looked down at the remaining men on the ground, and flicked her cigarette to the side. The cigarette fell onto a piece of straw that could serve as a fuse toward a bale of straw.

Most of the remaining people managed to get onto the wagon without much difficulty.

The thin Trick Greene easily bounded onto the wagon and looked down to the last couple to climb on the wagon. "Come on folks, we're a little behind schedule."

Jez looked at husband Richard. Without moving her thin lips, she whispered in her caustic voice, "Dear, I do not believe we should be seen on a hay wagon."

Richard looked up toward Trick. "We will enjoy the day and walk."

"You sure? It's a little bit of a walk."

"We're good," Jez said and waved for the group to go ahead.

Trick waved to the driver of the tractor and yelled, "Head them up and move them out!"

The deep thumping of the two cylinders of the powerful tractor came to life and inched forward. The wagon moved with a jolt and Hagar the hippie fell on the floor of the wagon. The other visitors had already found their seats on the hay bales that lined the wagon. "I've not been on a hay ride since I was a little girl," said Maddy. Sitting across from her the Mennonite Sarah said, "I wish I could say that."

"I have never been on a hay wagon," said Hagar, "It's a nice break from the craziness." His companion reached down and took out a brownie from the purse. Hagar took this as a sign it was okay for him to eat another brownie. He looked into her dark brown eyes, "Butterfly, it is times like this that I know why I love you so much." Her brown eyes softened.

President Nash and Dr. Blowfish had argued for weeks about the best way to transport the visitors around the hospital. Blowfish argued that many of the people had never been in a taxi and they would feel like royalty being transported in a procession of taxi cabs.

Nash countered, "We don't even have a taxi cab service in Weston. It would cost us a fortune to get enough cabs from Morgantown and Charleston to cart the visitors."

"You got to spend money to make money."

Nash tired of Blowfish's simplistic ideas. "A hay wagon ride is one of the most relaxing things a person can do. You sit with some people you don't know, you're forced to talk with them because of the close confines; and most importantly, people appreciate the more simplistic things of life. People on a hay ride are forced whether they like it or not, to enjoy life."

Blowfish insistently said, "We want these people, or visitors as you call them, to feel good about what we do. We want them to feel important. Hauling them around in a wagon is demeaning."

"It's nostalgic. Besides, what could go wrong?"

The majestic thumping tractor pulled the hay wagon with its ten visitors around to the back area of the main building. The two tanned walking visitors, Richard the III and Jez, lost distance with each rise of a piston in the John Deere.

Light conversations exchanged between the visitors on the nostalgic hay ride. They asked the others sitting next to them about where they lived, what they did, number of children, what they thought about the visit. The visitor group evolved into a group of people respecting their differences.

The half-finished cigarette that was flicked to the floor of the hay wagon by Debbie caught the edge of a piece of straw. The edge of the dried straw glowed red.

Ahead of their tractor, the visitors saw another tractor pulling its visitors to the cafeteria. A few of the visitors looked back toward the end of the massive building and saw another John Deere tractor pulling a group of visitors. A mutual feeling developed between the visitors of being free from life's daily hassles and burdens. The dialogues that had started out the day with judgments of others had changed to light-hearted conversations filled with joy and joy of life.

"Whoa—whoa," screamed Trick. Jana looked in the direction of Trick's head. She grasped the sides of her daughter's head with her stubby calloused hands and forcefully turned her child's head away from the shocking disclosure.

A tall male patient stood with his pant legs and white underwear pulled down to his ankles. He stared in the direction of the wagon of visitors. The patient worked his massively hung penis with two hands. The women on the wagon had never seen such an endowed man in their bedrooms. The men had never seen such a hung man in their high school gym classes. Among the staff and professionals of the asylum, the patient was nicknamed "tripod."

Maddy turned her face away from the patient. She stole a look to see most of the visitors were still looking in the direction of the patient. Maddy turned her head back in the direction of the freak of nature.

The patient worked his penis harder as he looked in her direction. She managed to pull her head up to look at the goofy looking face of the man and she smiled. The patient returned her smile and then his face turned to look of torment. The workings of his hands grew stronger and faster. His low hanging large testicles swung harder. He screamed and ejaculated a full stream of sperm three feet from his body with each of his three tugs on his cock—the patient screamed again and squirted another three loads.

The man raised his head up and looked back up in the direction of Maddy. "Thanks. I needed that."

"No problem," said Maddy. A pink glow filled her cheeks.

Trick jumped down from the moving wagon. He looked back at his visitors on the hay wagon and said, "Sorry folks. I need to take care of this. No big deal. I will meet you in the cafeteria."

Trick walked past the patient and entered a door to the asylum.

The thumping of the tractor continued its journey on the backside of the asylum. The now cherished friends said to each other things they would never have said to a stranger.

"I didn't know a man could be that big."

"Is that normal for a man to be able to squirt on and on?"

"He was probably about to faint due to all of his blood leaving his head so he could masturbate."

"What is masturbate?" asked Juli Jo of her mother.

"We're going to do our birds and bees talk tonight," said Jana.

The tractor continued its two-cylinder powerful rhythmic thumbing. The tractor and wagon passed a long line of patients standing outside a single door of the huge asylum. The man on the tractor took over as tour guide and screamed back to the visitors, "That was our old cafeteria and we are using it today to make sure all of the patients are fed!"

Due to the large number of people to feed during Community Day, there were two active cafeterias at the Weston Asylum. Cafeteria B, the original and rarely used cafeteria, was located in the basement of the main building. Cafeteria B had not been in use since the last Community Day.

Huge rough-cut limestone blocks lined the interior walls of Cafeteria B. Rusty metal light shades dangled from wires. The wooden table-tops were stained various shades of rustic red and black. For the past year the patients ate in the newer Cafeteria A. Since it was Community Day, the majority of patients were relegated to Cafeteria B, the old cafeteria in the basement. Since it was the older and a much smaller cafeteria, the food line for the patients started at 11:00 a.m. and continued until 2:00 p.m.

Over the cone-shaped speakers that were sporadically screwed into the outside wall of the limestone building a pleasant female's voice announced, "Code Blue on the grounds of the forensic unit, Code Bloooo on the grounds of the forensic unit." The visitor group hay wagon had just passed the outside of the forensic unit. The satisfied patient pulled up his underwear and pants. He ran toward the walking overly-tanned visitors.

Tripod, the well-endowed patient, spoke in words so fast it was difficult for the couple to follow. "They're after me." The couple with sweat-drenched arm pits looked at each other and then back to the patient.

"They're all Russians," screamed the crazed man, "Can't you see! Can't you see even this building is a Russian building! Nuclear missiles are in the basement! Help me! Help me please!"

Jez grabbed an arm of her husband.

"Don't you understand?" The man's rounded eyes were intense. His rounded eyes looked possessed. "There's a tunnel that goes from here to the Kremlin. Help me!"

The sweaty couple stood still like scared rabbits.

"Fuck you."

Men wearing all white came running out of the building.

The patient ran toward the old farm.

The rich overly-tanned couple looked at each other with blank faces. Richard broke the tension and silence. "Well, that was different." Sweat drenched Jez continued her blank stare. She then screamed, "I have never, ever, had such a demeaning experience!" The bank president held his arms out to his sides in a feeble attempt to dry off the drenched armpits of his Izod shirt. The couple was in the initial stage of dehydration.

"I saw everyone getting off the wagon at the far end of the building," said the sopping wet Jez, "that must be where the cafeteria is." With her head low, she managed to hobble in the direction of the distant wagon. Her husband hobbled to her side. Beads of sweat fell off their down turned heads. Because of drought conditions, the dirt road instantly sucked up the moisture from the drops of sweat.

The couple's steps grew lighter as the two found a common point of discussion. The couple bolstered about how their proletarian efforts of walking were worthwhile because they had a story to tell the other visitors about a patient who had come up to them wanting help to escape. As if they had surpassed the group, Jez bragged, "Wait until the other people hear what happened to us."

16

A light breeze fanned the sweaty faces of the visitors sitting on the hay bales around the wagon. Seth, the man of Mennonite faith, said, "I think I am finally cooling off." A tiny yellow flame came to life. The cooling breeze also lit the red spark of the straw attached to the bale of hay Hagar sat on.

The thumping of the John Deere tractor severely slowed down to a chugging suggesting the engine could easily miss a beat and the engine would die. The visitor group had arrived at their destination, Cafeteria A.

The thin figure of Trick Greene ran toward the wagon. "I hope you are all okay. I had to take care of that situation with the patient."

A tiny flame of fire danced between the legs of Hagar and a bale of hay. The hippie did not feel the burn so he did not move.

Dan the man leaped across the bed of the wagon and pushed the hippie to the side. He kicked the fire out without much effort. The athletic elderly man stood before the group with a slightly pronounced chest. The now bonded group gave a roaring cheer and applause.

Seth spoke without thinking. "It would have gone out anyway. These bales are wound too tight; it would be difficult for a little flame to ignite a bale. There was plenty of time." Because of the astonished looks of the other visitors, the Mennonite farmer realized he spoke too soon. "Of course, a bale of hay is extremely volatile, and I am grateful the man put it out so quickly."

Trick walked to the hitch of the wagon and said, "Inside there is chilling air conditioning." The visitors jumped up from their hay bale seats and swarmed their way to get off the wagon.

On Community Day a few of the more cooperative patients were served in Cafeteria A. The cafeteria was a building separate from the main hospital. It sat in the southwestern part of the campus.

Trick Greene escorted his small group of visitors into the cool Cafeteria A.

Maddy was the first to enter the cafeteria. "This could be a cafeteria from any large high school. It's wonderful," she said as she looked back in the direction of her husband. Milo was all smiles.

There were two serving lines in the 5,000 square foot room. The facility was clean and bright. Two lines of visitors had already formed waiting in line for their lunch. The cafeteria was built one year ago due to a bond from a previous Community Day. The table tops in Cafeteria A were plastic as were the chairs. Large pink-and-green patterns of daisies speckled the tabletops and chairs. Abundant four-foot-long fluorescent lamps in the ceiling cascaded the room with excessive glaring light similar to a pharmacy. And, there was air conditioning.

Trick was back and in complete control of his visitor group. "We do need to be moving on if we are going to be able to finish the tour on time for tonight's firework display. The people standing on the pink line are served beef-and-noodles, mash potatoes, and green beans. The green line on the floor is for people wanting hamburgers and French fries." Trick raised his arms in a gesture as if he was moving a herd of cattle to move.

As the group moved its way toward the juxtaposition of the two lines, Trick Greene felt compelled to enlighten his group further, "A few of the patients are being fed in the other cafeteria where we saw them waiting in line."

That last statement by the round sunglasses figure was another one of his lies because most, not a few, of the patients were being served in Cafeteria B.

Sarah wearing a head cap asked Trick, "Are the patients sitting around in different groups so we may talk to them?"

"No." Without hesitating, Trick explained, "They sit in groups based on their diagnosis." With no appreciation of people's privacy Trick pointed at each table as he spoke. "The depressed sit with depressed people. Over there are the schizophrenics. They're all paranoid at what the others at their table are thinking. The bipolars, when they can manage themselves, sit with bipolars. The alcoholics sit with alcoholics. Next to them is the table of druggies."

The 'druggies' as they were labeled by the professionals and nonprofessionals of the hospital were people supposedly suffering from chemical dependency issues. The crazy thing was that many of the druggies were not psychologically or physically dependent on drugs. A number of them had been caught smoking marijuana and the judges gave them a choice of jail time or hospital time.

The alcohol counselors didn't know what to do with the druggies. The marijuana users were not there to change. They mocked the Alcoholic Anonymous meetings. One day, all of the druggies in the group said their names and claimed they were alcoholics, even though most of them did not have an alcohol problem. During the daily AA meetings, druggies tended to question everything. The druggies questioned why we were in the Vietnam War. To the druggies, everything was a conspiracy about power and how money controls peoples' lives. The twelve-step counselors could not keep up with the druggies statements. The supposed therapeutic response of the counselors became such a ritual that the druggies would not wait for the counselors' intervention when they declared broad claims about social injustices. The druggies would respond first, "Yeah, I know, denial. I deny a problem." The druggies were not liked by the patients or the staff at the asylum even though many of the employees of the hospital and a couple of the AA counselors smoked marijuana.

The too-tanned couple arrived at the cafeteria. Their clothes were drenched due to their hike on such a hot, humid day. Richard opened the cafeteria door for his wife. In her low cut dress, she entered the cafeteria with her jaw held high. Her eyes scanned the faces looking for some recognition. There was none.

Jez feigned a need to fix her shoe and bent over exposing her wrinkled breasts. Only one patient and Trick Greene bothered to check her out.

Trick Greene's face squashed in a look of disgust. He had been with older women, but he disliked the woman. The new tour guide did not bother to help the tanned couple who had decided to walk instead of ride on the wagon. He turned to his emotionally bonding group who were engaged in conversations between and within couples. "When you get your food trays let's meet over there by the window."

The closeness of waiting in line, the coolness of the cafeteria, and the sharing of experiences had evolved into a day of newfound friendships. Trick's visitor group was laughing as they sat at two of the plastic tables. The light-hearted conversations were moments of listening, sharing, and bonding. The diverse couples of the mother and daughter dressed in pink, the long-haired young hippies, the Mennonite couple, and the elderly couple had bonded with the other couples. Their similarities were much greater than their differences. The group had discovered one of those wonderful experiences of what Thanksgiving dinners are supposed to be about, what life is supposed to be about.

The overly tanned woman and her husband walked to a third table because the seats at the other two tables were filled. Jez slammed her food tray on the table with the intent of gaining the visitors attention. Dramatically she raised her right hand to her chest and said, "You would not believe what happened to us."

Not giving her chance to continue Trick quickly said, "You decided you were too good to ride on a hay wagon and ended up getting caught in a rain shower?" He looked out a window and turned back to the woman. "But, it's not raining." Jana chuckled and Seth smirked.

Richard did not like confrontation even though he was responsible for millions of dollars at his bank. He attempted to save his wife from humiliation. "We talked to a patient. This patient..." Jez interrupted her husband. "No, let me tell it. You do not know how to tell a story. When we are at parties, you tell the story and I always have to correct you and fill in the best parts."

The bank president sat down, picked up his fork, and took a bite of green beans. *She's on her own for the rest of the day. It is time she learned.*

The recently bonded diverse group of people enjoyed watching the melt-down of the pretentious couple. The group stopped eating; they glared in the direction of the tanned woman. Jez erroneously believed her great appearance and putting her powerful husband in his place had gained the curiosity of her story.

To assist the attentive group to see her wrinkled breasts she placed her hand on the back of her husband's chair and leaned over toward the group. In a whisper, "A patient ran up to us thinking this place was a Russian facility." She looked at all of her fellow friends sitting together at the other two tables.

Jana asked, "Was he a tall man?"

"Yes."

The remainder of the bonded visitor group took turns and questioned the tanned lady not allowing her to finish her story.

Dan asked, "Was he wearing white underwear?"

"How the hell would I know?"

Debbie asked, "Was his manhood about a foot long?"

"What?"

Hippie Gal smiled and asked, "Did you see his multiple orgasms?"

"What are you people talking about?" asked Jez. She felt a unified assault being gauged against her by these lesser people. She opened her mouth in a feeble attempt to continue her story only to be interrupted again.

"Once satisfied did his face change from a crazy look to a satisfied man?" asked Maddy.

The tanned lady never finished her great story about a patient believing the Asylum was a Russian outpost. She sat down and in silence with her husband they picked at their food. They were too hot and embarrassed to eat.

At the two full tables of visitors, the group easily resumed the conversations they were having before the overly tanned couple arrived. Juli Jo's pink bibbed overall mother waved at a woman sitting with another group of visitors in the distance.

Trick Greene was not allowed to be one of the tour guides because he had an extensive history of fabricating events that never happened. His behavior of telling lies was similar to an obsessive-compulsive disorder. Trick knew he had this pattern; he just couldn't stop himself from telling lies. Most of the people at the hospital knew to take Trick with a grain of salt. For Trick, it was a delight to be a tour guide with the naïve townsfolk.

Coming from the numerous, three-inch, ceiling speakers was a bizarre blend suggestive of Lawrence Welk with elevator Muzak.

Trick went rogue. "Our new cafeteria, as you will notice, has a sound system." His voice was loud enough to gain the attention of all of the visitors sitting at his table. "This music is not just any music. The soundtrack was originally of a Beetles theme by Apple Productions."

Trick briefly stopped his pronunciations. His eyes searched for dissonance. None were found.

The visitors at the second table stopped eating and the people at the two tables waited to hear what concoction the Beetle haircut Trick Greene was going to produce. Trick was not aware that one of the repercussions of his group bonding was their questioning some of the validity of his stories.

Trick leaned over toward the relatively safe Mennonite woman and said, "If you listen to the album backward it obviously says, "Sounds your own." The music is at the forefront of a major breakthrough in the treatment of schizophrenic patients."

"Show me the album that says backward "sounds your own" and then tell me what the heck this has to do with these people being crazy?" demanded the rational Sarah.

In a gesture of gaining time Trick leaned back from the Mennonite lady and he declared, "The tape was pirated to Paris… France and it was designed to interfere with the brain waves that cause people to hear voices. It is still in the experimental stage."

"That's a lie," said eleven-year-old Juli Jo.

"What's a lie?" countered Trick, trying to buy some time.

"What you just said."

Still trying to buy some time to rethink the situation Trick questioned the kid, "What did I just say?"

Juli Jo's pink attired mother remained silent during this most recent episode of her pretentious child. Jana believed her daughter was doing exactly what she should do when confronted with ridiculous situations of life.

The four-foot-eight Juli Jo screamed an open declaration of defiance. "What you just said."

How did the kid know Trick could not follow a straightforward dialogue?

Young Juli Jo patiently waited for Trick's response to her question. After giving him enough time to prove he could not follow a dialogue, Juli Jo answered her own question, "You said people are cured by this music in the ceiling."

In an imprudent attempt of retreat, Trick tried to gain some face and glared at the pig-tailed, pink stirrup pants, and pink-and-yellow striped top girl. He demanded, "What's your name, girl?"

"Juli Jo," said the girl in a boastful manner.

"What, your parents didn't know whether you were a boy or a girl, so they gave both names?"

"I don't appreciate that," shrieked the pink garbed coal miner mother. "Mister, you apologize to my daughter!"

In a gesture that was supposed to suggest compassion, Trick slightly angled his head and said, "Juli, I do apologize for you having a boy and a girl's name." Before her mother could respond...

An ear-piercing rhythmic sound of an alarm went off in Cafeteria A.

17

"Bleep…bleep…bleep…" screeched the alarm in Cafeteria A. Jez screamed, "Shit, now what?" Maddy, the overweight teacher who wore a sunflower dress, labored her large body under the plastic table to safeguard herself from a nuclear blast. Milo shouted, "The crazies are taking over the asylum!"

One of the questions on one of the intelligence tests is, "**What should you do if in a crowded area a fire alarm goes off?**" Screaming, "shit," ducking under a table; or screaming, "Crazies are taking over": is not one of the higher scored responses on the intelligence test.

The visitors had not heard a fire alarm since they were in high school. The visitors at the three tables who did not overreact sat still. They looked in the direction of Trick Greene for some guidance.

Bolstered by his recent prominence to tour guide, Trick Greene took command of the situation, "Don't worry folks. I am sure this is a false alarm, but we are still required to walk outside for a few minutes. Please follow that group going out the door and I will go last and follow behind you."

Seeking a safe refuge from the supposed escape of crazy patients or fire, groups of visitors scattered under the large trees outside of Cafeteria A. A thankful light breeze flowed under the canopy of the walnut and oak trees providing some refuge from their return to the extreme humidity and heat.

Trick gestured his small group to come around him. He was going to enlighten them of the most recent gadgets at the hospital, fire alarms.

Trick visually checked out the face of the young girl to establish she was not going to cause any more problems. Once satisfied he returned to his boastful tour guide voice, "The fire alarms were installed one month ago. Needless to say, we are still trying to control the patients from pulling the alarms. When they were initially installed, three false alarms were pulled the first day by patients and ten false alarms pulled the second day. Following the second day…well, it took a couple of weeks and numerous false alarms; they installed mechanisms that spray blue powder paint on the patient's arm that pulled the alarm. That didn't stop the alarms, so they caged the alarms so that a person needed a key to pull the alarm. Apparently, they did not get the cages completed. But, mark my words; before the day is out, we will see someone with a blue arm."

A pear-shaped woman casually walked toward the group. The only thing out of place was that she had a blue arm. The woman seemed to be oblivious to the blue paint on her arm.

Trick Greene, in his newfound leadership role of being a tour guide, thought he would exhibit to the visitor group his keen mental health interviewing skills. He waved in the direction of the woman, "Hey, Sarah Sue, got a minute?"

"Sure Trickster, what's up?"

"What have you been doing today?"

"Not much, I went to group this morning. I think it's helping. I feel better."

"Excellent. What did you eat for lunch?"

"I had the noodles; they were really good."

With that last comment, she looked at the visitors to get their acknowledgment that the food was good. The visitors not being sure what they should do cautiously raised their heads up and down in agreement that the noodles were good.

The Trickster knew he had an easy prey for displaying his keen psychological skills, "Why Sarah Sue there's blue paint on you. How'd you get that?"

"Did you put it on me?"

"Why no, I just saw you and I don't have any blue paint cans do I?"

Trick held out both his open hands for her to see. He further questioned Sarah Sue, "Did you pull the fire alarm?"

"No, you aren't supposed to pull the fire alarms, I think Dave Steinkuehler did."

Trick Greene in his attempt to display his keen mental health expertise further questioned his subject, "Sarah Sue, where were you born?"

"Pluto."

"You mean the planet Pluto?"

"Yes, it is cold there because it is so far from the sun. It snows all year round. That's where I learned to ski and skate."

"How'd you get to Earth?"

"Spaceship."

"By yourself?"

"No, there were other people, but they drowned. The spaceship landed in Orange Crick Lake and then it sank. I'm a great swimmer and I managed to swim to the top of the water then I walked to the farm. The spaceship is still there at the bottom of the lake, but it is so deep nobody can find it."

"Don't you miss your family?"

Sarah Sue's facial expression abruptly changed to a hostile look and she yelled at Trick, "You stop that!"

Trick took a step backward from his subject. "Stop what?"

"Quit taking my thoughts. Quit it!"

"What are you talking about?"

Sarah Sue's eyes looked like she was possessed by the devil. Her face squished and her eyes emanated a laser beam stare at Trick. She took a threatening step toward Trick. Sarah Sue seemed to grow in size.

A deep, reverberating, booming voice put a stop to this pending precarious situation, "Sarah Sue you don't want to go there."

All heads turned toward the figure calmly walking to the group. It was the other physician assistant who had removed the man from the visitors' room and had also been on the Acute Unit, Mack Johnson. The calm deep voice continued, "Sarah Sue, why don't you and I leave these fine people alone and we'll go see if we can't round up some lemonade and we'll get that blue stuff off your arm." She nodded her head in a coquettish manner. Sarah Sue grabbed the black man's massive upper arm. Mack looked toward the group and requested, "Please excuse us," and the two proceeded down the sidewalk as if they were going to a dance.

Similar to the unison smiling of all of the characters in *A Charlie Brown Christmas*, all of the visitors grinned, even the too tanned couple. Walking toward the group was their original tour guide, Ashley. In her bright colored mod shift and orange stockings, took her time walking in a poised manner. As she approached the group the milk-white skinned woman confidently said, "Thanks for taking over for me Mr. Greene; I will now be able to finish the tour with the group." She straightened her dress.

Trick with slumped shoulders looked at the group "I enjoyed meeting all of you and I wish you the best."

Of course, he could not leave them on that note and he had to finalize his salutation with, "And remember, the next time you go crazy, please remember the Weston Asylum." A couple of the people got the sarcasm and the majority of the group looked to the ground and did not respond. The visitor group was glad he was leaving.

"Was everyone able to finish their lunch?" asked the sprightly Ashley.

She got the in-unison affirmative head nod from the group.

"Well, then let's get back on the tour. Please follow me."

The group walked along a wide sidewalk; when the group encountered patients on the sidewalk, the patients stepped off onto the grass to let the tour group past. Dr. Nash had instructed the department heads to inform the patients about appropriate protocol during Community Day.

Glad to be back with her tour duties, Ashley picked up with her rehearsed dialogue. "Over here is the infirmary and it is where people get medically evaluated upon their arrival. Most of our patients' medical needs can be taken care of on campus. There are two surgical rooms for emergencies. Otherwise, for the surgeries we cannot handle we send them to Jackson Memorial Hospital or to Clarksburg Memorial."

"How many medical doctors are on staff?" asked Dan the man.

"Right now there is one medical doctor. Two other physicians in the community are on an as-needed basis. During our heyday, during the 40s and 50s, we had four medical doctors on full-time status."

Dan's mouth and eyes tightened and he further questioned Ashley, "What happened to all of the doctors? Did everybody just get better?"

"Not exactly."

The ethic-driven social worker for the second time abandoned the prepared script of Dr. Nash. "There was a major change in the 1950s. Following World War II was when the drugs Thorazine and Imipramine were discovered. Thorazine is an antipsychotic medication. When people take their medication sometimes the voices go away and they are not delusional. It was also during the 50s that Imipramine was discovered by accident. That is an antidepressant. If depressed people take their Imipramine as prescribed, then their depression is lifted. As a result, people do not need to come to the hospital. There was a loss of over 50% of our patients in the last ten years. I know medication alone is not the answer. In the future, there could be a lot of people living in the streets or in jails, just like we did before Dorothy Dix if we don't do something different."

Dan continued to question, "Do you think that would be a good idea for these big old institutions to go away?"

"Absolutely not. As you can see, pretty much everyone here is on some type of medication and they still need the structured care of our facility. If left to their own impulses they would be getting into too much trouble. They would end up in the streets or prisons much like their predecessors before the asylums were built."

Ashley lost the attention of the group.

Fifteen feet away from the group sat a slightly balding patient on a bench. The visitor group moved their attention away from Ashley toward the middle-aged man. His empty exposed hands were in a cup-shape and he moved his cupped-hands in the direction of the group as if asking, "Would anyone want some from my refreshing bowl?"

Ashley smiled and clarified, "That's Fred Wood. He's a World War II marine veteran and he still thinks he is on a battleship in the Mediterranean. Their small fleet of ships had been attacked by Nazi planes. His battleship was the only one to survive of their fleet. The ship's propellers had been annihilated by a rear attack of a torpedo dropped from a plane. The stern of the mighty ship was completely submerged. Due to the quick work of the sailors, they had closed the hatches to not allow water into the other passageways of the ship. One of the closed hatches kept them from gaining access to their food supply. The bow of the ship rose a full forty feet in the air. The ship was a sitting duck for air and sea attacks. Their major source of food was an emergency supply of Spam. All of the seamen knew there was no way they were not going to get to land alive. They were going to die a sea burial. Four days the entire ship mainly lived on a limited supply of Spam. To this day, the delusional patient is offering people some Spam."

Milo asked, "How do you know so much about this man's story?"

"He's my uncle."

Ashley yelled, "Isn't that right Freddie?"

"Please, take some Spam," was the best her uncle could muster.

A few silent, awkward seconds ticked by. Most of the visitors looked at the man with his open cupped hands. The hippie couple moved closer together. Jana's eyes moistened. The Mennonite couple stood and stared. They did not move. The elderly, smoking, dancing lady grabbed the upper arms of her husband. Richard did not move. Jez picked a burger from her nose, flicked it on the ground, and walked over to a tree trunk and sat down.

Eleven-year-old Juli Jo broke the stillness of the group. She walked up to the World War II veteran and pretended to take some food out of the man's fictitious bowl. Pretending to eat the make-believe Spam, Juli Jo lifted her hand to her opened mouth. The veteran spoke to the girl, "Remember to know which lifeboat station is yours."

Juli looked past the man's drug-induced yellowed eyes into the black of the man's pupils. "I will."

The veteran got that spark in his eyes that people get when they secure contact with another person.

Ashley lightly brushed the corner of her eye and smiled. *Juli Jo has the touch.*

18

Following the advent of psychotropics, nerve medications, most of the mental health professionals failed to actively listen to their patients; they became lazy. Once the professionals had their beloved diagnosis, their label of the person, many of the mental health experts did most of the talking during their 'therapeutic' sessions. The art and science of psychotherapy had changed from being an expert on the development of a therapeutic relationship to a tutorial of things the patient needed to do: take medications, make friends, exercise, go to church, don't drink alcohol, and change negatives into positives.

A pill and the not-wanted advice could only do so much.

The patients and professionals of the asylum felt trapped. The patients felt trapped because nobody seemed to really understand their disorder and their feeling different; subsequently, patients felt alone and not understood by their mental health practitioners. The professionals felt trapped because treatment hinged on patients taking their medication. Patients would go through expected times of relapse and the only answer was to increase the medication or change their medication. The professionals doing psychotherapy, talking therapy, no longer felt responsible for developing a therapeutic relationship that was conducive to change.

Dr. Katie Carmel did not feel trapped by the confines of society. She grew up knowing how to work with frightened animals. Carmel had been raised on a small farm in Southeastern West Virginia. The farm always included some livestock. They had their cattle, hogs, and chickens. When it was time to load the animals in the back of the truck for slaughter, it was always the young Katie's job to load the animals because she could load the scared and stubborn creatures without a fuss.

Her father and brothers had to use the newest gadget, a cattle prod; a four-foot long tube filled with 'D' batteries that delivered a strong electrical jolt. The animals would jump and move but not always move in the desired direction; and, sometimes they would turn on the proprietor of the cattle prod.

Young Katie, however, would cut off a limb of a live tree and calmly talk and tap the sides of the animals' necks with her flexible stick guiding them to the loading shoot. This same knack she had with the animals she had with people. She knew when to talk softly and when to tap and when to use a good sharp snap.

Periodically people were admitted to the Admissions Unit who did not talk with any of the professionals. Who could blame the patients? Historically, every time they talked with the non-empathic mental health professionals, they got labeled with a diagnosis and were questioned, "Are you taking your medication?"

Dr. Carmel was one of the few professionals at the Weston Asylum who took the time, and had the talent, to truly listen to her patients. She cared about the patients.

During the earlier Admission's Team morning meeting Carmel was assigned to be an interim leader due to Blowfish's outburst toward Psycho. There had been a scream in the hallway during the meeting and Carmel helped a physician assistant take down an agitated patient. Upon return to the Admissions Team room the professionals, the Team decided to send a frequent flyer, Ms. Jenkins, to the Acute Unit.

Following the questionable decision to keep Ms. Jenkins in the hospital, Carmel was aware they had a lot of cases to review by the eleven o'clock deadline. She questioned the group, "Who has seen Crik Stone?"

All of the professionals sitting around the T-shaped table in the room said they were unable to interview the man; Crik Stone refused to answer any questions, he refused to talk.

Toad, the social worker assigned to his care, also said, "This Neanderthal is dangerous; I think he's manipulating."

"Do we need to use derogatory names?" Carmel wanted to control any unnecessary, demeaning theatrics in her room.

The social worker replied, "Well he is. The guy looks like a caveman. He's huge and his long unkempt blond hair, muscles that don't stop, and his eyebrows and jaw stick out just like a caveman."

Carmel hesitated and leaned back in her chair in an obvious gesture of deciding whether to take down Toad or let it slide. The room waited in anticipation.

"What is in the Admissions Note of Crick Stone?" asked Dr. Carmel.

Toad read the Admission Note of the psychiatrist, "Crik Stone is admitted from Jackson Memorial Hospital. Patient and his live-in girlfriend had an argument. She threatened to leave him, so he cut on his forearms. This man has a long history of cutting. The patient has welts on his forearms where he has cut on each forearm numerous times over the years. During his cavity search, a concealed razor blade was found in his mouth."

Toad, in her never-ending search to gain power within the Admissions Team room abandoned the admitting psychiatrist's notes and added her evaluation, "The guy is on a one-to-one suicide watch. Hell, he ain't going to kill himself. I tell you he's manipulating. He has been in prison for a good part of his adult life and at least one reported time he was raped while in prison. He just wants people to feel sorry for him."

Carmel knew there were too many cases to discuss. The time would come to highlight to Toad how she was destroying the functioning of the Admissions Unit. Carmel asked the social worker, "Does it say why he was in prison?"

Toad turned the page of the Admissions Note and said in a defeated voice, "He killed his previous girlfriend."

"With what?" questioned the interim leader of the Admissions Unit.

After looking down at the chart again, the ill-prepared Toad said, "His hands, he strangled his previous girlfriend with his hands."

In a modest voice, Carmel said, "Crik Stone is one of my patients. I will see him this afternoon. If I can't get anything from him, we will decide tomorrow what to do with this guy."

The remainder of the Treatment Team meeting was no different than other days. The usual bickering and out-right name-calling proceeded when one member had information another did not—just another day in paradise.

The number of admissions was horrendous. Following the Admissions Team meeting, Carmel had seven people to meet that afternoon. Usually, she met three to four patients in the afternoon.

When people are hot, tired, and placed under stress; they make mistakes. Dr. Carmel was hot, tired, and stressed.

19

Crik Stone, the patient who was admitted with a razor blade in his mouth, was on a one-on-one suicide watch.

When patients arrive at the hospital, they are given a shower and a cavity search. Crik Stone had a razor blade concealed in his mouth. He was placed on one-on-one. A physician assistant or nurse must accompany the patient everywhere he went on the Admissions Unit.

Following the Treatment Team's meeting, the all too familiar "click…click…click" of the high heel shoes announced Carmel was on the Admissions Unit. The psychologist, in the yellow polka dot dress; sauntered past the blond, long-haired, seated man who stared at the floor. He did not look up to hear the trumpeting entrance of Carmel's shoes.

The pounding of the heels stopped a few feet away from the massive man. Carmel's head turned back to glance to where Crik Stone was sitting. His head despondently hung toward the concrete floor. He supported his head with his huge red-tanned hands. His elbows were on his knees. Knowing he was the man she must later interview, Carmel turned her body to face the large muscular man.

In a tone of voice, that was more befitting of a dentist saying she was going to be late for a benign teeth cleaning, "I am Dr. Carmel, a psychologist. I need to grab a bite to eat. I will be back in a few minutes to ask you a few questions."

Dr. Carmel did not wait for a response.

She brusquely turned and there was the infamous "click… click…click" of her heels as the lady in the yellow polka-dot dress sashayed away.

The blond haired man looked up from the floor as Carmel walked away. The heavy steel door opened and closed as the woman left for her routine lunch.

Twenty minutes later Crik Stone sat in the same chair with his dazed stare to the workings of the concrete floor. The various shades of gray of the floor were moving in a concerted dance as if in preparation to attack his mind. The darker spot closest to his left foot was the leader of the grey army that threatened his mind. Some of the soldiers of the black spot had already entered his mind. He must focus, he must remain focused on their movements. To lose a second of concentration was to risk being overpowered by the black spot and to go crazy.

The metal-to-metal clicking of the interworking of the lock within the steel door at the end of the hall announced that someone was entering the unit. Crik Stone continued to stare downward toward the floor never risking losing sight of the black spot. His massive strong hands supported his head.

The distinctive "click...click...click'" of Dr. Carmel's white-patent high heel shoes announced she was back on the unit. Carmel picked up one of the hallway chairs as she got within striking distance of Crik Stone. The physician assistant motioned for her to move her chair farther away from the homicidal patient. Carmel did not move back; she sat the chair down at a 60-degree angle from the patient. She leaned over and rested her elbows on her thighs and rested her head in her delicate hands. Her long black hair hung toward the floor. She stared down at the floor.

The mirrored figures remained fixed for about a minute.

Not raising her head, Carmel softly broke the silence, "Mr. Stone, I am Dr. Carmel. I am a psychologist and I need to ask you some questions."

She did not dare to look up from the floor. Unlike the other psychologists, she did not use a standard opening or ask patients how they felt. She went solely on her guts.

Continuing in her soft voice, she asked, "Bad day?"

Following a prolonged ten seconds, in a low flat voice, he spoke. "Bad day."

Giving him five seconds, she mimicked his response; but, she expanded, "Lots of bad days?"

"Lots of bad days."

"It's just a fucking merry-go-round."

His head remained fixed on the black spot and its soldiers. Crik Stone answered in a somber voice, "Are you going to fuck me or what?"

In a calm voice, Carmel asked, "Does the pain ever stop?"

"Sometimes… sometimes with my live-in or when I have good weed."

"Is this a good woman you live with?"

A prolonged silence.

Dr. Carmel chuckled.

Crik Stone raised his head.

He didn't chuckle.

Similar to what a mother does with her newborn child, Carmel raised her head to empathetically mirror his gesture.

Crik Stone branded a penetrating threatening glare into her pupils. His eyes did not move from his target's eyes. His message was clear. *Don't fuck with me bitch.*

Their eyes focused on their respective targets.

His chest rose.

Carmel's chest rose and her heart rate raced.

The physician assistant shifted in his chair.

Carmel asked in a composed voice, "This woman you live with may be good in some ways and not so good in other ways?"

His eyes never wavered. He said in more of a grunt than a word, "Yeah."

Stone's eye's slightly relaxed.

Her eyes never wavered. "At times she can love you like nobody ever has. She cares when nobody else cares. She alone is the only person who knows how much you hurt."

Crik Stone's chest allowed movement and he took in a deep breath.

Carmel took in a deep breath, "Then other times she can take the life out of you. You can do no right in her eyes. Her anger, her rage can be overwhelming. During these times it is like she is possessed by the devil. It's as if she knows which buttons to push to make you feel like a worthless piece of shit."

A deep and resounding, "Yeah." His eyes slightly relaxed.

Carmel had previously worked with similar patients; she knew Crik Stone was still not ready to let go of his paranoid stare.

"Maybe she is not what you need right now." Her comment was light but explosive. She had brushed this man's mental world followed by a definitive tap.

The massive previously homicidal Crick Stone leaned frighteningly forward toward Carmel and bellowed, "No! She's not good for me! I do love her, but she's not good. I need my own place. I get disability, $226 a month. I need help finding a place. I can't read or write."

"So, you must have felt at times like you were stuck living with her. What is her name?"

He hesitated to answer.

Carmel feared that with this fairly benign question she might lose him. She waited.

"Karen"

"With Karen, at times you must have at times felt stuck and that you didn't have a choice. She made you feel that you needed her."

"Exactly."

With that affirmative statement, the psychologist knew she was on a correct path.

There are many different paths to helping people. The idea is to find a path that will help the person move in a constructive adaptive manner. Carmel continued talking with Crik about his relationship with Karen. Crik and his girlfriend were perhaps both suffering from a borderline personality disorder. They were caught in a vicious display of projective identification. In other words, the relationship was a mutual setting up of their partner of what they hated about themselves; all the while, accepting how their partner sets them up for what they value.

Crik's head returned to look at the pattern of the movement of the concrete floors. The various shades of grey had stopped their dance. The black spot remained by his left foot.

Seeing his head return to the downcast position, Carmel asked, "Where'd you go?"

"Nowhere, just thinking."

Carmel told Crik she was going to talk with one of the social workers, who would then talk with him about finding an appropriate place for him to live. Carmel got a social background: his years growing up, his education and work history, his various crimes and imprisonments, his drug and alcohol usage, and his severe sexual abuse. She had more than enough information to support her main diagnosis of a borderline personality disorder from this uncooperative patient who had not spoken to any of the other professionals.

She then preceded to list in layman terms, to Crik Stone, the experiential and daily-life symptoms of a person suffering from borderline issues. His eyes came to life as he made direct eye contact with the psychologist. "Shit, it's like you've been living with me."

Carmel requested that she would like him to stay at the hospital for a few more weeks so that he could feel more solid before he left the hospital; it would give them time to find suitable living arrangements for him.

Crik Stone agreed to sign a voluntary commitment and move to 246, the Acute Unit.

A signed voluntary commitment, with an uncooperative patient, was a major feather in an Admissions Treatment Team member's cap.

Her next patient was going to be more docile; but, he was going to be more troubling for Dr. Carmel.

20

It was approaching mid-afternoon. Carmel had four more patients to interview. Because she was confident about her interviewing skills, Carmel did not always take the time to review the patients' charts before interviewing them. If there were something significant in the Admitting Note that she missed during her interview with the patient, she'd return later in the day, or the next day, to clarify with the patient.

The next patient to interview was Bob Burns, the patient Blowfish had transferred to the Acute Unit without the treatment team's signatures. Following the correction of Blowfish's misguided transfer, Bob Burns had been returned to the Admissions Unit.

Carmel stood beside the nurse's desk on the Admissions Unit. A slight upturned grin rose on Carmel's mouth as she recalled the morning meeting. *Bob Burns was not even Blowfish's patient. Pedro was his psychiatrist and Pedro forgot that he met the man. When he remembered that he did meet with Burns; he said things like Bob Burns being a nice boy, My Three Sons and some Oedipal issues.* Carmel was concerned because she did not have time to review his chart and there was much she did not know about Bob Burns.

When the Community Day visitor's group toured the Acute Unit, earlier in the morning, Bob Burns was erroneously on the Acute Unit. During the morning visitor's group tour, pig-tailed Juli Jo talked with Bob Burns. When Juli Jo walked away from Bob Burns, he silently mouthed the words, "It's okay."

Standing beside the desk that sat halfway down the hallway, the yellow polka dot dress psychologist asked the nurse who sat at the desk, "Is Bob Burns outside of his room?" The nurse pointed in the direction of a man sitting alone playing solitaire with a deck of cards.

The "click...click...click" of her white patent shoes and her flowing dress gained the attention of the sleepy looking Bob Burns.

"Mr. Burns, I'm Dr. Carmel; I'm a psychologist. I need to ask you some questions."

The sleepy looking man came to life. "Okay."

"Let's talk at the end of the hall. It is more comfortable there and there are fewer people."

When Dr. Carmel was able to get patients to cooperate, she liked to meet with them at the end of the hall where there were two chairs, a couch and a coffee table. The main reason for the different venue was the coffee table. She had something to prop up her legs.

When the two reached the end of the piss-yellow hallway, Carmel sat on one of the chairs and routinely rested her feet on the coffee table. She crossed her tanned athletic legs. The shortened dress draped to the floor.

Bob Burns, a twenty-three-year-old Caucasian male, sat on the couch. He looked well-groomed in his button-down plaid shirt and blue jeans with the pant legs rolled up.

Not being governed by set structured interview questions, the psychologist questioned, "So, Mr. Burns, you look sleepy; yet, you seem pretty chipper."

"I feel pretty good. People have been decent here. But I am tired."

"So, what brings you here?"

"I hear voices."

Dr. Pedro had briefly described Bob Burns' symptoms at the Admissions Treatment Team meeting and he insisted Bob Burns needed psychoanalysis due to some Mommy issues. Carmel was already confused about why this man was at their hospital. He did not exhibit any of the negative symptoms that were so common with people who were psychotic: monotonic voice, apathy, or flat affect. He seemed okay given that he was locked up in the Weston Asylum. More importantly, he did not have the deadened-lifeless eyes that were so characteristic of psychotic patients. He just seemed like a nice guy who was sleepy.

Carmel in a nonchalant manner asked, "And what do these voices say?"

"Bang and escape."

In a surprised tone of voice, "That's it?"

The young Bob Burns countered in a sarcastic voice. "Yeah, do you want more?"

"Kind of."

"Kind of what?"

"I was kind of expecting more."

"Would it help if I was from Mars?"

"Not really. It depends on what you mean by 'help.'"

"Would it help you do whatever you do here for me to say I came from Mars?"

"Not really. Are you from Mars?"

"No."

"Then it won't help. Where are you from?"

"My mother's belly."

In an exacerbated voice, "I mean where were you raised?"

"Fairmont."

Dr. Carmel was annoyed and felt like she was being toyed with. He seemed rather normal, too normal. Most people who were locked up in a mental hospital because they heard a couple of non-threatening words would be pretty upset at the idea of being locked up. He didn't seem upset; he didn't look depressed, his speech was logical. Burns was a puzzling patient for Carmel.

"Tell me more about the voices. When did they start?"

"About two months ago."

"Did anything significant happen two months ago?"

"Nothing in particular. Last December I graduated from the University of West Virginia in American History. I was lucky to find a job as an adjunct teacher at Glenville High School; but, I hope to go back to school and become a history professor eventually."

To test the waters about this questionable American History Admission, "Who was the fourth president of the United States?"

Without hesitating, "If you don't include Jefferson's two terms, it was James Madison."

"Who was his first lady?"

Again, without hesitating, Bob Burns answered, "Dolley Madison."

"Everything okay with the job?"

"Yeah, it couldn't be better. The students, even the jocks, seem to enjoy my classes."

"Any idea why you started hearing 'bang' and 'escape'?"

"No idea."

"Does it bother you?"

"Yeah, they can happen at any time; especially when I am under more stress. But, I have pretty much gotten used to them now."

"I'm confused. At first, you said they bother you; but, then you said you'd gotten used to them. Which is it?"

"I guess it's both. Sometimes they still bother me and other times they don't."

"Why did you decide to come in now instead of two weeks or two months ago?"

"My girlfriend had an aunt that was hospitalized and it did her some good. She thought I should get help."

In a chipper voice, "You have a girlfriend?"

"Yes."

"How is that going?"

"Okay, but we have our problems like everyone else."

"Yes, everyone does have problems in relationships. What type of problems are you and, what's her name?"

"Gina."

"What type of problems are you and Gina having?"

"Nothing much. She just thinks I'm too bossy and I think she is too laid back. We have different personalities."

After talking with Bob Burns another 30 minutes and asking the classic questions about his background, his drug/alcohol usage, and his present life; Katie Carmel was stumped and she found nothing remarkable about his past or present.

The patient broke the predictable questioning of the psychologist and asked, "I hear you can get a free haircut here?"

Carmel answered his question with a brief question. "Yeah?" She did not attempt to conceal her dropped jaw and slightly downturned head. "I don't get it. You are here because your girlfriend's aunt went to a mental hospital, and I assume she got some help, so you decided to come here because you hear two words. But, more remarkable to me, is that of all the bizarre feelings and thoughts you must be experiencing by being here in an asylum, you ask about a haircut."

"Can I, can I get a haircut here?" asked the well-groomed plaid shirt patient.

"I will tell the social worker to schedule you for a haircut. I am stumped. I have no idea what is going on with you."

"Me too."

"Bang and empty?"

"Bang and empty."

21

In his second-floor apartment, the lop-sided-face Dr. Nash slouched in a tufted black leather chair. His face was less demented because the muscles of his mouth and his one good eye were relaxed. The once salesman persona had mutated into an information gathering machine. Nash's dilated pupils were dark holes taking in all matter. He devoured data from his personal history, five senses, and his sixth sense.

His thoughts raced. *Something going on in my hospital is wrong. It does not belong here. It is evil.*

Nash could not put his finger on what "it" was. The president of the Weston Asylum knew in his gut that something, or someone, was not right. Historically, his gut-feelings had a good batting average.

Western civilization was celebrating in the year of Dewey Nash's birth, 1909. A wonderful future for society was predicted by the number of new inventions and major progress in the arts and sciences.

The tree of life grew a disfigured branch when Dewey Nash was an 11-month old infant. His beloved Pentecostal preacher father died in a railroad accident. His mother had turned to booze for comfort. As an only child, he had to learn to fend for himself.

As an infant, the president of the asylum had to decipher whether his alcoholic, abusive mom was in a safe or dangerous mood. The seed for his future paranoid states-of-mind was planted. His unexpressed anger toward his mother fueled the paranoia. Over the years, the young Dewey Nash's talent of unconsciously picking up on his mother's thoughts, feelings, and behaviors grew in accuracy. As an infant, he learned to walk *not* because of an instinct to explore. He learned to walk because of an instinct to escape.

During the weekends, when his mother would go on major binges, he stayed with his loving maternal grandparents. Maama and Paapa had provided him the needed love to grow. They had laughed at his mistakes and repeatedly hugged him. He was treated like an adult during their ventures to the garden. They even gave him a small plot of the garden for him to grow his loved sunflower plants.

When he did risk telling Maama and Paapa how his mother would put her mouth around his wee-wee, the grandparents were quick to minimize his fabrications and they reminded him he should be a good boy because his mother loved him very much. His grandparents had a 6th-grade education and had been isolated in the same holler for their entire lives. People don't talk about such things as sucking on a boy's penis and they told the infant Nash he should never repeat such blasphemous words again.

"Your mother loves you."

The young child felt an awkward way of feeling understood because they did not slap him for saying such a thing.

By the time he was three years old, he could easily tell when his mother had those sick eyes; he would disappear into his bedroom and hide under his bed. Except for the first time, she subsequently always found him under the bed. She would grab one of his kicking ankles and scream, "Why do you do this? You've totally destroyed my life. I sacrifice everything for you!" His body would go limp after she threw his slight body on top of the bed. He was no match for her overwhelming frightful strength. "Honey, you know I love you more than anything on this planet." The abuse always began with a light touch to his face.

His new safe spot became the closet in the bedroom. Dewey Nash learned to take care of himself; he hoarded cereal, a plastic canteen of water, and an empty pickle jar in the closet.

The sound of the somnambulant footsteps to the closet door was guaranteed to be followed by his mother's drool, "You do not love me…You need to be the man of the house…You have to quit thinking only about yourself."

The following day she always begged for the infant's forgiveness followed by, "We will not talk about last night."

The times of his mother's remorse became less frequent.

When the infant Dewey Nash matured to a child, his fear turned to rage. For the first time in his short life, he felt pains of safety. He felt sane when he screamed back. He discovered he could get her to cry. Anger became a friend. The deadening blanket of fear was replaced by assaulting bouts of anger. The anger brought hope, change, and control.

His newfound rage twisted their relationship into a sick duet. She'd scream, he'd scream, she'd cry…and then he would comfort his mother. She was all he had. He was all he had.

The neighborhood kids avoided him. The "Nash Kid," who would become president of the Weston Asylum, had to create his own mental world where he was above all others. As a boy, he created a mental world where he was special and everyone else was wrong. He fabricated a magical world where one day other people would recognize his genius or would be forced to accept his superior power.

His mental world had split into all good or all bad; there was no gray. On some days, he believed he was a child destined to be great; other days, he believed he was a child destined to destroy, he was evil. His changing moods also effected how he viewed other people in his life. On some days, people: his mother, neighborhood kids, and even grandparents; were untouchable great people; other days, they were evil. Life was good or evil. People, including him, were good or evil. His moods would easily switch from good and evil.

At the tender age of four, Dewey had polio and half his face was paralyzed. With time he gained some movement on the right side of his face.

On the first day of first grade, his nickname was, "The One-Eyed Monster."

The boy was alone in a school building filled with cruel children. He knew he was different from the kids in a bad way. His anger mounted to the intensity of a mounting volcano.

Following a mistaken voice of faith, he had told his teacher he did not complete an assignment because his Mother had again put her mouth around his wee wee; the teacher called the newly formed Children's Bureau.

Two days later a police officer showed up at the house. It was 3:00 p.m. and his mother had the strong stench of alcohol on her breath. She denied ever doing anything wrong to her beloved child. "He is my little man. I would never do anything to hurt him." The police officer never did talk with the little Dewey. Being a devoted Methodist, the police officer recommended she go to church.

With her devil-child in hand, Mrs. Dewey did follow the advice of the policeman and walked the one block to the local Pentecostal church. She attended the Sunday services two times.

One year later, seven-year-old Nash walked alone to the three-times-a-week venture to the Pentecostal church. The seven-year-old Nash had discovered God. For him it stuck. He found his asylum, his peace, his purpose, his savior. From the pulpit, the preacher told the congregation, told Dewey Nash, "God forgives all sins and only the elected few—the believers in Jesus Christ—would go to heaven." The lost child had been promised eternal love if he had faith. Young Nash felt accepted by the congregation. They taught him he was special; how there were the 'believers versus the nonbelievers of their faith,' the 'us versus them.'

Unlike the majority of the evangelical congregation, the didactic teachings fueled an already present schism in the young Dewey Nash. He contained his anger within the walls of the church. Away from the congregation, he was different. He had become proud that he was different.

On the playground, he would beat the teasing, weaker nonbelievers with a furry of sheer hatred. The first time he was sent to the principal's office there was a harsh hand spanking, the second beating was with a board, and the third beating was on his naked back with a freshly cut hickory stick. With blood flowing down his back Dewey broke his silence with the principal, "I am doing them a favor by beating on the weaker ones by saving God the time and trouble of teaching them the errors of their ways. They will learn. God loves you if you believe in Jesus. I love you."

Dewey Nash had a reason to live. There was hope.

Following the three trips to the principal's office, he was no longer called the one-eyed monster on the playground. The kids learned to leave him alone.

Dewey Nash no longer felt alone because he knew, and accepted, the kids and teachers at school were sinners. *They are going to hell.* Dewey had uncompromised faith in Jesus and had faith he was going to heaven. Following the third beating, he would no longer go home after the school bus dropped him off at the end of the day. Instead, he walked to the one-story white church that lacked a steeple. Usually, the young pastor was waiting for him and they would discuss the scriptures. When the pastor was not there, Dewey would sit in a pew and pray.

During adolescence, most young people question their childish beliefs of an anthropomorphic God, of a white-bearded man sitting on a cloud, and they develop a more mature, personal, spiritual belief; or, they leave the institutionalized teachings of their upbringing.

For the adolescent Nash, his religious beliefs were that of a six-year-old. He had discovered his purpose in life by virtue of the fundamentalist teachings. Questioning his childish beliefs never happened for the adolescent. He had found his home. There are the believers and there are the nonbelievers. *There is them and there is us.* His black and white thinking easily fit with his developmental years of love for a mother and hatred for his mother.

At the age of 13, he performed some of the sermons at his Pentecostal church. His voice rose in a feverish pitch and the congregation raised their arms swaying back forth screaming for the Holy Spirit to enter their souls. Reaching a crescendo, the pubescent Nash screamed at the congregation, "Do not think that I have come to bring peace to the Earth; I have not come to bring peace, but a sword. Matthew ten thirty-four." He leaned on the lectern. The eyebrow of his good eye reached to the heavens. The youth's deep voice rose from the depths of his hatred toward the 'thems.' "These words of Jesus confirmed we are chosen.

Our brief lives are to fill the Holy Spirit within all the souls we encounter. Sometimes words alone are not enough."

Words were not enough for the adolescent Nash. The Roaring Twenties was a time of the 'thems' sinning. The fifteen-year-old Nash burnt down a Speakeasy in the early morning hours. Unknown to Nash, a hobo had broken into the Speakeasy after it had closed. The hobo died in the fire. Nash was never a suspect in the crime.

As a young man, Nash created a splinter Pentecostal church. One of his parishioners of the church was a psychiatrist. Nash encountered one of those 'ah-hah' experiences where everything seemed to make sense. The clouds seemed to open. He could save sick souls and be an all-powerful doctor; he could be a psychiatrist. He could fix the 'thems'. It was a perfect fit for the demented man.

The intelligent Nash did graduate from medical school specializing in psychiatry. During his residency, he met a Mennonite nurse. She asked him to marry her. He felt loved; and, for the first time in his life, he could feel love for another, his wife. Their relationship stopped the good and evil battle in his head. He could for the first time appreciate how a person could be frustrating without hating them.

Unfortunately, the brain pathways are not completely malleable. Nash remained with a heightened sense of paranoia.

He would go through sprees of being on a constant mission of scanning his environment for threats.

Dr. Nash was equivalent to the ultimate, poker-faced, player of life: picking up on other peoples' tells.

His eerie ability to pick up on peoples' secrets led him to believe he was in touch with the cosmos, the Holy Spirit. He could even predict future events.

The adult Nash believed he was a prophet blessed by the Almighty Father.

One week before Community Day, Dr. Nash's supernatural skills were tested.

22

A baseball diamond was on the southern end of the front lawn of the asylum. Gazebos dotted the lush forest of deciduous trees that filled the northern tip of the lawn: oak, maple, cherry, birch poplar, and alder. The trees in the small forest were enormous compared to the majority of trees in West Virginia. A few generations ago lumber barons had raped West Virginia of its trees. The asylum's modest forest was one of the few virgin tracts in the state. A smaller sycamore tree grew by a small pond. Under the shade of the tree, two men engaged in a heated discussion.

In a squeaky, high-pitched voice, Nash chastised Flattop, his Chief of Maintenance. "You don't know for sure if the fireworks will arrive on time, your people are not trained in pyrotechnics, and you didn't check out the insurance coverage. What do you know?"

Flattop replied with an unrelated answer. "As a boy, I lived in the Thurstone house, over there." Flattop pointed in the direction of a bridge crossing a stream. "From our front porch I saw the burial of the greatest president of the asylum." Two veins protruded from Nash's neck. He could not believe Flattop changed the topic. "My god man, we have a week to go for the greatest firework display in West Virginia and perhaps the greatest in the United States."

Flattop believed the newly appointed president of the asylum needed to know some history of the place. In his laid-back tone, Flattop said, "Dr. James Sycamore was buried in an urn. I never heard of cremation and I didn't really understand what it was until I was in middle school."

The ramblings of Flattop provided president Nash some time to think. With his left hand, Nash rubbed the cheeks of his face and said, "Yes, I've heard of Sycamore and he was a great benefactor of this community. I believe he managed to find funding for two wings of the hospital, six ancillary buildings, a grass tennis court, and a dance hall. Dr. Sycamore also secured funding for the local bank and a Baptist church."

Relieved that he was no longer being scolded, Flattop smiled and enthusiastically said, "Yes, the town worshipped him; so, they put his ashes in an urn and buried him on this front lawn. We could be standing on top of him right now."

Nash focused on Flattop's words and *the town worshipped him*. In a subdued voice, Nash asked, "But, if they buried his ashes on the front lawn wouldn't there be a marker?"

A tilted head and dropped jaw from Flattop suggested a need for clarification.

Nash restated, "Wasn't there a monument, a stone with his name, a rock, or something to know where Dr. Sycamore was buried?"

The chief of maintenance straightened his head; he said in a deep contemplative voice, "Now that you mention it, I don't remember ever seeing them putting a monument over the site. I do remember, I think, of a place where there was no grass for a while but that could be my imagination."

Nash's egotistical mind went wild. *I need to find this urn of the ashes of the dead president and put it on display for Community Day. The people may then associate his great deeds with the great deeds I am doing. I must find the urn.*

No further mention of the pending firework display was made. The emphasis became finding the dead president's ashes.

Flattop was a grade school kid when he witnessed the burial of president Sycamore's ashes. The appearance of the lawn had changed a lot over the 40 plus years; Flattop's memory had also changed over the years.

Flattop spent the next couple of days on the Weston Asylum lawn with a Geiger counter trying to find the urn. Community

Day was one week away. The micromanager Nash periodically stood on his apartment balcony to watch the maintenance man waving his Geiger counter over the lawn. The prolonged absence of finding the urn only heightened the paranoid Nash's obsession to find the urn.

Nash knew where he was going to display the urn. Similar to all of the levels of the hospital, there was a major intersection of hallways under the clock tower. On the third floor, in the middle of the intersection, was a statue of Michelangelo's David. It was a bronze piece and was of significant financial value. Nash wanted to move this piece of art to a closet because he considered the nude male statue to be distasteful.

The one meter in height replica of David was anatomically correct of the statue in Italy. The major difference was that, due to staffs' and patients' rubbing David's manhood, the statue's penis was a shiny bronze while the rest of the statue was a darker aging blue-grey. It was time for the statue to go and Nash was going to find a more appropriate replacement—the ashes of a dead president of the hospital.

Flattop had some positive readings with his Geiger counter that turned up three spoons, 12 coins (three from the 1800s) and one tobacco tin. During the beginning of his search, he had a tractor with a back-hoe digger following him. When the Geiger counter ticks gained in frequency Flattop dutifully moved to the side and pointed at the spot. The man on the tractor hoisted the huge metal claw into the air and ripped open a huge hole in the ground. Numerous eye-sore craters were the result in this once tranquil setting.

One spot was not meant to be dug into; it was not an old Indian burial ground.

When the tractor's back-hoe clawed into the earth, at the prescribed spot, the tractor was swallowed by a large sinkhole. They had accidentally discovered one of the old tunnels that had been in disuse for decades. The unused tunnel connected the hospital to the jail. The next day it required a crane to lift the tractor out of the sinkhole.

Nash liked things to look clean. His once-manicured lawn looked like it was attacked by a group of enormous prairie dogs. Nash's old friend, anger with its accompanying defense of obsessive thoughts, rose with vengeance. His once political demeanor soured to a face with one rounded eye demanding attention.

President Nash directed Flattop to replace the tractor with a maintenance man carrying a shovel.

Flattop remained persistent in his quest and they kept digging holes with shovels in the yard. One day before Community Day, Nash had enough. The paranoid, but supposedly sensitive-to-the-happenings-of-the-cosmos president of the hospital; left his commanding view from his balcony. Because Community Day was only one day away, he dashed down the stairs, ran out into the front yard, and slackened to a fast walk up to Flattop. "I needed to get outside, care if I just tag along?"

Based on the number of holes he had dug, Flattop believed he was doing a great job searching for the urn. He responded to the president, "Of course not. I could use the company."

Nash in his best humble voice requested, "Try hovering your contraption there to your left a little bit."

The Geiger counter continued it's relentless, "tick...tick... tick..."

"Look a little bit more to your left."

"tick...tick...tick..."

In a sickening attempt to be polite, Nash begged, "Please, just ahead, take just a step forward."

"tickity..tickity..tickity..tickity..tickity..tickity..."

Dr. Nash snatched the shovel from the maintenance man and the administrator manically dug. He hit something hard. The man in the three-piece striped-suit went down on his knees. His manicured hands viciously dug around the object.

Nash's mind raced. *It has to be the urn. It must be. I foresaw the urn was here.*

Seeing the president's frantic possessed digging, Flattop and the other maintenance man took a half step backward.

Nash turned his head in an act of affirmation and smirked at the two reposing maintenance men.

His head leaned closer to the buried object and his hands gained a determined thrashing on the sides of the rounded object. The maniacal clawing was interrupted by brushing off the dirt from the exposed portion of the metal object. Some shiny portions and a blueish tint were evident. Nash returned to scouring the sides of the object. Once enough of the dirt was removed he forced his hands under the belly of the object. He attempted to pull the object out of the ground. One side slightly budged. His hands thrust underneath the opposing end of the object. He again forced his small hands under the belly of the object. It came free.

He raised the object above his head.

It was the magical urn.

Not one of the three men on that prodigious day was consciously aware that Dr. Sycamore's remains were buried under the shade of the only sycamore tree on the property.

When Nash had stood up from finding the urn, Flattop saw something he did not like. His boss looked disheveled: a greased strand of hair hung over an eye of the usually exacting man. The voice of the president of the asylum was comfy, too smooth. "You got the fireworks display completely covered--right?"

Flattop's hand rubbed the flattop haircut of his head. He said, "Yeah, but you got to realize I spent a week out here with one of my workers and...." Nash, in his still too-controlled voice, interrupted Flattop. "No, you either tell me tomorrow's firework display at the end of Community Day is going to be a total success or you resign now."

"Oh, it will be good."

"No. Not good. It will be great with no mishaps, right?"

Flattop looked in the direction of Nash with frowned eyes and nodded his head in an up-and-down affirmative direction. "I **swear, on a stack of bibles**, nothing is going to go wrong."

Flattop thought the priority was finding the stupid urn. Flattop had not spent the needed time to check out the weather conditions. He was not aware of the complicated and intricate nature of pyrotechnics. Too many unreturned phone calls to the firework company had resulted in a message to his secretary, "We can do only so much. We're going to leave the product and you are responsible there on." Flattop had no idea of the insurance liabilities of a fireworks mishap; he thought the insurance stuff was the responsibility of the financial department, or of the state.

Following Flattop's **swearing on a stack of bibles** that everything was going to be okay, Nash felt impelled to verify the import of the Community Day's firework display with his lackadaisical Head of Maintenance. "Well, you promised me six weeks ago we would be astonished by a great firework display. If we do, then your job is secure. If you don't, you will be looking for employment elsewhere."

The stature of David was replaced by the great discovery of the urn. It was an ornate urn with a relief of the Weston Asylum that surrounded the container of the dead man's ashes. The urn was a dark blue and the relief of the hospital was solid gold.

The statue of Michelangelo went to the basement.

On that memorable day, president Nash had walked back to the building with a down-turned head. He was not depressed; he was in contemplative thought of everything that needs to be secured by tomorrow's Community Day.

Entering his second-floor apartment his mental list of things to verify and complete before the all-important Community Day, turned to other thoughts. Nash reclined in his black leather tufted chair in his apartment. It was not a time of celebration.

The paranoid thoughts returned. *I don't know what 'it' is. Something, or someone, is in my hospital and does not belong here. It is here to make me fall. It is beginning to crowd me.*

Nash stood up from his favorite chair and walked with no intention. *It is getting too close. It's in the staff. The disease has taken over a staff member.* For no purpose, a hand stroked the top of the fireplace mantel. *Someone has leaked to the hospital credentialing board. They are going to make me fall. I must not use the phone anymore. I must hold my meetings in other rooms. Maybe we need to meet outside and away from the building.*

The man, a once defeated infant, aimlessly walked around his apartment in thought. The respect of being president of an asylum was not enough; the power of his relationship with his wife was not enough. He was losing it.

The old schism of love and hate returned.

Nash walked to his newly purchased transistor, Sylvania, stereo console. He opened the wooden lid and turned the volume knob of the radio. Simon and Garfunkel sang one of his favorite songs, *"I am a Rock, I am an Island."*

Nash's mind strained to get him back on track. He sang with the song and his nasal voice joined. "I am a rock; I am an island...I am a rock...I am the rock of Gibraltar...nothing can stop me."

Walking to relieve himself in the apartment bathroom, Nash's mind returned to his safe prophetic world.

Garfunkel should go solo: Paul Simon is holding him back.

23

The visitor group stood with large rings of sweat under their armpits. The once lively visitors stood motionless and speechless in the scorching heat. In the cemetery, there were no trees. Most of them even refused to look at some of the headstones from the 19th century. Some of the visitors were pale. The high humidity and heat was getting to them. Following their lunch in the air-conditioned cafeteria, the group had visited the old farm. Following a tour of some abandoned barns, the group had gone to the asylum's cemetery where there were over 100 graves. They were told by Ashley there were perhaps 500 or more bodies in the cemetery but the number was unclear because the majority of the patients didn't warrant a gravestone—because there was nobody to come and visit them.

The slow-moving group waddled to the hay wagon and lumbered up from the wagon tongue to their previous sitting pattern on the bales of hay. The too-tanned couple, Jez and Richard, opted to ride the hay wagon this time.

Micromanager president Nash came to the rescue. He told all of the tractor drivers to be sure they had an ice box filled with Coca-Cola, Pepsi, Dr. Pepper, Fanta, Hires Root Beer, and chocolate milk. There were no water bottles.

The lively conversations of the visitors had returned by the time the hay wagon stopped in the front of the main building. The limber ultra-thin Ashley jumped off the wagon. She straightened her smock. "We are back where we started the day, and we are going to go inside so you may see a new addition to the asylum." Eleven of the twelve visitors bottle-necked at the front of the wagon and waited their turn to use the hitch of the wagon as a step.

Juli Jo jumped off the wagon and ran to the side of Ashley. "Where are we going now? Are we going to see some more patients? I think they are nice." Before Ashley had an opportunity to answer any of the hyper-girl's questions, the pig-tailed girl pointed to the baseball field in the front of the asylum, "I play baseball over there."

"Good."

"It is good because I am good. I am better than any of the boys," said the eleven-year-old in her pink, stretchy, stirrup pants. "Did you know I hit more balls than any of the boys? I mean you being a girl: you are a girl aren't you?"

The last comment did it for Ashley. "Kid you need to settle down. Go find your mom and stay by her side," said Ashley in a caustic voice.

All, but one of the visitors, managed to get off of the hay wagon without incident. Hagar's foot slipped off the wagon hitch and the side of his face caught the PTO of the tractor. Blood poured out of a gash on the side of his cheek. The blood ran down his cheek and dropped onto his tied-dyed T-shirt.

Milo, the accident insurance salesman, handed the hippie a white handkerchief. "Here, it's clean."

"It's okay man; I don't need to blow my nose," said the hippie.

Harmony walked to his side. Her delicate fingers soothed his cheek underneath the gash. "You got a bad cut." Hagar rubbed the cut on his cheek. When he pulled his bloodied hand away from the cut, he took Milo's offered handkerchief.

Ashley, in her mod shift orange and yellow dress, did not move. In a matter-of-fact-tone-of-voice, she said, "You might need stitches for that."

Hagar said, "I'll be fine. If I need to, I will tape it closed when I get home." He turned back toward Milo and pulled the handkerchief away from his cheek. "Thanks for the handkerchief." The gash spurted out some blood. Milo frowned, "Sure, anytime…Maybe you should keep it and just apply some pressure. It can't hurt…I mean applying the pressure can't hurt… Well, I mean…just keep the handkerchief."

Ashley was not in a mood to babysit. *The idiot got what he deserved for coming here so high.* "Let's get inside where it is a little cooler."

The twelve visitors, for the second time of their tour, ventured into the robin egg painted walls of the main entry.

A thankful sigh erupted from the group when they shuffled into the cooler cavernous entry hallway of the stone building. A nurse wearing all white clothing passed out hand fans to the visitors. The fans were a simple construction of a square piece of light cardboard stapled to popsicle-stick handles. The pictures on the cardboard depicted the scenes of the Stations of the Cross when Jesus walked to his pending crucifixion. The fans were donated by the First Baptist Church; Richard was a deacon of the First Baptist.

Maddy and Milo, the Mennonite couple, and the elderly couple took fans. The long-haired hippie couple did not take fans, nor did Juli Jo or her mother.

Concerned about the apparently long day on her unfit visitors, Ashley made her best attempt at compensating. In an overly-enthusiastic voice, she said, "I would like you to follow me to a recently discovered majestic urn that contains the ashes of one of the past presidents of the hospital. We will take our time walking up to the third floor. When we get to the second floor, we will take a short break."

The group broke off into two smaller clusters. Half the group hiked up the northern staircase and the other half slowly climbed the southern staircase. The divided mostly overweight groups huffed and puffed their way up the stairs. When the two groups reached the second level, Milo and Maddy paraded straight for the floor ashtray. He hacked as he pulled out his Old Gold cigarettes from the brown jacket he was carrying. The overly tanned couple was immediately behind them followed by the elderly dancer. Harmony pulled a cigarette out of her purse for the two to share. Within seconds the landing area was filled with a small cloud of second-hand smoke.

Juli Jo coughed and nobody paid her mind.

In her rehearsed voice, Ashley said, "As you may recall, behind that door is where we were earlier today, Unit 246. The unit behind you is Unit 244."

"Who goes to 244?" asked the elderly Dan.

"People who need a little more care," said Ashley.

"What kind of care?"

Without hesitating, "It can vary. Many of the people had not lived with friends or relatives for some time, so they go there to get used to being around people." In a chipper voice, she pointed to two wooden doors and said, "Please look to your side over there; one door is the apartment suite for Dr. Nash and the other is for the chief psychiatrist. Dr. Nash owns a house that is off campus. Because he works so many late hours, he also has this apartment at the hospital. The chief psychiatrist, Dr. Blowfish, lives in his apartment in this magnificent building. As many of you know, the remainder of our doctor's live in the houses that line the road on the south side of the campus. Please, let's make our way to the next floor."

Silhouettes of two people emerged from the shadows of a hallway. A patient was escorted by a physician assistant. The patient was the friendly Bob Burns. He was being escorted to get a haircut.

Juli Jo ran toward the patient and screamed, "Bang!"

The lethargic Burns worked up a gentle smile.

That was not enough for the spunky Juli Jo, "Empty!"

Bob Burns nodded his head up and down and grinned. He put his hands on the sides of his head and he leaned down toward Juli Jo with large rounded eyes and screamed, "I'm going crazy!"

Juli Jo shrieked in delight.

With the fun exploited with one venture, it was time for Juli Jo to find another adventure and she went scurrying up to the third floor.

The wheezing visitor group clambered to the third floor. Due to the extreme heat and the demands of the walking tour, many of the visitors had grown a new layer of oily skin. The group was desperately in need of a bath.

After all the visitors arrived at the pivotal point of their venture, the third floor; Ashley turned and pointed to the urn in the middle of the lobby. "Just yesterday, this urn containing the ashes of one of the past presidents of this hospital was discovered buried in the front lawn. Inside this urn are the remains of Dr. James Sycamore. He was president of the hospital from 1888 to 1929. I am confident most of you have heard of him: he was the benefactor for many of the original buildings in Weston. Two of the more noteworthy buildings he funded are our large red brick Southern Baptist church downtown and the Citizens Bank of Weston which was completed one year after his death. For you out-of-towners, if you have not been to the bank, you need to stop by before you leave. It is one of the finest examples of art deco architecture in the East."

The tour guide in orange stockings walked to the side of the man wearing the Izod shirt. "We are fortunate for the president of the bank to be here today as one of our guests." Ashley moved an arm in his direction with her palm up in a gesture requesting him to say something.

In the manner of a politician he did not miss a beat and immediately began speaking. "As Ashley told you, inside the bank are wonderful art deco sculptures and paintings. We are in the process of restoration due to the recent relaxation of regulations by President Nixon."

Ashley straightened her dress and said, "We feel very fortunate to have been able to find Dr. Sycamore's remains to put on display 40 years later for your benefit. He was a great man and donated much money to the hospital when funds were difficult to find following World War I. During his presidency we added six of the buildings out back. It is his picture that you saw when you first entered the hospital. Due to the acute intuition of our present president Nash he discovered Dr. Sycamore's remains buried under the only sycamore tree on the property."

President Nash had hinted to Ashley to mention his name when the visitors saw the great man's urn. After completing Nash's request to mention his name, Ashley said, "Please take a few seconds to view the great workmanship of the urn that had been buried for forty years."

Why did the obsessive compulsive Nash leave an unprotected urn on a pedestal? Shouldn't ropes had been set up to keep people at a distance; or at least, the urn should have been protected by a glass display? Or, the pedestal could have been higher so that the following would not have happened.

Eleven year-old Juli Jo saw something of interest outside the window. She abruptly turned away from her mother. The pig-tailed girl's left hand caught the bottom of the urn.

The urn rolled on its bottom resembling a basketball weaving around the hoop. The visitors stared at the rotating urn and stood in stark fear. The eyes of the visitors fixed on the urn rotating in a helix pattern.

The urn fell to the concrete floor with a series of clangs.

The ashes exploded from the urn.

The men's pant-legs and women's exposed legs were dusted with the contents of the urn.

Visitors screamed in agonizing shrieks as if the ashes were burning through their skin. Some pranced around as if the floor had become electric. Maddy, who fainted early in the morning, fainted again.

A tired sigh flowed from Ashley's dropped jaw. Her mouth quickly changed to a grimace and her eyes grew taught.

In a desperate attempt to regain some composure of the group, the social worker screamed, "No problem! Please! Please calm down!"

The group stopped their contagious jumping after hearing the trusted yelling of the social worker that there was no problem.

All eyes of the visitors looked in the direction of the trusted social worker for refuge.

Ashley let out a long sigh and in a placating voice the social worker said, "At the request of the deceased president's relatives we had his remains placed in a different urn. We sent his ashes to the relatives. This urn is the original urn and it just contains cigarette ashes."

The fainted Maddy came back to life and Ashley did not want to deal with her. The visitors with ashes on their pant legs and calves looked relieved.

Taking full command of the situation, Ashley said, "And, do not worry about the ashes. At the end of the tour I will write down your names and addresses. I'm sure the hospital will mail you a check to get your clothes dry cleaned."

The visitors turned toward each other giving an approving nod.

Perhaps to avoid punishment, Juli Jo did not stop her run to see something of interest outside of the window.

She saw the long-haired man, the psychologist lady who called Jesus. He sat by a pond outside.

Actually, the pond was a reflective pond and was only two feet deep. Due to the insistence of the insurance companies, the original deeper pond was filled in years ago following too many effective suicides.

From her perch, Juli Jo saw the pretty doctor in the yellow polka dot dress walking toward the long-haired man. It did not take a prophet to know the preadolescent's thoughts, "Maybe he'll grab her boobs again."

As Dr. Carmel approached the pond, the psychologist lit a Virginia Slim cigarette.

Noah Holiday (AKA, Jesus) sat by the pond and took off his shoes and socks. Dr. Carmel walked up to him, "Giving it another try?"

"Yeah, I swear, yesterday I made it two steps."

"I needed to take a break. Mind if I watch?"

"No. But, but if you have the faith, you can pray."

"I will." Dr. Carmel stepped to the side as Jesus rose to his feet.

She bowed her head in an act of prayer.

Jesus stood at the water's edge. He looked to the heavens and raised his arms in thanksgiving and praise. He solemnly lowered his arms and stood in silence and prayer. His head slowly rose.

Jesus' right foot extended over the water. He slowed his rate of breathing. He felt the Holy Spirit entering his body. The man became a living spirit. His corporal right foot lowered to the smooth surface of the pond. Only one-half an inch of water covered his foot. His foot sunk no further.

His right foot sunk no further because he was at the edge of the graded pond and his foot was in mud. The light movement of his left foot also sunk no further than one-half an inch in the water.

The man, now spirit, further extended his right foot over the water. He gradually allowed the physical foot to descend six inches.

After three minutes, Noah Holiday was five feet away from shore standing in water up to his knees. He turned and despondently looked at Dr. Carmel. His face was similar to that of a child with a broken toy.

"Shit."

"Give it time Jesus."

24

President Nash did not want the visitors of Community Day to tour the Admissions Unit for a good reason. The vast majority of the patients on the Admissions Unit were on an involuntary 72-hour hold: they had threatened to harm themselves or other people. Many of the patients came onto the Admissions Unit with anger issues. The cure, locking them up against their will, did not always help them with their anger issues.

The Admissions Unit was a lively place.

"James, telephone call," yelled a robust female patient in the admissions hallway.

Midway down the piss yellow hallway, a nurse sat behind a desk. She yelled back, "Levida, quit your lying!"

James methodically did his Thorazine shuffle down the long hallway to the pay telephone. Levida held the phone up in the air for James to retrieve. The nurse behind the desk reminded James for the umpteenth time, "James, don't you go down there, she's lying."

Hearing the nurse give away her ruse, Levida had some options: (1) put the phone back in its cradle and return to her room, (2) apologize to James and the nurse, or (3) rip the phone off the wall."

Levida ripped the phone off the wall and threw it in the direction of a placid patient suffering from dementia.

The nurse at the desk picked up the phone. In a mundane tone of voice, the nurse said, "Code Blue on Admissions." Not waiting for a response from the person on the other end of the line, she hung up the phone.

The intercom system of the hospital came to life. The chipper voice of a woman announced, "Code Blue, 382, Code Blooo 382."

Levida was a frequent flyer and she knew within 20 seconds she was going to be assaulted by a group of people, they would take her down to the concrete floor, and a nurse would pull her pants down and administer a hefty dose of Thorazine in her butt. She would then be physically escorted to the seclusion room where she would stay for at least 24 hours.

Levida decided she was not going to give up easily. *James did have a call.*

She boldly walked toward a new young male nurse who was running in her direction. Levida had a determined look on her face and in her walk. As she marched toward the nurse running in her direction, her calloused hands tightly clasped into fists; her massive arms boldly swung at her sides. When the young new male nurse was within a few feet, he spread out his arms and lowered his shoulders in an ill attempt of grabbing her.

Levida sidestepped. With her right arm, she blocked his feeble left arm to the side; with her left fist, she delivered a decisive blow to his temporal. The man was out cold before he hit the concrete floor.

Levida straightened and looked down at the unconscious man.

Within a few minutes, Levida laid flat with three physician assistants and one nurse laid on top of her, one nurse injecting a hefty dose of Thorazine in her butt, and six other people hovered over her.

Dr. Katie Carmel walked out to the hall to see if this recent code was one of her patients. Seeing it was not one of hers she looked at the nurse sitting at the desk, "Is there a full moon out tonight?"

"No. But, they are well on their way to the moon."

"The astronauts or the patients?"

Carmel returned to the chart room behind the nurses' desk.

The psychologist decided it was going to be a long day, so she was not in such a rush. After completing the dictations of patients she had met in a hand-held tape recorder, Dr. Carmel decided just to relax and review the charts of the patients she still needed to see. Her remaining patients had never been to the hospital.

Carmel believed she was in a groove.

Following her asking the location of the first patient she was going to interview, Carmel sashayed away from the nurses' desk, "click...click...click," the hoop of her skirt pitched outwards. The flamboyant figure's white patent shoes passed the telephone that was pulled off the wall by Levida.

A demented man sat on the floor; he was talking into the handset of the broken phone. Carmel overheard some of the man's comments. "Yeah, they are holding me against my will. What do you mean you won't help me? You're the fucking police. Did you hear what I said?"

Carmel mused, *Could be another code working his way up.*

Dr. Carmel in her yellow polka dot dress and white patent shoes turned her head back down the hall and continued her infamous catwalk to her patient's room, "click...click...click."

A male patient abruptly jumped in front of Carmel.

"Sorry, doc. It's these outrageous erections that last forever and it drains all the blood from my head, so I get a little lightheaded." Not feeling in the mood, Katie Carmel looked at his crotch where he had a minor erection. She said, "Looks like you need a blood transfusion buddy. You look a quart low."

Carmel did not wait for a response and continued her catwalk to interview her next patient.

The psychologist took four strides to her patient's room and a patient sitting in a chair pathetically asked of her, "Can I go to my room now?"

Dr. Carmel replied, "That is up to Dr. Blowfish."

The lock-door order was one of Dr. Blowfish's great therapeutic techniques. When a patient spent too much time in their room: and not mingling with other psychotic patients, Blowfish would write a lock-door order. When the patient woke in the morning they were escorted out of their room, their door was locked, and the patient could not get access to their room until it was evening and time to go to bed. Nothing was provided regarding psychotherapy, the learning of social skills, or anything of value. Patients on lock-door orders sat in the hallway rehearsing in their heads how much they hated the place.

Dr. Carmel knocked on the patient's door. Based on the downstairs Admissions Note, Carmel knew the 36-year-old Caucasian woman was from Indiana. The woman had driven six hours to West Virginia. The woman and her husband had recently separated. Following the marital breakup, the woman had stayed in the house with her 16-year-old son. The problem was the son wanted his mother to move out of the house; and, he wanted his father to return to the house. Upset by the recent marital separation and the emotional loss of her teenage son: the woman mentally lost it. She ran to her car and started driving.

Before crossing the Ohio River at Parkersburg, the patient took a bunch of pills to calm her nerves. She had an intense fear of driving across bridges. The woman took about half a bottle of her imipramine which is hard on a person's heart and can cause a heart attack.

Once the patient drove across the bridge, she either called the police or called friends in Indiana who then called the police. The patient did remember the police bringing her to the hospital.

Carmel clarified with the woman, "You have every reason to be overwhelmed and confused. Long-term relationships and relationships with our kids are not meant to end abruptly. You have every right to feel like you are losing it."

The woman told Carmel about how she hurt and her husband was the meanest son-of-a-bitch on the planet (even though she lived with him for a couple of decades).

Carmel empathically listened and it seemed the psychologist was saying things which only made the woman hurt more. "You must feel so alone...Even your closest friends and relatives do not understand...At times you must feel like just calling it quits." The patient cried, the cries turned to wales as the unrelenting psychologist appeared to be heightening her pain. After only a few minutes of Dr. Carmel's emotional charged statements the patient said, "Finally, someone understands."

Carmel did feel the pain of the patient, but she also knew the patient did not need to be at the asylum. She said a paradoxical statement to the suffering woman. "You can stay as long as you need." Even though this woman had some histrionic tendencies, Dr. Carmel was confident that after being on the unit a day or two the patient would find a relative or friend who would be of more help during her traumatic time of transition.

"Code Blue 382, Code Blooo 382."

Carmel left the overly dramatic patient's room to meet with her next patient. A gathering of staff assembled outside of the restroom. Tempted to not ask one of the nurses, but she did, "What's going on?"

"Cindy is in the bathroom and is trying to shit in the trashcan, but she's missing."

"Oh."

Cindy was one of the patients who came from the regional jail. Cindy suffered from psychosis. She believed her miscarried child of three years ago lived and haunted within her. Cindy is psychotic and may also be manipulative. Patients referred from the jail simply did not want to go back to jail.

Somehow a rumor got started a long time ago in the regional jails that inmates who were sent to the hospital would get a reduction in the number of days they had to stay in the jail for every day they were in the hospital. This was not true. If they arrived at the hospital with 28 days to serve, no matter how long they spent at the Weston Asylum, they would still fulfill their 28 days in jail upon their release from the hospital.

God was admitted to the Admissions Unit from the regional jail the day before.

Six of the seven specialties of the Admissions Team had met with the patient yesterday, except for the psychologist. The psychologist was Dr. Carmel. During this morning Treatment Team meeting, the professionals unanimously said the patient was manipulating his psychosis and he needed to go back to jail. If Carmel agreed, after she interviewed him, then he was returning to jail this afternoon.

The man, God, was another inmate who erroneously was told his days at the hospital reduced his days at the jail. Bottom line, he might be psychotic, but he was manipulative and he needed to serve his time.

Dr. Carmel had seen this scenario many times of inmates using their mental illness trying to get out of jail. She trusted the Treatment Team's decision and planned to tell the man he was going to be discharged in the next couple of hours, as soon as arrangements with the sheriff's department to come and transport him back to jail were completed by the social worker.

The nurse behind the desk in the hallway pointed out the jail-referred soon-to-be-discharged patient to Dr. Carmel.

The man, God, heard the distinctive "click...click...click" of Carmel's white patent shoes striking the floor. When he looked up and saw the athletic legged, yellow polka-dot dressed psychologist approaching him his pupils dilated.

His enthusiasm was to wane quickly.

Tired of manipulative psychotics, Carmel's opening comment to the man was, "We are going to discharge you back to jail today."

"You can't do that."

"Why not?"

"I'm God."

"That's okay."

"You don't understand. I'm no better than when I got here."

"What symptoms do you have?"

"I thought I was God when I came in and I still do."

"Well, that's okay. I can't tell you who you are."

"I'm getting confused."

"If you say you are God, who am I to say you're not? I'm Dr. Carmel; it's good to meet you, God." Carmel extended her hand to shake his hand in greeting.

He extended his arm and limply shook her hand. As if a light bulb went off in his head, he abruptly pulled away his hand and exclaimed, "You don't get it. I really think I'm God!"

"That's okay."

With that, she turned and walked away to meet her next patient, "click...click...click."

Something about Carmel's physical appearance, persona, or smell pulled patients to her; she could not walk down the hallway without a patient wanting to talk with her.

On her way to meet her next patient, a patient violently grabbed her arm and in a staccato voice said, "Lady, you look sane, I tell you I don't belong here. I just made it all up. I just wanted to go fishing with my girlfriend. I'm not crazy."

Carmel mustered the patience to listen to the man's incessant dialogue. She ended her conversation with the patient telling him she would see what she could do to help him out.

One of Dr. Carmel's responsibilities following the Treatment Team's decisions was to tell patients where they would go following their customary three days stay on the Admissions Unit. Many were glad to return home, or wherever they had been living, or not living. Many were glad to go to one of the Acute Units where they could continue to get a place to sleep and be served three regular meals a day. A few did not want to return home, or from wherever they came.

Then there were the frequent flyers who knew how the asylum worked. Sometimes she had to tell them they were going to Unit 244.

Unit 244 was strictly for the ornery patients, the agitated patients, the patients who got mean. Some of the staff referred to unit 244 as the bad-boy-bad-girl unit. Word got around to patients on the Admissions Unit about 244. Nobody, even the agitated patients; did not want to go to 244. When patients were told by Dr. Carmel they were going to 244; they tended to get more violent.

Carmel usually enlisted the presence of a physician assistant when she had to tell a patient they were going to Unit 244. Because some of the physician assistants were called to work other units due to Community Day, Carmel feared she had to meet with an agitated patient solo.

Dr. Carmel's face lit up: her eyebrows raised, her smile broadened, and her arms opened; as she saw Mack Johnson strutting down the hallway. She sashayed up to the side of the muscular man and enveloped his taut right upper arm with both her hands. Pleadingly, she looked into his eyes and asked, "I have to tell a patient he is being moved to 244. Would you mind providing me your presence?"

"I would do anything for you," he replied in his deep reverberating voice.

The two arrived at the patient's door. A couple of knocks on the door did not warrant the verbiage that emanated from inside the room, "Fuck you! Fuck your Momma! And Fuck yourself! Get the fuck away from my door!"

Mack turned toward Dr. Carmel, nodded, and opened the patient's door.

The male patient looked like a live skeleton with bleached skin and clothes hanging on him. He was all skin and bones. Eyeballs bulged out of the sockets of his skull. Even though he had been given a shower, when he initially came to the hospital, the patient looked disheveled. His long disheveled hair would put Einstein to shame. The bulging-eyed patient sat on the edge of his cot and due to having little fat he was able to pull a foot up to his mouth. He chewed on his toenails.

According to the chart the man huffed butane as a teenager. He would stick a lighter in his nose without a flame and snort the fumes until he passed out. He then went on and huffed paint and paint thinner until eventually, he worked his way up to mainlining amphetamines--speed. The guy had fried his brain. He was paranoid and believed the people of a Lutheran church had put seeds in the walls of his house. The seeds, over days and weeks, ultimately gave birth to angel demons. He could see and hear the angel demons. They wanted to kill him. Sometimes the demons would infiltrate under his skin and they would do their demon dance.

Before his admission to the asylum, the skeleton-man had plans to blow-up the Lutheran church, the source of the angel demons. When he went to the farm store and purchased some dynamite, the man behind the counter called the police.

The patient's working diagnosis was substance-induced psychotic disorder. He unequivocally believed the people on the Admissions Unit worked for the Lutheran church and they had planted seeds in the walls of his hospital room.

Seeing the massive Mack Johnson enter his doorway, the skeleton man removed his foot from his mouth and loudly yet slowly enunciated, "Stay...the...fuck...out...of...my...room!"

154

Mack ambled toward the patient and spoke in his calm, deep voice. "You don't want to go there. We can do this the hard way or the easy way."

The two had a stare-down for a few seconds.

It wasn't Mack's voice or his size; there was something about how he carried himself that most people, including flagrantly psychotic people, knew you do not want to mess with him.

Mack continued, "We are going to send you to another unit. Get your stuff ready."

A stupefied glare, a dropped jaw, and slightly turned head on his face was the best the amphetamine brain-dead patient could do. With that, Mack exited the room.

When Mack Johnson and Katie Carmel got about ten steps away from the room, there was a loud bang of a wooden chair thrown against the door and a scream, "Fuck!"

Mack turned toward Katie and said, "Miss, I need…I mean doctor, I need to take care of this. You go ahead and do whatever you were doing."

"Thanks, Mack. I do appreciate you in the fullest sense of the word."

Mack returned to the agitated patient's room.

Carmel strutted to the nursing station.

The previously seen patient from jail, who claimed he was God, walked up to Carmel and firmly grabbed her upper arm. With her free arm, Carmel delivered a round-house slap to God's head. The patient instinctively let go of his grip and took a step back. Similar to a child being spanked for the first time, he stared at the psychologist with a look of astonishment. *You hit me!*

The two stared at one another. His eyes rounded. Her eyes couched in a tilted head in a gesture requesting, *you want more?*

God, the patient, pulled out the full guns in his attempt to not go back to jail. "I'm suicidal."

Carmel's face was that of an innocent playground girl. In a slowly enunciated, high-pitched, sing-song voice, "You are suicidal?"

"Yes, you can't release me back to the jail because I will kill myself."

A broad smile erupted from Carmel's face exposing all of her white teeth. The strong, sarcastic, and adult woman's voice returned, "I am so glad you told me that. Because when we discharge you back to jail, I will request the social worker to call the regional jail ahead of time and inform them that you are suicidal. They will put you in a paper gown and they will strap you down in a chair so you will do no harm to yourself."

God looked in total disbelief at the yellow polka-dot dressed woman as she strutted back down the Navajo piss-yellow hallway.

25

Unit 246 was the Acute Unit where the visitors began their day. The Acute Unit was a safe unit, compared to the Admissions Unit. It was especially subdued on Community Day because a few of the more cantankerous patients were transferred off the unit.

Community Day was coming to an end: it was late afternoon. The visitors were in the final ventures of their tour. They will still see the fantastic library and be dined again in the cafeteria. Then they will witness the greatest firework display in West Virginia; and perhaps, in the United States.

Since the staff of the Acute Unit had more time on their hands, Unit 246 was the hotbed for hospital gossip. According to policy and procedure there needed to be only one nurse at the nurses' desk halfway down a hallway unit. It was common for two nurses to be at the nursing desk halfway down the hallway of Unit 246.

The seated white dressed nurse said to the standing nurse, "I think it went really well today."

"I do too."

The seated nurse with her hair pulled tightly into a softball sized bun said, "None of the patients got mean."

"That's because Nash had all the mean ones taken off the unit."

"I know. But those who are left didn't get mean."

The standing nurse in a chic French hairstyle with a long pullover said, "That's because they are snowed out of their gore."

The skinny seated nurse wearing the large hair bun said, "At least nobody jumped off the building this year."

"That's because Nash had all the doors going to the roof locked."

"I like Dr. Nash," said the seated Southern Baptist nurse.

"I don't trust the guy," said the chic hair Methodist nurse.

The seated skinny Baptist nurse slightly turned in the direction of the other nurse as if to accentuate her words, "The hospital has changed since Nash became president of the hospital."

"Yeah, if you're into the evangelistic holier-than-thou preaching he does."

"President Nash has been saving souls since he came here."

The irregular-church-attending Methodist nurse said, "Yeah, thank goodness we had the Crusades and witch burnings. Well, the Catholics and Muslims did all the killing in the Crusades."

The Wednesday-evening and Sunday-morning, regularly-attending Southern Baptist nurse countered, "My uncle was recently saved. He was drinking fire-water every day and had his own still. The doctors said he pickled his liver so bad he had six months to live. That was a year ago. He began attending the Holy Crossroads Church at Jane Lew and was baptized. He's still alive. The doctors say it's a miracle."

"You mean he went to that serpent-handling church?"

"Yeah. It's saved his life."

The heavy mascara and fake eyelashes Methodist nurse could not believe her ears. She thought the Baptist nurse seemed normal. "I went to one of those churches once. They scream and talk-in-tongues. They sound like a bunch of kids screaming some gibberish. That's just like when Nash came back to the hospital last night like he does every Wednesday and Friday. He goes into a patient's room and you hear that wild screaming, just like they did at that snake church I went to...you've heard the screaming."

The hair-in-a-bun Baptist nurse had a different interpretation of the events, "He goes to selected patients' rooms to release the demons who took over patients' souls. The demons don't come out quietly."

The French hairstyle, Methodist church nurse defensively maintained, "When he's in a patient's room Nash insists for none of us to go in the patient's room. He always has a little doctor's bag. I bet he has a snake in it; and, he's scaring the shit out of the patients."

"You're crazy. His only concern is the welfare of the patients."

"I bet you five bucks he's got a rattler," declared the chic haired Methodist nurse.

"You're on."

"Because of Community Day, we both have to work late tomorrow. When he comes to our unit tomorrow night, I'll try to take a quick peek into his black doctor's bag." After thinking about what she had just said, the Methodist nurse said, "Or I'll get someone to check Nash's black bag."

26

Ashley's group had been to the Acute Unit, cafeteria, farms, cemetery, gym, barbershop, theater, and pool. They witnessed Juli Jo knocking over the urn of the past president's supposed remains.

The visitor's group last stop of the day, before dinner, was the hospital's library. Their church-donated fans moved at a slower pace: they strode down one of the cooler hallways on the first floor. The unified visitors engaged in lively discussions.

The ultra-thin social worker stood erect in front of two massive wooden doors. Ashley yelled, "Folks! Folks!" Out of respect for Ashley, the group politely quit talking.

Ashley ran her hands down her sides straightening her chic dress. She said, "These towering heavy doors are the main entrance to the library. Dr. Sycamore purchased these doors from an abandoned cathedral in Italy during the 1920s." Hagar had a look of slight confusion. Ashley fixed her gaze on the long-haired man and clarified in a slow rate of speech, "Dr. Sycamore was the president of the asylum a long time ago; it was his ash remains you thought had spilled on you." Removing the red handkerchief from his cheek, he said, "Yeah, now I remember." All of the group, but not Harmony, chuckled. Ashley rolled her eyes in her head in an act of tiring of this long-haired, unkempt, bloodied hippie.

Not wanting to lose the attentiveness of her group, Ashley turned to the towering wooden doors and grabbed the two massive iron door knobs. She firmly twisted the balls in her hands, leaned back with all of her sparse body weight, and partially opened the two massive doors. At chest level, she pushed two flattened hands against one of the doors to fully open the one entry. Ashley did the same exercise of using her body weight and fully opened the second door to expose the library. The social worker walked to the center of the grand portal and straightened the sides of her dress. The lithe body, silhouetted by the light from the library, raised her arms toward the heavens and she proudly announced, "Welcome to the library."

It was a site to be seen that rivaled most public libraries and some college libraries of the day.

With her arms still pointed to the sky, Ashley turned and walked inside. "Come on in and relax. This is one of the coolest rooms in the hospital. The entire visitor group, even Juli Jo, strolled inside with a measured pace of reverence. When the small group passed through the massive entryway, they splintered off in fascination of their surroundings. Each person moved in methodical steps and up-turned heads in an attempt to emotionally grasp the essence of the colossal library. The walls of the library contained so many shelves of books that nobody could have read all of the books in ten lifetimes. A balcony went around three of the walls with more bookshelves on the second floor. Leather chairs and couches, the massive fireplace---and the spectacular windows adorned the library.

Three enormous windows opposite the grand doorway extended from the floor to the ceiling. The windows had an arch at the top and stained glass figures were in the middle of the arched colored glass.

Ashley stood next to the first window. She straightened her dress and said, "The library is based on the Vanderbilt's Biltmore library in North Carolina.

Ashley's voice brought some focus to the overwhelmed visitors of the visual splendor of the room. "I see many of you are looking at the stained glass windows. Each one depicts a significant event in the history of psychology," she pointed to the first window. "This stained glass window depicts the Weston Asylum when it was first built. As I mentioned during the beginning of the tour, it was during the mid-1800s that this cherished institution was built, as were other asylums east of the Mississippi. Our building, our home for these people, was and still is a major contribution to helping the mentally ill."

Ashley pointed to the second window and said, "This stained glass window is of Sigmund Freud. He awakened society to the role that our unconscious plays in our daily lives. The dark creature above his bearded face symbolizes the unwanted frightening impulses that lie in our unconscious. People do things for reasons they are not totally aware. In the next twenty years, I am positive there will be extensive research into the area of the unconscious so that people will no longer have to suffer."

The third stained glass window was of a mortar and bowl.

"And the final window represents medication," said the tour guide. "As I noted earlier in our tour, the 1950s was a major turning point in the treatment of mental illness with the discovery of nerve medications for helping people inflicted with an illness."

Jana asked, "Why are the first two windows rough and the third window is smooth?"

Ashley straightened the sides of her dress and said, "The original stained glass depicted a brain and a scalpel which represented the frontal lobotomies they use to do at the Weston Asylum. Since we no longer do lobotomies at the hospital the stained glass was changed a few years ago to the mortar and bowl that you now see."

The pig-tailed Juli Jo asked what she considered to be a more important question, "Why do you always rub your dress before you speak?"

"It's just a habit. Do you have any habits?"

"Yeah, I like to eat dinner." Juli Jo was bored; she ran to the wooden spiral staircase. Nobody, except for Ashley, took notice of the absent girl. Out of the corner of her eyes, Ashley watched as the child ran up the spiral staircase. *The kid will be safe up there. There's just a bunch of books. There is nothing up there for her to get into trouble.*

The social worker finished her architectural tour of the library and concluded, "Please, let's take a break. Someone will be bringing us refreshments soon. Wander around the room or just find a seat and be comfortable."

The elderly Dan skirmished around the room like an obnoxious little boy in a candy store. He discovered a small cherry and walnut inlaid wooden box on a desk. Dan, the man, opened the lid of the decorative box, "These are expensive cigars."

"Yes," consoled Ashley, a distance away from the desk. "Please help yourself to one of the cigars. I understand they are from Panama and are supposed to be pretty good." Richard, Hagar, Hippie Gal, Jana, and Milo rushed to the fancy box to smoke a good cigar.

Dan retrieved one of the cigars, removed the cellophane wrapping, and stuck the large end in his mouth. He reached for a desk lighter placed by a crystal ashtray. As he was about to light the cigar, he said, "I usually smoke Swisher Sweets or Crooks." Ashley delicately moved between some of the visitors. "Please, let me assist you," as she nimbly took the cigar out of Dan's mouth and turned the cigar around in her tantalizing light-skinned fingers. She opened a small drawer of the desk to retrieve a cigar cutter. Ashley cut the closed end of the cigar and said, "It will draw much smoother if you smoke it this way." She pointed to the end of the cigar she just cut.

Ashley slipped the cut end of the cigar into the smiling mouth of Dan and lit the cigar for him. This was just too fancy and too much for the visitor. Debbie smoking a cigarette glared a penetrating stare at Ashley.

The remaining cigar frugalities' eventually managed to cut and light their expensive dollar cigars. A heavy yellow and orange cloud lingered over the group of cigar smokers. Richard took a strong puff from the Panama cigar and looked at the bloodied hippie man standing next to him. "Good stuff." "Yeah, this is pretty good shit," said Hagar. He removed the bloodied handkerchief from his cheek and exposed his wound. The cut stopped bleeding, but it was obvious by the deep cut that it would leave a scar.

The pair puffed on their fine cigars as they walked to one of the leather couches and reclined. Hagar relaxed his legs on the coffee table. Richard, as he also relaxed his legs on the coffee table, said to the long-haired man who sat next to him, "You really should get some stitches for that cut or at least make sure you don't get it infected." The tie-dyed shirt guy took a puff of his cigar. "It is what it is."

The odd couple on the couch shared personal stories and all was going well until the tied-dyed shirt guy asked his new buddy, "What do you think of our new president?"

"You mean Nixon?"

"Yeah."

The bank president and deacon of the First Baptist church slightly shifted on the leather couch. "I'm concerned. He only ran on fear tactics. He told America that due to all of hippies rioting he was going to create law and order in our cities."

The hippie drastically turned to face his new buddy, "I know exactly what you mean. Sometimes it's like he wants to create a police state."

"It is," said the president of the local bank. "Most of my friends are scared of him. And then I can't believe they went ahead and voted for him. And the scariest part for me is that he is sending our young men by draft to Vietnam and promises he will win the war because of his great leadership. The man is scary."

Taking another puff of the Panama cigar the hippie leaned back into the couch and looked in the direction of the cherub paintings on the ceiling of the library. "I can partially understand why your friends voted for Nixon even though they did not like him because the alternative was Humphrey. He would never have been against Vietnam because he needed Johnson's support. Picking between Nixon and Humphrey was like picking between two evils."

Richard raised his cigar in the air and Hagar reciprocated by raising his cigar in the air. The odd couple had fully bonded.

Because nobody would talk to Jez, she stood at the end of the couch and overheard the odd couple's discussion. She gingerly walked to the opposite side of the coffee table the two men's feet rested upon. She looked down at the cigar smoking buddies.

By her moving from the side of the couch to towering over them, the two men knew she had something to say. In an act of silent expectation, the men simultaneously took a draw from their fine cigars. Their wondrous powers of prediction, even the stoned hippie, were accurate. The woman had something to say.

"I couldn't help but overhear what you fellas were talking about."

Keeping her legs straight, the standing Jez leaned over and moved the ashtray one inch closer to the couch. In the process of the supposedly unknown reason for her gesture of moving the ashtray, she once again exposed her aged, deep-cut, cavernous breasts. Her husband rolled his eyes upwards. *Not again.* The hippie man, forced to look, could only think. *Ouch!*

Once she had given her boys enough time, she stood upright. "Both of you know, well at least my husband should know," she stared at the Izod shirted man on the couch, "That Nixon won by a landslide victory of 301 to 191 electoral votes."

"Why do you recall the exact numbers? You don't seem like you'd be interested in politics." The hippie, active in a number of presidential protests, shifted his legs from the coffee table to the floor and sat upright. He looked in the direction of his new buddy on the couch. The president of the bank shrugged his shoulders in a gesture of, *she's all yours.*

Hagar was ticked by this woman interrupting his conversation with his new buddy. "What was the popular vote?"

"The what?" Was the best intrusive woman could muster.

Hagar spoke in a slow-paced voice as if she was someone who did not understand the language of English. "The people. Who did the people vote for?"

Because she had been so proud that she had memorized her Daddy saying Nixon won by a landslide of 301 to 191 electoral votes, she did not know how to respond; hence, she did her best. "Well, duh they voted for Nixon you stupid ass."

The tie-dyed shirt guy leaned comfortably back on the leather couch and placed his feet back on the coffee table and said, "Nixon won the popular vote by **only** seven-tenths of one percentage point."

The newfound buddy in his Izod shirt said, "Honey, he's trying to tell you that the people were not confident of Nixon as you make him out to be. Nixon is a power-hungry maniac. We're just going to see if he can use his thirst for power for more good throughout the world."

Harmony had been scanning the numerous fascinating books of the library; she sensed she needed to go to the couch where her boyfriend was retired. As she walked up to the two reclining buddies and the standing woman, she heard Jez say, "The United States is the greatest nation of the world and we need to build our military and close off all immigrants coming into our world until we can figure it all out. Once we get our house in order, then everyone around the world will be happy."

Harmony lightly touched the overly tanned woman's upper arm. "I know what you mean. The goal, we, the United States of America, is working toward is a true appreciation of variety."

The too-tanned lady frowned.

Harmony took a step back from Jez and said, "I heard you say we all want to be happy."

"Yes, that is the goal of life, to be happy."

Harmony reached down to Hagar with an open hand. He gave her his cigar. The hippie girl's protruding lips deliberately caressed the long, hard, thick cigar. She took a steady draw on the cigar and turned her head to the side to not blow smoke on the overly tanned lady. Jez, who was raised to do everything right, to be perfect, frowned upon seeing the precocious young girl smoking an obvious phallic symbol in public. Harmony returned Jez's frown with a devilish upturned smirk.

Harmony reached into her purse and produced a brownie. "My grandmother baked brownies that guaranteed people happiness. I would love to share a brownie with you."

Jez was jealous of the friendship the boys had developed on the couch. She wanted a friend. Jez took the brownie and said in a chipper voice, "Thanks, that is so nice of you." Harmony smiled at the boys on the couch and looked back at her new girlfriend. "This brownie is a little darker than the other brownies I brought— it has more sugar in it."

Jez downed the large brownie in three bites.

"Cool!" screeched the youthful Juli Jo from the balcony.

All of the visitors' heads, and Ashley's head, ferociously looked upward in the direction of the obnoxious pig-tailed girl. The adults had had enough of the antics of this little girl. Juli Jo managed to find something to quench her hyper thirst for adventure. Juli Jo stood in front of an open space between the bookshelves. She somehow had managed to find a hidden lever that opened a bookshelf. The bookshelf was a hidden door.

"Juli Jo, please close the bookshelf!" screamed an inimical Ashley.

With ease, the girl pushed the heavy bookshelf back against the wall; and, the bookshelf closed like a door, and then dropped one centimeter into place to be aligned with the other bookshelves of the of the perfectly aligned bookshelves of the library.

Milo stood by the large fireplace and exhaled a puff of smoke. He looked in the direction of Ashley and asked, "Where does that go?"

Ashley was not told how to handle this situation. Only two people in the hospital were aware of the secret doorway. Ashley was not one of them.

Being quick on her feet, Ashley created a fabrication. "That is a second exit in case there is ever a fire." She did not know the real purpose of the hidden doorway or where it led. Ashley's thoughts frantically raced. *What need was there for a secret room to be built in a mental hospital? What type of forbidden things happened in the past in a secret room? What forbidden things might still be happening? Why is the room in the library? Nash frequently uses the library.*

A dark figure stood in the shadows of the massive entrance of the library.

Ashley's dangerous thoughts about the secret room were quickly buried when she saw the distinctive figure. She waved to the man as if he was a long-lost friend. Her wide smile displayed her white teeth that could sell one-thousand tubes of Crest toothpaste.

The man in the shadow mimicked the happy wave and returned a half smile. President Nash was so proud of his social worker. He had warm deep-down feelings for her much like some uncles feel for their nieces.

Nash waved a second time, turned, and walked back down the long dark hallway.

As he strolled down the Navaho yellow hallway, his thoughts were betrayed by his overly-broadcasted sneer. *This has been a splendid day. What could go wrong?*

27

The visitors had been to the library and were then treated to a fine dinner in the cafeteria. The visitors were transported from the air-conditioned cafeteria to a fireworks display they would never forget. Twelve hay wagons, filled with enthusiastic visitors, were pulled by twelve tractors. During the next hour, the tractors would make the loop: from the cafeteria to the front, and then back to the cafeteria, to pick up more visitors and back to the front. The people on the hay wagons engaged in lively conversations.

On Ashley's wagon, Jana said to her daughter, "I love you." The pig-tailed girl quickly answered back. "I love you more."

The pig-tailed, pink bib-overall mother returned, "No I love you more than all the stars."

"I love you more than all of the trees in West Virginia," said her daughter.

"I love you more than all of the sand on beaches throughout the world."

The cognitively and hormonally growing preadolescent was embarrassed by this life-long charade and finalized, "I love you more than all of the electrons, protons, and neutrons."

The overweight mother's eyes teared and she hugged her little woman.

Ever since their encounter in the library, the capitalistic bank president and his wife had united with the hippie people. They ate together in the cafeteria. The guys discussed the future of the world. Harmony allowed Jez to lead the discussion into how women are not appreciated by their husbands. On the hay wagon, the too tanned woman frequently touched the hippie girl, giggled, and her reddened eyes sometimes stared into space to be followed by another giggle.

The Mennonite couple reveled on about the architectural wonder of the main building. Seth said to Sarah, "It would take generations for our church to even cut the stone, let alone build such a structure."

Milo and Maddy did not speak because she had a headache.

Debbie flicked her cigarette ashes onto the floor of the wagon; the ashes were cold by the time they hit straw. She looked at her elderly husband, "I was going to wait until we got home but I cannot wait any longer. That young floozy of a social worker was hitting on you when she put that disgusting cigar in your mouth. You seemed like you liked it."

"I did like it."

In the wagon in front of Ashley's wagon, kids played King of the Hill pushing each other off the wagon. Ashley yelled to the maintenance worker who drove their tractor only five feet behind the front wagon. "John, make some more space between us and the other wagon." He raised his hand and slowed down to allow more space between the tour groups.

Ashley's wagon of visitors turned the corner of the massive building and the visitors were greeted by the Weston High School band playing, *Honky Tonk Woman*. Music played outside brings a fresh dimension to life. Maddy's headache appeared to have stopped; she spoke to her husband. "This reminds me of when we were dating."

The bank president elbowed his new hippie friend and pointed his head in the direction of one of the numerous trees on the front lawn. Trick Greene, the physician assistant with the Beetle haircut and John Lennon sunglasses, leaned against a tree. The white attired physician assistant was attempting to impress a Glenville State College coed with his musical knowledge.

"You know who does that song the band is playing?" The girl's shoulders dropped. "No, I don't. Do you?"

"It's the Rolling Stones. They're a bunch of wanna-be Beetles."

"I like the song."

"You ever seen the Stones perform?"

"No, you?" It was not clear who was hitting on whom at this time in the relationship.

"I saw the Stones perform live on the Ed Sullivan show. The singer has lips like a girl. They look old, especially the guitarist. They'll probably be dead within a decade."

The young college student rubbed the back of her head and her feet shuffled in the grass. Trick allowed her time to embellish in his profound musical knowledge and his presence.

She broke the silence: her brown eyes inquisitively looked into Trick's eyes, "Who are the Beetles?"

Without answering the coed's question, Trick turned and meandered away to find some other game.

When the wagons entered the front lawn, the day-long visitors were treated to a sight they had never seen. The craters in the search for the urn had been filled in and the front lawn was carpeted with olive-drab sheets of canvas from World War II wall-tents. The tents were on loan from the National Guard in Fairmont. The townsfolk were once again treated to an unaccustomed treat, sitting on cloth instead of the itchy bug-infested grass.

Jez pointed in the direction of the freshly carpeted grass. She grabbed Harmony's arm and in too loud of a voice said, "They carpeted the entire front yard." Harmony grinned a devilish grin, "It is good." Not getting the desired response, Jez's eyes squinted in the direction of her husband. "Look at that. The entire yard is covered for us to sit." Picking up his wife was overreacting; he said in a dull voice, "They did." Not getting a reaction, the overly tanned woman yelled so all on their wagon could hear, "They gave us a place to sit and watch the fireworks. There's no bugs' crawling up our dresses." The last comment about bugs soured any positive reaction from her audience.

The tractor's two-cylinder engine slowed to a thumping cadence and the wagon came to a stop at the edge of the canvas. The visitors again bottlenecked at the front of the wagon waiting their turn to step down onto the hitch of the wagon and then onto the ground. Juli Jo again jumped off the wagon. Jez stood too close to the edge of the wagon. She fell off. She was fine. Jez immediately went to the hitch to help Hagar because she knew he needed help because he fell off the wagon earlier and he had cut his cheek. It was her sophomoric attempt to make it clear to the others that he was wounded, not her. She lightly touched a cheek of Hagar and asked, "Are you okay?"

"I'm good. You okay?"

"I feel wonderful. Life is wonderful."

It was dusk and the temperature had dropped a thankful 15 degrees. A cold front from the southwest was assaulted by a warm front. It promised to be a hell-of-a-storm.

Most of the visitors paid no heed to the possibility of a ferocious storm because the cooler temperature and breeze was such a welcomed relief. The Baptist church hand-fans went to the ground. The visitors sat or laid on the canvas sheets enjoying the refreshing cool breeze.

Following a day of feeling like royalty, compared to the patients' lives, the townsfolk were in a superior-holier-than-thou mood and a few were in a thankful mood. The children ran around playing hide-and-go-seek. High school couples tried to find places away from the view of their parents to smooch. Everyone had a wonderful picnic experience at the end of the day; except for one person, President Nash.

The paranoia had never left Nash. It was not his life-long paranoid creature that haunted him this time. It was not a fabrication from his childhood. This paranoia was real.

Nash, in his hyper-vigilant state of mind, knew the sudden change in temperature could mean violent storms. A thunderstorm could be the ruin of a perfect Community Day. *I devoted too much time, effort, and bullshit for this day.* He decided to speed things up for the final orchestrated festivities.

Nash doggedly worked six months to convince the Board of the hospital to fund a major fireworks display on the evening of Community Day. He pleaded with the Board, "You have to spend money to make money." Nash wanted to provide the biggest firework display the visitors had ever seen so they would walk away and talk about the fireworks for years to come. Following profuse times of negotiation, the Board finally agreed to purchase an astronomical sum of $6,000 of fireworks. Two new automobiles could be purchased for that price.

The plan had some major flaws.

The fireworks did not come with pyrotechnicians. The setting up of the fireworks and the detonation of the fireworks were to be executed by Flattop's untrained maintenance workers.

One of the crudely constructed wooden fireworks chutes sat in one of the partially filled in holes previously dug by Flattop in search of the President Sycamore's urn. The fireworks chute sat at a precarious angle.

The dried-out leaves of the generous crowded trees formed a canopy over the lawn. The summer's drought was the worst some had seen since 52.

The only opening of the trees was the driveway entrance and the area where the visitors sat on the canvas. The visitors' picnic area was encircled by tall bushes dried out due to the drought conditions of the summer.

Behind the tall dried-out bushes was where the maintenance workers did not have the personnel and equipment to keep the grass mowed. The yellowed grass had grown an outrageous three feet high and it looked like a wheat field.

The paranoid and intuitive Dr. Nash mentally took note of the above possibilities. All of his obsessive-compulsive detailing of Community Day could be ruined by a freak of nature.

Nash bowed his head and prayed to the Almighty God to suspend the coming electrical storm until his Community Day was complete. *May my blessed father come to my home.*

On a wooden stage, a man from the Methodist choir sang the lyrics of the song, *In the Year 2525*. The cooler, but fatigued crowd gave light applause at the closing of the song.

Before the singer could turn to walk away from the microphone, Nash leaped two steps at a time up the stairs leading to the stage; he tersely grabbed the mike and commanded in a salesman's voice, "We at the Weston Asylum appreciate all of you making time for coming out here today. We hope it has been a good visit. We are going to start the fireworks display a little early because we know most of you fine folks get up early and we don't want to have to keep you overnight."

A unison thankful laugh echoed from the large group. Jez howled too loud.

Looking in the direction of the fireworks chutes, Nash tried to hurry things up. The wooden chutes had been crudely constructed with numerous splinters of the wood sticking out of the chutes; and, more dangerously, splinters inside the chutes. The president of the asylum again spoke into the microphone, "Flattop, will you be ready in about five minutes to begin the show?" Flattop looked in the direction of Nash with frowned eyes and nodded his head in an up-and-down affirmative direction.

Besides the: severe drought conditions, a tilted chute, overgrown grass, an umbrella of prematurely dried leaves on the trees, chutes with splinters; there were the incompetent lay pyro technicians who were trying to hurry up their schedule.

What could go wrong?

Trying to buy some time, Nash looked back in the direction of all of his wonderful life-sustaining visitors, "Please, everyone stand."

"May we pray?" The sea of people stood and lowered their heads, the children stopped running and bowed their heads and a few of the adolescents kept smooching. "Oh Father in heaven, Almighty God who sees all and knows all, we ask for your blessings of these poor lost souls of the Weston Asylum who had to endure needless mental suffering and strife. Many of these fine people, just as the Beatitudes, encountered ridicule and shame throughout their ostracized lives. Many, prior to coming to our sanctuary in the hills of West Virginia, were inflicted with untold horrors of physical punishment and even sexual indiscretions."

Nash's voice rose to a crescendo. "Some sinned. They sinned against men and women in unconscionable ways! Worse, they sinned by turning their back upon the Holy Word! Might the Holy Spirit open her hands to the everlasting light of Jesus Christ?"

Nash's wife said he would double his votes for a new bond if he referred to the Holy Spirit in the feminine form.

His evangelical voice faded to a lower level. "May our patients find the peace they so wantonly seek with your words of the Holy Scriptures? We give thanks to you Father Almighty who has blessed the countless people who work at the Weston Asylum with the courage and daily emotional strength to provide unending care and love to these lost souls. And most importantly, Jesus, we ask that you bless these fine outstanding employees of the Weston Asylum who provide a safe haven for our community. Without the fine community folks who made time to visit us today, our missionary work at this sanctuary in Weston would not have been possible and the patients would otherwise be turned out into the streets or prisons. Amen."

The sea of visitors echoed a solemn, "Amen."

Nash looked in the direction of the fireworks chutes and gave an affirmative nod downwards for Flattop to start the fireworks.

Because other members of his maintenance crew were looking in the direction of the stage, Flattop turned his head toward the stage. His boss's head emphatically nodded up and down.

Flattop nodded his head sideways.

Flattop felt rushed.

People like Nash get caught in grandiose decisions that nothing can go wrong and they end up making stupid and harmful decisions. Nash wholeheartedly believed Community Day must end with his spectacular and unforgettable firework display. The president of the asylum was obsessed that he must gain the monies for the next bond.

The cool breeze picked up to a cool wind. The prematurely dried leaves broke free of the trees. The sky of the front lawn was a deluge of prematurely dried leaves fleeting their way to the ground.

A blue, dark, ominous front spanned the overhead sky of the Asylum. Half the sky was dark. The other side was bright.

Some of the townsfolk ran to their cars to avoid the obvious storm.

The president of the Weston Asylum desperately requested, "One more song before you will see a fireworks display that you will never forget."

Nash looked in the direction of the Weston high school band director. "Could the band play one more song for us?"

The band director shouted some orders to the Weston High School band and she requested the male singer to return to the microphone. The director raised her baton. The band played and the singer sang, "Sugar Sugar" by the Archie's.

Nash ran over to where Flattop and his men were working. A few mixed words exchanged. The heated conversation ended with Flattop saying, "I **swear, on a stack of bibles**, nothing is going to go wrong."

At the close of "Sugar Sugar," a much-desired sound was heard by everyone at the asylum.

"Phoooop.'" The first firework headed to the split dark-and-light sky. The firework left a trail of light during its takeoff to the heavens.

BOOM!

The first firework exploded like a cannonball.

"Phooooop," the second firework took off.

"Phooooop," a third took off.

"POP." The second spread a wonderful golden umbrella of light over the audience. The desired "oohs" and "ahhs" sprung from the rounded mouths of the crowd.

"POP." The third firework spread green spokes of light, similar to spokes on a bicycle wheel. When the green spoke-lights reached the end of their journey they each popped into six small red umbrellas. The "oohs" and "ahhs" turned into roaring applause from the audience.

The fireworks display continued for another 15 minutes. The townsfolks stood from their canopied floor; they laughed and yelled. They had never seen such a magnificent fireworks display.

The grand firework display paused for a full minute.

Because some of the audience thought it was the end of the fireworks, they walked to their cars.

The cold front canopied the Weston Asylum. The once split sky was completely darkened.

The cool wind stopped. The gloomy stilled sky promised a hell of a storm.

With the stopping of the wind and the darkness of the sky, the remaining visitors were silent.

The young kid, Juli Jo, noticed a spark by one of the crudely-constructed angled boxes of fireworks. She pulled on the arm of an adult next to her, but the man was engulfed in what might happen next; he did what most adults do with children, he ignored her.

From the sidelines, Nash ran up the steps, two at a time, leading to the stage. He grabbed the microphone for one last time of the evening. Out of breath, he announced, "A couple of months ago we had, shall we say, a visitor to our fine facility." A few of the townsfolk understood his poorly hidden break of confidentiality. "This, visitor, had written a song; all of us here at this facility fell in love with it. I hope you do too. On the sides of the stage are gigantic screens where we laser beam the words of the song on the screens. Please, sing along if you like. (The gigantic screens were only ten feet by ten feet. The "laser beamed words" were from two overhead projectors).

A young, clean-cut-looking man with round glasses walked onto the stage. Nash walked off the stage for the final time of the evening. The young man stood in front of the microphone and nodded his head in the direction of the high school band director.

And then it happened.

The following event will be discussed amongst the townsfolk of Weston for decades. The telling of the event will be handed down through several generations.

The band vociferously played the song, *Take Me Home, Country Roads,* which would be popularized by John Denver.

Exhilarating sounds of, "phoop...phoop...phoop...phoop...phoop" erupted from the chutes.

And before those five fireworks could reach their zenith, phoop...phoop...phoop...phoop...phoop."

The sky filled with fireworks. The crowd stood and joined the smiling singer singing the song.

"Take me home, country roads
Almost heaven, West Virginia."

The fireworks turned the darkened sky into day. The visitors had never imagined such a display in their entire lives.

The emotional toned singer found his pinnacle with the words:

"Blue Ridge Mountain, Shenandoah River,
Life is old there, older than the trees
Younger than the mountains, growing like a breeze."

The townsfolk were lost in the moment. Their "oohs" and "ahhs" changed to the merriment of crazed laughter of amazement.

And, before the lights of the original ten fireworks reached their descent, "phoop... phoop... phoop... phoop... phoop."

The singer, band, and visitors— continued in their resounding enthusiastic singing. A few of the townsfolk begin dancing equivalent to the crazed dance mania during the medieval times.

"phoop...phoop...phoop...phoop...phoop."

And over the microphone came the credenza for the folks of West Virginia.

"Country roads, take me home
To the place I belong, West Virginia,
Mountain mamma, take me home
Country roads."

For the next three minutes, the midnight-blue sky was lit by humankind. The townsfolk laughed in wonderment. It was a pandemonium of joy and the visitors got lost in the immediacy of the moment.

Dan the man and others cried. The Mennonite couple and others fell to their knees in prayer.

Experiencing a never-before profound connection with God, Jez removed her clothes and gyrated her naked body in front of God and everyone.

Nash stood on his apartment balcony.

He witnessed the naked dance of his co-deacon's wife, Jez.

Nash's face relaxed.

His unbalanced eyes balanced out. *It's a perfect conclusion to a perfect day.*

Day Two
(Friday, July 18, 1969)

28

Following the grand fireworks display from the previous night, the front lawn of the Weston Asylum is littered with trash. Today, the doors are locked to the townsfolk. Unorthodox things happen behind closed doors.

"Fuck you! Fuck you bitch! You eat shit! You are shit!"

The screams are directed at Dr. Carmel. The psychologist looks out of the open window of her musty smelling yet to be renovated antique car. Behind a heavily screened window and barred window; is the shape of the amphetamine, toe-nail-biting, psychotic man. Yesterday, she had the unpleasant venture of telling him he is going to Unit 244, the bad-boy-bad-girl unit.

Carmel takes in a breath. She exhales a long sigh. Her head turns away from the man in the window; she stares at the limestone walls of the facility. *He's already managed to get into solitary confinement.*

The attractive driver in the parked 1940 Buick does not move for several seconds.

Carmel's present love is her antique car. The massive, all steel automobile is powered by a straight eight engine that necessitates a long front hood with two rounded fender wells covering the front wheels. The staff openly refers to her antique car as, "The Cock Mobile."

Today, Carmel is dressed in looser clothing, because of the high temperature and humidity following last night's storm. A heavy metal click announces her opening the car door. Her long, athletic legs exit the suicide door of her black Buick. When she stands upright from the auto, there is another scream from the window,

"Looking good bitch!"

She does not bother to look at the window. Carmel saunters toward the grand steps of the Asylum. The psychologist lightly touches the pronounced fender well of her mechanically sound, but yet to be off-the-frame restoration, motor car.

The innocent gesture demanded another scream from the window.

"Fuck you bitch! You want some real balls to touch? They are up here waiting for you!"

Her once-blank stare into the stones of the asylum turned into raw energy. The psychologist's head turned to the window. Her emerald green eyes and thick dark eyebrows fixated with intensity on the man in the window. Dr. Carmel lost it. "You fuckin amphetamine freak! Your marble-sized balls and tiny penis might satisfy a hamster!"

"Fuck…you!"

The usually composed psychologist cheats a glance at her surroundings to see if anyone else was around.

She stealthy walks up the steps in the main portico of the Asylum. Uncharacteristic of her walk, her head tilts down toward the limestone steps. A powerful thought takes over as she hikes up the steps. *Why me? Please, please make it stop!* She was not referring to the extreme heat.

"You fucking whore. I bet you fucked three patients in the back of that car at one time. You know you are a fucking whore!"

Her eyes moisten as she enters the robin-egg blue painted main hallway.

At the conclusion of last night's magnificent fireworks display, President Nash informally asked Dr. Carmel to join him for an early breakfast. "Say 7:30 the Doctor's Lounge?"

Carmel initially hesitated to respond. *He's just going to brag about how his Community Day was a success.* She then recalled the scheduled Administrative Hearing that was to be held today because of her suspected bad call of sending a frequent flyer to the Acute Unit. *They are going to crucify me. I need to gain some power.*

"Thank you, Dr. Nash. I would love to join you for breakfast in the Doctor's Lounge."

Immediately following last night's fireworks display a fierce thunderstorm pelted the town of Weston, West Virginia. Five thousand homes were without power because trees were blown on the power lines; and, because of lightning striking a transformer. As the sun rose, the storm left the town of Weston in a sauna. The result of the storm was increased humidity, combined with another day of scorching heat. Due to the expected excessive heat, Carmel decided to wear looser more comfortable clothing.

It has been only during the past six years that psychologists are allowed to eat with the real doctors, the psychiatrists, medical doctors, in the Doctors' Lounge. The room is reminiscent of the old men's club. Even though psychologists are now allowed to eat in the Doctors' Lounge, Carmel had never been to the Doctors' Lounge to eat. She did not want to participate in such an ostentatious activity that neglected the workings of the nurses, social workers; and, especially, the patients.

Upon entering the room, she's aware of the powerful scent of cherry pipe tobacco. The room is ordained with oak wood throughout the room. Two large tables that seat ten are protected with tablecloths from India. China dinnerware and silverware are placed at each setting. Leather couches and chairs line the walls of the room. The Doctors' Lounge, similar to the suite of the carpet-lined Administrative Offices, has air conditioning. Carmel has difficulty accepting such a pretentious room exists in the old Asylum.

Carmel awoke this morning with the belief that she must win a war. She must make a statement. Similar to the effect of her polka-dot altered dress from yesterday, Dr. Carmel is wearing clothing common for the decade. As a compliment to her hip-hugger, bell-bottom, blue jeans she is wearing a loose-fitted top that exposes her navel. She blatantly seeks the scandal created on the long-running TV series, "I Dream of Jeannie."

The exposure of her stomach accentuates her taut tummy.

Besides her exposed navel, Carmel decided to take a bolder step this morning when dressing.

The spaghetti-strings of the loose top accentuate the deep plunge of a fitness fanatic. The thin material of the top is not masked by a bra. The air conditioning of the Doctors' Lounge has the attention of Carmel's nipples. Cowgirl boots further highlight her imposing height and the pronounced sound of her gait.

Seeing Carmel walking toward him in her "cool'" outfit, Nash stands from his chair and says, "Nice boobs...I mean boobs...I mean boots."

Carmel returns President Nash's smirk with a snarl. She pulls a leather and wooden chair away from him, casually sits down, and moves the chair closer back to Nash. The two are sitting dubiously close to each other.

Nash is wearing a platinum colored double-breasted suit.

"I don't think I've seen you wear this suit," says Carmel. "Are you wearing this power suit because of today's Administrative Review?"

The president of the asylum works the knot of his tie and says, "You got me. Sometimes things can get a little out of hand during those meetings and I save a few of my suits as a reminder to people who are in power."

Because the two are so physically close together, Nash cannot conceal his attempt to sneak a peek at Carmel's breasts. Carmel feeling comfortable with her sensuality is accustomed to the looks she creates. Nash recalls the testaments that thou shalt not lust.

His red face forecasts his next statement. After clearing his voice, "We've been pretty up front with each other. If I might, you may want to consider an outfit that is less wanting."

"I understand and thank you."

A tall black man, wearing all white, approaches Nash and Carmel.

Looking up at the man dressed in white, Nash sneers with his half-upturned smile that is accentuated by his thin mustache. In a nasal voice, he requests, "May I have the omelet with ham, onions, green peppers, and a Coke. Is there any orange sherbet left from yesterday?"

"I don't know sir—I will check."

"Thank you."

Carmel looks into the black man's eyes; their eyes do not meet. She says, "I'll have a banana."

His eyes, meet her eyes. "Thank you."

Nash raises one eyebrow. "So, what did you think?"

"Think about what?"

"What did you think about yesterday, Community Day?"

Her emerald green eyes focus on the black eyes of Nash, "I knew that was why you asked me to breakfast. You already know what I think."

"No. Now that it's happened, what do you think? Come on, dammit; you got to admit it was a total success."

Nash is like a kid at Christmas. He is overwhelmed by good feelings. He wants to get Carmel on his side because she holds too much informal power within the Asylum.

In an exacerbated voice Carmel questions her boss. "Do we really need to rehash this? You are not going to change your mind and I am not going to change my mind."

Staying composed; the Bible-thumping Nash keeps his dark eyes connected with her sea-green eyes and says, "The number of people who attended yesterday exceeded all expectations. The power people of the community already endorsed the bond for the next election. The charitable contributions will triple last year's donations. Any way you look at it, yesterday was a total success—admit it."

"Can't you hear or has your memory just totally left you? Don't you remember us going over this yesterday morning?" Carmel knew this was the agenda for the breakfast.

Carmel moves a flock of her thick dark hair around an ear; she recites to the president of the Asylum, "It is totally outrageous that you allowed people to come to our hospital to view our patients, people who are suffering, people who are inflicted. They're people damn it. If you had your visitors come to the units without the patients and see how we actually work it, would be another story. You used our patients as freaks of nature."

The elderly Nash placed one of his hands on the thigh of the psychologist. As he leaned closer to Carmel, a smirk grew across Nash's face. He says in an easy-going tone, "Are you that idealistic to think we are able to provide the care that we do, just based on government funding? We would be providing care in canvas tents instead of this fine facility if it was left up to you? Are you really that stupid? Why do you always fight me?"

Carmel pushes his hand off her thigh.

She makes a verbal stand within the confines of the Doctor's Lounge against the: we're-holier-than-thou, we're different from the little people, we're god-like.

Carmel screams, "Bullshit! Just as many things in life, there are numerous roads to the same goal. The end does not justify the means."

Recalling his recent 45 record on salesmanship, Nash pulls out the big guns; he agrees with her. "You are right: the end does not justify the means. What we provided the people of Weston and the surrounding counties, was an opportunity to see what really happens at our facility; and, to see the great work that you and the rest of the staff do to help these suffering inflicted souls."

"Like I said yesterday, it was a zoo, it was a human zoo." She loses her composure and shouts, "Its sick!"

Nash reaches out with an arm toward the attractive woman and lightly grasps her forearm; he moves his head closer to hers.

For some reason Carmel does not draw away.

His face is alarmingly close to Carmel's face.

In a deep whisper of a voice, he says, "You've heard the gossip on the streets as far as the wild tales people distort about what really happens here. It is much better for them to see the truth that is less bizarre than the local gossip."

In her mimicking, deep, composed voice; Carmel whispers back, "The way it was done yesterday, it still remains a human zoo. You don't even foresee what is happening around you. Your type of reasoning, your people, is going to—"

Nash pulls back, "Who's my people?"

"Your people, people in power positions, men whose focus is money and ethics are left out the window."

"I'm a psychiatrist. I entered this profession to help people not to make—"

"Let me finish." Carmel interrupts Nash. "Your people, who are obsessed about finances, at the neglect of the impact of their decisions on people's lives; are going to be the demise of your beloved institution...why are our numbers decreasing every year?"

Before Nash can answer, she answers her own question,

"It's because of drugs: medication, pills, psychopharmacology, or whatever fancy name you want to give it. Why can't we do both, medication and psychological treatment? It's almost like the medical people do not realize that changes in a person's environment causes a change in the person's brain structure.

The psychologist stands. She glares down at the president of the asylum.

He knows she's not done.

The psychologist is on a maniacal journey of winning a war.

She continues her wrathful venture at Nash. "The recent praise of medications being the panacea for all our mental health concern is no different than the hoopla that was around when they first started doing lobotomies. We know what ended up happening to the Pulitzer Prize winning psychiatrist who discovered the surgical technique. One of his patients killed him. I fear we may be on a similar road with this outrageous increase of emphasis on medications. Because people like you, who focus on just the bottom line, the insurance companies are going to pay for the cheaper meds and offensive brief Band-Aid treatments. Your beloved institution is a dinosaur. The insurance companies, and the government, are going to close the asylums."

The waiter in the white clothes brings out their food.

Carmel returns to her seat. The hardy debate continues throughout their meal. For being such compassionate enemies they seem to mirror one another. During the remainder of their conversation, they look in the other's eyes without wavering.

Following their breakfast meeting, Carmel sashays her way to Acute Unit 246. There is enough time for her to get her Thursday morning therapy session, prior to the 9:00 a.m. Admissions Treatment Team meeting. Her therapy session is with Jesus (AKA, Noah Holiday).

A familiar, but different, pounding of Carmel's shoes smack the concrete floor of the Acute Unit. Unlike the heels of her white patent high heel shoes, a heavier more distinctive sound of her cowgirl boots pounded the concrete floor, "crack...crack... crack."

29

If patients require more care than a three day stay on Admissions, they are usually sent to one of the acute units. The units provide the structure of a mental hospital; and, more importantly during this contemporary age, time to figure out what meds and what level of meds the patients need. In rare cases, the patients get to work with a psychologist in psychotherapy. Jesus (AKA Noah Holiday), is one of the patients that gets to see a psychologist for therapy.

Dr. Carmel pageants down the hallway of the Acute Unit to Jesus' room. She is trying a new form of psychotherapy on the man who claims to be Jesus. Instead of attempting to help her psychotic patient to rationally gain insight, or to cognitively talk delusional people into how their delusions are ridiculous, Carmel tries to join with Noah Holiday's delusions. Instead of fighting him, she agrees with his delusion. She assumes he is Jesus.

She had told Jesus (AKA, Noah Holiday) during one of their first sessions that she was experimenting on a new way of doing therapy.

The psychologist wearing a loose top, hip-hugger bell-bottoms, and cowgirl boots—knocks three times on Noah's door.

"Yeah, come on in."

Carmel swings the door open and stands with her legs spread.

Jesus sits on his bed, cross-legged in a lotus position with opened hands atop his knees.

Casually, Carmel moves her hand from her hip to pulling back a lock of hair behind an ear. *He looks more mature, more like a man.*

Perhaps his newfound maturity was because he had been to the barbershop and had his long hair and beard trimmed. Or, he was sitting cross-legged wearing a white shirt and white pants instead of his childish striped shirt and blue jeans.

"You look, older but younger. There is something about you."

Jesus smiles, "I went to the barber and he trimmed back some of my wild hairs on my head and beard."

"There's just something fundamentally different," she says. Carmel looks puzzled. "I can't put my finger on it."

"Maybe it's because my skin looks alive because of all of the itchy hairs on my neck and back. I'm going to take a shower later; then, I'll look like your old Jesus."

"Nope, there's something else about you."

Not moving from his seating position, Jesus grins. With a broad smile, he says, "Because I soaked my pants in the pond yesterday: Mack gave me a physician assistant's white pants and shirt."

Carmel smiled.

"Well, I didn't keep up on my washing."

"Maybe that's it. That must be why you look different to me. You do look like a physician assistant or a male nurse; and, I am used to seeing you in one of your striped shirts. I'm sure that's it."

Carmel's eyes fix on Jesus's strong upturned calloused hands.

Jesus is a freelance carpenter when he's not in a mental hospital.

Her eyes move up from his hands to his eyes. She asks in a chipper voice, "Jesus, are you now practicing Buddhism?"

In a caricature of a meditative monk voice, Jesus says, "No grasshopper, I am practicing some meditation techniques that I picked up in the East a couple of centuries ago."

"Shall we go to our regular meeting place for your therapy?"

"As you wish," says Jesus in a slow deep voice.

The couple walks to what use to be the staffing room of Acute Unit 246. Similar to the Admissions Unit, the Acute Unit's staffing room was moved to a larger corner room with more windows. The old staffing room is no longer in use except for Carmel's therapy sessions.

Dr. Carmel has had six psychotherapy sessions with Jesus in this room.

After unlocking the heavy, grey, steel door, "Huh, someone's been here," says Dr. Carmel.

"How do you know?"

"Our regular chairs facing each other have been moved."

The barefoot, dressed-in-all-white Jesus sits down at a wooden chair close to a window.

Carmel walks to the other side of the room to retrieve a chair. As she scoots the chair toward Jesus' chair she leans over and unwittingly exposes a full naked breast to Jesus. Her patient can't help but stare. Jesus, Noah, is a man. Dr. Carmel's eyes remain fixed on something outside the room's windows. She sees the moon.

Jesus does not stare out the window. He does not stare at the moon.

Still bent over looking out the window of the seductive moon, the attractive psychologist says, "They will be landing on the moon in two days."

"Yeah," was the best Jesus could say. He sits more erect in his chair.

"Have you been to the moon?"

"No," his eyes never move from her hanging bare breast.

"Just think of being the first person to walk on that soft moon dust that nobody else has experienced."

"I'd like that," Jesus says in a low soft voice.

Turning to face Jesus, "I would have thought you had been to the moon?"

Catching the placement of his eyes, Carmel stands upright. Her cheeks develop a flushed glow.

In a quickened voice Jesus attempts a recovery, "Yeah, I was on the moon but I was a spirit so I couldn't really feel it, touch it, I mean I couldn't touch the sand, the moon dust."

She sat in the chair across from Jesus. She crosses her long legs. Her blue jean, bell bottom, blue jeans fit her like a second skin. Jesus resumes a lotus pose in the wooden chair. In their sophomoric movements, the two pretend as nothing had transpired.

Dr. Carmel says in a poorly-framed statement, "Let's just do it. I've had a question I've wanted to ask you for the past couple of weeks."

The strong-jawed man leans slightly forward. "Go for it."

"In this second coming, were you born of a virgin?"

Jesus leans back. He assumes a softer contemplative voice. "No. I know the Scriptures don't say anything about my second birth. It's kind of a downer given the hoopla all of you made about my first birth. Father just created me as an adult this time and he took care of my social security number and all that necessary stuff to prove my existence."

With a frowned brow, Carmel asks, "Your father?"

"Yeah, God."

"But I thought you are God."

His entire face grins; he says, "I am; but, I am not."

"You sound like a Buddhist."

"Why do people need to label everything? I'm God."

Unconsciously making a risky move of leaning toward Jesus, or God, "I thought you are Jesus."

"I am."

"And you're God."

"I am; but, I am not."

Carmel abruptly questions, "Who's on second?"

"What?"

"Old joke, sorry." She uncrosses her legs and leans slightly forward. "So, you are God, Jesus, and I guess the Holy Spirit."

"Yes."

"But you're not?"

A broad smile fills Jesus' face. In a whimsical tone of voice he says, "By Jove, I think she's got it." In a more serious tone, "I think the Jews got it best. When Moses asked, 'Who shall I say sent me,' I replied, 'I AM.' The idea is I am nameless. For humans to try to comprehend me is equivalent to an ant trying to describe to another ant, using ant language, what it means to be a human being. It's just not going to happen. First of all, an ant cannot fully fathom the essence of the higher consciousness of a human being; and secondly, if they could, their language is too archaic. Humans likewise cannot comprehend me; let alone they cannot communicate about my higher level given their archaic languages."

Jesus takes a contemplative moment. "Are you Jewish?"

Carmel frowns. "No, I am not Jewish?"

The two are feeling the heat and humidity of the day. Beads of perspiration are working their way to the skin of the two. A heavy bead of sweat rolls down the sides of Jesus' eye and his pronounced cheekbone. "The Jews do not speak my name for to do so is to put me in a box. They seem to get the idea of not turning me into an idol."

"So why Christianity and Islam, given the Jews captured your indescribable essence the best."

Jesus' eyes relax. The man, the patient, has finally found someone who seems to hear. "Human's discernment of me has evolved as is apparent in the Bible. I began in the Garden of Eden in a human form walking with Adam and Eve. As the story goes, there is a flood because some angels came down and had sex with the women who birthed giants. I get mad, so I flood the planet. Did this happen? Yes and no. I did get mad and there was a flood."

"You got mad?"

"There is no love without anger. Can we come back to that later?"

Carmel leans forward. "I'm all ears."

Jesus wipes the sweat from the side of his face and pulls back the sides' of his long hair with both his hands; he wraps the hair around his ears. In an animated voice, "Since the development of the Old Testament, humans changed how they view me, that is what I am trying to say. Personally, I like the first creation story the best. I miss the good ole days when things were simpler."

"What first version?"

"There are two creations stories, the seven day version and the Adam and Eve version. They don't match and even contradict one another. In the first I supposedly created—plants, then animals, then humans. In the second—I created plants, **then humans**, and finally animals."

In a high pitched school girl voice Carmel says, "I didn't know that, are you sure?"

"Yeah, I've read the book."

"I thought you wrote it?"

"Nope, humans wrote it. I provided the impetus. I thought with the Documentary Hypothesis coming about in the 1700s, most people would by now quit reading the book literally. The Documentary Hypothesis does a clean job of explaining how many of the contradictory stories in the Bible are due to sociopolitical events happening at the time of the authors of the various books of the Bible. Most theologians accept the Documentary Hypothesis; they're just a little slow about letting their flocks know about it. I mean you can only let people know so much, look at how Darwin's theory totally upset the apple cart."

A scream and people shouting in the hallway interrupt Jesus and Dr. Carmel.

For three days a patient has refused to take a shower. Given the sultry heat, and the neglect of taking a shower or bath, the patient stinks.

Carmel and Jesus stop talking. The couple listens to the screams.

"I'm not going to shower! You can take that bar of soap and stick it up your ass!"

Over the hospital-wide intercom system comes the all too familiar pleasant voice of a woman, "Code Blue 246; Code Blooo 246."

The cross legged Jesus sitting in a chair lowers his feet to the floor. He enlightens Carmel, "That's Jackson. He's scared the FBI has been following him. He thinks the FBI rigged the showers with chemicals that will eat his skin. Can you blame him for not wanting to take a shower?"

Carmel had attended a Southern Baptist church as a child. As an adult, she periodically attended church on holidays and when bad things happened. For her, a lot of the things Jesus had been talking about made a lot of sense.

She was precariously moving from her role of being a clinical psychologist to being an enthusiastic student. She was perhaps coming prey to his manipulative unconscious yearnings.

Many psychotic people develop a crude understanding of the basis of their delusions. Just as many, if not most, people are manipulative.

The enthusiastic Carmel leans toward her calm patient and wants to know more, "So the Bible is a misconstruction of how you evolved?"

"Yes and no."

With a gleeful fun-filled gesture of wonderment she says, "Of course."

Within the darkened room, Jesus had evolved from being a boyish psychotic patient to a reminder of Carmel's old college professors. Her emerald eyes were wide.

"For some people, the description of me in the Old Testament did not meet their needs. So, the Christians added me; the Muslims added Mohammed following me. It is still an Abrahamic religion founded on I AM and the Golden Rule. Those two things are accurate, most of the rest in The Book humans embellished or created for a variety of reasons. I am evolving with the universe, or universes; and, I am changing. The humans' interpretation is…wanting."

"Wait a minute; you said earlier human's perception of you is evolving. Now you are saying you are actually evolving. I thought you are supposed to be omniscient and omnipotent?"

The two participants share a moment. They look into the depths of each other's' eyes. The laughing couple says in unison, "Yes and no."

They found a therapeutic connection.

Jesus moves his hands from lying open on his knees, to turning his hands face down on his knees. He leans slightly forward to his newfound student. He continues, "I am not the same God that I was billions of years ago. There are just some slight changes; but, actually critical changes. Have you ever heard of process theology?

Carmel shifts in her chair. A cowgirl boot accidently strikes the big toe of the bare foot Jesus.

"Sorry"

"It's okay. I'm used to it—Have you heard of process theology?"

"Nope"

"I don't think it's in the *World Book Encyclopedia*. It's the idea I am always the same, but I am changing. If I may, I am evolving much like the creatures on Earth."

A pained look materializes in Jesus' face. "Kate, can I tell you something, something I have never told anyone?"

Only family and close friends; or when Noah wants to piss her off, ever referred to Katie Carmel as 'Kate'.

Carmel's body stiffens. She fears the wondrous moments with this patient, this man, this man who has expanded her questioning her archaic religious beliefs; is going to ruin it by doing something psychotic and stupid. "I would be humbled to hear what you have never told." In her bones, she believes she has never met a more sincere man in her life.

"There's a darker side to me. It has been getting stronger lately. I'm having feelings I've never felt or had a need to feel. I'm having doubts."

"Doubts? Doubts about...?"

"Doubts about my existence: whether there is a God."

Catching herself, before saying, *"That's human,"* Carmel asks, "How long have you had these doubts?"

Since he has been evolving in the past few billion years, she expects his questioning the existence of God, should be at least a few million years.

"I've doubted myself ever since I sat down in this room."

30

The heat is unbearable. It is only 8:55 in the morning. The rise in the humidity due to last night's thunderstorm has turned the Admissions Treatment Team's room into an oven. All of the windows are open; there is no breeze. The two plastic rubber plants appear to be drooping from the pervasive heat.

The customary sitting around the T-shaped tables, similar to the accustomed church parishioners sitting in specific pews, are filled with their usual occupants; except, one chair is empty.

A few of the Admissions Unit Team members fan themselves with patient's charts.

The heat does not sour the animated discussion within the room.

"This is the greatest thing we've ever done," says Psycho, the Admissions Treatment Team head.

"It's going to be televised on Sunday," says the animated voice of Dr. Heering, the impotent chief psychologist with the large protruding ears.

"I'm too scared even to watch it," claims Toad, the social worker.

"This shows to the Ruskies what it is to be an American. We can do anything we put our mind to doing."

In a feeble attempt to regain some lost power within the dynamic forces of the Admissions Team, Dr. Blowfish declares, "Nine years ago Kennedy said we would do it and by God, we will."

The male nutritionist asserts a rare comment, "It's a scam, or in you guys' language; it's a delusion. The whole thing is a fake to convince the Ruskies we are better. It's just like, how did they take the close-up pictures of the Saturn Five rocket without the camera getting destroyed in the process? Duh. They overlaid a video of a Saturn Five taking off with a video of a fire display. You've undoubtedly heard they already filmed the landing in Arizona; that is what you are going to see on Sunday."

There is no movement in the room. Silence pervades.

Following a few seconds, squished faces turn to drop-jawed faces sitting next to them, a couple of faces turn toward the heavens.

Psycho, not wanting to waste his valuable Treatment Team meeting time on some idiotic kid's beliefs, does a rare humane gesture. He changes the topic, and questions the Team, "What did you think about last night's fireworks?"

The Admissions Unit meeting room returns to chatter.

"That was something my mom will remember for the rest of her life."

"It was like night turning into day."

"And then the music, the song of John Denver's *West Virginia* was amazing. It was amazing how the fireworks went with the music. It was just amazing; the fireworks exactly matched the beats of the song."

"The entire Community Day could not have gone better."

The occupant of the only empty chair of the room enters the doorway.

"Crack…crack…crack" echoes the pounding of her cowgirl boots on the concrete floor. The lively chatter continues as Carmel hurries to her seat,

"I think we should get Ashley a card for the great work she did."

Most of the heads in the room followed the grand entrance of Carmel.

"We should also thank the folks in the cafeteria; they worked hard to serve that many extra people."

Before she reaches her customary chair, Carmel attacks her beloved team members, "And how do you think our patients performed?"

She sits in the empty chair to the right side of Psycho. The psychologist hands a paper sack to Psycho and scans the faces of her cherished team. "Our patients, people whom we are entitled to help, what did we do? We moved the agitated out of view, and we snowed the rest with Thorazine. And then, and then, we put them on display. Boy, I am proud of what we do here. Sometimes it feels like I was zapped from another time to the craziness of this crazy institution. You're all nuts."

Psycho opens the paper sack handed to him from Carmel. Inside are ten Push-Up ice cream bars.

During yesterday's meeting, Psycho had demanded ten push-ups from Carmel for being late again. She promised him ten Push-Ups and delivered. Psycho looked at his partner to his right and smirked. He knew he could not allow too much independence of his team. Psycho was not going to let Carmel's antics of consistently arriving late to be acceptable. "Dr. Carmel, as I know you are aware we had an inordinate number of admissions this past week. We need to start on time and we are going into another apparently crazy weekend. Is it a full moon?"

The faked-moon-shot nutritionist says in an awkward way of trying to gain face, "No, I think it's waning"

Psycho decides he has enough time to take this idealistic flamboyant Carmel, who consistently runs late to his meetings, down a notch in front of the team. In his all-too-calm of-voice, Psycho looks to the psychologist sitting next to his right. He asks, "Dr. Carmel, do you remember yesterday, in my absence—"

Carmel already knows this is not going to be good.

In his righteous voice, Psycho continues, "—you moved Ms. Jenkins, the woman in the wheelchair, to the Acute Unit because of a supposed suicide threat. Ms. Jenkins is a frequent flyer and I believe you knew that."

The usually silent chief psychologist with extruding ears, lounging on the couch, quickly follows the lead of Psycho. "Dr. Carmel, I know that Psycho, Dr. Blowfish, and myself were not here to help on this call; but, you dropped the ball on this one. Dr. Shivangi is extremely upset by this referral to her Acute Unit. She petitioned for an Administrative Review this afternoon at one, or 1300 Psycho's time. We made time during our Administrative Review to discuss this questionable referral to the Acute Unit. Can you make the meeting?"

The diplomatic Dr. Carmel scans the room with slits for eyes--*it is a war and not a battle*. She decides to win this one, "Of course, I would like to attend and clarify the referral."

"The meeting will be at the Administrative Conference Room at one," decrees Dr. Heering in a rare-heard authoritarian voice. His large protruding ears appear to flap out farther from his head. In a weird sort-of-way, it is similar to those reptiles that expand their ears, so they appear threateningly larger. Dr. Heering along with Psycho, are finally going to put the uncompromising ostentatious Dr. Carmel in her place.

A heavy silence and a lot of wide eyes, shroud the members of the Admissions Treatment Team. They cannot believe what they just heard. Carmel is being called to the carpet because of some whiny, manipulative woman. The Admissions Treatment Team members knew because they signed the paper for Miss Jenkins to stay in the hospital and to go to the Acute Unit, their integrity is also being questioned.

The call for the team to move the patient to the Acute Unit was perhaps an emotional decision following Dr. Carmel's courageous efforts to subdue a belligerent man who tore off the bicep of the physician assistant and sent two nurses to the hospital. Perhaps the Treatment Team had been overwhelmed by the heat, the number of admissions, and then the reportedly histrionic suicidal threats of Ms. Jenkins. At the time, it seemed a good call.

All of these reasons are just excuses for a bad call.

31

Psycho, the ex-Navy psychologist in charge of the Admissions Unit, is cognizant of the sorrowful faces following Dr. Carmel being called to the carpet for yesterday's bad call of keeping a frequent flyer in the hospital. Psycho handles this situation as he tends to handle all situations. He gets down to business.

In his stoic military voice, Psycho commands, "What do we know of Jack Smack?"

The social worker designated the patient reads the psychiatrist's Admissions Note. As if she had written the choppy notes, the social worker recites, "Thirty-six-year-old Caucasian male was admitted to the hospital because he was running naked in the downtown streets of Glenville by the stop light. Patient had a BAC of .34. He has a prior history of admission for alcohol and substance abuse. Patient claims to drink 12 beers to a case per day and uses THC and benzos. Patient does not like speed. Mr. Smack was admitted to Change (the chemical dependency unit of the Weston Asylum) and is referred to Admissions from Change because he claims to be hearing voices. He attended the Change program two months ago. Patient has been in three rehabs in New York State and other rehabs. This man admittedly has three to four DUIs and at least 10 PIs."

Psycho interrupts the social worker's readings of the psychiatrist's Admissions Note. In a drill sergeant's tone of voice he asks, "Why is this guy even on our unit? Why is he not at Change getting drug and alcohol treatment?"

Carmel calmly answers, "He claims to be hearing voices, but he told me he doesn't really hear voices. He just wants out of the

Change program. It's a turf. Change does not want to deal with him. He does not hear voices. He admitted that to me. They don't want him and they turfed him to us because of his aggressive behavior on their unit."

Psycho wants to keep the momentum, "We got a druggy on our hands and Change does not want him and I do not want him. Where do we go?"

Carmel again interrupts the flow of the usual communication pattern of the psychiatrist- speaking–before-a-psychologist. She says, "When I interviewed him, I asked him what he wanted. He said he wanted to go to a Salvation Army in St. Petersburg, Florida. He has a sister living in St. Petersburg."

Following some dialogue with the various professionals, including the psychiatrist, Psycho unconditionally says to the social worker, "Call his sister. If she is willing, get him a bus ticket to St. Petersburg tomorrow."

Turfing unwanted patients to other states is a common practice amongst the asylums. It is one of those hidden wonders of tax-payer monies at work. If patients are agitated, the answer is to turf them to another state. It is not that difficult because a mental health professional simply reminds the patient how lonely the patient feels without some relative or lover who once cared for them in another state. Once they get to the other state, all will be well. Public funds are readily available for this shuffle boarding patients between states.

The professionals of the Admissions Unit are particularly proud of how they were able to secure funds one month ago to fly a blatantly psychotic patient to their home in Costa Rica. The goal was not to get them with their beloved family as it was to get the patient out of West Virginia.

Psycho's eyes fixate on the social worker's eyes. His head is slanted downward. "Make sure you get him a bus tomorrow and ship him out to St. Petersburg." Psycho turns to the psychiatrist, "Make sure he has a good dose of Thorazine before he leaves."

"I will."

Psycho's voice slightly lowers to a conversational tone. "We got a newbie, a Ralph Rawlings."

The social worker Toad scrambles through the stack of patient files in front of her looking for the patient's chart, even though a list of the order of patient presentations for the team meetings is given to all members at the beginning of the meeting.

A couple of the members of the Admission Team's peanut gallery look downward in a gesture of submission to support her antics that she is so much wiser because she is supposedly busier than everyone else on the Admissions Unit. Most of the faces around the T-shaped tables drop; because once again, they are being forced to endure the antics of this social worker attempting to convey she is so busy.

Toad believes she is superior to everyone else on the Admissions Unit and in the hospital and maybe the world. In her mental world, she takes pride that she tells it like it is. In Toad's world, she says what people do not have the balls to say. The social worker does not appreciate there is a major difference between being assertive and being a narcissistic-power-hungry wanna-be.

Toad boasts she smoked marijuana as a teenager. She consistently reminds everyone on the Admissions Team meetings she was addicted to marijuana (even though THC is not physically addictive) and she beat her addiction. The team has long ago tired of the following, "I can't understand why all these drug addicts cannot just quit?" Toad is another personally disturbed mental health professional.

Toad is in her third marriage with eight children. She drinks way too much red wine every night; but, she does not like the hard stuff.

Toad finally finds the right chart. She flips through the chart incessantly looking for the Admissions Note, even though the Admissions Note is always at the opening of the chart. Most of the professionals of the Team are accustomed to her antics to look busy.

Psycho has met with her two times to tell her to stop her obvious looking-busy antics.

Finding the Admissions Note that is in the front of the chart, Toad reads the psychiatrist's Admission Notes, "Ralph Rawlings is a 26-year-old Caucasian male admitted for depression and suicidal ideation." Toad raises her head and says, "The Admissions Note is otherwise not completed."

Dr. Blowfish, the psychiatrist who had erroneously referred two patients yesterday without the treatment teams' signatures, believes he is now going to gain face in front of the Team. "Yes, I was the admitting psychiatrist yesterday for Rawlings. Two police officers escorted this extremely belligerent man to the hospital. Rawlings was swearing and he even threatened the police officers' lives and their children. Any sane man knows you do not threaten a cop. The patient was out of control. There already was a 72-hour hold on Mr. Rawlings, so I admitted him. It was black and white. I will finish the Admissions Note after I meet with him this afternoon."

In an attempt to ally herself with the all-powerful Blowfish, who has connections with the president of the hospital, Toad chimes in following Blowfish's declaration. "Yes, this man is definitely a suicidal and possible homicidal maniac. The guys downstairs told me when they did the strip search he punched one of them squarely in the jaw."

Unbeknownst to Toad and the other team members, Carmel's eyes' are laser-thin splits spitting uncontaminated electromagnetic waves directly into the eyes' of Toad.

Toad is not aware of the challenging stare from Carmel. The gossip-focused social worker goes on to clarify, "Once Rawlings was on the unit, one of the nurses told me he cussed her out using the 'F' word and he said he is calling his attorney and is suing everybody in this place. Been there, done that. How often are we threatened by lawsuits? Daily."

A few of the Admissions Team members in the peanut gallery provide her the much-sought-after chuckles.

One of the many daily contradictions of the Weston Asylum happens.

The male nutritionist, who had earlier volunteered how the moon-shot was a fake, speaks again. This will be the third time he has spoken during this meeting. The last time he ever spoke at a meeting was months ago.

In an innocent, juvenile voice, the young nutritionist says, "But the Admissions Note says he was admitted for depression and suicidal ideation. He just sounds angry for being hospitalized and humiliated."

Blowfish, the admitting psychiatrist, poignantly looks at the nutritionist. Blowfish is going to attempt to save face after his bad call of moving two patients yesterday without the team's signatures. He stands up and looks down at the nutritionist who is sitting in one of the outer chairs by the wall of the Admissions meeting room.

The psychiatrist in his best deep doctor's voice commands, "I went to medical school and had nine years of extensive training in mental disorders. One of the first things I learned, and that you people need to learn is that depression and anger share the same coin. People who are depressed harbor much anger. People who are angry harbor much depression. Some psychiatrists quote the words of dermatologists, 'When it's wet, dry it; and when it's dry, wet it.' It's all about conflict and frustration. Some people express their frustration via depression and others express their frustration through anger. Depressed people harbor much anger; angry people harbor much depression. It's that simple. Does that help you for why this depressed man came in being so angry?"

The power structure of the Admissions Unit is based on knowledge about the patients that nobody else has been able to obtain.

Carmel turns her head to the man sitting next to her. Psycho turns his head to face Carmel. She is smirking and says nothing. He smirks back at the woman who he had only moments before chastised for coming late for his meeting. Even though the two have major personality differences and vast differences in their therapeutic styles, Psycho has a deep respect for Carmel's evaluations. He knows she is withholding information.

Psycho asks the psychologist who has been assigned Ralph Rawlings, "Did you interview him?"

"Yes."

Silence around the table.

Carmel deems it is now time to speak, given that all the chest-pounding is over and nobody has any other info on the patient.

She speaks.

"Ralph Rawlings wanted to go fishing. It's that simple. He pulled me to the side as I was seeing my patients on the unit yesterday; Ralph Rawlings physically pulled me to the side, so I listened to what he had to say."

The following is the conversation that transpired between Dr. Carmel and Ralph Rawlings.

"Lady, you look sane, I tell you I don't belong here. I just made it all up. I just wanted to go fishin' with my girlfriend. I'm not crazy."

The man has a crazed look in his eyes as if he can't take it anymore and he's going to lose it.

Dr. Carmel, being in a harried mode to see her assigned patients, asks the anxious man some simplistic questions, "So why didn't you go fishing?"

Ralph Rawlings praises, "Oh thank you, lady, thank you for listening. Can I tell you my story?"

At this juncture of this recent encounter, Carmel is more aware of her next patient who she needs to see. She is already growing leery that this is just another manipulative patient. In an obvious indifferent voice, Carmel again asks, "So why didn't you go fishing?"

"Well, we were, we were, lady. Wednesday night we decided, Jenny and me. We decided we would call into work and say we were sick so we could spend the day fishing."

There is a tired expression on the face of Carmel and she is fully aware of being tired of being called 'lady.'

The twenty-something skinny man recites his story at a hurried pace, "So….so I called sick into work this morning. It was at six in the morning because I knew nobody at work would be there at that time. But, before I could get out of the apartment, work called me back and said I needed a medical excuse. Well, Jenny is just gorgeous and I wanted in her pants so bad. Is this okay to say?"

Still offended by the "lady" comments, the best Carmel could muster is, "Anyway, you wanted to go fishing with a woman."

"Yeah, so I went to the Emergency Room at Minnie Hamilton and told them I was suicidal. Doesn't that make sense? I mean, I had no injuries and how can you prove if someone is depressed? I was desperate. I know I made a mistake. I am sorry. I am so sorry."

Not feeling in the mood of being a Catholic priest taking a confession, Dr. Carmel tries to expedite the process, "So, you go to the Emergency Room and claim you are depressed. No doubt you had to sit there for a while."

"That's it. I did. It was insane. I sat there for two hours and Jenny is waiting at her parent's house. I called her on the payphone to let her know I was going to be late, but I could tell in her voice she was reconsidering our going to the river. I did what any guy would have done in this situation; I left the ER to go to Jenny. But in the process, two pigs picked me up."

The patient, Ralph Rawlings, was not aware of the following details of how the police got involved.

When the intake worker at the ER of the hospital finally came out and announced, "Ralph Rawlings," and there was no response, the intake worker of the ER went by the book. She explained over the hospital phone to the psychologist on the psychiatric unit of Minnie Hamilton that a depressed man was walking the streets of Grantsville. The psychologist on the inpatient unit diligently signed a 72-hour-hold paper. The judge's signature was previously signed without hearing the scenario. His signed paper was taken from a stack of signed 72-hour-hold papers.

A 72-hour-hold paper requires a QMHP (psychiatrist's or a psychologist's signature) and a judge's signature. The neophyte psychologist requested the patient to be picked up by the police and taken to the Summit Center for an outpatient evaluation to rule out suicide potential. In the vast majority of cases, a 72-hour-hold meant to take the patient for a three-day stay at the Weston Asylum.

Dr. Carmel begins to get intrigued with Ralph Rawling's story. Her interest is obvious in her lighter less judgmental voice. She asks, "Two police officers pick you up?"

"Yeah. I mean I was at Jenny's parents' house and Jenny and her parents saw the whole thing. The pigs asked if I was Ralph Rawlings. I said, "Yeah." The next thing I know I am in the back of a cruiser going down highway 33."

Following a few questions related to his mental status, Carmel did not waste any more of her limited time, "I will see what I can do."

After giving her synopsis of her interview with Ralph Rawlings, she questions the Treatment Team. "Dr. Blowfish, I liked your analogy with the coin of depression and anger. Toad, we sometimes respect your gossip-way of obtaining information on our patients; but, I must admit, if I were mistakenly forced to be here, I would be angry and easily say "fuck" to anyone who gave me an unwanted shower—The guy just wanted to go fishing."

BOOM! IN YOUR FACE!— races the unexpressed thoughts of Dr. Carmel.

The peanut gallery looks like a bunch of the *Charlie Brown Peanut* characters with their unanimous smiles.

Carmel has gained a notch on the informal power structure of the asylum.

More importantly, she has gained a notch of confidence for her pending Administrative Review on her supposed bad call of the frequent-flyer.

32

In the scorching heat, the sweat-soaked Admission Team members' are treated to an Admissions Team event version of a Mohammad Ali boxing match.

The members of the Admissions Treatment room have witnessed the battles going back and forth. Carmel was down for the count following Psycho, Heering, and Blowfish telling her she had to go to an Administrative Review following a bad call. The woman in a wheelchair was a frequent flyer and the patient had once again feigned a suicidal threat to stay in the hospital. Carmel had a partial recovery from the blow when she conveyed information of a malingering chemical dependency patient that resulted in him being turfed to Florida.

Carmel is on a roll. The question is whether she will go down, or will she keep counter punching in this exciting arena of the Admissions Unit? The Admissions Team are all ears.

Carmel appears to have been injected with a mega-dose of testosterone. She sits erect in her chair and her eyes are wide as she scans the room. She patiently waits at the head of the table for the next round to begin.

Psycho regains control of his people and says, "Dr. Carmel's evidence is overwhelming. All of the disciplines need to see fishing boy by 1500 today." A brasher voice of the ex-Navy man's voice continues, "Let me personally know your results. Given there is no strong evidence to the contrary, we will discharge Mr. Rawlings at 1600 hours." Psycho makes a point to verify that Blowfish is looking in his direction. "Once we gain everyone's signature."

Psycho's overarching goal is to keep his meeting going and to move patients off his unit. "What is going on with this Bob Burns? This patient who claims to hear voices saying "bang"' and "escape"?"

Dr. Pedro, the elderly, short-term-hire psychiatrist, knows he needs to gain some recognized power within this room of characters who behave like a bunch of wild-cats working on an oil-derrick. He is accustomed to working with hospital professionals who defer to the intelligence of the psychiatrist, a medical doctor, a real doctor. Pedro is not familiar with having to prove his psychiatric knowledge to those beneath him.

Dr. Pedro believes he is prepared for this meeting.

In his best imposing voice, Pedro says, "Because Psycho, Dr. Heering, and Dr. Blowfish had to leave our meeting yesterday; I again will make it even clearer that this young man is suffering from a pronounced oedipal issue. For some of you in the room not cognizant, it is the accustomed story of a boy falling in love with his mommy."

Most of the members of the peanut gallery exhibit a sour facial declaration—their faces are squished with looks of, 'that's sick.'

Dr. Pedro, a trained Freudian psychoanalyst with over six years of training analysis, sees some of the soured faces. He clarifies the oedipal conflict. "Yes, yes it is disgusting, a boy having sex with his mother. But the theory is sound. We have instincts, just like all creatures have instincts for food, water—and sex. You put a five-year-old boy and five-year-old girl on an island; come back in 15 years, there will be three or more people on the island. If there are no monkeys on the island to model, how did the extra people materialize? How did the children learn to have sex? They did not learn; it is an instinct, it is natural."

In an effort to maintain momentum, the elderly Pedro without-a-real-job continues, "Sex is an instinct just like the need for food and water. We can easily gain food and water in our society; however, if we're horny—that's a different issue because society, via our parents, tries to control this strong sexual impulse. Who in this room has ever had a five-year-old child of an opposite gender: a niece, nephew, neighbor, or student; flirt with them?"

Dr. Pedro gains only two assenting nods. The Team members are not about to risk their stature in the power-hierarchy of the Admissions Treatment Team for an old psychiatrist who will be gone within a month.

The Team does not move. They sit in their chairs similar to mice in a room where a cat has entered. They have been here before; they can feel it in their bones. There is a cat in the room.

Psycho swirls his right hand in a circle in the gesture of, *get on with your findings.*

Pedro erroneously interprets the quiet and motionless behaviors of the Team members. He believes he has gained the much-desired respect of the Admissions Team. In more vigorous voice, Pedro says, "'Bang' and 'Escape' are the two words our young Mr. Burns hears. To me, this is the most blatant example of an Oedipal conflict I have encountered in my 40 years of psychoanalysis."

Carmel has heard enough. Her mouth opens to speak.

Upon seeing Carmel about to speak, Pedro raises his hand in a gesture of, *speak to the hand,* and says, "Yesterday, I ordered psychological testing on this man. His Rorschach was most revealing to support my hypothesis."

Carmel now feels more secure because the psychiatrist, Pedro, has entered her territory, psychological testing. She places her hands on the wooden table and leans forward. She glares in the direction of the old man. His eyes do not meet her eyes.

In a deep and finely enunciated voice, Carmel asks, "So, what did the psychological report have to say about Mr. Burns?"

The elderly psychiatrist rubs the top of his bald head. "Well, the psychologist who did the testing did not get an opportunity to get the written report back to me. However, he did give me Bob Burns' responses to the inkblots. The projection of the patient's unconscious onto the inkblots fully supports my hypothesis."

Carmel looks at Psycho, another psychologist, she demands, "He's a psychiatrist; he has no training in psychological testing. Why is he interpreting Burns' responses? This is a dark comedy about to happen."

Carmel feels safe letting her cat out of the bag. She knows psychiatrists do not have training in psychological testing. *Whatever this old coot comes up with I will flatten him.*

Psycho is a die-hard behaviorist of the 1960s. He is amused by the psychoanalyst's words. However, he cannot let go of the thought that this discussion is based upon some absurd idiosyncratic interpretations of some ink spilled on paper—he's intrigued.

Carmel cannot believe what she sees in Psycho's face. He appears to be intently listening to the psychiatrist.

Psycho, the Tomcat in the room, makes a bizarre move. He wants all of the mice around the table to hear how bizarre of an interpretation Pedro is going to present. Psycho shifts in his chair. He moves his butt to the edge of his chair and leans back; his broad shoulders are braced by the back of the chair. *Pedro's interpretations of Bob Burns' responses to the inkblot test are going to be so far-fetched that it will only serve to show the Admissions Team how great the systematic approach of behavioral psychology is.*

In his relaxed sitting position, Psycho appears to be interested in the inkblots. He says to the Freudian psychoanalyst, "Doctor what do you make of the inkblots?"

Psycho turns toward Carmel with a non-concealed leer.

Every muscle fiber in Carmel's body tightens. She wants to flip Psycho off.

Mistakenly feeling comfortable and thinking he has gained the favor of the all-powerful Psycho, the for-hire psychiatrist giggles. He says, "It was Bob's, Mr. Burns' response to the second card that gave him away. As is well known (an ill-conceived attempt to gain power), the second card is the color shock card. The psychologist always administers the inkblots with the statement, "I am going to show you a series of inkblots. I want you to tell me what you see." Due to these standardized instructions, patients are given the mindset that the ink-blots are all black. However, on the second card, there is blood red. This challenges their present mindset. Their emotions rise because of the challenge.

Troubled, Carmel leans back in her chair. *This Freudian psychiatrist does appear to know something about the artistic and subjective sequence analysis of the Rorschach inkblot test.*

Dr. Pedro places his hands on the table and leans forward. His thin eyelid eyes look directly in the direction of the wide emerald eyes of Carmel. Pedro asks Carmel, "What did Burns respond on the color card?"

Emanating from the smirk on her face, Carmel says, "And how the fuck should I know what he said?"

The usually bold Admissions Team members remain silent and do not move. They know Pedro is the victim, Carmel attacked first; but something unexpected happens. A Tomcat appeared in the room, Psycho.

The elderly Pedro repeated himself, "The change from all black inkblots to blood red in an inkblot challenges the patient."

Carmel waves her hand in the air in a gesture of dismissing his comment, "I know about the color card."

Due to the silence of the room, Pedro believes he has gained his much-needed power. "Bob, Mr. Burns said he saw, "A spaceship going off and there is the red shooting out of its back." His spaceship is the white interior of the black ink. He is angry. You say black ink and he says white space—he did not respond to the black ink. He responds to the white space; a spaceship is what he said. He's a walking time bomb ready to go off because he did incorporate the red saying it is the fire of the ship blasting off. The man cannot control his rage."

Carmel attempts to present a poker face to the Team. *Where'd this psychiatrist get his knowledge? He seems to be on target except for the anger or oppositional tendencies being uncontrolled. Is there a pattern of Burns' responses to the inkblots on the remaining responses?* Carmel makes a conscious effort to remain silent.

Pedro sits back in his chair comfortable with the idea he has Carmel's attention.

Similar to the workings of many elderly people, Dr. Pedro may be losing some of his short-term memory, but he has accumulated a wealth of knowledge over his years. Due to his years and interest over those years, he'd asked his psychology friends how the inkblot test worked. His psychology friends only introduced him to the artistic and subjective sequence analysis of the inkblot, where the interpreter looks for patterns of how subjects project themselves onto a vague stimulus like an inkblot.

Pedro believes he has Carmel under his power. He moves on with his deeper interpretation of the white spaceship response. "Because all that white in the middle of the black ink is clearly a vagina and the red are the open lips. He is an angry man because of past vaginal issues."

"Are you real?" screams Dr. Carmel. "What—what is your training in the interpretation of the Rorschach. I know a subjective sequence analysis is an important part of an interpretation of the responses; what objective, scientific, interpretive system did you use?"

A voice from the peanut gallery screams, "Get him!"

The outsider psychiatrist asserts himself, "Mam, I was in six years of Freudian training psychoanalysis and my entire training is how we project ourselves onto life. Do I need to say more? Or, do you need me to explain how paranoid people see a paranoid environment, or how lovesick couples see life as wonderful?"

"I don't care you had six years training. If you take two years of shit and add another four years of shit, you still end up with shit."

The peanut gallery hoots and howls at this clean, decisive blow.

Psycho does not move. A Cheshire cat's smile grows from the corners of Psycho's mouth. Psycho loves this. Even though Pedro is not aware, Psycho knows that Pedro is going down for the count.

Carmel questions the pompous Pedro in a calm definitive voice, "What standardized, scientific, interpretative system did you use? Did you use Rorschach's, Klopfer's, or Exner's?"

Pedro becomes aware he is going down a steep slide within the confines of the Admissions Room. Following Carmel's last question, about the interpretive system he used, the old man realizes that the behaviorist Psycho is not going to come to his aid. No person in the room is going to come to his aid.

The once minuscule spots of sweat confabulate into rivers running down the deep chasms of the furrowed face of Pedro.

In a final act of desperation, Pedro looks toward Psycho.

Psycho, the Tomcat in the room of mice, does not look at Pedro. The rarely relaxed and poised figure of Psycho is turned toward Carmel, waiting for a final take-down of this psychiatrist.

Carmel is tired of this week being ongoing battles. In a stoic tone, she asks Pedro, "May I look at Mr. Burns' responses to the inkblots and his other test results? I will score his Rorschach responses using the scientifically reliable and valid interpretive studies of Exner."

Pedro tries to save face within the all-important Admissions Team. "Of course you may." In a gesture similar to a defeated warrior handing his sword over to the victor, Pedro slowly hands the psychologist's test report of the patient's responses to the inkblot to Dr. Carmel.

Pedro did not hand over the patient's test results on the other psychological tests that Bob Burns had taken. The other psychological tests did not suggest any mental disorder.

"Thank you," says Dr. Carmel in a coy, sly, and all-powerful manner upon receiving the patient's responses to the Rorschach Inkblot Test.

Because the psychiatrist still believes, based on previous decades of deference from other mental health professionals due to his having the initials "MD" behind his name, the old man makes a final gesture of authority. Dr. Pedro says, "Oh, Bob Burns also needs EST because he is so depressed. I plan to administer his shock treatment tomorrow along with many of my other patients."

Carmel goes into uncontrolled fighting mode, "What the fuck? You analyze Bob Burns as having an oedipal issue upon one meeting with the man and a fake interpretation that is more of a reflection of your oedipal issues than the patient. And now, with your blind ignorance, tell us he needs electric shock treatment.

Psycho, the psychologist in charge of the treatment team and a strong **dis**believer in projection and anything that has to do with suggesting an unconscious motivator for behaviors, charges ahead, "Dr. Carmel, unless you can provide other evidence against Dr. Pedro's findings, I must support the psychiatrist."

Dr. Pedro believes he has won in this amazing turn of events and he further exclaims, "I am going for a 60-day hold on Bob Burns following his scheduled EST tomorrow."

Dr. Carmel explodes, "What psychologist is going to sign this hold? I am the assigned psychologist."

The Tomcat comes out of left field. None of the mice in the room saw the following coming.

Psycho, the head of the group, the behaviorist having no training in the Rorschach, dictates, "I will sign the hold."

Carmel gets a blow and falls. The team members' hearts race in anticipation of how Carmel will respond.

She tightens her grasp on the summary paper of Burns' responses to the inkblots.

The remaining hour of the Admissions Unit proceeds in a solemn tone. Carmel is uncharacteristically quiet.

Knowing she has the Administrative Review at 1 p.m., she scores Bob Burns' responses to the inkblots during the remainder of the meeting. Because she was trained in her doctoral program and internship on the newly developed Exner system, she will be able to score it in only 20 minutes.

Out of the corner of his eyes, Psycho sees Carmel scoring the Rorschach. He does not stop her. He wants to hear the results of her supposed scientific evaluation of the inkblots.

During the concluding minutes of the Admissions Treatment Team meeting, Carmel hears the words, "…so we are sending Hesus to Acute."

Dr. Carmel raises her head from her scoring the Rorschach. She screams, "Jesus is already on the Acute Unit! I am seeing Noah Holiday in psychotherapy on the Acute Unit. What is wrong with you people?"

Carmel sees the look of horror on the Admission's Team members' faces. The mice have returned. She is the defeated cat in the room. The Admissions Team members stare at her as if she just walked out of a bloody automobile accident.

The lower jaw of Carmel drops. *This is not good.*

Psycho, like any good warrior, knows the enemy is more similar than dissimilar. He comes to Carmel's rescue. "If you would've been paying attention, you would know we've been discussing a woman who claims to be the Gnostic Jesus. Didn't you see her on the unit? She is wearing a gown with primitive African designs and has an over-sized hood covering her thick black hair. Were you even listening when we wondered what is going to happen when she meets Noah Holiday, the original Jesus, on Acute? I know Dr. Carmel that the Administrative Review this afternoon must be on your mind, but while you're in my room, I would like you to attend."

Carmel is baffled: she did not hear the discussion about the second Jesus on the unit and the discussion of what will happen when the two Jesus' meet. In a high pitched voice, she says, "I've worked hard with Noah Holiday and he is making progress. Now, you people are going to play mind games so you can all get your spectator show of what happens when two Jesus' meet."

Psycho looks down at his watch and taps the crystal cover.

"I guess we're done," says Psycho.

Psycho has done his job. The meeting promptly ends at 1100.

33

Carmel bolts and bounces out the Admission's Team door. She hopes she can complete an interview with one of her assigned patients, Carlos Lopez, before noon. She plans to complete a quick interview with Carlos, drives home to change clothes in preparation for the Administrative Review, and return for the meeting by 1:00 p.m. She lives five minutes from the hospital. Because of her growing grandiosity, she believes she can make the ridiculous schedule.

During the Admissions Treatment Team meeting, the social worker read the psychiatrist's Admission's Note on Carlos Lopez when he was admitted yesterday afternoon. The social worker emphasized Carlos was very delusional upon this admission. Carlos is another frequent-flyer. Unlike the frequent flyer of Ms. Jenkins in the wheelchair, Carlos usually gets into trouble warranting his admission.

Yesterday a telephone call was made to the police and the volunteer fire department of Weston, West Virginia. Carlos Lopez, wearing an aluminum-wrapped skull-cap, stood on top of the four-story Citizens Bank of Weston. With outstretched arms, he screamed, "The Martians know, the Martians know! They've had a base on the dark side of the moon for centuries. They know we are coming. They are going to destroy Earth!"

Carlos Lopez had previously been admitted to the Weston Asylum three months ago because he knew his neighbors at Alum Bridge were Russian spies. He did the most sensible thing to do when you find out spies are living next to you. He burned down their house. Fortunately, nobody was home.

Due to his many hospitalizations, Dr. Carmel and Carlos knew each other. In an awkward way, they were friends in Carlos' world and Carmel's world. During his last few admissions, Carlos had developed a game with the psychologist. When the fifty-six-year-old man would be walking by Dr. Carmel in the hallway, he would point his index finger at her face and say, "You're crazy."

One day Carmel was not in a hurry. She stopped her typical "click…click…click" pounding of her heels and turned around to face Carlos. Dr. Carmel walked up to Carlos. They stood in that uncomfortable zone of invading one's space. She looked directly into Carlos' eyes. He returned the look with a concerned facial expression. Carmel said in a calm voice, "No, Carlos, you are the crazy one."

His disparaging face broke into a child-like smile and he said in a high-pitched voice, "I know."

A few weeks after the above encounter she met Carlos in the vending machine room. Most of the time, following his stay on the Admissions Unit, Carlos did get sent to one of the acute units. During one of his stays on the acute unit, Carlos gained enough privileges so that he could walk around the hospital and outside. In the vending machine room, he stood looking at a Coca-Cola machine.

"What's up?" quipped Dr. Carmel.

"It's my birthday and I want a soda, but I only have a nickel."

One of the major rules of the hospital is never to give money to patients—it blurs the therapeutic alliance. Giving money can turn a professional relationship into a friendship.

"Here's a dime, have a happy birthday on me my friend," said Dr. Carmel.

Carlos' eyes watered. Carmel had never seen him tear. She reached out to him and he reached out to her. He gave her a tight authentic hug.

Out of curiosity, Carmel later called the acute unit. She asked the nurse, "Would you mind looking in Carlos' chart and tell me his birthdate?"

The day was not Carlos' birthday.

Following this morning's Admissions Treatment Team

meeting, Carmel is doing her high step walk to Carlos' room. She hopes his medication has started to take effect so he will not be full-blown psychotic. She hopes his Martian delusion has subsided so she can get her interview done in 30 minutes, and then drive home to change into more appropriate clothing for the 1:00 p.m. Administrative Review meeting. The hurried Dr. Carmel arrives at Carlos Lopez's door on the Admissions Unit.

In her rushed state-of-mind Carmel rapidly bangs on the wooden door with her knuckles. An agonizing few seconds later the door opens. It does not look good. Carlos is still sporting his aluminum-wrap skull-cap and is wearing a T-shirt with a picture of the Milky Way on the front of the shirt.

In a fake Italian accent, Carlos quips, "Do you speak Italian?"

In a stupefied look and equally stupefied voice, Carmel can only muster, "No."

Carlos slams the door shut.

The situation does not look promising for Carmel to complete a quick interview. He still has the aluminum foil skull cap and is wearing a Milky Way shirt. Carlos has somehow combined his Martian delusion with speaking Italian, even though he is of Spanish background.

Nonplussed and being used to uncooperative patients, Carmel appeases to their previous encounters for a foundation. She incessantly bangs her knuckles three times on the wooden door and pleads, "Carlos, this is Dr. Carmel. I am the psychologist who gave you a dime for a Coke. You know, the crazy woman. I need to ask you some questions."

The door swings wide open. "Nice tits."

The door slams shut.

Carmel shouts to the closed door. "Carlos, I am your psychologist on the Admissions Unit; there is a limited amount of time I can see you! If you want a different psychologist, let me know and I will happily turn you over to another psychologist!"

The patient's door swings wide open as if to announce the presence of someone of significance. The believer in Martians on the dark side of the moon, and the man who speaks Italian sticks his chest out in a childish manner. He says, "I am the world's greatest psychologist." Within a few seconds, Carlos has managed to transform himself into the world's greatest psychologist.

Trying to find some semblance of mutual purposes Carmel says, "Being the world's greatest psychologist, you know I need to ask you a few questions. Let's go to the end of the hall where I can put my weary legs on the coffee table."

As the two figures walk pass the nurses station, where there are three nurses talking about West Virginia Universities' football legacy and WVU being a party school, Carlos points with his index finger in the face of Dr. Carmel. In his best Italian accent, Carlos says, "She's a lunatic." Carlos is still fixated on being the world's greatest psychologist and he is aiding these nurses in making a diagnosis. The three nurses provide Carlos what he desired—they chime delightful giggles.

When Carlos and Carmel reach the end of the hallway the three nurses at the nursing desk are all ears.

Carmel raises her cowgirl boots onto the coffee table and she asserts, "Being the world's greatest psychologist you know I need to ask you some questions."

"No, I ask the questions," claims the world's greatest psychologist in a bogus imitation of an Italian accent.

Carmel knows this is not good. He is still delusional. She looks at her watch.

In his cheap imitation of Italian speech, the Spanish-speaking Carlos asks in a staccato tone, "What was the name of the first man-made satellite in space?"

Carmel does not know where he is going. She answers in a questioning voice, "Sputnik"?

Quickly, Carlos, the world's greatest psychologist, next questions his patient, "Who was the first to do an orbital venture?" His stubble face, needing a shave, has a strong, silly grin; as if, *I got her.*

"John Glenn."

Carlos rubs the three-day growth of his beard. "I am thoroughly impressed by your intelligence. Most of my crazy patients say Alan Shepard, but he did not go orbital. Sunday, in two days, people will land on the moon. Who is the third astronaut who does not get to land?"

"That's not fair," squawks Carmel, "The other two are all over the news."

"Okay, who is the guy with Neil Armstrong that will set foot on the moon?"

"Carlos, this isn't fair. I don't know. His name sounds something like "bumble bee." Hell, I don't know."

Without providing any more time for his patient to qualify her response, the world's greatest psychologist stands up from the couch. His arms reach toward the heavens and frantically wave as he scrambles back to his room screaming, "You're impossible— you're impossible—you're impossible to work with!"

Carmel tilts her head back in a defeated gesture. The three young nurses at the desk delightfully laugh. Carmel looks toward the nurses. With a full smile, a tilt of the head, and uplifted shoulders; she coveys the message, *I tried.* The nurses fully reciprocate with gleeful smiles.

Dr. Carmel drives her 1940 Buick to her home and she changes from her braless spaghetti-top attire to a business suit. The pin-striped suit is a jacket and skirt. The skirt is a comfortable one-inch above her knees; not exposing her athletic thighs, yet risk revealing her pronounced calves. An eloquent pink blouse, with only two buttons left untouched, conceals any cleavage. She slips on Go-Go boots to conceal her athletic calves.

More important than the change of clothing, is her change of attitude. Unconsciously, following the morning's trials, Carmel's mental dialogue of, *win the battle,* has changed.

I must lose this battle to win the war.

34

Yesterday, when Carmel was left in charge of the Admissions Unit, she had emotionally decided, with the support of the Admissions Treatment Team, to move a frequent-flyer to the Acute Unit. The patient was a woman confined to a wheelchair and had a history of sporadically appearing at the doors of the Weston Asylum demanding to be admitted. The patient's major form of attempting to get admitted was a pseudo-suicide attempt, including the usual supposed drug overdose. This time, her pseudo-suicide attempt had moved to a more dramatic and risky form, maneuvering her wheelchair into traffic—all the while, timing the movement so she knew she could not get struck by a car. The woman needs some type of mental health intervention; however, a prolonged stay at the asylum for a false frequent flyer was a forbidden unwritten rule of the hospital. There are also the ethically-bound and government-enforced policies of care in the least-restrictive environment.

Dr. Shivangi, the head of the Acute Unit, filed a complaint against Dr. Carmel for the bad call. It required an Administrative Review.

Shivangi is in the process of attempting to gain U. S. citizenship. She was raised in India and her parents are of royalty. She had attended medical school in Great Britain and completed her residency at a VA medical facility in San Francisco. Shivangi and Psycho are very similar: both served in the military and are protective of their respective units.

In the Administrative Conference Room sits the major players of the hospital: Dr. Nash in his tailored platinum power suit, Dr.

Blowfish in his lime-green Sears-and-Roebuck suit (representing Psychiatry), Dr. Heering sporting way too much Hai Karate cologne (representing Psychology), Head of Nursing in her white dress, Head Nurse of the Admissions Unit in her white dress, two young Patient Advocates wearing blue jeans and striped shirts, and Psycho in his customary polo shirt (representing the Admissions Treatment team). And for some reason, the doc-in-the shop was present. Dr. Pedro, the psychiatrist who cannot find steady employment, is wearing a 20-year-old suit and white shirt with yellow stains on the collar.

Dr. Sarah Shivangi, the team leader of the Acute Unit, has shoulder-length grey hair and wears a long-sleeve denim shirt with matching blue jeans. She is one of those rare people who somehow manage to balance a soft, yet firm, approach with her staff and the patients. People who work with her feel like she is a mother figure, but they know not to cross her. Today someone has already pushed one of her buttons.

Shivangi's stern eyes look toward President Nash. "It is already 1:03 and Dr. Carmel is not here. We can proceed with her issue once, or if, she arrives. There is no need for her to be here for the other allegation."

"Whoa, whoa, what is going on here!" shouts Psycho. "According to the agenda, Dr. Carmel is intimately involved in the first allegation. I like, and demand, meetings start on time, just as much as you." Psycho smiles at Shivangi. "I know Dr. Carmel is aware of the time of the meeting. Her comments may be necessary in regard to the issues in the first allegation."

Psycho and Shivangi are friends; and, they have similar personalities—they like a good fight. When there is a difference between Psycho and Shivangi, particularly when the issue is a transfer of a patient to Shivangi's Acute Unit, their friendship is pushed to the side. Each tries to outdo the other.

Their similar personalities necessitate Shivangi defends getting on with the meeting. "I can understand if this was just another team meeting. This is an Administrative Review with possible severe repercussions. All of the people in this room knew what time the meeting started." The grey-haired leader stares in the direction of President Nash for affirmation.

Psycho looks toward Nash with a stern taut face. Blowfish in his lime green suit also turns to Nash. He doesn't bother to hide his sneer.

A wrinkled forehead on the power-dressed president of the asylum betrays his confusion. Nash rubs his thickly greased hair and the wrinkles in his forehead fade away. He breaks the silence of the room. "I like to begin a scheduled meeting on time just like anyone else. If you break that rule, people learn they can come at any time." Nash slowly closes his eyes and rubs his chin. "I do not want to start precedence, but I do. Given the circumstances, we will give Dr. Carmel until 1:15 to arrive. If she is not here at that time, we will then begin the meeting."

Dr. Shivangi heard the words of the president. She has already lost a minor battle. *It was a skirmish. By the end of this day, I will win this war against the holier-than-thou Psycho and his people.*

At 1:14, Dr. Carmel struts into the room. Her pink blouse accentuates her femininity. Her pen-striped suit projects power. *This does not look good. It looks like one of the all-too-familiar "boys club" meetings.*

Carmel walks to the one empty chair in the middle of the table.

As the woman is sitting, President Nash says, "Dr. Carmel, you have not attended one of our Administrative Reviews. We are first going to investigate the subduing of the patient on the Admissions Unit yesterday; and then, we will discuss your referral of Miss Jenkins to the Acute Unit."

Carmel nodded her head in affirmation.

President Nash says, "First of all, there was the terrible outburst yesterday on the Admissions Unit. A physician assistant sustained a severe tear of his bicep and two of the nurses were placed in the hospital."

He looks toward the Head Nurse of the Admissions Unit (who filed the complaint) and the president of the asylum says, "You wanted this particular case to go up for review because members of the Admissions Unit did not intervene. Please tell us more about why this incident warrants investigation."

The white-attired demonstrative woman does not hesitate. "The doctors and other professional men and women of the

Admissions Unit just stood there and did nothing. I also include women because this is the 60s. Has anyone heard of the feminist movement? Women should have to put themselves at risk in Vietnam, or on our unit, just like the men. The problem is even the men do nothing; it is solely left up to the nurses and the physician assistants to subdue an angry patient. The professionals,—the doctors, psychiatrists and psychologists; and the social workers, physical therapists, occupational therapists, and nutritionists— just stood by and watched. In my ten years at the hospital, I've never known any of them to intervene during a code. My nurses, my nurses are required to put their lives in jeopardy while all the professionals sit by and watch the show. This is bullshit."

Nash strokes his red tie and interrupts the nurse, "This is not the Admissions Unit; I would appreciate if we could contain the unnecessary foul language."

"Bullshit," screams the Head of Nursing of Admissions. "I am tired of this holier-than-thou mentality that creeps throughout the hospital. I will cuss if I feel like cussing—dammit. You don't know what it has been like up there this past week. Have you seen the number of admissions this week? Do you feel the outrageous heat? It is over 100 degrees on our floor."

The Head Nurse of the Admissions Unit nurse takes a brief break in her tirade and turns to see a room full of wide-eyed people.

She takes in a deep breath and turns back toward Nash. In her harsh school-mum voice, the nurse continues to lecture Nash. "Toad broke down in tears yesterday because she again didn't have the time to go to lunch. One of my nurses, and a nutritionist were also in tears because they just can't keep up this crazy pace in this outrageous heat with these patients who are not adequately treated. It's fucking insane."

Nash began to speak.

The nurse held up an open hand and halted his attempt to speak. "I dare—I dare you to come up today and just try to take over my job. I would love to be one of the carpet people in the administrative offices. Hell, you have air conditioning in your beloved carpeted offices."

Due to so much emotion in the room and feeling attacked, Nash again opened his mouth in an attempt to speak.

The distressed eyes of the nurse kept Nash from interrupting a time of silence.

All of the players in the room were accustomed to emotional meetings. To go against the all-powerful Nash, was a sin. The room was silent.

The Head Nurse of the Admissions Unit in a more subdued voice asked of the president of the asylum, "May I continue?"

"Please do."

Staring down the president of the asylum, she screamed, "How the hell could you know what we are going through? All I want is some help, some help for my nurses. Why would any man, assuming he has some balls in his pants, sit idly by and watch women get the shit kicked out of them? The only—the only person, the only professional on that unit, with any balls, was Dr. Carmel. Did she hesitate? No. Did she risk exposing herself on the unit because she was wearing a dress? Fuck yes."

Crocodile tears flowed down the nurse's cheeks. People at the Weston Asylum are used to tears. The tears usually have no impact on the staff. A couple of eyes in the room are watering. All faces in the room are turned in the direction of the president of the asylum.

The unexpected happens.

President Nash negates the customary, lengthy, and discussion of the matter. "You are right. I fully concur. There is no reason an able-bodied man, the protector of women, should stand to the side while women are being persecuted." His voice softens. "Why don't you and I meet so that we might tone down your presentation a little; together we can take this matter to the Policy and Procedures Committee for review?"

The nurse's tears cascade down her cheeks and her hiccupping voice thanks the president. "Thank you— thank you— thank you, sir, for listening."

The one-good-eyed Nash leans toward the nurse. "God is on our side."

The professionals around the table are not sure what they heard. Does *Nash want to put the people with a degree at risk with a belligerent patient? Was it just the men, or does it include women? He's breaking tradition. This is wrong.*

Somehow, all the professionals around the room forgot that the dressed in white nurses also had a degree.

Shivangi knows she is not going to get involved in a take-down with an agitated patient, *that is why we have physician assistants*, she smiles in the direction of Nash.

Nash retains his soft pastoral voice and rubs his slight mustache. "Shall we move to the second issue on the agenda? Dr. Shivangi, you expressed a concern about a bad call to your unit."

Shivangi appears to be a collegial person, particularly since she is attired in a blue jean shirt and pants. More importantly, to convey her being a good person, she constantly smiles.

The Head of the Acute Unit believes she is prepared. In a slight British accent, she summarizes her concern. "Dr. Carmel referred Ms. Jenkins to the Acute Unit. We, at least my people, and most of the people of the Admissions Unit, are trying to keep this woman out of the hospital. She is a histrionic woman who only leaves her home because she wants attention."

The gray-haired Indian smiles.

Shivangi looks at everyone in the room. "We all know this, we all know Ms. Jenkins." She gains the needed confirmatory nods from three of the professionals sitting around the investigation table.

Shivangi raises her hands above the sides of her head, wiggles her fingers, and says in a girlish voice, "When I saw Ms. Jenkins was coming onto our unit, I must admit that I blew my cap." Her voice drastically switches to a deep Indian accent. "This is a ridiculous and absurd referral. She should never have been transferred, let alone admitted into the hospital."

A period of silence announced that Shivangi was done.

President Nash raises his one good eyebrow. He looks at Carmel and asks, "Any rebuttal?"

The asylum is filled with battles, as are all organizations. A difference is that in the Weston Asylum the battles were more open.

The professionals surrounding the table are waiting for a historical battle between Shivangi and Carmel. The personalities of the women, the history of their wins and losses at the asylum, their ability to take down the administration at key times; promised a major catfight.

All of the professionals look in deference to Carmel awaiting her response. There is no movement in the room.

Carmel, in her business attire and sitting erect in her chair, takes the time to look at every face in the room.

"It was a bad call," says Carmel.

It was in a tone of voice as if she was admitting she forgot to take out the trash, no big deal.

Shivangi screams, "Damn straight it was a bad call!"

"I know it was," says the smiling Carmel.

For the second time of this meeting, the unprecedented happened.

Dr. Nash intervened without listening to the incessant dialogue of the professionals around the table. "There, I think we have it. The heat is crazy, we work with crazy people, and we also work with patients."

He gains his necessary chuckle from a few of the professionals in the room.

Nash believes he needs to clarify to the people in his room why he didn't want any more discussion of the matter.

The platinum power-suited president asks, "Dr. Shivangi, when is the last time you worked on the Admissions Unit?"

"You know. I have never worked on that unit."

The once-collegial looking and denim attired Shivangi turns to looking like a biker chick. Every muscle fiber in her body is ready for a cat fight and the president is taking her down before the fight begins. *It's not about the patient. He's making me lose in front of other people. He's making me look like a fool.*

President Nash looks comfortable with his decision. His face looks balanced. "Dr. Shivangi, were you in this room just a few minutes ago when the Head Nurse of the Admissions Unit described their conditions?"

Shivangi can't believe it. *It was a bad call. Carmel is going to get off.*

The best Shivangi can do is drop her jaw in disbelief and negatively nod. Her narcissistic wound has left her dissociating;

she's emotionally leaving the room because she cannot believe what is transpiring.

President Nash, without asking input from the group, lifts the left side of his mouth in an attempt of a smile. He looks in the direction of Carmel and says, "I've never heard such honest and courageous words during my brief tenure at the hospital. I fully appreciate the stress your unit has been under and I will see what I can do with massaging the budget to get more assistance during these peak times."

With that concluding remark, the president of the Weston Asylum raises his hands in the air, "Okay, I guess we're done."

Following the meeting, Dr. Nash waits until everyone left the room; he lays a hand on the back of Dr. Carmel.

"I liked the change into the business suit, nice touch."

In a chirpy voice, "Thanks."

The platinum power-suit Nash briskly walks out of the Administrative Review meeting. His walk is more sharp than usual.

As president of the Weston Asylum, he decided without the usual bickering of Administrative Review commentaries: all professionals, not just the nurses, must help control the physical acting out of the patients; and, he acknowledged the strength of Carmel that she made a mistake. Based on his years of experience, Nash knew a single incident of a mistake was, a mistake. However, a pattern of mistakes was worthy of his attention.

Omnipotent thoughts easily emerge in Nash's mind. *Maybe I will tithe an extra 5% above my usual 30% this year.*

In the distance, Nash sees the thin legs of Ashley. The social worker enters the hospital's library. Through the hospital's grapevine, Nash heard many stories about the social worker going beyond the call of duty during yesterday's Community Day. Nash feels proud of his social worker—much like some uncles may feel toward their nieces. This married and devoutly religious man has feelings toward Ashley he rarely feels toward his other employees. *She's a good kid. I think she likes me.*

In his customary polo shirt, Psycho stands waiting for the slow elevator to take him to his unit. The middle-aged athletic man ironically refuses to take the stairs. Twice he has been trapped in the antiquated elevator. His mind is focused on what he needs to get completed this afternoon. The clanging of the elevator bumping against the loose tracks becomes louder.

Psycho's head rises in anticipation of the door opening. An undesired sound gains his attention. The sound of her Go-Go boots echoing off the Navajo piss-yellow walls made a pronounced incessant pounding, "quack...quack...quack." Psycho moves one foot closer to the elevator door. Carmel's steps gain in frequency as she plans to rectify Pedro's earlier ostentatious and detrimental interpretations of Bob Burns' Rorschach responses.

During the morning Admissions Treatment Team meeting, Dr. Pedro, the psychiatrist with no formal education in the interpretation of the Rorschach Ink Blot Test, surmised that Bob Burns hearing the two words "bang" and "escape" was a result of a severe Oedipal Conflict. Pedro, the elderly shop-for-a-doc psychiatrist, concluded at the earlier meeting, "Burns is having a psychotic break due to his ambivalent love and hate of his mother."

The door of the elevator opens and Psycho dashes inside. Carmel grabs his upper arm. He turns to face her. "You did a good job at the Review meeting," says Psycho. "Honesty tends to go a long way. Okay, I complimented you; may I get on with my work?"

In a hurried and determined voice, Carmel says, "Dammit, Psycho, this is not one of your times to be so dramatic and patronizing."

The elevator door bangs into the pin-striped suited psychologist's arm. She lets go of her hold on Psycho and enters the elevator with him. The dated elevator drops one inch. Carmel's eyes look toward Psycho for reassurance. He takes a step back and leans on the wall farther away from the door. "It's been doing that the past couple of weeks. I already called maintenance."

Carmel makes a bold move, not giving him time to push the third-floor button, she steps toward him and grabs the ex-Navy officers' powerful upper arms. "I had some time during our meeting to do a quick scoring of Burns' Rorschach, you know the patient who only hears the words "bang" and "escape"?

Psycho, the Behaviorist, already has heard enough about this stupid inkblot test during his Treatment Team meeting. He exhales and asks, "So whatcha got?"

Still holding both of his arms, "The guy is a bad call, I don't know why he is here, but he's not psychotic." Carmel slowly blinks her eyes at Psycho.

"Carmel, are you flirting with me?"

"Fuck you, Psycho. This is serious. I'm trying to get your fucking attention." She let go of his arms and takes a step back.

Psycho leans away from the wall of the elevator and moves closer to Carmel. "Your idea that Pedro is making a bad call is based on your interpretation of those inkblots?" asks Psycho. He pushes the button for the third floor. The antiquated elevator jolts and begins its slow shimmy to the next floor.

Carmel shifts to a poor schoolgirl persona. She runs a hand through her hair, shifts her hips and in a softer voice says, "Pedro, psychiatrists, in general, should not be interpreting the Rorschach in the first place, let alone doing any form of psychotherapy. They are trained in drugs; that's it. And everyone knows, if reliably scored, the Rorschach is the best test to pick up psychosis. Even though you were not trained in the Rorschach, you surely read how, if it is reliably scored, is good on picking up psychosis."

The elevator abruptly stops and the door does not open.

"Okay, you got lucky today with the Administrative Review," says Psycho, "Just because you think you're on a roll gives you no right to be so condescending. You do realize that others of us also have graduate degrees? Perhaps your specialty in the psychodynamic field does not make you holier than the rest of us."

Psycho pulls a Swiss Army knife out of his front pocket. He opens the longest blade.

Carmel continues in a matter-of-fact voice, "Based on the Exner interpretation of Bob Burns' responses, which was standardized on similar grounds as your beloved MMPI test, Burns is not psychotic. He does not score like a group of people suffering from psychosis. In fact, he looks sickeningly healthy."

As he works on jimmying the elevator door with his knife, Psycho asks, "What about the Oedipal issues that Pedro says Burns wants to bang his mother and thus feels empty?"

With her open-handed arms out to her sides, she asks, "What boy does not want his Mommie? We know research already suggests we marry people similar to our parents."

As Psycho pushes the door of the elevator to the side, he commands, "Hold this open."

With both hands, she holds the elevator door open, but there is still the door on the floor to open. They are one foot short of the third floor.

Carmel continues her plea, "Haven't you ever had a niece or little neighbor girl flirt with you? But this oedipal stuff is not the issue with this case. Bob Burns is not psychotic based on the scientifically validated evidence of the Exner system."

The elevator again drops an inch. Carmel's again looks toward Psycho for reassurance. He looks calm and says, "Usually it only drops when at a floor. This is the first time it has dropped when it's stuck between floors." Since Psycho does not appear alarmed, Carmel says, "Burns does not need shock treatment and he especially does not need to stay here for 60 days. He is no danger to himself or anyone else. The man just doesn't belong here. I interviewed him. I found nothing."

Psycho with his Swiss Army knife in one hand pushes open the door of the third floor. He throws the knife onto the third floor and tells Carmel, "With one of your hands hold this door open. Can you do that?"

"Who is condescending now?" asks Carmel.

When he does his minor jump up to the third floor, Psycho moves his right muscular arm to stop any movement of the two doors and reaches down to Carmel with his left arm. "Okay, I'll talk with Pedro," sighs Psycho.

Carmel looks up to the man freed of the elevator.

"Damn woman, I got the doors. Grab my arm and I'll try to heave you up. I told you I will talk with Pedro."

He easily pulls her safely out of the elevator. She falls into his chest. Instinctively he lets go of the elevator door and embraces her.

Psycho does not immediately let go of Carmel. There is no protest from either the man or the woman. Psycho drops his arms and Carmel takes a step back. She asks, "Why don't you take the stairs?"

As he is turning away from her, "The elevator's faster."

Psycho walks toward the Admission's Unit Navy gray door, without bothering to turn around, he shouts, "Do me a favor. Call maintenance again and remind them the elevator's not working."

"Sure, and thanks." Dr. Katie Carmel is on a roll. It is as if nothing can go wrong.

Psycho waves an arm in the air. His mind does a mental review of what just transpired in the elevator. *This inkblot shit is driving me crazy.*

Carmel doubts whether Psycho will take the time to talk with Pedro this Friday afternoon. Bob Burns' EST is scheduled for tomorrow. She is fatigued from having to fight so many battles. Yet, she also feels she is on a roll.

She turns and walks toward the door of the stairway. The large wooden heels of her Go-Go boots pound and echoes off the floor of the asylum, "quack....quack....quack."

On the Admissions Unit, a nurse walks up to Bob Burns in the hallway. He is reading *Of Mice and Men*. The cooperative patient is once again wearing blue jean pants with the pant legs rolled up. The young nurse in her best professional voice informs him that Dr. Pedro scheduled him for EST tomorrow.

"What is EST?" asks the cooperative young man.

"It is shock treatment."

The nurse did not expect the following words to come from Bob Burns.

"What the hell is wrong with you people? I only hear two words. I don't belong here. I'm part of a grand experiment being conducted throughout the United States at several hospitals. Lady, I am saner than you ever hope to be."

In his excited state, Bob Burns did not mean to personally challenge the sanity of the nurse with his statement, "I am saner than you ever hope to be." However, those were the only screaming words the young nurse heard coming from the patient's mouth. He had challenged her. He had challenged one of the workhorses of the asylum.

The nurse's eyeballs roll upward in their sockets and the nurse, now pretty much blind with her eyelids half-closed, turns her head toward the nursing station and nods her head up-and-down.

Throughout the hospital come the all-too-familiar words, "Code Blue 382…Code Blooo 382."

Bob Burns cannot believe his ears. *They've called a Code on me.*

Being in an asylum is crazy enough for the young man. But to have a Code called on him is beyond the synapses of his brain. He begins to dissociate; everything becomes surreal. It feels like he is in another dimension of life. It's as if he is underwater and objects grow a vague haziness instead of their usual distinct outlines. Time slows down and yet speeds up.

A physician assistant and two nurses bolt out from the room behind the nurses' desk in the hallway. The people in white are coming for him. They appear to run in his direction slowly. Nonexpressive patients are stepping away making a path for the attackers. In the opposite direction, his numb but keen ears hear keys enter the steel door to the unit. Bob Burns indolently turns his head to the door and sees four men slowly running in fast gestures toward him. The nonexpressive patients move back toward the piss yellow walls of the unit.

The physician assistant from behind the nurses' desk gets to Bob Burns first. It is a clean side tackle.

Burns' head strikes the seat of a metal chair as he goes down. A major artery on the side of his forehead bursts open and blood gushes and drains down his face making him blind in one eye. Not preparing for the tackle, Bob Burns' nose crashes against the concrete floor. His nose breaks his fall. A distinctive cracking sound from his broken nose vibrates up through his skull to his eardrum. For the first time in his life, the acidic taste of blood fills his mouth.

Knees are forcefully thrust into his back and thighs. A nurse quickly binds his wrists behind his back with a leather strap. The nurse, who called the code, clumsily binds his ankles together with another leather strap.

The physician assistants and nurses stand up from the debilitated man who looks like a cow being prepared to be branded.

Bob Burns' face is lying in a pool of his blood.

Four nurses and four physician assistants stand over him.

The patients of the unit do not move, with a stare similar to frightened children, they gawk at the incapacitated man.

Bob Burns believes he feels someone pulling down his trousers. The patient is mentally losing it. Of all the thoughts he could materialize in his mind, Bob Burns recalls a childhood memory when he saw those pig-faced people on the TV series the *Twilight Zone*. It is all too bizarre to comprehend.

A dull hypodermic needle is injected too high into his buttocks and strikes his upper hip bone. Burns screams in pain.

Following the misguided injection of Thorazine, the training nurse who delivered the hypodermic in his upper hip tries to convey in a tone that she is one of the bold take-no-shit Admissions Team members, "He'll sleep well tonight."

Completely disregarding the presence of the training nurse and her inept words, the physician assistant on the Admissions Unit asks, "Where's he going?"

The neophyte nurse who signaled the code takes command of the situation and says, "He has EST scheduled for tomorrow; he freaked out when I told him. He needs to stay in solitary until his treatment tomorrow. Then he's definitely going to Acute for 60 days." She places her hands on her hips in an ill-conceived attempt of displaying her power.

Bob Burns hears but does not hear. He hears the words, but there is nowhere to place the words in his brain—he can't believe his ears.

Three men in white clothing bend over to lift the limp form out of his pool of blood. One man wraps his arms around Burns' ankles, the second man wraps his arms around the patient's hip, and the third man wraps his arms around the defenseless patient's shoulders. One man says, "Now remember, use your knees and not your back. We don't want anybody to get hurt. On the count of three."

The three men in white managed to lift bloodied and traumatized Bob Burns without incident.

The doorway to solitaire is lower and thinner than customary doors. It was built that way so it would be more difficult for agitated patients to kick open the smaller steel door.

The physician assistant carrying Burns' shoulders stoops and ducks his head down to enter the confined space; in the process, he bangs the back of Burns' head into the steel doorway. Burns is so helpless, so defeated, no sound emits from his mouth. The physician assistant quips, "Sorry."

Tomorrow, people will discover that a lot of things happened on Friday, July 18th, 1969. An intoxicated United States Senator drives his car off a bridge on Chappaquiddick Island and there is a woman in the car. She tragically dies and the United States Senator gets off for any misdoing. A photograph will be taken of a creature in the woods of California. The picture of the beast, which is a cross between an ape and human, will spawn decades of search for Bigfoot. President Nixon's speechwriter, William Safire, has been given the unthankful job of writing a speech for the President should the astronauts not survive the moon landing.

"These brave men, Neil Armstrong and Edwin Aldrin, know that there is no hope for their recovery. But they also know there is hope for mankind in their sacrifice. These two men are laying down their lives in mankind's most noble goal: the search for truth and understanding."

The national events do not detour the magnitude of what is about to happen at the Weston Asylum.

36

The echoing "quack…quack…quack" sound of the wooden heels of Go-Go boots draws the attention of the staff and patients on the Acute Unit. Carmel's eyes narrow as she sees the staff look in her direction. The psychologist is on another mission to stop an unnecessary injustice.

As Carmel hastens onto the Acute Unit, Hesus, the self-proclaimed female Gnostic version of Jesus, is walking up to Noah Holiday, Carmel's Jesus.

Hesus wears an oversized hooded gown that partially conceals her rich black curly hair. Hesus' downturned face is obscured by the hood. Primitive drawings of people adorn her gown.

Due to the antics of the Admissions Treatment Team sending another Jesus to the Acute Unit, the therapeutic breakthrough Jesus and Carmel made this morning (Jesus saying, "I've doubted myself ever since I sat down in this room.") is threatened. Another Jesus will probably easily awaken Noah's psychosis that he is Jesus.

The two Jesus' are facing off on the Acute Unit. It is a psychiatric reenactment of the *Gunfight at the O.K. Corral.*

Because of her recent victories of so many battles, Carmel believes she can also take care of this pending disaster.

Elsewhere in the hospital, another person is feeling good and is a tad grandiose. President Nash believes he is in the groove of his life. His brisk walk down the hallway is accompanied by his whistling a light tune. He feels omnipotent. Following yesterdays' successful Community Day, and especially following the extravaganza of the fireworks with music, Nash decides to take a well-deserved break. He walks to the library to read the *Wall Street Journal*. Within the comforting solitary confines of the library, he hopes to find his most recent intellectual hobby, a new article on the X and Y Theories of management styles.

During his walk to the library, he sees an obese woman wearing a plain, print dress. His face lights up as if he has seen an old lost friend. It is uncharacteristic of Nash to be excited about seeing a patient. The exceptions are the women Nash meets for his mysterious Wednesday and Friday night "therapy" sessions on the Acute Unit. This patient is scheduled to be his therapy session for this Friday evening.

The president walks up to the patient. With his crooked, polio-stricken, half smile he finely enunciates, "Remember Ms. Parkins, we meet for our therapy session this evening."

Frowning, and then smiling, the middle-aged woman slurs the words, "Yes sir."

Nash softly lays a hand on the woman's shoulder. A cross between a groan and a slight scream belches from her mouth. He removes his hand and says, "Today will be a day I know you will remember for the rest of your life." The patient has a frightened look.

"It will be fine," says Nash. He abruptly turns and continues his light walk to the library to read his newspaper. His brisk walk is accompanied by his whistling John Denver's, *Take Me Home, Country Roads* song.

It is late-afternoon on Friday and the heat and subsequent humidity following last night's thunderstorm become increasingly unbearable. Nash opens one of the opulent doors to the extravagant library. Tens-of-thousands of books line the two-story room, a fireplace, the reminiscent sweet smell of cigar fumes, and a wooden spiral staircase that leads to the balcony to the second floor of books—and, a secret door that eleven-year-old Juli Jo had discovered on Community Day. Only two of the five people in the room are aware of the secret door.

Ashley, the social worker, sits in a corner of the room. Her tight blue jean pants accentuate her thin legs. Because Nash has always been an X manager, an administrator who must know all and control all of his subordinates, Ashley tries to escape being noticed; she quickly looks back to reading her magazine, *Cosmopolitan*. She sneaks a peek— all seems to be well— he does not look in her direction.

Unlike the carpet peoples' offices, the library has no air conditioning. Walking to the newspaper rack, Nash removes his tailored shiny platinum jacket; he significantly loosens his red tie and unbuttons the top two buttons of his white shirt exposing his abundant white chest hair. Nash reclines in a leather chair and unfolds his *Wall Street Journal* to find the most recent article on the X & Y Theory of Management.

During the next 20 minutes the president of the asylum and the thin-legged social worker read their articles of interest. Both of them fear, but hope, they might be caught catching glances from the other.

Two young psychiatrists, a man and a woman, and a female psychiatric nurse are having a lively conversation by one of the large windows of the library. The three walk out the library agreeing to go to a local bar for some refreshments to celebrate the end of the week and to play out whatever else is on their minds.

Nash and Ashley are alone in the library for the next five minutes.

Nash stands up. He casually walks to the spiral staircase. Ashley abruptly lifts her head. The two figures in the large room make eye contact. The mutual eye contact is sustained a little longer than just a casual recognition of the other.

Nash turns. He does a deliberate, slow, and methodical trek up the spiral staircase.

On the Admissions Unit, Bob Burns is in solitary confinement with half his face covered in dried blood. The impact of the IV of Thorazine has kicked in; he feels no pain. The walls are padded with white canvas. A sickening stench in the room and yellow stains malign the otherwise white canvas walls. Uncannily, his confinement has allowed him to think. Well, it really is not that uncanny because there is not a Code being called, he is not being tackled, his head is not driven into a chair, he is not driven to the concrete floor breaking his nose, he is not having his pants pulled down, and he is not picked up by three men driving his head into the frame of a doorway. A little solitary confinement has given him a chance to take in what has transpired.

Even though Bob Burns is experiencing the deepest need to sleep he has ever experienced, he forces himself to rise to the barred open window. He sees his one hope out of this craziness, his one God-given opportunity—he thinks he sees eleven-year-old Juli Jo hiding behind a bush on the front lawn. She is playing kick-the-can with some of her friends. The girl looks different from the pink cladded pig-tailed girl of yesterday. In his drugged state, Bob Burns struggles whether it is the girl. *It could be her older sister.* Instead of pig-tails, her dark hair is pulled back into a ponytail. Instead of a too cute pink outfit she is wearing blue jean short shorts and a Pittsburgh Pirates T-shirt. She looks much older than yesterday.

In a hysterical, desperate attempt, the blood-drenched Bob Burns screams, "Girl…girl!"

Juli Jo turns her head toward the window. The girl sees a crazy man's face covered in blood. A couple of her girlfriends also turn their head upwards. Juli Jo realizes it is the funny man who played the game of "bang" and "escape" with her. Yesterday, Juli Jo would scream the words to Bob Burns, who would then look horrified and act crazy.

"I need your help. Come closer."

Juli runs in the direction of the window. One of her girlfriends, who also heard the crazy patient screaming, grabbed her just in time. "You know, if you cross this road, then you go to prison."

Juli has played for years on the front lawn of the asylum. She has frequently had fantasies of rescuing a falsely imprisoned political figure. Even though she is only eleven years of age, Juli has seen the violent political protests on television. She has thought many of those protestors made sense. In the imaginative, idealistic mind of a young girl, she believes she must rescue her friend. She must expose the terrible doctors and people in authority of the Weston Asylum. *The future of the world is dependent upon me.*

Juli runs across the road that circumscribes the asylum and races thirty feet. She stands below the third story window. The girl shouts, "There's blood on your face like a crazy man!"

Seeing her closer and hearing her voice, he knows it is the girl from yesterday. Even in his drugged state of mind, Bob Burns knows he must gain the trust of the girl, "You look older than you did yesterday."

"That's because my Mom made me wear those prissy clothes. I'm also going to turn twelve tomorrow," shouts the young Juli.

Believing he has the initial trust of the girl, the bloodied Burns says, "I need you to do a very grown-up thing. I am not supposed to be here. I'm part of an experiment." Amazingly, even though Bob Burns is drugged to the hilt on Thorazine, he perceives he has lost Juli with the word "experiment." In a pathetic fatigued voice, Burns says, "I'm tired. I'm just so tired. You got to help me. You are my only hope."

And then the miraculous happens.

"I know. I know you are not crazy." The zealous girl jumped up and down. "Ever since you silently told me everything would be okay yesterday morning I knew you weren't crazy. Are you here because you're one of those—objectors of something?"

Burns does not know how to handle all his conflictual feelings: his feelings of helplessness, hope, and stupidity. *I never should've volunteered for this stupid experiment.* The bloodied-faced lethargic man tries to get closer to Juli and leans against the screened bar window. He pushes his hands, in an act of desperation, against the heavy, metal screen. *How can I convey all of what has transpired to this middle-school kid, she's my only hope.*

"You're right. I do not belong here. Me and some scientists wanted to know if people would be admitted to a mental hospital if they said they heard two voices."

Juli treads two steps to the stone building, "I know. I know. You hear "bang" and "escape.""

"That's right! You're right!" *I think she really understands.* "There's nothing wrong with me. I was just pretending. Juli, do you ever play pretend games?"

"All the time."

"I was pretending, but they do not know I was pretending. The people here are going to give me shock treatment tomorrow and hold me here another 60 days."

"That's not right."

Juli understands.

"I need you to call the professor who is doing this experiment, the man who created this pretend game. His name is Dr. Alan Samuels; he's at Glenville State College."

Juli speaks to her mother with words of wisdom way beyond her years, "I know I fibbed about things in the past, but this is true. You have to hear me." Juli's eyes tear. "I know he's not crazy and he's about something bigger than I can understand, it's an experiment about something." And then, the girl pulls out the big guns that youngsters rarely do, "You are crazy if you don't listen to me."

Because Juli was such a special kid, and because she had a special relationship with her mother, she was heard.

In his meticulous manner, Nash continues his slow hike up the spiral staircase. Ashley is not aware of what is happening to her. She feels like she has been transposed to another dimension, another time. Ashley is numb to her surroundings. Things are real but not real. The young social worker is scared, but is not scared. Her feelings are so wonderful; she has never felt such feelings.

Ashley stands and walks toward the spiral staircase. An oversized button down white shirt emphasizes her thin legs.

Nash cheats a looks to see if she is following. *She looks much younger in that big white shirt.*

Eleven-year-old Juli's mother frantically searches for Dr. Alan Samuel's phone number (the supposed psychologist conducting an experiment) in the white pages of the telephone book. No luck. She searches in the yellow pages under "psychologist." There is no listing. Jana does not allow the thought, her daughter might have been duped by a crazy person, to enter her mind. Jana knows a neighbor whose daughter is taking psychology classes at Glenville State College. The only information she gains is that:

there is a Dr. Samuel at Glenville State College, he is a published psychologist and he is a great teacher. There is no way to contact this psychologist to see whether Bob Burns' claim to be a part of an elaborate psychology experiment is true. Their friends agree to call back if they can find Dr. Samuel's telephone number.

A neighbor is also in the room with Juli Jo and her mother. Jana says to the neighbor, "That young man did not seem like the other people we saw on the unit. He looked like some nice college kid—he just looked so sleepy." The neighbor heard from a friend that worked at the asylum that they drugged the patients, particularly for Community Day. The neighbor is a volunteer fireman at Weston. The neighbor has complete faith in Juli and takes an awkward command of the situation. She calls the emergency phone number of the fire department to dispense the fire trucks to the Weston Asylum.

With a similar gesture of faith, Juli's mother knows a friend in administration who works at Stonewall Jackson Memorial Hospital. She calls her friend. An ambulance is dispatched to the Weston Asylum.

Juli, the girl turned woman, has had enough. She grabs the telephone and calls the police, "There is a man that is at the Weston Asylum who should not be there. He is a part of an experiment and they are going to hurt him tomorrow."

In an act of providing credence to her young daughter's story, Juli's mother takes the phone away from Juli; Jana provides some details supporting this man does not belong at the asylum.

Nash steps up to the wooden balcony. He looks down at the social worker striding to the staircase. He patiently waits at the top of the stairs.

She reaches the bottom of the staircase.

In a somnambulant state of mind, the young Ashley climbs the wooden staircase to the awaiting crooked-faced Dr. Nash.

Ashley spoke first. "I saw you earlier walking to the library."

"I saw you enter the library—there is something I want to show you."

The platinum suit Nash walks in the direction of the secret doorway. In her numbed state-of-mind, Ashley dutifully follows him along the balcony of book-filled shelves. Nash stops at the shelves that little Juli Jo had discovered yesterday.

Nash pulls on a book that is an enclosed lever that partially opens the bookshelves. The bookshelf rises a tad and scoots out a tad. Ashley's numbed state has moved her to another universe. She is simply not here. Ashley is: scared, excited, fearful, elated, and sexually intrigued with the father figure.

She innocently asks in a child-like manner, "What happens in that room?"

Nash easily opens the bookshelf that sits on numerous ball-peen tracks. The opened shelves expose—a hallway.

The crooked smile Nash says, "I just saw you reading a *Cosmopolitan* magazine. In my apartment, there is one of the originals. Because of the great work you did yesterday during Community Day, I would like to give the first edition."

The married Ashley, not recovering from her previous conflictual emotions (*what is behind the bookshelves*), can only say, "What?"

"Would you like an original, first edition, 1888 *Cosmopolitan*?"

Stupefied by all her conflictual emotions, the young social worker blurts, "Yeah, yeah; but, I thought there was more."

"More?"

"You know? The hidden room. The hidden bookcase opening? Well, I guess it's not a hidden room."

"I'm lost, my child. You thought there was a room behind the bookcase?"

Ashley replies in her girly-girl voice, "Yeah."

"Oh, some doctor added this door in the 40s, so he did not have to go out the library doors and face patients. He was rather odd. I just like to use it to get to places faster. I noticed earlier you were reading a *Cosmopolitan* magazine. In my full appreciation of you making Community Day a success, I would like to give you a copy of the magazine I acquired from the 1800s. I enjoy collecting first editions of magazines, journals, and books. I would like to give you this first edition of *Cosmopolitan* only because of the work you have done. I wish I had a hundred social workers like you."

Recovering from her previous devious thoughts, Ashley can only say, "I thought you wanted more."

He raises his one good eyebrow a little higher; he questions, "You did? Let's go to my apartment and get that magazine."

As the pair approaches the door of the president's apartment, it is the first time that Ashley begins to question. *Why would a man, a psychiatrist, a president of an asylum; take the time to collect an original Cosmopolitan?*

37

President Nash owns a gated estate twenty-five miles from the asylum, During his employment interview, he insisted on having an apartment in the hospital. He told the Board members, "To run an efficacious hospital takes more than 40 hours a week. In this day-and-age, it is a 24/7 job."

It's odd nobody at the asylum knows the real reason Nash stayed at his last asylum for only one year.

As Nash and Ashley tepidly walk to his apartment, Nash whistles, "Take Me Home, Country Roads." Ashley stops walking. Nash turns back and takes a step closer to the tight blue-jeaned and oversized white-shirted Ashley. She says, "Last night was so wonderful. I've never experienced anything like last night's firework display. It was just—."

Nash raises one eyebrow in anticipation.

"—it was—I don't know, wonderful. You are such a wonderful man to give that to us." Nash's one raised eyebrow lowers and he smirks.

The couple enters the domain of the presidential suite of the asylum. The two married people concoct angels and devils on each of their shoulders. The devils on their left shoulders mimic, *It's okay. It's just a magazine.* The angels on their right shoulders are silent. Their masks, keeping the relationship platonic, waver.

The apartment is refreshingly cool. The window air conditioners run 24 hours a day. The living area is grand: 1800s antique furniture, red velvet curtains, and black-and-white photographs of the asylum decorate the walls.

Nash moves his left hand to Ashley's upper back and leads the petite social worker to his kitchenette. "Would you like a glass of wine?"

Ashley can only muster, "May I?"

Removing his hand from her back he insists, "One drink is always okay."

Not waiting for a response, he opens a cabinet and pulls out a bottle of one of his favorite dry wines. From the same cabinet, he removes two wine glasses. The president of the asylum pours the perilous fruit into the glasses. Ashley cannot believe she is standing in the president's apartment sharing wine with the older man.

Ashley rarely drinks alcohol. She has drunk a favorite wine of her husbands. Her husband's favorite wine is Mad Dog.

Following her initial sip of the dry wine, she hesitates in contemplation. Before speaking, she takes another sip. "This is wonderful. I never had wine like this."

The pretending masks defending the two from their lustful feelings lower. Nash lifts his glass into the air, "To us." Without thinking, Ashley raises her glass in the air. "To us." The invisible devils on their left shoulders are winning.

Nash again lays a hand on the upper back of Ashley. "Come, let me show you the rest of the place." He leads her through the living area of the apartment to French doors that open to the president's balcony.

The young Ashley and the powerful Nash stand together on his prestigious balcony. They regale in the activities of the front lawn. Patients wander around in the front yard. Some of the patients suffer from tics, a crippling side-effect of the drug Thorazine. They jerk their heads to the side. Maintenance men are picking up the trash and removing the canvas sheets left over from last night's firework display. One group of children is playing a game of baseball. Another group of children is playing kick-the-can. The asylum provides a rare large flat area in the hills of West Virginia for children to play. Never has there been an incident of the children being hurt. Only the more docile patients are allowed on the front grounds.

Ashley feels exposed drinking a glass of wine on the balcony. The paranoid Nash, because of his ever-present ability to pick up on people's thoughts and feelings, says to Ashley, "Let me show you the rest of the place."

The tea-totaling social worker dutifully follows. She is getting a slight buzz from the wine. Nash refills her glass of wine.

"This must sound crazy, but let me show you the bathroom," says Nash.

Entering the green-and-white tiled bathroom, the first thing Ashley notices are the two toilets. Ashley asks, "Why two toilets. I mean that is just too weird that there is one for the man and the other is for the woman. Who would want to go to the bathroom with someone sitting next to them?"

Nash chuckles and says, "The one is a bidet."

"A bidet?"

"I will show you later how it works," says the warmed Nash in the air-conditioned suite. "Let me show you the final room, the bedroom."

He flips up the light switch to his bedroom; a black-light turns on. A green and blue fluorescent poster of Jesus illuminates against a distant wall. Ashley's eyes dilate and she sees numerous dark crucifixes and abundant unlit candles.

"Very few people have seen this room," says Nash. "This is my inner sanctuary where I gain peace in my relationship with God."

Nash looks at his Timex watch. He taps his wristwatch and says in a hurried voice, "Oh, it is getting late. There is my usual Friday patient I see on the Acute Unit. Please, return another day."

Ashley's jaw drops. She runs her hands down the sides of her white shirt.

Taking his customary control of the situation, Nash escorts her back to the living room where there are some bookshelves. From the shelve containing numerous psychiatric journals, he pulls the first edition copy of *Cosmopolitan* magazine.

He hands the original copy of *Cosmopolitan* to Ashley; he does something that feels awkward to Ashley, but not so awkward, given their most recent unacted upon transgressions.

With outstretched arms, Nash steps closer to Ashley and gives her a tight hug. He presses the side of his face against the side of her face. Moving back, but while still embraced, they make prolonged eye contact. He says, "Thanks again for everything you did yesterday during Community Day. I do not know if I can ever convey how much you mean to me."

Ashley is numb. Poor Ashley feels like she has been hit on the right side of the face and before her head can swing the entire direction from the blow; she receives a left swing to her head.

With his hand again on her upper back, Nash leads Ashley out of his apartment. She pithily stands outside of the apartment in a daze. *What just happened?*

Nash pours another drink of wine and returns to his balcony. His eyes scan his property, his empire.

In a hurry to meet a regularly scheduled patient on the Acute Unit, the president of the asylum returns to the living area of his apartment. He strips off his power suit and neatly folds his clothes on the fainting couch. Naked, he walks straight for his bathroom.

Five minutes later he takes a hot shower.

He returns to the living room and puts back on his power suit. Since he is in such a good mood, he decides to look more casual and does not wear his red tie. He picks up what looks like an antiquated doctors' bag before leaving his apartment.

Briskly walking in a wide hallway of the asylum, Nash's left arm slightly swings the black bag; he resumes whistling, "Take Me Home, Country Roads."

At dusk, he will meet with his usual Wednesday and Friday patient. It is always a different patient he meets. The fundamentalist Nash, even though he is an administrator, believes it is his responsibility to help these poor souls. Due to his evangelical Christian background, Nash believes he must personally provide effective missionary work in these peoples' lives—these people who have sinned. He knows the pills of his fellow psychiatrists, and the talking therapy of the psychologists, are of little help with these poor misguided souls who need the help of the teachings of the Holy Bible.

On the Acute Unit, the inevitable showdown between the two Jesus' is about to commence. In one corner there is Noah Holiday. During his morning therapy session with Carmel, he questioned whether there is a God. In the other corner, there is Hesus. The gowned woman who claims people must find God through insight, through personal experience and not through indoctrination.

The attire of the two Jesus' matches their ideology.

Following a shower, Noah Holiday is returning to his room. He is inappropriately dressed with only a towel around his waist. Wearing only a towel on the Acute Unit is forbidden. At the minimum, a robe is required after taking a shower. It is odd that of all days Noah decides to walk in the hallway with only a towel.

The day must be predestined. What transpires cannot be just an act of coincidence.

His long hair is wet; strains of water flow down his body and highlight his muscular features. Noah Holiday sports a six-pack. His muscular arms are framed by his broad shoulders. Physically, he is a match for the woman in the gown apparently seeking his crucifixion.

The obese Hesus wears a gown with an over-sized hood covering her head. Her locks of thick hair are pulled to the front. Onlookers, staff, and patients, can only partially see her face due to the expansive hood of the gown. Primitive human figures are printed on the gown.

Hesus sways her broad hips. She waves a pointed figure in the direction of sinfully toweled Noah. She screams, "You—you!"

There is no response. Noah continues his methodical walk on the unit.

In an evangelical emphasis of the syllables, Hesus screams. "Jesus!"

Noah turns toward Hesus.

Hesus runs to the man.

She is immediately upon him. Her head turns side-to-side, a finger waves in the air, as she screams, "You say you are Jesus?"

The two Jesus' stand face-to-face. They stare at each other for an inordinate amount of time.

The staff, professionals, and patients had anticipated this inevitable battle. All are silent as the two Jesus' face off.

Fearing that Noah Holiday meeting Hesus could result in a setback, Carmel came to the Acute Unit believing she could prevent a major fallout. Carmel stands off to the side waiting to see whether she needs to intervene.

Hesus again wags her large hips and throws a finger in the air. "You think you are Jesus?" she asks and commands.

Noah Holiday quips, "I don't know."

Hesus is caught off balance. "What do you mean you don't know?"

Jesus, in a dumbfounded look, makes no response.

Sensing an easy prey, Hesus attacks, "You, you claim to be the supposed Jesus who gives us all these wonderful cute sayings and doings that are on the bumper stickers of old peoples' RVs about optimism and just a bunch of goody-two-shoe shit. I thought Jesus was human. To be human is to accept the dark dimension."

Noah utters, "I think you're acting crazy about all of this."

Not to be outdone, Hesus vigorously gyrates her body and shrieks, "I know you're crazy!"

In a calm voice, Noah says, "I know you are crazy."

In a zealous voice, Hesus lets it rip. "If you're not crazy, you're a liar—Jesus. You lied about Mary! My people...the Gnostic scriptures fully wrote down that you "knew" Mary. You fucked Mary! The Gnostics knew about you and Mary. That is why I exist. You're either crazy or a sick pervert who preaches abstinence but fucks!"

Noah Holiday bends his head down to the concrete floor. His long wet hair hangs toward the floor covering his face.

Every person's eyes, even the drug-induced patients' eyes are wide.

From the side of the confrontations is a familiar striking of shoes against the concrete. Noah Holiday lifts his head.

Carmel walks up to the towel-cloaked man. She grabs his hand, "We need to talk." She pulls him in the direction of her make-shift therapy room on the Acute Unit.

"Who's this bitch?" shouts the Gnostic Hesus, who has supposedly balanced a dark-and-light side of life and has so much insight into life. "Yeah, yeah, I would walk away too if I had a good looking man grabbing me."

Hesus gains the laughter of the professionals, staff, and patients standing around watching the escapades unfold.

Feeling too omnipotent, because she had won so many battles today, Carmel loses it. The psychologist turns around to face Hesus.

Carmel slowly enunciates, "Fuck—you."

38

Nash unlocks the door to the Acute Unit; he hears everyone laughing. Nash continues whistling as he strides down the long hallway toward the nursing desk. He carefully sets the black doctor's bag on the desk. In a high pitched voice, Nash asks one of the nurses, "What's going on?"

The Methodist white-attired nurse says, "The two Jesus' met."

"I heard that was going to happen." The president of the asylum rubs the side of his head and asks, "Who won?"

With a smirk on her face, the Methodist nurse says, "I think Dr. Carmel."

Nash is still anxious about something happening in his hospital that is beyond his control. In his peripheral vision, he sees two people walking to the end of the hall.

Carmel and Noah Holiday walk together to the old conference room without further incident from Hesus. Unlike this morning, when Carmel was wearing her braless spaghetti-string top, it is now Noah Holiday, following a shower, who is underdressed wearing only a towel.

Noah sits in one of the two chairs respectfully placed at a slight angle. The placement of the chairs is left from their therapy session this morning.

Katie Carmel removes her striped business jacket and hangs it on the back of her chair. She sits in the chair opposite Noah Holiday.

Carmel casually questions, "So how are you doing?"

"Not good. I've been troubled ever since we met this morning, so many thoughts and so many feelings."

"So many thoughts and feelings?"

"Yeah, I question whether God exists, whether I exist."

"You are feeling lost because you question not only the existence of God, but even yourself."

"Fuck you."

Carmel's face squeezes with a look of unexpected horror.

Noah's eyes appear possessed. In a deepened voice he yells, "You sound like a cheap whore therapist! I've had to hear all of that parroting bull-shit from other shrinks. I thought you were above all of that. I thought you gave a shit."

Keeping her composure, Carmel stares directly into his pupils and asks, "Who's the whore in the room?"

Noah's face squishes. "What?"

"You heard me. Of all the words you could use; you used the word "whore." I asked you, "who is the whore in the room?""

"Fuck you."

"We've been there done that. Maybe I am in left field; but, you are, or were, the one who claims to be the Almighty. I don't. I can't help to wonder if there is something more to all of this you didn't tell me."

Noah Holiday looks past Carmel. In a contemplative voice, Jesus says, "It's Hesus; she brought up my past, a past I don't talk about. For the past couple of centuries, people worshipped my life, my death, and my ultimate transfiguration. I was important to people; I was Jesus—I was God. I felt important. But this damn crazy Gnostic comes into my life while I'm imprisoned at this crazy house and she exposes me just as they had done centuries ago. It's too crazy. She, the Gnostics, not only half got it; they got the story straight."

He desperately looks directly into Dr. Carmel's eyes for validation that it is okay to proceed.

Her lips lightly part in a state of wonderment of what is to transpire.

Carmel nods her head.

Jesus continues his rambling. "Hesus, the Gnostics knew I was not celibate. Mary and I had a relationship. The paternalism of the Catholic Church had to conceal my sexual relationship with Mary because of the supposed profound writings of St. Augustine who was a party boy in the fullest sense of the word: drinking and sexing, until one day he saw the light—he decided he should be celibate. The fucker supposedly became impotent. So what does the Catholic Church do during their coming out years at the beginning of the fourth century? They embrace the fucker's teachings. Augustine, to the demise of his marriage, decides sex is bad. He's going to be a good boy. Fuck that. To have sex is normal; it can be and is holy. Because of him, sex is a bad thing. It is all so crazy. I mean we now have the pill. We can be blessed with each other's presence without having to worry whether 'are we emotionally ready or financially ready?' It's fucking insane."

Jesus abruptly stops his discourse and throws Carmel for an unexpected loop. He questions her.

"Are you on the pill?"

Without hesitation, Carmel emphatically states, "Don't go there. It is irrelevant whether I am taking the pill or not. Our focus is you." Carmel does not feel comfortable where this is going. *Not only is he sexualizing our therapeutic relationship, he's running. He's hiding in a bunch of theological mumbo-jumbo to avoid the original pain. I'm losing the Noah I had gained this morning.*

In a more animated voice, as if he has to get this out of his internal prison, "It's just so crazy. I mean look at DeVinci's painting of the Last Supper. Mary is obviously sitting to my right. Her hair has a flow, her skin is smooth, and her features are clearly that of a woman. Once again, an artist has to expose the truth. It keeps getting crazier so what does the Catholic Church do? They idolize the painting even when they preach not to turn me into an idol. The whole thing is too crazy. I mean I was a man. I was horny. I wanted to be with Mary and I was with Mary. Why does that have to be concealed? It's just crazy.

Carmel maintains her unwavering eye contact with his dilated pupils. *He's perseverating on the word "crazy." I might be losing him.*

Outside of the make-shift therapy room, Nash disappears into the back offices where the professionals review their charts and write their notes after meeting with their patients. He absent-mindedly leaves his black doctor's bag on the nursing desk. The president of the asylum enters into a jovial conversation with the various professionals of his flock in the rooms behind the nurses' desk.

Two nurses sit at the nurses' desk on the Acute Unit. The two nurses stare at the black bag sitting on the desk. Their eyes rise to each other's faces.

One of the nurses says, "There it is."

"Yep."

Yesterday, the same two nurses had a $5.00 bet whether Dr. Nash had a snake in his doctor's bag. The Methodist nurse had bet there was a snake in the bag. She based her bet on the facts that Nash would come to the Acute Unit every Wednesday and Friday night, go into a patient's room alone, always insisted to not be interrupted, and following a few minutes; there was always screaming of the patient similar to a snake-handling assembly she had witnessed at the Jane Lew church. The Baptist nurse opposed the beliefs of the Methodist nurse and supported her fellow Baptist, Dr. Nash. The Baptist nurse claimed he was only helping these poor souls not to follow the path of the devil and he was helping the female patients to embrace the Holy Spirit in their pitiful souls. The Baptist nurse believes it is a powerful emotional process to experience the Holy Spirit: there is no snake involved.

And there it sits before the two betting nurses — the black bag.

The Methodist snake-believing nurse says to the Baptist nurse, "Open the bag."

"I'm not going to open the bag. You're the one who believes there's a snake in the bag. You open it."

"That's stupid. I'm not going to open a bag with a poisonous snake."

Dr. Blowfish, Nash's supposed right-hand man; the man who always had Nash's back covered, the suck-up, the brown-noser;

walks up to the nursing station and overhears the conversation between the two nurses.

The following dynamics are so similar to families, football team rivalries, and corporate systems theory; it barely needs repeating. Sometimes our staunchest enemies are those we are closest.

Blowfish says in his deep doctor's voice, "I could not help what the two of you were saying about Dr. Nash." In a hollow nonauthentic voice Blowfish attempts to gain some validation of his facade, "I can reassure you, Dr. Nash only has the welfare of our patients as his major concern. I will open the bag."

Even though Blowfish attends Wednesday night and Sunday morning services at his Methodist church, he silently believes that he will prove this Baptist micromanaging Nash has a snake in his bag. He is willing to risk getting bit by a snake to expose his golfing buddy.

Blowfish walks up to the black bag. He is on a mission. He wants to expose his boss.

39

Dusk has arrived at the Weston Asylum. A red sky is the background for a few determined ill-fated splatters of virtuous white clouds making their final manifestations of the day over the pristine mountains of West Virginia.

The two figures in the room look exhausted. One is the woman wearing a striped business skirt, a pink blouse, and Go-Go boots. Dark circles are under her eyes. The second exhausted-looking figure is the towel-cladded man with his long wet hair dangling to the sides of his head. The two have connected on being tired, tired of fighting. One is tired of fighting the politics of the hospital; the other is tired of the politics of fighting life.

Carmel is **not** only worn down by the politics of the hospital. She is also plagued by her internal struggles.

Carmel is scared and feels on precarious grounds with her therapeutic work with Jesus. *I'm scared that Noah Holiday may recede into a more primitive form of psychosis. I do not know if our therapeutic relationship is strong enough for me to confront him.* Carmel is fully aware of how her *thoughts* of her fear may hinder her work with Jesus. Just as an animal knows if you harbor fear; people, and particularly patients, are sensitive to picking up the fear.

Tucked away in a separate lobe of her brain, Carmel simultaneously has unconscious feelings of being invincible. Today she has been the recipient of many successes: the morning success with Noah questioning whether there is a God, successfully turfing a manipulative alcoholic to St. Petersburg, successfully taking the time to gain information on the guy who just wanted to go fishing and coming out clean from the Administrative Review. She *feels* in the groove. She *feels* she can do no wrong. She *feels* untouchable.

The simultaneous unconscious *feelings* of invincibility and *thoughts* of fear for her patient sets her therapeutic relationship up for a precarious outcome. Based on her feelings of invincibility, will she boldly intervene—risking throwing her patient deeper into a psychosis? Or, will she allow her *thoughts* of fear detour her from making a powerful therapeutic intervention?

Carmel desperately wants to keep the pace of this morning with Noah; however, the encounter of Hesus with Noah Holiday is a major threat. Noah is an intelligent man, as apparent by his rudimentary theological background. A few minutes ago, during their earlier session, Carmel fears he was gaining momentum on his psychotic slide as evident by his perseveration of the term "crazy." Perhaps he was telling her he feared completely losing his mind; his repeated usage of the word "crazy"' was his way of conveying to her he is regressing to a more primitive psychotic state.

His last comments to Carmel were, "*It's just so crazy*. I mean look at Da Vinci's painting of the Last Supper. Mary is obviously sitting to my right. Her hair has a flow, her skin is smooth, and her features are clearly that of a woman. Once again, an artist has to expose the truth. *It keeps getting crazier* because what does the Catholic Church do? They idolize the painting, even when told to not turn God into an idol. *The whole thing is too crazy*. I mean, I was a man. I was horny. I wanted to be with Mary and I was with Mary. Why does that have to be concealed? *It's just crazy!*"

Carmel's intuition, based on years of experience, suggest that Jesus' conflict is not so much about Hesus. *There's something more about Hesus' presence on the Acute Unit. The Gnostic Hesus disclosed Jesus' hidden sexual relationship with Mary.*

It was beyond the comprehension of the theologically naïve Carmel that there was a possibility of a relationship between Jesus (God) and a woman

In the building-block interpretation of the Holy Bible, the King James Version, there is no mention of a sexual relationship between Jesus and Mary. However, in the excluded Gnostic books, there are strong references to a relationship. And then, there is the Da Vinci painting of a woman sitting to his right. Carmel is close to a revelation. *Perhaps a key to Noah Holiday's psychosis is related to having sex with a forbidden person.*

As most people tend to do, Carmel listened to her readily-available unconscious *feelings* of omnipotence. She asks, "You said earlier you had an intimate relationship with Mary. Is there...."

As if he could read her mind, Jesus interrupts her. "Fuck you!"

Carmel once again, in a slow fatigued voice says, "We've been there. We've done that."

On the Admissions Unit, Bob Burns, the man who claims to be a part of a grand experiment, is completely snowed from the Thorazine injection. Bob Burns lies with dried blood covering half his face; his broken nose still needs attention. He is asleep.

The reddish dusk of the day creeps into the barred windows of the solitary confinement room. Beads of sweat gather to join the steams of sweat that flow over the blood-stained unconscious man's face. Because of the powerful Thorazine injection, the sting of the salt from the sweat does nothing to assault his wounds.

Little Juli's mother, through a friend's help, finally gets Dr. Alan Samuel's phone number. Earlier, the blood-stained face of Bob Burns had screamed out his window for Juli to find Dr. Alan Samuel.

The Glenville State College professor is doing a grand experiment throughout the Eastern United States about the inappropriate admission of people to mental hospitals. Dr. Samuel sent mentally healthy people to the asylums. These healthy people were told to tell the professionals they were hearing two neutral words, just two words. They did not hear voices telling them to kill themselves or someone else. They heard two benign words. Dr. Samuel wanted to know whether any of these mentally healthy people would be hospitalized.

Following a few introductory comments between Juli's mother and Dr. Samuel on the telephone, the psychologist goes ballistic. "What? He called out to your daughter? His face is full with blood? They're going to give him shock treatment tomorrow? They want to hold him another 60 days?"

Juli's mom screams in the phone, "You mean he's not crazy?"

"Hell no!"

"Earlier, we called the volunteer fire department, the police, and an ambulance."

This last comment by the woman sunk Samuel deeper into his emotional abyss. "What the hell? There is no fire and nobody is yet injured." The experimental psychologist hangs up the phone without getting the caller's phone number.

Dr. Samuel is in a state of panic. Because it is late, he calls the home phone number of a friend who works at the FBI department at Fairmont, West Virginia to report the false imprisonment. The experimental psychologist gets an answering machine. Based on his emotions of fear he does not leave a message. Samuel is not thinking rationally.

He flips the cards on his Rolodex searching for his FBI friend's work number. Even though it is late, he hopes they will contact his friend. The phone on the other end of the line rings.

A chipper voice answers the phone. "FBI-Fairmont."

Samuel screams into the mouthpiece of the black phone. "A person is falsely imprisoned at the Weston Asylum and they are going to torture the man—like they do our soldiers in Vietnam."

The still happy voice of apparently a young person on the other end of the telephone line says, "Watcha say?"

The usually soft-spoken research psychologist unexpectedly responds, "You fuckin bitch." He slowly enunciates the following in a staccato voice. "I said someone is erroneously hospitalized at the Weston Asylum in Weston and they are going to torture him tomorrow. Can you hear that? Can you understand that?"

The voice on the other end of the telephone says, "And you arrre...?"

Dr. Samuel inhales a deep breath. He moves the telephone handset from his ear and slowly inhales and exhales. He begins his practice of the Rule of Three: counting to three and then responding. *One...Two...Three.*

Following his brief relaxation exercise, he slurs, "You God-Damn-Fuckin-Bitch. Can't you hear? There is a man going to be tortured tomorrow."

The woman on the other end of the line was not at all accustomed to emergency calls. The number Samuel called was mainly for agents to contact other agents about meetings or to leave a message for one of the agents. It was not an emergency number for the FBI.

The young receptionist apparently had no alternative in her world and said, "Fuck you. Who do you think you are talking to? I am the FBI. I pressed the button and we are right now tracking the source of this call. Your pathetic little balls are mine."

Samuel was not to be outdone. "You fucking cunt."

He slams the black phone into its cradle.

Samuel's experiment going wrong interrupted his usually refined interpersonal skills.

Wearing his one-piece pajamas, with Mickey Mouse figures and built-in slippers, the psychologist runs out of his faculty housing apartment at Glenville State College.

The college professor leaps into his yellow VW bug and commences his drive on the 27-mile treacherous winding road to the Weston Asylum. Dr. Samuel is on a mission to save his reputation, to save his getting tenure; and of course, to save Bob Burns.

The three figures at the nurses' desk at the Acute Unit are still trying to decide what to do with the black bag that Nash left on the nurses' desk.

Dr. Blowfish, the suck-up of Nash, has all-too-willingly volunteered to see what is in the black bag.

Partially to expose his virility in front of the two nurses, and unconsciously to expose his contempt for Nash, Blowfish walks up without hesitation to the black bag, grabs the zipper, and unzips the top of the bag.

No snake.

The nervous laughter of the three bonds them in their misdeed.

The Methodist snake-believer nurse, sensing it is safe, reaches into the bag and carefully pulls out its contents. It is a fanciful frilly dress. She holds the dress up to the front of her body modeling the dress. In a further admission of defeat, she holds the thick-strapped dress with bright florid patterns close to her body to show the two onlookers.

Seeing the content of the mysterious black bag, Blowfish, unwilling to admit defeat, questions the two nurses. "And you say the women always scream when **he** is in their room for only a few minutes?"

Taking the prompt from Blowfish, the snake-believer Methodist nurse resumes her negative stereotype of Nash. "Oh my God. He dresses like a woman. He's one of those cross-dressers!" Her grasp on the dress' straps loosens and the girly-girl dress falls to the floor.

The Baptist nurse dutifully picks up the dress and frantically pushes the delicate dress back into the black bag. She does not zip the top of the bag.

Blowfish attempts to cover his poorly hidden agenda of creating a split, an unnecessary schism between coworkers. In a naïve voice, he questions, "Why would a man, a psychiatrist, the president of our hospital; bring women clothing concealed in a black bag?"

The initial snake-believing nurse provides some never-before-heard evidence, "I heard he was let go from his previous hospital because he was having the female patients give him a blow-job in his apartment at the hospital." In a demonstrative voice, the Baptist church woman screams, "Nash is wearing women clothing. He's one of those transsexuals. He's doing that instead of snakes. It's no wonder they scream."

"He's a pervert," shouts Blowfish.

"Who's a pervert?" questions Dr. Nash exiting from his impromptu meeting with some of his professionals in the rooms behind the nurses' desk.

"Pervert? No, I said 'desert,'" qualifies Dr. Blowfish. "I was telling the nurses how my wife makes this exquisite New York cheesecake.

"Oh." Nash reaches to pick up his black bag. The paranoid Nash sees that his black bag is unzipped.

The hypervigilant president of the asylum scans the faces of the three people hovering over his black bag. Nash sees three children in adult forms that look like they have been caught with their hands in the cookie jar. His paranoid feelings return. *There are demonic forces happening in my hospital.*

Nash's mind races on how to intervene. *Chastise the three in front of each other, focus on Blowfish and make him a model for the weaker two, fire the weakest nurse, hit the nurse with a smug on her face, pray, run, or piss my pants.*

Like the ball of a roulette wheel, his racing thoughts come to an abrupt and a determined decision. He opts for the most common defense mechanism of human-kind.

He denies the bag was ever zipped.

Nash picks up his unzipped black bag and takes a step toward Ms. Parkin's room. Earlier in the afternoon, on his way to the library, Nash told her to be sure she was in her room around dusk because he had a special surprise for her.

As he takes a second step away from the nurses' desk, he tersely stops and looks back in the direction of the nurses' desk. His eyes penetrate the eyes of Blowfish. "Make sure we are not disturbed."

"Yes sir, consider it done," squeaks the two-faced Blowfish.

In his platinum power suit, Nash walks in an erect manner to Ms. Parkin's room. The three figures behind the nurses' desk watch the president of the hospital enter the patient's room. As the door slowly closes, the three return to their excited conversation.

The Methodist nurse, who originally believed there was a snake in the bag, is the first to speak in a grimacing voice. "The fucker's a pervert. I once had a husband who could only get off only if he wore diapers. This is the same thing."

Blowfish and the Baptist nurse look at each other to verify that was more information than they needed to know.

The Methodist nurse in an evangelistic voice further declares, "Nash's doing amoral sinful acts. The women he sees screech that frightening scream; it is a scream similar to CPS taking away their children. Something terrible is happening every Wednesday and Friday when he goes into their rooms. That we know."

Blowfish, taking account of the situation, needing to bolster his previous impotent response that he said "desert" instead of "pervert," attempts to man control of the situation. "These things happened in the past of this hospital; I will not be a part of it continuing."

"A part of what?" asks a deep, reverberating, masculine voice.

Mack Johnson, the confident black physician assistant wearing his all-white uniform cascades his easy walk toward the three.

One of the two married nurses, who had a steamy one-night affair with Mack a couple of months ago, declares, "Nash is going into female patient rooms, and then he puts on a dress, and then he has sex with them."

In an uncharacteristic, effeminate, shrill voice, Mack Johnson screams, "Whhaëëët?"

Johnson's one-night affair nurse continues, "He goes into the women's rooms every Wednesday and Friday evening. The women always...."

An unadulterated vicious female scream discharges from behind Ms. Parkin's door.

Blowfish takes command of the situation. He looks in the direction of the Methodist nurse and commands, "Call a Code, then call the police, then call the Adult Protective Services hotline."

As required by his position of being a physician assistant, Mack Johnson responds to the scream and sprints down the long hallway toward Ms. Parkin's room. As Mack gets closer to the patient's door, the all-too-familiar words are announced over the hospital intercom.

"Code Blue 246, Code Blooo 246."

Nash and Ms. Parkins are standing very close to each other. Upon hearing the Code, Nash's one good eye squishes and his once devilish smile melts into a convoluted frown. There is no time to escape. He only has time to scream out of frustration, "Now what?"

The steel door of Ms. Parkin's room blows open and slams against the wall.

Nash thinks he sees the figure of Mack Johnson. It all happens so quickly. He is not sure who tackles him to the floor.

The initial hit from the intruder fractures one of Nash's ribs. Nash goes down hard to the concrete floor.

Due to years of practice, Mack Johnson uses his body weight to hold down the president. He grabs the president's two wrists and spreads Nash's arms out in a cross-like gesture. To verify incapacitating his victim, as not taught in the take-down manual, Johnson thrusts his right knee into the president's groin to confirm the perpetrator is completely helpless.

The two men's faces are inches from one another.

Perspiration from Johnson's face drops into the eyes of Nash.

The president of the hospital has a look of disbelief and then of hopelessness. Nash's eyes move from Johnson's face to the figure of the standing Ms. Parkins.

Mack Johnson's eyes follow those of Nash.

Ms. Parkins, in her Prince Valiant hairstyle, is standing and wearing the new fancy dress over her clothes. She pulls up on the thick straps with her thumbs in a gesture to show off the dress to Mack Johnson. With tears flowing down both her cheeks, she says in a child-like voice, "Isn't it the most purdy thing you have ever seen?"

The powerless Nash, and the heavy gigolo Mack Johnson lying on top of him stare at one another.

Nash gurgles through the splatter of blood coming out of his mouth, "Sometimes...to give...even the simplest of things...are the most...valuable and life-giving."

For the second time of the early evening, an effeminate, shrill a voice reverberates throughout the hallway of the Acute Unit. "Sheeit!"

40

Mack Johnson's once lackadaisical walk turns to a walk of disdain. He shuffles to the Acute Unit's nurses' desk. His face is covered with sweat due to the heat and the humidity of the day, the recent physical take-down of the president, and—his fear of unemployment. He rightfully believes the staff and the patients of the Acute Unit are mutely laughing at him.

Only one person in the hallway has the balls to express what is on everyone's mind. A feeble elderly patient with missing teeth, whose delusion is he has no arms, says to Mack Johnson, "You fucked up."

Without looking up, "Thanks for that."

During the hot and humid summer months of West Virginia, the movement of the deer population is miniscule compared to hunting season during Thanksgiving. Usually, around dusk, Bambi and her mother are safely tucked away resting on some of the beds of the needle-pine trees.

There is a reason for the cliché, "They stood there like a deer looking in headlights."

It is illegal to go deer hunting using spotlights because the deer just stand there and stare at the light. When driving a car, and a deer would perchance be standing on the road, the deer stare at the headlights of the car waiting for the structure to hit them; thus the saying, "Like a deer in headlights."

None of the above about deer is on Dr. Samuel's mind as his yellow VW bug swerves across the yellow lines on the curvy, mountainous, two-lane Highway 33 from Glenville to the Weston Asylum.

Dr. Alan Samuel is the mastermind behind Bob Burns being hospitalized. Bob Burns is only one person who is a part of his $1,520,000 NIMH grant-funded experiment to expose how asylums are hospitalizing almost any person in emotional trauma so the hospitals might keep their beds full. Since the advent of psychotropics during the 1950s, nerve medications, the beds have been less full. The mental hospitals have been admitting anyone who enters their doors so they may attempt to keep their beds full—to keep the money flowing into the hospital.

Bob Burns, the man with a broken nose who is now in solitary confinement with dried blood covering half his face, volunteered to be a part of Dr. Samuel's experiment. Burns was instructed by Samuel to go the Weston Asylum and to say he heard two voices, "bang" and "escape." Otherwise, Burns was instructed by Samuel to act normal during his admissions interview; and if heaven-forbid, he should be admitted, to act normal while in the asylum.

What could go wrong?

Dr. Samuel can only hear the words from the telephone call, "Electric Shock Treatment tomorrow followed by a 60-day hold" as he drives the dark road to the Weston Asylum.

Samuel sees it all transpire in slow motion.

A dark shadow is on the road.

The deer turns its head in his direction.

Samuel is going way too fast. He manages to hit the car horn at the last second.

The deer stands and looks at the headlights. It does not respond to the beep of the small car.

Samuel, a Southerner, does not realize the doe will not move.

The professor attempts to swerve to the side to miss the deer. He is too late. His light-weight vehicle bumps the hind end of the deer.

The car swerves off the road. The car teeters risking leaving the bank and going into the mountain river.

The doe limps across the paved road, gains a full walk, and leaps up the side of a mountain.

The pajama-wearing psychologist abandons the teetering VW. In the darkness, he stands on the narrow shoulder of the secluded two-lane highway.

Samuel is in luck. A pair of lights is coming in his direction. Having no history of hitchhiking, he naively believes this person will pick him up. He extends his right arm out into the road with his thumb in the direction of the bright Milky Way. With his free left arm, he waves toward the oncoming vehicle in the gesture that it is an emergency.

The ridiculously oversized monster-truck slightly swerves to miss Samuel. The professor is engulfed with the smell of diesel fumes as the truck speeds by.

Fifty feet past the hitchhiker the truck leaves skid marks as it comes to a sliding stop. The unknown driver of the monstrosity puts on his emergency lights.

The tall psychologist runs to the monster truck. As Alan Samuel clumsily climbs into the passenger side of Monster Truck, he sees something not expected. His hysterical and anxious thoughts of rescuing Bob Burns are detoured. The driver of the Monster Truck is the least thing Dr. Samuel expects. The driver looks the same as he does on the TV series; but, he is dressed differently from his television character.

Ted Cassidy, better known as Lurch in the hit television series, *The Adams Family,* is on his way to a high school reunion in his hometown of Philippi, West Virginia. Samuel stands about five-foot-eleven. When the psychologist climbs into the passenger seat of the monster truck, his head barely reaches Ted Cassidy's shoulders.

Samuel temporarily forgets his mission to rescue the bloodied Bob Burns. The college professor sees something that does not fit within the synapses of his current way of looking at life.

The strong-jawed Lurch is wearing black leather pants and a leather vest with no shirt. Samuel feels small in the massive truck sitting next to this gargantuan super-star wearing all black leather.

When Ted Cassidy turns to face the hitchhiker in the passenger seat, Samuel sees something that makes him feel not only small; but helpless and scared. Ted Cassidy wears red lipstick and dark black mascara.

In his deep Lurch voice, Ted Cassidy questions his newest rider. "What do you like?"

Unbeknownst to all of the various rescue teams heading toward the Weston Asylum, they are on their way to being on social media, television.

Because of the calls of Juli and her mother about the wrong imprisonment of Bob Burns, because of the call of Dr. Samuel about his imprisoned Bob Burns and because of the telephone call of the nurse on the Acute Unit concerned about Nash wearing a dress with patients; every emergency vehicle in the remote vicinity has been called: regional services, statewide services, and even federal services were summoned. The vehicles on the move include an ambulance, three black/white police cars, a water truck, pumping truck, and ladder truck from the volunteer fire department, two National Guard helicopters, an Adult Protective Services van, and the FBI.

Actually, the FBI was not on the way to the Weston Asylum because the FBI agents never responded to their beepers.

In Carmel's make-shift therapy office she once again hit a therapeutic rupture. Carmel is trying to find a way to free Noah Holiday of his delusion of being Jesus, "You said earlier you had an intimate relationship with Mary. Is there…"

"Fuck you."

"We've been there a bunch of times."

Based on an omnipotent *feeling* Carmel intuitively knows she is close to helping her patient break his psychosis. Believing she has a therapeutic relationship with Noah, she thinks she can emotionally push him harder. What she is not aware of is the tenacity of her feelings of being omnipotent.

Carmel's mind races with a hunch for a pattern. *There are his references to "going crazy," a "whore," and his uncharacteristic cussing and using the word "fuck."*

She thinks she has enough information to drop an interpretation: a light, very risky, tap based on their previous dialogue.

She says, "It was not your fault."

Jesus' eyes turn the size of silver dollars.

He looks terrified.

His hands rise to the sides of his face and he bends over violently sobbing.

Jesus looks like a defeated man.

Unbeknownst to Carmel and Jesus, National Guard helicopters are flying from Charleston, West Virginia over the construction of the highway 79 corridor. Numerous emergency vehicles are also driving to the Weston Asylum.

From the west of the Weston Asylum, is an ambulance with its red lights bouncing off the close houses contained within the mountains. The ambulance speeds to an impending disaster at the asylum.

On Main Street, going south, are three police cars driving to the brand new stoplight at Main and 2nd Street. On Main Street, going north, are the Volunteer Fire Department vehicles. From the east, on 2nd street, is the Adult Protective Services van.

All of the drivers of these emergency vehicles had been to Community Day and witnessed the crazies. The drivers of the emergency vehicles had witnessed the memorable fireworks display. The drivers of the emergency vehicles are on a mission. They are not fully clear what is— but they are on a mission.

At the new stoplight in Weston, following the accident between the ambulance, a police car, a fire department pump truck, and the Child Protective Services van; a call goes out for another ambulance. The remaining emergency vehicles venture their way to the Weston Asylum.

The FBI personnel never return the call from their beepers. Their lack of response will result in a review of policy and procedure.

The thumping sound of the menacing helicopter blades, that Americans have heard on the televised Vietnam War, are approaching the outskirts of Weston, West Virginia. Locals walk down from their porches to their small front yards to see the darkened silhouettes of the two helicopters.

41

Toad, the social worker from the Admissions Unit, cannot hear the thumping of the helicopter blades as they approach the Weston Asylum. She is deaf to her surroundings because she had an epiphany. She can admit she was wrong about Bob Burns.

In her diligent venture of gaining power, Toad had earlier in the day approached Psycho, the head of the Admissions Unit. Psycho told her that Carmel had scored Bob Burns' responses to the Rorschach inkblot test. Carmel determined he was not psychotic. Psycho further admitted to Toad that he thought Carmel was right. Bob Burns is not psychotic.

In her never-ending attempt of trying to gain power, Toad believes she must find Dr. Carmel to inform her that she agrees with Dr. Carmel that Bob Burns is mistakenly hospitalized. He's not psychotic; Toad will do whatever it takes to get him released from the hospital. Toad will then gain favor with the more powerful psychologist and the power structure of the Admissions Unit.

Toad is on a mission.

Dr. Carmel's last powerful interpretation with Noah Holiday was a risky broad statement, "It was not your fault."

Following Carmel's empathic statement, "It was not your fault," Noah's deadened eyes awaken.

His strong veined hands rise to the sides of his face. He leans over violently sobbing.

The scantily towel-covered Noah Holiday is hunched over. His long, wet hair hangs to the sides of his face concealing the look of terror, pain, and defeat in his face.

He screams in agony. Tormenting hiccups burst from his bowels.

His dramatic response was sparked by the statement, "It was not your fault."

Still attired in her pink blouse, pin-striped business dress, and Go-Go boots; Carmel sits erect in her chair, opposite the emotionally breaking man. She waits for a disturbing protracted two minutes.

Silence fills the make-shift therapy room.

Carmel does not listen to her *feelings* of omnipotence, only questions her *thoughts*. *I've pushed him too hard too fast. He's regressing back into a deeper psychosis.*

With his hands to his head, Jesus does not move from his defeated posture. His long wet hair hangs down the sides of his face concealing his expression of loss.

From his bowels, erupt the words, "I hurt—I hurt so much—I hurt so much."

Carmel, still not listening to her emotions that she is all-powerful, goes for the jugular. She says, in a mesmerizing soft voice, "It's time to let it go."

Jesus mumbles something unintelligible.

A soft voice, "I can't hear you."

A dead voice, "I had sex with my sister."

The room is silent.

The faint sound of a mosquito entering the room prompts the breaking of the prolonged silence.

Noah Holiday says, "She was eleven, I was sixteen. I knew better. I did. But it kept going on for a couple of years. She never protested. Our parents were sicker than us. She looked up to me. I was there for her. We needed each other. Do you understand?"

Carmel tries to follow, "Now, looking back— you were all she had."

"I do. I do know what I did was wrong. But you're right. All we had was each other. At the time, all we had was each other."

The muscles of Carmel's face relax.

The eyes of the delusional man (who believes, or believed, he is Jesus) scans the concrete floor for an answer.

Not finding a retreat in the workings of the concrete floor, "When my sister and I were together, my beliefs stopped that aliens were controlling my thoughts. I was crazy back then."

Noah raises his head to look at his therapist. "I mean…I got a reprieve for a few hours when I was with her. It was as if she understood. She was the only person who understood. She made the first gesture. She wanted me. I knew it was wrong—but I also wanted her—I needed her. I thought if we were together, she would not abandon me. She made the craziness stop. I now know I was wrong for what I did.

As we got older, I saw a psychiatrist and the medications seemed to help. My sister started dating older guys; our times together stopped. Following her first date with—I remember him so clearly—I hated him so much—Ben Steinkuehler. From that day forward, neither one of us made mention of our past. We both eventually seemed to be doing better and we were okay with it all.

The room was silent, except for the noxious flight of the mosquito.

Noah broke the silence between the two. "My sister eventually married the asshole. I wondered if it was because of our relationship, but I don't think it was."

Carmel slumps further down in her chair.

Noah felt safe to continue.

"One night, my sister and her new asshole husband came to my apartment to supposedly check on me. They had a lot to drink. He called me a "sick fuck." She'd told him about us. She'd told him about what we did. She didn't do anything to stop his drunken rantings. He said he was going to report me to authorities and I would be locked up for the rest of my life."

The room is completely quiet.

The mosquito landed on Noah's beard.

Noah's voice is solemn. "After they left my apartment and on their drive home, on Hwy 33, they hit a deer. Their car swerved into the river. They both drowned."

Carmel leans forwards and lays a hand on the top of Noah's hand. "What a terrible thing to have to carry with you."

Noah shrugs his shoulders.

Carmel returns to leaning back in her chair.

The mosquito hikes up the bearded man's face.

In his deadened voice, Noah recalls, "It was the day of my sister's funeral when they were lowering her coffin into the ground— I became Jesus. Because of your love, I now know I am not. I am not Jesus. I'm just so lost."

The defeated Noah Holiday raises his head and looks directly into Carmel's eyes, "I hurt, I hurt so much."

A much-needed eye contact with another human is formed. A relationship is formed.

Carmel's eyes moisten.

She stands and spreads her arms to the feeble man. He stands and his towel falls to the floor. The two tearing figures embrace.

Outside the Weston Asylum, the remaining emergency vehicles are making their way up the long entrance of the Asylum. The police cars, volunteer fire department trucks, and other emergency vehicles with their red-bubble-gum lights rotating on top of their vehicles are parading up the driveway.

Noah Holiday sees the reflection of the emergency vehicles' lights reflected off the ceiling of the make-shift therapy room. Dr. Katie Carmel is not aware of the red lights.

The families living along the perimeter of the asylum walk off their front porches into their small front yards. They hear the ominous thumping of the helicopter blades of the two National Guard helicopters making their way to the Weston Asylum. As the menacing helicopters approach the Weston Asylum, they turn their white-naked-ten-million-candle-power search-lights on the massive limestone building.

Running up to the nurse's desk of the Acute Unit, Toad (the wanna-be administrator) asks the two nurses at the desk, "Is Dr. Carmel on the unit?"

The Methodist nurse quickly prompts, "She's in a therapy session with Noah Holiday."

"I know where she does her therapy."

The squat social worker scrambles to the room.

The Baptist nurse attempts to interrupt Toad's crusade, "You can't go into a therapy session unless it's an emergency."

In Toad's mental world, she has something that is life-threatening. Bob Burns, the man in solitaire should not be hospitalized. Toad must gain power.

Toad opens the door to Carmel's make-shift therapy room.

The severe, naked, white searchlight of the lead National Guard helicopter shines in through the windows of the room.

The effect is a snapshot.

Toad is numbed by what she sees.

Noah Holiday lies on his back on the wooden conference table. Katie Carmel is on top of him. Both figures are completely nude, except for the dark nylons and Go-Go boots of Carmel.

The attending reflection of the red lights of the emergency vehicles making their way up the long driveway to the Weston Asylum gives the room a surreal effect of being a whore house.

Noah Holiday pays no heed to Toad's presence. He has never been with a woman, except for his younger sister.

Noah Holiday (no longer AKA Jesus) feels a female mosquito, that has a slight tear on her left wing, land on his wrist.

He slaps the insect.

A bloodstain is left on his wrist.

Two days later, July 20th, 1969; humankind lands on the moon.

Two Years Later

Mack Johnson:

The physician assistant, with the uncompromising deep voice, leaves the Weston Asylum. He becomes a leader in a national movement of helping fatherless African-American youth.

Noah Holiday:

Due to his therapeutic work with Dr. Carmel, he is completely free of his Jesus delusion. He stops his heavy medication regime. He has delightful, but infrequent, bouts of believing he is Mr. Spock on the popular Star Trek television series. Every once and awhile, he sees and hears Captain Kirk. He does not tell his new wife about these delusions and hallucinations.

Dr. Katie Carmel:

She loses her license to practice clinical psychology and invests in a small farm outside of Glenville, West Virginia. Repulsive to her neighbor farmers, she becomes a goat farmer. Her business is making and selling goat milk soap. It goes international, mainly due to the marketing skills of her new husband. Noah Holiday is instrumental in making a linkage between the goat soap and religion. Dr. and Mr. Holiday are active in many of the Vietnam War protests. There is just one minor problem; she just can't understand why her husband has to sometimes wear collarless monochromatic clothing and waves goodbye with his palm exposed separating his two sets of fingers making a 'V' shape.

Dr. Blowfish:

He remains imprisoned to work at the Weston Asylum for the remainder of his years.

Dr. Alan Samuel:

Lurch, Ted Cassidy the actor, and Dr. Samuel did arrive at the asylum that fateful night. Ted Cassidy dressed in black leather and red lipstick was on his way to a high school reunion and all of the alumni were instructed to wear a costume. Due to the politics of the asylum, Samuel was not able to stop the inevitable shock treatment of Bob Burns. Dr. Samuel subsequently limits his research to honey bees and roly-polies.

Bob Burns (the patient who heard two words):

Because the emergency personnel and professionals of the asylum were focused on Dr. Carmel having sex with her patient, Bob Burns was the recipient of Electric Shock Treatment on Saturday. Following his EST, Burns' short-term memory has never been the same. He sees numerous psychiatrists following his "rape" at the Weston Asylum. None of the medications help him. He remains anxious with panic attacks, poor sleep, and he cannot concentrate. He turns to cocaine.

Juli Jo:

The girl excels at school and lives at the library reading everything she can about psychological disorders. Juli wants to be a psychologist like the nice lady she met at the asylum.

Toad:

Due to drastic cuts of federal funds for mental health services, psychologists' services are reduced and are replaced by the less expensive social workers. Toad replaces Psycho. She is the head of the Admissions Treatment Team.

Ashley:

The benevolent, yet assertive Ashley continues her social work at the Weston Asylum. She dies in 1971 due to electrolyte imbalances. Anorexia will be recognized by the American Psychiatric Association as a life-threatening diagnosis years after her death.

Trick Greene:

The Beetle-look-alike came out of the closet. He quit working at the Weston Asylum. Trick and his boyfriend takes over the management of his mother's flower shop in the township of Burnt House.

President Dewey Nash:

Following the two days escapades, Dr. Nash prayed to Jesus for an answer. He heard the words of Christ. *You know what you need to do.* Nash put in his resignation at the asylum and began a crusade of providing adequate clothing for homeless people. The enterprise looks promising to go international.

Weston Asylum:

Mainly due to the advent of medications, the Weston Asylum slowly dies and eventually becomes a major tourist attraction.

The Patients

When the Weston Asylum closes; the patients, the people who did not ask for a confusing life, to be different, were ostracized to the streets or prisons.

Epilogue

(The Story Behind the Story)

Bob Burns, the character who heard the two neutral words of "bang" and "escape," is based on an actual experiment conducted in the 1970s. Due to the advent of medications, the beds of the great asylums were not full. The asylums were admitting people who did not need to be hospitalized.

Asylums needed to keep their beds full. It was about money.

In 1973, the Rosenthal study was published in the highly acclaimed journal, *Science.* Eight people, with no mental health history, went to 12 psychiatric hospitals in five states. They claimed to hear voices of neutral words. Unlike the novel, once they were admitted, they said they no longer heard the words (Bob Burns said he kept hearing the two words once he was admitted). In the experiment, all of the people were admitted to the 12 hospitals and were diagnosed with a severe mental disorder. Their length of stay ranged from 7 to 52 days. The average length of stay for these mentally healthy individuals was 19 days.

The incompetent, abusive, and negligent care of the severely and chronically mentally ill has a long history.

During the majority of the existence of civilized humans, the diagnosis and treatment of people with mental disorders was juxtaposed with religion. It was believed that a mentally ill person must have sinned (so god punished them; therefore, they must be ostracized); or, the mentally ill were possessed by the devil (so humans punished them to make their bodies intolerable for the devil).

Before the advent of the asylums, most of the people who suffered severe and chronic mental disorders were forced to live in the woods or were imprisoned. People, who were mentally crippled—who believed they were Jesus or their mother was the devil—were kicked out of their communities and forced to live in the forest. Or, these mentally imprisoned people were incarcerated with criminals.

Due to the courage and persistence of a woman, a rational and compassionate mental health revolution occurred around the time of the Civil War.

During the mid-1800s, Dorothy Dix had witnessed the inhumane confinement of people inflicted with severe and chronic mental disorders in prisons. Dorothy Dix resolved it was her mission to provide sane and meaningful care to these mentally ill people. She was a major force in the construction of the munificent asylums. Her overarching theme was to provide an emotionally and physically safe haven for these troubled souls—an asylum, a safe refuge.

Her unwavering, empathic conviction resulted in the creation of the asylums.

Three critical incidents during the second half of the 20th century resulted in the demise of her asylums: (1) the advent of antipsychotic and antidepressant medications during the 1950s, (2) the Community Mental Health Act of 1963 and (3) the beginnings of managed care during the 1980s.

The discovery of medications for mental health treatment was a major breakthrough for helping people suffering from mental disorders. Antidepressant and antipsychotic medications were discovered during the 1950s. The voices and the delusional thoughts stopped for some of the patients. It was, and is, a major revolution in mental health care for the chronic and severely mentally ill.

Before the 1950s, when townsfolk walked past the Weston Asylum, they would have heard the tormented screams of the mentally tortured patients. When psychotropics were introduced, the screams from the asylums were drastically reduced.

For a society that was cutting on patients' brain as a cure for psychosis (frontal lobotomies), taking a pill was less obtrusive and also effective. The answer for mental health was discovered.

Embracing psychopharmacology, in 1963 the federal government took a bold move by passing the Community Mental Health Act. Federally funded community-based mental health agencies were to be set up in every county so people could get their relatively inexpensive medications—and also provide some limited psychotherapy.

The 1980s was the beginning of managed insurance companies. Managed health care reached its zenith during the 1990s. Insurance companies sought the cheapest forms of treatment. The insurance companies severely cut back on the number of people admitted to mental hospitals and, once admitted, how long people were allowed to stay in the hospital. Managed care was the fatal blow to the few remaining large mental hospitals.

There is some good news regarding the treatment of the severely and chronically mentally ill.

Based on the American Psychological Association's website, 25 percent of young people suffering from a psychotic break, who get immediate treatment, can function socially and occupationally within six months to two years. They can develop healthy relationships and to be gainfully employed without ongoing treatment. Another 35 to 40 percent of people who have a psychotic break at a young age; are able, with medication and psychotherapy, to live relatively normal lives without the structured care of a hospital.

What about the remaining 35 to 40 percent of people suffering from psychosis?

Where do they go following the closing of an asylum, a safe place?

The following is the crux of this novel.

One-third of the homeless population is suffering from schizophrenia. Our contemporary society has placed humans on the moon and has been searching for the beginning of the universe. However, our contemporary society's treatment of the severely and chronically mentally is strikingly no different than our historic barbaric ancestors. Before the building of the asylums, for centuries, families would cast their demon-inflicted relatives out to live in the woods. In the 21st century, we cast them out to live in the streets.

Besides living in the streets, a staggering number of people suffering from psychosis are imprisoned. Isn't that what society did to them before the asylums? Wasn't it the detestable imprisonment of the severely mentally ill that prompted Dorothy Dix to take a stand for these people who needed a safe refuge, an asylum?

The statistics from numerous sources highlight how there are more severely mentally ill people in prisons than there are in psychiatric hospitals. The American Psychiatric Association estimates that one in five of prisoners in our expensive prisons is seriously mentally ill. The numbers are even more staggering for female inmates. Particularly amongst the regional jails, it is rare that a person who suffers from psychosis gets medication, let alone some form of effective psychotherapy.

For over a decade, United States citizens have witnessed on social media the numerous school shootings by seriously mentally ill people. The number of people killed by school shootings far exceeds the number of Americans killed by terrorists in the same time period. Efficacious treatment— accountability of the mental health practitioners—is nonexistent.

One possible solution for the severely and chronically mentally ill: Reopen the asylums, or adequately fund a similar housing situation that would provide a **truly** therapeutic environment. During the grand days of the asylums, a major form of intervention was to provide jobs on the farms or the ancillary services. It gave the people a purpose for living. More importantly, increase research funding on the **efficacious** treatment of people with severe and chronic mental disorders.

With increased expenditure in this area of mental health, we will be more likely to curtail the numerous shootings going around the United States. We will save lives. And, during this age of economic concerns, we will be able to: in the long-term, and maybe short-term, save money. This cost saving venture would be an excellent venture for an economist or psychologist to do for a dissertation. It is time that society woke up about the terrible injustices these poor souls have been inflicted.

People suffering from psychosis do not have a strong lobbying effort because their thoughts are disorganized. The televised saddened faces of cats and dogs appear to have a stronger charitable campaign compared to the saddened inflicted people with a severe and chronic mental disorder.

C. S. Lewis' words are applicable to the history and current problem of society dealing with people who suffer from mental disorders.

Terrific energy is expended—civilizations are built up— excellent institutions devised, but each time something goes wrong. Some fatal flaw always brings the selfish and the cruel people to the top and it all slides back into misery and ruin.

I hope this dark comedy/psychological thriller of a novel has been an entertaining and enlightening read. More importantly, I hope this novel provokes you to make a minor donation of $10.00 to the Visionary Grants program of the American Psychological Foundation. This program supports research, education, and projects to solve social problems.

Ten-percent of the author's proceeds from the book goes to the Visionary Grants program of the American Psychological Foundation.

People do not ask to have a mental disorder. You may make a difference in the funding of a research and education program that will have an impact on effective mental health interventions. Ten dollars can go a long way.

There are several avenues to donate:
- www.apa.org/apf/donate Please do not be intimidated by the questions. In the second category of questions, 'DONATION INFORMATION,' simply type in your donation amount and immediately under that type in

'Visionary Grants.' Then go to the bottom of the page to enter your credit card information.

- Snail Mail Address:
  American Psychological Foundation
  750 First Street NE
  Washington, DC 20002
    - If by check: make payable to American Psychological Foundation: Visionary Grants Program.
    - If by credit card: include name on card, account #, expiration date, and signature. Include information that it is to go to the Visionary Grants Program.
- Contributions by phone: (202) 336-5843

The one thing psychologists may agree upon is that life is ultimately about giving—it is moving beyond a narcissistic world to an empathic understanding.

I want to acknowledge you, the reader. That is what this novel is about—it is about you for taking an interest in the mental health care system.

A list of asylums and a few spooky architectural wonders offering tours

The following is a brief list of asylums and architectural wonders of the past. Most of these facilities offer tours.

Arizona
13th Floor, Phoenix
Yuma Territorial Prison

California
Preston Castle
The USS Hornet
The Winchester Mansion

Colorado
The Asylum, Denver

Delaware
Pea Patch Island

Florida
St. Augustine Lighthouse
The Spanish Military Hospital

Georgia
Oatland Island

Idaho
The Old Idaho
   State Penitentiary

Illinois
The Ashmore Estates

Indiana
West Baden Hotel, IN

Kentucky
Waverly Hills Sanatorium
USS Nightmare

Louisiana
The House of Shock

Maryland
Point Lookout Lighthouse

Massachusetts
Danvers State Lunatic Asylum
Medfield State Hospital
The Hoosac Tunnel
The Hammond Castle
The Houghton Mansion
Salem, the Witch City

Michigan
Seul Chiox Lighthouse
Traverse City State Hospital

Missouri
The Darkness

Montana
Bannock Ghost Town

New Hampshire
Haunted Overload

New Jersey
Burlington Prison

New York
Rolling Hills Asylum
Willard Asylum for the
    Chronic Insane
H. H. Richardson Complex

North Carolina
USS North Carolina

Ohio
The Haunted Prison
    Experience, Mansfield
7 Floors of Hell: OH
Athens Lunatic Asylum
Mansfield Reformatory

Oregon
Heceta Head Lighthouse
The Shanghai Tunnels

Pennsylvania
Pennhurst Asylum
Terror Behind the Walls,
    Eastern State Penitentiary
The Field of Screams
ByBerry Mental Hospital
Eastern State Penitentiary
Nemacolin Castle

Rhode Island
Belcourt Castle, RI
The Sprague Mansion

South Carolina
The Old City Jail

Tennessee
Old South Pittsburg Hospital

Texas
USS Lexington Museum on
    the Bay
Yorktown Memorial Hospital

Virginia
St. Albans Sanatorium

Utah
Old Tooele Hospital

Washington
Thornewood Castle
Manresa Castle

West Virginia
Trans-Allegheny Lunatic
    Asylum
Moundsville Prison
Mummies of Philippi, Bodies
    from the Weston Asylum
Ghost of Silver Run Haunted
    Train Tunnel, North Bend
    Rail Trail

Wyoming
Haunted Frontier Prison

CANADA
Century Manor Insane
    Asylum, Ontario, Canada

Acknowledgments

A novel requires the work of numerous people. I am indebted to Rob Kerns, Dr. Megan Gibbons, Dave Bernier, and Kathryn Wood for editing an earlier proof of the novel. When I wrote the novel, I purposefully wanted to include sex—sex sales. Thanks to the comments of Dr. Gibbons many, but I am sure not all, of the sophomoric sexual innuendoes were eliminated.

I am also indebted to a once good long friend, Jerry Kelly. He read a few pages of a proof of the manuscript and he emailed back to me that the novel didn't interest him. Because of his heartless comment, I did make changes to make the novel move faster. Only a good friend could make such a comment. I have not spoken to him since—just kidding.

I met the founder of an editing service, *Inspiration for Writers, Inc.*, at a writer's conference—Sandy Tritt. She has been a personal God-send throughout this process. Based on our personal meetings and emails she walked me through the publishing process. One of her associates, Geoffrey Fuller, provided the needed line and copy editing. I definitely need to thank Cat Pleska of *Mountain State Press* for providing unselfish insights into the publishing process.

I fully appreciate the people who own the copyright of the 49 lyrics I used from a John Denver song.

An author could not find a better publisher than Cathy Teets of Headline Books, Inc. My emails to her would always get a response within an hour. It is no wonder her company achieved 2017 Independent Publisher of the Year. The publisher and I also played around with making the cover of the novel marketable. We worked well together.

The place of the novel is set at the Weston Asylum in West Virginia. The asylum closed in the early 1990s and was purchased by a private individual in the early 1990s. He reopened the asylum for tours and it is now known as the Trans-Allegheny Insane Asylum and boasts over 30,000 visitors a year. The interiors of asylums are usually very similar with long wide hallways interspersed with patient doors. Many of the interior features are based on other psychiatric hospitals I have worked or on other sites.

I worked for one-and-one-half years at an older asylum that was originally constructed in 1854. It housed some of the most severely and chronically mentally ill in the western part of the state. I worked on the Admissions Unit where people initially arrived at the hospital and they were blatantly psychotic.

Some of the patients on our Admission Unit tried to conceal their hearing voices or that they were psychotic. After six months of work, I was finally able to empathize with these poor souls. When I did learn to experience their lives, too many times these poor souls would cry because it was the first time someone lived within their experiential world. You could see their deadened eyes come to life once we connected. It is a humbling experience. This connection with a blatantly psychotic person needs further research.

I acknowledge the people who suffer from severe and chronic mental illnesses who taught me so much about the constant confusion of being inflicted with a severe and chronic mental illness...and the aloneness.